PRAISE FOR
A MAN IN UNIFORM

"Taylor's twisting plot is rich in romance and disturbing in its implications."
—*ELLE*

"Equal parts historical novel and Agatha Christie–style thriller . . . [with] unexpected and page-turning twists and turns."
—*NEW YORK POST*

"An awfully enjoyable romp. Taylor writes clearly and transparently, leaving nothing to abstraction. The book moves along at such an admirable clip that it's hard to believe it won't carry on without you if you dare put it down."
—*TORONTO STAR*

"A literate thriller . . . Today, the Dreyfus Affair continues to serve as a bracing reminder . . . that we dare not have blind faith in the willingness of our leaders to defend our most cherished rights and freedoms. Taylor's engaging novel, in creating a detailed historical world, reminds us of that ever-present danger."
—*GLOBE AND MAIL*

"Transports readers into late-nineteenth-century Paris."
—*HISTORICAL NOVELS REVIEW* (EDITORS' CHOICE)

"An engrossing mystery that neatly bridges literary and popular fiction."
—*CHATELAINE.COM*

Also by Kate Taylor

Madame Proust and the Kosher Kitchen

A MAN IN UNIFORM

a novel

Kate Taylor

Broadway Paperbacks
New York

Copyright © 2011 by Kate Taylor

All rights reserved.
Published in the United States by Broadway Paperbacks, an imprint of the Crown Publishing Group, a division of Random House, Inc., New York.
www.crownpublishing.com

BROADWAY PAPERBACKS and its logo, a letter B bisected on the diagonal, are trademarks of Random House, Inc.

Originally published in hardcover in Canada by Doubleday Canada, a division of Random House of Canada Limited, Scarborough, Ontario, in 2010, and in the United States by Crown Publishers, an imprint of the Crown Publishing Group, a division of Random House, Inc., New York, in 2011.

Library of Congress Cataloging-in-Publication Data
Taylor, Kate, 1962–
A man in uniform : a novel / Kate Taylor.
I. Dreyfus, Alfred, 1859–1935—Fiction. 2. Spies—France—Fiction. 3. Treason—France—Fiction. 4. Trials (Military offenses)—France—Fiction. 5. Lawyers—France—Fiction. 6. Jews—France—Fiction. 7. Paris (France)—Fiction. I. Title.
PR9199.4.T38M36 2010
813'.6—dc22   2010017621

ISBN 978-0-307-88520-3
eISBN 978-0-307-88521-0

Printed in the United States of America

Cover design by W. G. Cookman
Cover photography courtesy of the Musée des Archives Nationales

10 9 8 7 6 5 4 3 2 1

First Paperback Edition

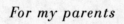

For my parents

On October 15, 1894, the French army accused Alfred Dreyfus, a captain in the artillery, of passing military secrets to the Germans. On December 22, a court martial found Dreyfus guilty of treason and sentenced him to life imprisonment.

What follows is a work of fiction.

Those who truly love justice have no right to love.

—ALBERT CAMUS, *The Just*

A MAN IN
UNIFORM

There was something small—and apparently alive—at the bottom corner of the cot. The thing was scratching at his toe. In gentler circumstances, he supposed this would be irritating, or even frightening. Was it a beetle? Or worse yet a mouse? But in this long night, he found the tickling sensation on his right foot a small comfort. Here was an event to mark the undifferentiated time stretching to dawn; another creature would share his vigil.

His captors had never given him a light, simply locking him in the tin shed at dusk and unlocking the door at dawn. On moonlit nights, he could just make out the shape of the small, bare room in the pale light seeping underneath the door. Other nights, he lay in darkness so complete he had to crawl across the dirt floor, feeling his way with his hands to find the bucket into which he relieved himself. In these climes, there was little perceptible difference between the longest and shortest day of the year, and all were uniformly hot. If he was lucky, he could sleep away eight or ten hours of these twelve-hour nights, but in the rainy season, overcast days forced him inside earlier and the water pounding on the roof over his head prevented him from sleeping. He would lie awake for what seemed like huge swaths of time, unsure if he had slept or not, confused as to whether he was at the beginning of the night or its end. Only the faint gray light from under the door could rescue him, propelling him into another day. Whatever its heat or its horrors—boredom, loneliness, humiliation—the day could not be worse than the half death of these nights in which he felt his own existence slipping away from him, drawing him down toward nothing.

The thing at the bottom of the bed seemed to have a hard shell, a carapace of sorts. He wondered now if it was a scorpion. He supposed there might be scorpions on the island, although his jailers had never mentioned the creatures, and they seldom failed to regale each other with descriptions of the local fauna. Making waving motions with their arms and hissing between their teeth, or jumping about like madmen and scratching their armpits, they would imitate the giant snakes and bands of chattering monkeys that roamed the jungles of the mainland. Although they never spoke directly to him beyond the occasional barked command or acknowledged his existence in their own conversations, these displays were surely aimed at him. These were the creatures that would drive him insane or kill him outright if he ever managed to reach the other side of a strait patrolled by sharks and piranha. "Care for a swim?" the guards would sometimes ask laughingly of each other, when they caught him looking out to the sea beyond his hut. His captors had no need of a fence to keep him here.

The thing was beginning to crawl up the leg of the loose canvas trousers he wore day and night. Perhaps it *was* a scorpion. Was its venom lethal? On some nights, he might have desperately hoped so, but tonight he could not even muster a death wish. The thing crawled a little higher. He finally shook his right leg and brushed it off with his other foot. There was a small noise as it fell to the floor and scuttled away.

Some time later, an hour or two as best he could judge, morning was announced not by light under the door but by voices outside the shed. Men working, apparently, giving each other instructions, digging, he gathered from the clang of a shovel against rock. Soon after, his door was opened and his breakfast—hard bread and a cup of water— was placed on the floor. He struggled to his feet. This morning his guard was the lieutenant, an unbending young man never given to the crude jokes and mocking insults of the others.

"You'll stay in here today," the lieutenant announced, "until the work is done."

He slumped back onto his cot. He had never stayed inside the shed on a dry day before; only the most ferocious storms could keep him here. Usually, he sat outdoors, with the overhang of the shed's roof providing either shade from the sun or shelter from the rain. He had been given a battered cane chair and table when he arrived, and eventually was permitted pen and paper. It had seemed a great breakthrough and, at first, he had written long letters home. More recently, he didn't bother, but simply sat and stared at the sea. He had also talked to himself, just to hear a human voice in the long hours of solitude, but now he didn't do that either, and when he tried to use his voice he found it was little more than a croak.

The men dug for much of the morning. They were convicts too, he concluded from the shouts directed at them. A gang must have been brought over from one of the other islands. They complained of the heat and called for water, but he supposed his windowless tin shed was worse. The heat was now becoming more than he could bear. The sides of the shed were burning hot. He lay in the middle of the room to avoid brushing against the metal. If he pressed his face to the floor, the dirt seemed slightly cooler than the air.

After a while, the digging stopped. It was replaced by some slower work, something heavy being moved about. There were cries of "Steady, steady!" or "Hold it!" but he couldn't figure out what the men were doing. It grew hotter still, and eventually the work stopped. The door opened. He looked up from the floor. The lieutenant had brought him another cup of water, but when he tried to stand he fell back. The lieutenant crouched and put the cup to his lips. After a sip or two, he downed the rest greedily. He tried to ask for more, but the sound that escaped his mouth was barely a whisper. The lieutenant said nothing and left. He fell back to the floor, despairing, but the man returned a few minutes later with a whole jug. It was the only time he recalled the lieutenant showing compassion.

Later, it seemed to grow cooler, or perhaps it was just the water inside him. The work had started again. The half light in the interior of the shed was growing fainter now. The work stopped. The lieutenant returned and held the door open. "Out."

He staggered out. It was almost dusk. There was no sign of the convicts but their work was evident. They were building a rough wooden palisade around the tin shed. Only one of the four sides, the front, was complete, but it presented a solid wooden wall. He could no longer see the sea.

ONE

Maître Dubon lifted his gaze from Madeleine's right breast, which was peeking out tantalizingly from under a crisp white sheet, and let it travel slowly down the bed, admiring as he did so how the draped cotton clung to her body in some places and obscured it in others. He glanced across the room and let his eye come to rest, ever so casually, on the ornate gilt clock that sat atop the dresser. It was twenty minutes before the hour.

"Well, perhaps it's time we get dressed." Still leaning back against the pillows, he waited a long moment before he made up his mind to move, and then took the plunge, pulling the sheet off his own body, swinging his feet to the floor and standing.

Beside him, Madeleine stirred and stretched an arm languidly across the bed toward an armchair. Dubon crossed over to it, picked up the peignoir that was lying there, and held it open for her. As she rose to her feet, she slipped her arms into it, drawing the fluttering layers of its wide lace collar over her shoulders and around her neck. He moved to his clothes, pulling on his undershirt, shirt, pants, and waistcoat, buttoning buttons as he did so, methodically but with no apparent haste. He turned to a full-length mirror that stood in one corner of the room and straightened his tie approvingly. Though only of average height, he had a big head, and a finely shaped nose, straight but for the sharp break that formed a little shelf at the bridge, and his features gave him presence. His hair was still good and thick, he always noted with pleasure, and the occasional strand of silver that now appeared at the temples added an air of distinction.

He picked up his jacket. "See you tomorrow, my dear."

"Until tomorrow," she replied. He kissed her affectionately on one cheek, gently patted the other, and left her padding about her small apartment in her peignoir and little satin slippers as he stepped calmly into the street. It was fifteen minutes to the hour.

Maître Dubon's day was a well-ordered thing. Its final goal, which the lawyer achieved without fail, was a seven-thirty dinner hour during which he shared a light meal with his wife, Geneviève, and his son, André. He also breakfasted with them at seven, and most days joined them for a large lunch at eleven, for he thought of himself as a family man and considered it his duty to eat three meals a day in the company of his wife and son, a duty he executed with affection.

From the breakfast table, he proceeded to the office, a pleasant walk, if the weather was fine, along the river and across the place de la Concorde to the rue Saint-Honoré, and so to his clients, who would visit him before lunch. They were prosperous burghers and people of society, and he drafted their wills and their contracts with diligence if no particular enthusiasm. The practice he had inherited from his father represented a limited set of legal permutations that he had long since mastered. The thrusts and parries of the courtroom, on the other hand, he left to others, simply passing on to a colleague the occasional unfortunate case that was headed in that direction. Returning home for lunch, he tried not to dally at the table and allowed himself only a single glass of wine, because after a few more hours in the office preparing documents and reviewing files, he would proceed to an engagement rather different from the dinner hour but to which he was equally faithful.

Between five and seven, Maître Dubon visited Mademoiselle

Madeleine Marteau in her apartment off the boulevard des Italiens. He had been visiting her there five days a week for the past eleven years, ever since he had rented the apartment for her in the seventh year of his marriage, when André had just turned three. He had met Mademoiselle Marteau, or Mazou as he called her, a few years previously; he had been introduced to her by a legal colleague with bohemian connections. In those days, she worked as a seamstress with a leading fashion house and had received many different visitors in a second-floor studio in Montparnasse. His attendance at her little gatherings and the occasional tête-à-tête had ceased briefly when Geneviève presented him with the joyous news of her pregnancy, but he had resumed the acquaintance soon after André's birth. Labor had strained Geneviève, and two things had become clear to him then. One was that his relations with his wife, while always cordial, were unlikely to become physical again anytime soon; the other was that if he wished to enjoy Madeleine's company, he needed to regularize their situation. And so, he rented the apartment off the boulevard des Italiens and attended her there faithfully Monday through Friday, arriving with the occasional box of chocolates or new handbag to augment the check he paid into her bank account every month.

His relationship with Geneviève, meanwhile, remained happy enough. She was thirty-nine now; he was forty-three, and friends and relations had stopped dropping hints about the joys of big families. It was sad, but there it was: André would never have, could never have, a brother or sister. Although Dubon slept beside his wife each night, their sexual relations were less than infrequent.

If it was important that he arrive home by seven, it was no less important that he present himself at Madeleine's door by five, for he considered himself, both at home and abroad, to be a gentleman and here too there were delicate social negotiations to be entered into before they could move to Madeleine's bedroom. Perhaps there was a new dress to admire or a recent concert to discuss over a cup of tea or a glass of wine. Maître Dubon may have visited Madeleine's bed more than two thousand times, but their relations remained enjoyably fresh thanks not only to Madeleine's sense of invention but also to his lack of presumption—or at least his pretense of a lack of presumption.

Yes, it was important to arrive no later than five, but Maître Dubon often liked to be there earlier or even make Madeleine a surprise visit on a Saturday morning after he had spent an hour or two in his office. His mistress was a highly attractive woman almost ten years his junior and it would be unwise to take her for granted.

So he was particularly annoyed when, on the following afternoon shortly before five on a day that was already running late, a sharp whistle sounded. As he lifted the speaking tube off the edge of his desk and put it to his ear, the clerk Roberge could be heard mumbling something about a visitor to see him. Roberge had never mastered the gadget, always blowing the warning whistle too loudly but then speaking too softly into the tube to be heard.

Dubon blamed the interruption on Lebrun's mother's cat. Lebrun was his regular clerk and knew that afternoon visitors were rare and certainly not permitted after 4:00 P.M., but his aged mother had fallen over her cat the week before and broken some bone, the location of which, being a delicate man, Lebrun would not name. He had craved Dubon's understanding—and a few days' credit from his annual holiday to attend to his relative. He had called in, as his temporary replacement, Roberge, a downtrodden character who floated around the quartier picking up work in various law offices when his weak health would permit. And so, on that day, it was the less-than-satisfactory Roberge who ushered a lady into the lawyer's office at an inconvenient hour.

The woman, a widow, entered the room with a firm but quiet step. Dubon guessed her husband must be six months' gone now: she was dressed head to toe in black, but not veiled. Instead, she wore a tidy little hat. Her hair was carefully pinned up out of sight, and the little that showed around her forehead was dark but not quite black, hinting that the unseen mane was a luxurious brown or perhaps a rich chestnut color. She wore no ornament of any kind, not even a mourning brooch, except for a gold wedding ring on her left hand. She wasn't old— perhaps thirty or thirty-five, certainly not yet forty, he estimated— and, if it were not for the sad contradiction between her youth and her bereavement, a man passing her in the street might not give her quiet figure a second glance.

Unless, of course, he had the gall to look her straight in the eyes. And what remarkable eyes they were, Dubon noted as he rose to greet her: a deep, deep blue, sparkling with an intensity that suggested widowhood had not dampened some quick spirit alive beneath her sorrows. Dubon was visited by a sudden image of her quite naked, her skin . . . He checked himself. Perhaps he had been staring.

"Madame, my apologies. I so seldom receive visits after four o'clock; you have startled me, I'm afraid." He paused and reached for her hand, then held it in his as though he might kiss it before letting it drop. "To whom do I owe the honor?"

"My name is Madame Duhamel. I apologize, Monsieur, for waiting until the very end of the day to call upon you—"

"Oh, not at all, Madame. You are most welcome. Please, do come in."

He adjusted the chair reserved for clients and swept a hand across it to invite her to sit down. Then, instead of going around and settling himself behind the large expanse of the desktop, he stayed in front of it, drew a second, smaller chair out from against one wall and sat down directly facing her. She made no move to take off her hat but sat there, clutching her gloves in one hand.

"The weather is still so cold, don't you find?" Dubon asked. "Almost unseasonably so. I always enjoy the spring, but here we are in mid-April and we are still bundled up in our winter clothes. If I may be honest, Madame, I would myself not say no to a ray or two of sunlight."

"Oh yes, a ray of sunlight . . ."

Her voice trailed off and she appeared puzzled, as though unsure why they were discussing the weather. She held his gaze now, and again her eyes arrested him. They darted and glittered. This time he was not imagining it: there was some humor there behind her evident grief. Indeed, she almost laughed, emitting a little sound that ended in a gulp.

"Oh, Monsieur, I suppose you want me to state my business."

"Whenever you wish, Madame. I am in no hurry."

And indeed, Dubon, who but moments before had felt annoyed at the interruption keeping him from Madeleine, was now happy to linger. She seemed hesitant, as though sensing there was specific etiquette to be employed when visiting a lawyer's office but ignorant of what it might be. Dubon found the effect charming.

She drew a long breath and shifted in the chair. "Maître. They do call you Maître, I suppose..."

"Oh yes, indeed. Lebrun, my clerk, always insists on introducing me that way to clients. That wasn't him who let you in. That was Roberge; he's just temporary. He calls me Maître too. My friends, on the other hand—"

She interrupted him here. "That's fine. I will call you Maître. And," she added, her tone serious now, "I will tell you my business."

"By all means, do go ahead."

"I come to you on behalf of a friend of mine..." Some skepticism must have shown in his face for she repeated it. "Yes, a dear friend of mine. She is in serious trouble but cannot risk coming to see you herself. Indeed, she does not know that I am here, only that I said I would try to make some inquiries as to what might be done to save her husband."

"Save her husband? What ails him, Madame?"

"Nothing that true justice could not cure, Monsieur."

"Well, Madame Duhamel. I am not sure you have come to the right place. A lawyer will get you the best justice he can, but as to whether that constitutes true justice..."

"Maître, please. Your reputation precedes you. Your work on the—"

"No, no, Madame, please, that is not necessary." Dubon did not want to hear her fabricate some tribute to his supposed credentials by dragging up his minor role in events now long past. He could only suppose someone had told her that his services came cheap by the standards of the rue Saint-Honoré. God only knew what a client might be asked to pay the society lawyer de Marigny, whose offices were across the street, or the much-praised Socialist, Déon, who was just one floor up and always willing to take on a high-profile cause.

"Please, do continue. Tell me about your friend's husband."

"He is an army officer, Maître, a captain in the artillery." Dubon began to guess the real reason she had come to his office; she must have learned of his family connections and judged they would be useful if her case involved the military.

"I will come to the point. There is no way to put it gently and you have perhaps read about the case in the papers. It caused some furor at the time: about two years ago, my friend's husband was accused of spying for the Germans. He was court-martialed, convicted, and deported to serve his sentence in cruel exile. Even now, he languishes on Devil's Island."

"But, Madame, his trial is then long past. Why seek legal advice now?"

"Because he is innocent, Monsieur."

"Madame, I am sure your friend is a charming person and a loyal wife—"

"Do not patronize me, Maître," she interrupted.

Dubon, unaccustomed to such directness in any lady other than his wife, drew himself up and began again. "No, I would not dream of it, Madame. So naturally, your friend believes completely in her husband's innocence."

"It is not a matter of belief; it is a matter of fact. The man is innocent. I have known him, well, many years. It is unthinkable that the captain is a spy."

"That may be, Madame. However, if the army has convicted him at a court martial, I don't see what possible help a lawyer could be now." Most especially, Dubon thought to himself, a lawyer with no current experience in criminal law and whose only knowledge of the workings of the military was limited to Sunday lunches with his wife's relations, however much the lady's informants may have billed him as the highly placed son-in-law of the late General de Ronchaud Valcourt. "I can only assume your friend's husband had the benefit of good legal advice at the time of the court martial?"

"Yes. I believe a Maître Demange undertook his defense. But clearly he did not succeed in forestalling a conviction."

She paused and looked down at her lap before raising her face to him. He found it was all he could do to stare straight back.

"Monsieur, I am . . . we are . . . increasingly desperate. It has been more than two years, two and a half, and the captain is seemingly forgotten. His brother is responsible for the family's attempts to exonerate him and win him a new trial, but makes no progress. No progress at all. I do not wish to undercut his efforts, or divide the family, but I despair that his approach will ever bear fruit. No one knows I am here today. I do not wish my friend to be associated in any way with my de-marche. I believe the family has made a mistake in simply proclaiming the captain's innocence, as though justice will ultimately triumph just because he *is* innocent. I have concluded that the secret to his release is to find the reason for his conviction. The army had evidence that someone was selling secrets to the Germans; the generals' mistake was to convict the wrong man. And you, Maître, you can find the real spy so as to exonerate the captain."

If it weren't for those unrelenting blue eyes, Dubon would have dis-missed the widow then and there. Who was this lady with such inflated notions of what a lowly barrister could achieve? He answered rather feebly, "But I am a lawyer, not a detective."

"Maître, you are both. Your very name is synonymous with justice. And you know the right people."

Dubon knew the former was pure flattery and the latter much nearer the mark. Still, it was gratifying that after all this time people still remembered his work for the Communards. He had been only a junior lawyer in those years after the Franco-Prussian War. Maître Gaillard had taken the lead on the file, defending the many Parisians who had seized control of their own city after the Germans had lifted the siege. When the new national government at Versailles finally de-cided to march on the capital and wrench control of Paris away from its citizens, the suppression of the Commune was swift and brutal. Dubon was little more than a boy and had never seen such bloodshed before or since. The army had shot the Commune's leaders on the spot and court-martialed thousands of others, executing anyone who had wielded a rifle or bayonet against the new government's troops, and jailing everyone else unfortunate enough to be caught on the streets, whatever their sympathies might have been. In the long years that fol-lowed, it was Maître Gaillard who had fought hardest to get new civil trials for these bit players and bystanders, and Dubon had been his young assistant.

But Dubon had given up criminal law long ago.

"My friend . . ." she continued, "is deprived of her husband and does not trust that his brother's attempts to free him will ever succeed. We must help her."

"I see," said Dubon. He took a long look at her before he asked, "And your husband?"

"My husband?" She seemed startled by the question, as though momentarily she had forgotten she had a husband. "My husband is gone. He has nothing to do with this."

"My condolences, Madame. He is recently deceased?"

"Oh no, six, seven months now."

"So sad, very sad. Could he possibly have been as young as yourself?"

"Five years older."

"Too young, too young. An accident perhaps?"

"An accident?"

"His death, I mean . . ."

"Oh yes, of course. An accident. But really, we need not speak of him."

Dubon noted with interest that she did not seem to have been a particularly fond wife. The thought gladdened him a little, although he did not stop to examine why.

"Well, Madame." He paused, knowing full well he should send her about her business but wanting now to prolong the acquaintance. "I will think on it and make some inquiries of colleagues. Perhaps I can find an advocate who would be more appropriate to your needs."

"No, Maître, really, it must be you."

"You flatter me. At any rate I will make my inquiries and contact you in a few days."

"Can I come again the day after tomorrow at this time, if it is not too inconvenient?"

It was not in the least convenient. He glanced at the wall clock behind her. It was twenty past the hour, almost too late to bother visiting Madeleine. He would have to ask Roberge to send his mistress a message telling her he could not come tonight. And the following day he would again be pressed to see her because he and Madame Dubon were to attend a ball at General Fiteau's. His wife was insistent that he be home early on such occasions so that she could discuss her costume with him and review the probable guest list. So, if his visitor came again in two days' time, on a Friday, he might be forced to make do without Madeleine until the following week. None of this was what he would have wished.

"Perfectly convenient, Madame. I am at leisure Friday afternoon."

"I will try to be here by four."

"I look forward to Friday, then."

"Thank you, Monsieur."

She stood and offered him her black-gloved hand. He took it and bent over it without touching it to his lips before slowly straightening himself and then letting it go.

"Until Friday," he said.

She smiled in response and walked out the door.

He waited until he heard her speak to Roberge on her way out and close the door of the outer room before he picked up the speaking tube and called the clerk into his office.

"You will have to send a message for me. The post office is at the corner," Dubon said as he opened a drawer and pulled out a blue sheet of paper. He sighed as he filled in the form. If Lebrun had been there, he would have taken a look at the time, readied the form himself, and been poised, without Dubon having to ask, to send the *petit bleu*. Paris's system of local telegrams was known affectionately by the blue paper on which the messages were written before being stuffed into glass containers, ready to hurtle across the city along a network of pneumatic tubes that connected all the post offices and then be delivered by hand from the nearest outlet. There was a post office down the street from Dubon's office and, but a few streets away on the other side of the avenue de l'Opéra, one next door to Madeleine's apartment. Lebrun actually could have walked the distance in less time than it took the messengers to pick up the telegram and deliver it, but Dubon would never have submitted him to the embarrassment of appearing on his mistress's doorstep.

He composed a brief message of regret and folded it over, addressed it, and handed it to Roberge.

"You can take it now and send it on your way home. I will lock up behind you."

"Yes, Maître. See you tomorrow."

Dubon tidied his papers and left the office ten minutes later. He walked down to the rue de Rivoli at a leisurely pace and entered the place de la Concorde at the northern corner, passing the statues representing the cities of Lille and Strasbourg, the latter draped in black ever since the province of Alsace had been lost to the Germans during the war. Since André was a boy, Dubon had joked to him that his father crossed all France to get home in time for dinner, for he then walked down the eastern side of the square and across the bottom, passing the statues of Bordeaux and Nantes as he reached the Seine. Today, however, he barely noticed the geography and walked by the work site where the new exhibition halls were being built at the bottom of the Champs Élysée without even checking on their progress. Absentmindedly, he traced his habitual route along the river and up the rue Bayard, still thinking over his conversation with the widow. There was some question about her story that he had meant to ask, a little inconsistency or discrepancy that was floating just out of reach. Whatever it was, it quickly evaporated as he pushed open the door of his home and walked into the salon.

"You're early." Geneviève greeted him in slightly accusatory tone. She was standing on the far side of the room, in front of its two heavily curtained windows. André was with her, his growing body jammed up against the delicate writing desk his mother had squeezed between the windows and the back of a long sofa. His school books were spread over the desk's impractically small surface and Geneviève stood at his shoulder, shepherding some piece of homework. André turned his head and, without comment, glanced back to where his father stood before returning his attention to his books.

"I had a client show up at the last minute but . . ." Dubon paused, remembering that he was early not late. Geneviève eyed him quizzically. "But I . . . well, I tried the tramway again. Really very quick." One of the new electric trams had been installed along the quay, and on cold days the previous winter, Dubon had come to prefer it to the crowded horse-drawn omnibus that served the rue de Rivoli. Geneviève herself had even tried it on a few occasions.

"Oh, the lovely new tram. It's a godsend, isn't it?" she replied. "I'll just see if Agathe can get dinner on the table at seven. It would be nice to eat early for a change." She smoothed her skirts and made her way toward the door Dubon had just entered.

"André, tidy up your books, dear, and take them to your room. Your father doesn't want your schoolwork cluttering up the salon." She glanced at Dubon as she passed him, and walked out.

"You don't need to tidy up on my account," Dubon said, smiling at his son.

André, however, was already bundling his books into his arms. He mumbled, "Doesn't matter," as he brushed by his father and was gone.

Dubon was left standing by the door, staring at an empty room. He crossed to a small table at his left, poured himself a short glass of red wine from a decanter and sat down in the one comfortable arm-chair Geneviève's decor permitted. She favored Louis XV, although the apartment itself was of a much more recent style. He removed an embroidered cushion from behind his back and tossed it over to the sofa, settled himself, and took a sip from his glass. It was the Château Cheval Blanc from '93, probably better cellared than drunk this young, but Geneviève, who ordered all their wine, permitted older vintages only when they had guests. He swallowed—the wine had not improved since the previous evening—and sighed lightly.

Yes, he was home in plenty of time for dinner.

TWO

Dubon watched his wife waltz away in another man's arms and noted with satisfaction that she was looking particularly beautiful that evening. Her blond hair was swept back in a sleek chignon, and her mother's diamonds sparkled convincingly at her neck. She was wearing a new dress he had bought her and that he admired not so much for its delicate shade of blue or finely tailored skirt as for its clever neckline, which succeeded in plunging without provoking. Most women of her age—those muffled matrons now sitting out the dance on the little gilt chairs that lined one wall of the ballroom—would have been unable to carry off such an uncompromising look. Geneviève, however, could hold her own against any of the debutantes swirling across the floor in their white dresses. She was in her element here, surrounded by her intimates, and it was the easy confidence of that familiarity as much as the pleasures of the dance that gave an extra light to her eye. Just now she was leaning a little closer to hear what her partner was saying in the midst of the din and laughed delightedly as they spun back down the room.

She was happy now, but as always her social anxiety during the preparations for a party had been pronounced if, in his opinion, utterly unfounded. He had arrived home in plenty of time, listened attentively to her instructions, and admired her dress, reassuring her that the neckline was appropriate and that he would stick to safe topics of conversation. The Fiteaus were old friends of her family, wealthier versions of the same titled Catholic military stock, and their annual spring ball was an occasion she had attended for years. Still, she had been irritable and impatient until the moment the carriage rented for the occasion pulled into the courtyard of the Fiteaus' *hôtel* in the heart of the Left Bank's aristocratic quarter. Her mood had lifted only as she stepped from it and ascended the wide staircase that led up to the spacious hallway where the host and hostess were greeting their guests. They could hear the sounds of the orchestra warming its instruments, readying itself for the first dance. Dubon had taken Geneviève's arm and they had moved together into a ballroom glittering with old-fashioned candlelight. The room, a long gallery with large windows at the front overlooking the street, ran the full length of the second story of the building, and they had proceeded slowly down it with Geneviève greeting friends and adding names to her dance card. At the end of the room, an archway led into a little adjacent salon where those who wished could sit out the dance. That's where Dubon was standing now.

"You're a lucky man."

It was his old friend Masson, coming up behind him and echoing his thoughts.

"Even if she is dancing with someone else," he added. They both laughed.

"She looks well. What about you? The law still keeping you happy? I keep meaning to come in about my will. Always putting it off. I suppose all your clients say that."

"Yes. Lots of them do. But I prefer you to the ones who are rewriting it every week."

"And for my first son . . ." said Masson, adopting the cracked voice of the aged, "nothing. To punish him for serving wine instead of brandy last Sunday."

"Exactly. Very trivial stuff compared to the affairs of state."

Masson worked for the Foreign Ministry. He and Dubon had been at school together, and Dubon had never abandoned the friendly habit of deferring to Masson's intellectual achievements. Dubon had been the good-looking one, the leader of his gang, and had shown early promise with the girls at the nearby convent, while the gangly and bookish Masson had been viewed with some suspicion by his peers, both for his unfailingly high marks and for his ability to talk his way around the grown-ups. He was the kind of friend one's mother was always inquiring about.

"Bah, the affairs of state," Masson said with an insouciance Dubon did not quite believe. "Developments that seem so momentous one year will be forgotten the next." The Baron de Masson, as the diplomat styled himself these days, had returned from a posting in Russia two years before, and Dubon was never exactly sure what it was that he was now doing. "Who will remember you or me when we are gone, Dubon? We are little people, eh? Private life is our true realm. Family, friends . . ." He gestured toward the crowd around them. "That's what really matters."

"What really matters, my dear baron?" It was their formidable hostess, Madame Fiteau, joining them in time to catch the end of their conversation.

"Yes, yes, off you go, dear," she added to the pimply, red-haired youth at her side, dismissing the younger of her two sons with an annoyed wave of the hand. An awkward Louis Fiteau beat what looked like a very welcome retreat from the ballroom into the salon.

Dubon wondered in passing at his discomfort—surely Louis Fiteau was at least five years older than his own fourteen-year-old André and mature enough to manage social occasions? He noticed that the youth was soon joined by an older man, an officer—tall but rather stooped, dressed in a baggy uniform and sporting a large white mustache—who seemed to have been waiting for him. The two disappeared through a small door in the salon's ornate gilt paneling that once closed behind them was almost invisible to the casual eye. Dubon turned his attention to his hostess, a large and determined woman not easily ignored.

"Masson was trying to argue, very unconvincingly I might add, that friends and family matter more to him than politics," Dubon explained. "But we all know you are a careerist through and through, my friend."

"Well, I don't think that's fair."

Masson seemed hurt, and Dubon belatedly realized he had perhaps been tactless. Masson's mother had come from an aristocratic line that could trace itself back centuries and she was always a high-strung character. His father, who simply called himself Baron Masson, was of humbler antecedents. He owed his title to a grandfather who had been useful to Napoléon, but the "de" in front of the surname was an addition his son had made only in recent years. The marriage between Masson's parents had been a battlefield and Masson was in his final year at school when his mother, after several very public displays of jealous rage, took herself to bed with the laudanum bottle once and for all while his father sought solace in the arms of his longtime mistress. Nobody seemed to care much what happened to the adolescent Masson until Dubon's parents took pity on him and allowed him to shelter in their less dramatic household. Masson had stayed with them for a full year during which he had slept in the room next to Dubon, who could hear him sometimes at night, crying himself to sleep like a little boy. After all the years that had intervened, Dubon still felt slightly protective toward him. A wife and children might have been a comfort to Masson, but he had gone into the diplomatic service directly after his graduation, traveled widely, and never married. Perhaps he did not want to repeat his parents' mistake. Or had the families of prospective brides worried that Madame Masson's notorious instability was a hereditary complaint?

"You have devoted yourself to the interests of the nation," Dubon assured him. "You have had little time for anything else."

"No, we don't think of you as a family man, Baron," Madame Fiteau piped in, "but if you were considering whether or not it might be time to marry, I know a very nice girl . . ."

"Ah, Madame. So thoughtful of you."

At that moment a rather aggrieved-looking young woman moved toward them.

"But not this one," Madame Fiteau added in a stage whisper. "Baron de Masson, Madame Verry. Her husband shipped out to Hanoi last week so we are doing our very best to keep her cheerful."

"Madame." Masson bowed.

"My dear, you met Monsieur Dubon earlier, did you not? Dear Geneviève's husband."

"I believe I have the pleasure of the next dance," Dubon said helpfully.

Madame Verry was a young military bride whom Madame Fiteau had taken under her wing in her husband's absence, making sure all the men danced with her. Their collective efforts did not seem to be having much effect: Madame Verry grimaced at Dubon, rather like one whose shoes were hurting.

"The baron was just telling us he's thinking of marriage," Madame Fiteau continued, and Masson laughed.

"No really, Madame, you mistook me. My work continues to keep me busy. It would be no kind of life for a woman," Masson replied.

"Nonetheless, you are not traveling so much these days."

"Not so much."

"But you are still keeping us safe from the Germans?"

"I do my best, Madame. They are, however, a formidable force."

Dubon thought he detected a double irony here, as Masson, adopting the pose of one humbly accepting praise for keeping an entire nation secure, seemed to mock his own false modesty.

But if the man was anything less than sincere, Madame Fiteau did not notice, and she explained eagerly to Madame Verry, "The Baron de Masson is one of our great allies in government. The general always says you show a remarkable understanding of military affairs for a civilian, Baron."

"He flatters me, Madame."

"What we need is another war," Madame Verry interrupted with vehemence.

"Another war, Madame?" Dubon asked, surprised.

"Yes, smash the Germans once and for all, pay them back for all the horrible things they have done."

Her anger seemed out of place at a party and was embarrassing her companions. Dubon could not think what to say, but Masson stepped in suavely.

"A decisive victory, you think? That is what is required?"

"Of course that is what is required. The government doesn't give the army what it needs. I mean, the English, say what you will about the English, but at least they know who keeps them safe. They don't stint their army or their navy. You wouldn't catch them letting the troops wander about in ragged uniforms."

Dubon wondered to himself if Lieutenant Verry—he assumed the man was only a lieutenant—was not too short of cash to have his uniforms made by a good tailor.

"Our politicians just don't understand," the lady continued. "All this talk about cutting the workweek. Nonsense put forward by the unions. The Socialists will ruin this country, just like they tried to in 1871. How are we ever going to win a war if men are afraid of a solid day's work? And the government panders to them; those politicians and bureaucrats, they'd rather not work themselves."

Masson raised an amused eyebrow for Dubon's benefit, but Madame Verry appeared not to notice she had insulted the baron's profession and sailed on.

"The army is not afraid of hard work—it can do the job—but it has to have the resources to do it."

"You are entirely right, Madame. One can't make something out of nothing," Masson said smoothly. "And where did you say your husband is garrisoned? Ah yes, in Tongkin. Fascinating place." He moved the conversation adroitly toward a discussion of the wondrous Orient until the music stopped and Dubon realized he must now take charge of the angry little Madame Verry.

He placed his arm around her and guided her confidently onto the dance floor. He thought nothing more tedious than women who attempted to maintain a serious conversation while dancing; he always found vague compliments and mild encouragement whispered in the lady's ear were all that was required, but Madame Verry was not to be dissuaded from her tirade and kept it up around the dance floor.

"Oh, entirely, Madame," Dubon shouted at her as he repositioned a gloved hand on her bony back and directed her away from a particularly exuberant couple rounding them on the left. "The army was never properly supported during the last war; the mistake should not be repeated."

He certainly hoped the mistake would not be repeated. He didn't blame the army for France's defeat at Germany's hands; he blamed it on Napoléon III's failure as a diplomat and tactician, and the last thing the new republic needed was another such fiasco. He didn't think it was worth clarifying his position to Madame Verry, however. She could hardly have been more than a babe in arms at the time of the war. As she opened her mouth again, he quickly interrupted her to point this out.

"But surely, Madame, you were not yet born . . ."

"No, but my father fought the Germans, and then he had to fight the Socialists to stop them from taking over his own country. Just imagine what Paris would be like today if those Communards hadn't been defeated. It would be anarchy."

"Ah yes. Just imagine." Dubon winced at the thought of how she might react if she knew his past. He had not only defended the Communards as a lawyer. During the brief, heady days of the Commune, as a young student with radical sympathies, he had run messages for them too. The leaders allowed each separate ward in the city to weigh in on every decision; swift young messengers were in high demand. He had done his bit—more than his bit—he would have been jailed had he been caught, but he had successfully disappeared back into his parents' house when the crackdown began. His involvement was his little secret; only a few old comrades knew, and Geneviève and Masson, of course, who tolerated his past. Well, perhaps *tolerate* was too generous a word: they were prepared to ignore it and keep his secret. He would pay a heavy social price if anyone in the Fiteaus' circle identified him as a former Communard.

"If we are ever going to win back Alsace and Lorraine from the Germans . . ." Madame Verry continued.

"I couldn't agree with you more," Dubon repeated, as he wondered how long this particular dance would last.

As he guided Madame Verry down the room, he glanced back enviously at Masson, who had somehow succeeded in keeping his dance card blank and was sitting with their host. General Fiteau, his large form overflowing the cane chair designed to hold the lithe figures of the debutantes, looked out at the dancers but did not seem to see them, as though distracted by whatever his companion had to say. Masson sat erect on the chair next to him and his trimmer physique with its square shoulders seemed to dominate the general's. The baron had always been tall and he had filled out with age; the gangly young Masson was now quite an impressive specimen, Dubon realized with some surprise.

Masson angled his torso slightly toward the general, offering advice or urging his opinion on the man. How assiduously Masson courted the military set, Dubon noted. If the diplomat who had graced the salons of Berlin and St. Petersburg felt Madame Verry and her ilk were beneath him, he certainly did not show it. Masson now gestured toward a couple who floated by as though to make some point and the general nodded almost sadly in agreement.

As Dubon watched them, he caught a movement in the corner of his eye. At the far end of the room, the little door in the paneling of the salon had opened slightly and a head now peeked out. It was the pimply young Fiteau. He peered about anxiously as though seeking someone. He then turned his head over his shoulder, as though a person in the room behind him had spoken, and quickly withdrew behind the little door.

Finally, the music stopped and Dubon could release Madame Verry, bowing effusively. She was scooped up again by Madame Fiteau and a relieved Dubon sank into the background, happily remembering that he was unpartnered for the next dance. He looked around, pondering his next social move, and noticed one of his brothers-in-law entering the ballroom from the salon. It was Major Pierre de Ronchaud Valcourt, Geneviève's older brother and eldest of her five siblings, resplendent in the blue tunic and red trousers of his regimental dress. He was a cavalry officer and held a position that kept him happily in Paris or in the provinces, drinking and card-playing with his colleagues when not exercising his horse. He had failed to inherit any of the military genius that had made his father so successful, but since the family had also failed to inherit any of the land historically associated with the Valcourt name, he had decided to follow his father into the army to supplement his share of the family income. Not that he resented this, since he lacked the imagination to think of any other life and was perfectly content with the company of his fellow officers, his pretty wife, and his two rather silly daughters and their many friends.

"Dubon! Over here!" he croaked in a stage whisper as he tugged on the lawyer's arm. He pulled Dubon toward him and then stepped behind him so that he was partly hidden from view. "Come and protect me from the captain. He's off on one of his rants."

And indeed, Captain Jean-Marie de Ronchaud Valcourt, the earnest younger brother whom Geneviève still affectionately called Jean-Jean, could be seen steaming across the salon in their direction, though he sailed by without a glance. His target, they realized, was General Fiteau, who was now standing with Masson but had also been joined by a lady, perhaps his partner for the next dance. They watched as Jean-Jean saluted his superior sharply before launching into a long preamble.

"He's got some bee in his bonnet about the artillery," the major explained, as he and Dubon eavesdropped tactfully from a distance. "Something about making the field guns quicker to reload if you could stop the recoil. He's probably right. He usually is, but it's beyond me." Jean-Jean, a young captain in the artillery with a passion for his guns, had inherited his father's professional understanding of war but lacked his tactical skills in dealing with the world beyond the battlefield. He was now clearly bothering his host.

"The recoil on the new 120 is ferocious, General," they heard Jean-Jean say. "It just hasn't lived up to our hopes. We are still wasting precious moments repositioning the guns and reloading them after we have fired. It's really a question of the brakes. The right advances in hydraulics—"

The general cut him off: "We mustn't bore the ladies with these technical matters, Captain. I'm sure what you say is right; you must take it to your superiors."

"I have spoken to—"

"I owe the marquise this dance," the general said decisively, turning to the lady and leading her away.

"What do you say, Dubon? Shall we rescue the boy?" the major inquired as they watched his brother now tagging after the general and the marquise.

"Captain," the major bellowed. "We need you over here. You've got to settle a little dispute I'm having with dear Dubon."

Jean-Jean turned toward the sound of his brother's voice and, in response to some frantic waving from the major, beat a rather awkward retreat toward them.

"I was just explaining to the general that the point is the brakes—" he began, but his brother stopped him.

"The general doesn't want to hear about your mad schemes, and neither do we. Tell Dubon something funny. He was forced to dance with Madame Verry and must be in dire need of some entertainment."

"But really, it can be done." Jean-Jean, not a man well equipped to produce jokes on demand, was not to be dissuaded from his original topic. "Major, at the very least you must care about the recoil because it frightens the horses. The last time I was on maneuvers—"

"Captain," his brother interrupted, for in public the family was in the habit of addressing one another by their military titles. "Really, if your idea is so clever, why are you parading it about at a party? Do you want those spies over there to hear you?" The major cocked his head toward a pair of dandies who had positioned themselves at the edge of the dance floor.

"Spies!" Jean-Jean was appalled. "How do you know they are spies?"

"Well, that's Schwarzkoppen from the German embassy and that's Panizzardi from the Italian. They are busy spying for their countries; that's what they do."

"But, Major, you must warn our host—"

"Jean-Jean." His older brother smiled indulgently. "General Fiteau *invited* them. He knows they are spies. Everybody does. All the military attachés at the embassies are spies, but one can't very well cut off relations with the foreign powers. Goodness, even an old cavalry officer like me knows how the system works."

"But this is an outrage," Jean-Jean persisted. "I assumed we were among friends."

"Oh, we are among friends all right—just don't go discussing state secrets with them, any more than you would go discuss them with your wife. Well, if you had a wife, that is." The major was always ready to poke fun at his brother's bachelor status. Now, to demonstrate how chummy everyone was, he called out.

"Schwarzkoppen. Come and meet my brothers; bring your Italian friend with you."

A rather sleek and self-satisfied-looking man began moving toward them, followed by a second, less commanding person. Dubon suddenly found Masson's tall figure at his elbow, quietly insinuating himself into the group.

"Dubon, I don't believe you have met Colonel Schwarzkoppen, nor Major Panizzardi," the major began. "My brother-in-law, Dubon. A lawyer, but we won't hold that against him. This is my brother, Captain de Ronchaud Valcourt. And the Baron de Masson," he added.

"Nice to meet you, Monsieur Dubon, Captain," said the taller of the two foreigners, as he and the Italian each shook hands with Dubon and Jean-Jean. They simply nodded in Masson's direction; apparently they knew him already.

"The colonel is with the German embassy, the military attaché," the major continued, leaning in toward Jean-Jean, feigning a conspiratorial whisper and repeating his previous accusation. "That means he's a spy, Captain."

Jean-Jean glared at his brother but said nothing.

"Ah, Major, if I were a spy, I would have succeeded in discovering where it is you have moved your little card parties," the German said. "I haven't seen you since the autumn."

"Oh, sh, Colonel. Not in front of my brother-in-law. He'll have my sister after me. Nothing wrong with a little gaming between gentlemen, but if Geneviève were to find out, she'd be horrified. Since our parents' deaths, she does like to play mother hen."

The major emitted a braying laugh and Dubon said nothing. The major's disapproving family already knew of his habit, but thus far his wagers were never so extravagant that he had gotten into serious trouble.

"I have not yet had the pleasure of meeting Madame Dubon, but I hear she is charming." Schwarzkoppen bowed slightly as he addressed

Dubon, who wasn't certain he really wanted to introduce this hand-some character to his wife.

"She's still busy on the dance floor, and she has promised me the first waltz," Dubon responded.

The major chuckled. "Schwarzkoppen, no man wants to introduce you to his wife. Your reputation as a lady's man precedes you."

Schwarzkoppen and the major now turned to an enthusiastic dis-cussion of their best bets for opening day at the Longchamp racecourse that Sunday while Dubon and the Italian mainly listened.

When the orchestra struck up a waltz, Dubon excused himself. "I must find my wife. It's a little tradition we have—a waltz."

He found Geneviève waiting for him at the edge of the dance floor. He slid his arms around her waist and drew her to him. Sniffing her familiar perfume, he felt, for the first time that evening, rather peace-ful. These dances were a touch of romance remaining in their other-wise practical union. Giddy with love and nerves, he had proposed to her in the middle of a waltz at just such a military ball eighteen years before. She had been something of a rebel in those days: a few months previously, she had rejected the young officer whom her parents had in mind. Dubon had felt it an enormous victory when he gained first her father's permission and then Geneviève's own consent.

"Lovely party," Geneviève said as they moved across the floor. "Ma-dame Fiteau always does the most wonderful job of her ball."

"Mmm," Dubon agreed without speaking, content to let the music, laughter, and snatches of other people's conversations flow over him.

"No, not until next year. It's been postponed again . . ."

"I haven't been able to find her all evening . . ."

"Well, they can hardly accuse the Republicans . . ."

And then, muffled but still loud enough to be recognizable for what it was, came the sound of a gunshot. The little door in the paneling through which the young Louis Fiteau had stuck out his head a few dances ago swung open. There was a thud as his body fell to the floor of the salon, landing heavily a few feet from the entrance to the ball-room. His hand was still clasped around the pistol with which he had just shot himself: a scarlet blotch appeared at his temple where the blood was seeping into his ginger-colored hair. A stooped fellow in an oversized uniform emerged more slowly from the same doorway. His face was partly hidden by a walrus mustache, but what could be seen looked ghostly. Dubon realized he was the same officer who had been at Louis Fiteau's side earlier in the evening, waiting for the awkward young man when his mother dismissed him.

"My God, I thought he was joking," the officer said as he began elbowing his way through the stunned crowd.

THREE

The general promptly put his military training to use. Within moments, he had cleared the salon and positioned a line of men, most of them young officers, across the archway, barricading his son's body from view. He looked up and caught Masson's eye. Dubon, standing stock-still with Geneviève still in his arms, instantly understood and began shepherding his wife and any other lady in his path down the ballroom, away from the salon and toward the main door that led to the hall. Masson was doing the same, having already forestalled Madame Fiteau, who had not yet seen her son's body, from coming any farther in that direction.

"Unfortunate accident . . . Nothing to do but remain calm . . . Best just to leave it to the general . . . Let's all move out to the hall . . ."

The cry had gone out for a doctor and as the crowd shuffled somewhat reluctantly away from the scene, a gray-haired man whom Dubon recognized as Geneviève's obstetrician came pushing by them. Even if he were the finest surgeon in France, Dubon doubted he was going to be of much use.

Once in the hall, the crowd moved with some relief across to the supper room, where people milled about asking one another what they should do. Dubon noted neither Masson nor Madame Fiteau was present. Wisely, the man must have got his hostess off into some private room. She was in for a shock.

They waited for about ten minutes before the general came into the room and spoke. His voice, normally booming, was a low monotone and would have been difficult to hear had a hush not descended: "There has been an accident with a gun. We have called the police. If you would all be so good as to remain here for a little while yet . . ."

There were solemn murmurs of assent and the general disappeared again. A few people now helped themselves to the glasses of champagne that had been poured earlier, ready for the guests, while others began surreptitiously selecting any food they could easily pop into their mouths, picking at the grapes on the pyramids of fruit at either end of the table or sampling the petits fours. The waiters who had stood idle when the crowd entered, unsure what role they should play, now began to replenish glasses. Soon the crowd was eating and talking quietly as the guests moved about speculating with one another on the young man's condition.

The ladies either did not understand or did not wish to understand what had transpired.

"Some kind of horrible accident . . ."

"I do hope he's all right."

"Poor Marthe. Her youngest."

The men, meanwhile, would avoid one another's glances. They could only guess there had been some kind of card game going on behind the little door, and that young Louis Fiteau had been losing heavily again.

After an hour or so, two uniformed officers entered the room briskly, commanding the crowd's instant attention. One stepped forward and introduced himself as Major Robin, and Dubon realized the general had called the military police.

"I am very sorry to have to tell you all . . . to announce to you . . . there has been an accident." There was a little cry around the room as he found the words: "Monsieur Louis Fiteau is dead."

❧

The death threw Geneviève into a social quandary.

"How is one to write a letter of condolence?" she asked Dubon at lunch the next day as she speculated, correctly as it turned out, that there would not be a public funeral. "They will be very lucky if they can get a priest to bury him."

"It's appalling, Geneviève," Dubon found himself replying with some heat, irritated by her concern over the niceties of the situation. "Just go over to the Fiteaus' and comfort the poor woman . . ."

"Really, the next day. It's far too early."

"We can't let them think they have been shamed."

"But they *have* been shamed. I mean, he could hardly have chosen a worse moment, right in the middle of his parents' spring ball."

"I don't suppose he planned it that way."

"I don't know about that. Perhaps he did, to get back at them."

"Why get back at them?"

"Well . . ."

"Geneviève . . ." Dubon was as much amused as exasperated. "You have already managed to obtain some gossip. What is it you know?"

"Last night I was speaking to—"

"I was with you the whole time after it happened."

"Not when you were getting our coats."

"So, while I was gone . . ."

"I was just speaking to the major."

"And what did your brother say?"

"That the young man had debts, heavy debts, and that the general was refusing to pay."

"What did the major think about that?"

"You mean did he think it wrong for a father to cut off a son like that?" Geneviève asked pointedly.

"Your father—"

"It never came to that with my brother," she said sharply.

"Did you tell him you hoped he learned a lesson?" Dubon persisted, sure his wife could hardly have resisted the opportunity.

"Oh, goodness, François, with the poor soul's body still lying on the floor? I didn't have the heart to say a thing."

❧

Dubon returned to the office after lunch and tried not to think about Louis Fiteau as he sorted through his papers. He could not banish the image of the young man's body sprawled out on the floor, however, and he wondered what he would feel if it had been his son lying there. His fatherly affection, often masked by routine or overshadowed by Geneviève's mothering, rose up in his throat as he thought to himself: My God, what if André got into some kind of trouble . . . He shook his head as if to clear it and tried to concentrate on the contract in front of him.

At about four, Roberge blew the whistle on the speaking tube and announced, "That lady's back," before slamming the thing down with a vigor that reverberated in Dubon's ear.

Sighing at the man's lack of grace, Dubon stood up and opened the door to find the widow standing there staring up at him. He blinked and stood aside for her to pass, feeling her skirts brush gently against his leg as she did so. He had meant to think that morning of another lawyer to whom he could refer her case, but his mind had been occupied with Fiteau's suicide. She was carrying a large envelope, which she handed to him without comment and then stood back waiting for his reaction, biting her lower lip with a set of fine, white teeth, like some child in front of a teacher. She was still dressed sedately in black but had permitted herself a little white lace collar that added to the girlish effect.

"Well, let's see what you've got," he said, attempting a cheery tone, before he walked around to his desk, opened the envelope, and removed the pages that were inside.

They were a thick pile of newspaper clippings surrounding the arrest, conviction, and deportation of her friend's husband, a certain Captain Dreyfus. Dubon remembered the case. There had been a furor about it two years previously, but he had completely forgotten the man's name. The convicted spy had come to be known simply as "the Jewish traitor" and the story eventually had dropped from the papers.

"These are newspaper clippings, Madame."

"Yes. A great deal was written about the case at the time, and I kept them all. I thought they might be of use to you."

"Yes, Madame. I expect they will. Very useful. But I was looking for the *legal* file."

"The legal file?"

"Yes. The documents relating to the court martial."

"Well, Maître, I don't . . ." The widow lowered her eyes. She appeared almost bashful for a moment as though she had been caught in some deception. "That is to say, my friend doesn't really have access to such material. It is in the safekeeping of her brother-in-law's lawyers."

"Not a problem, Madame. Just give me the name of the firm, and I'll liaise with them."

"No, Maître. You don't understand. When I told you my friend does not know of my efforts . . . that is to say, you must work independently of the family."

Dubon drummed his fingers lightly on the desk. Really, he did have to find someone else who could help this woman. He supposed the great Déon, the legal giant in the office upstairs, would only send her about her business.

"At least you can tell me the nature of the case against your friend's husband," he said, trying to suppress any tone of annoyance. "You did say the army had evidence of a spy."

The widow paused as though considering her answer and now raised her head.

"Yes, there was a document of some kind, I believe. A document the French intercepted on its way to the German embassy, a letter from someone within the ranks offering to sell secrets to the Germans." She paused again before continuing more forcefully. "But it was unsigned, Maître. I know that for certain, there was no signature. Why do they think the captain wrote it? They just picked him because they needed someone, they had to pick someone . . ."

"A scapegoat, you mean?"

"Yes, that's right, exactly. A scapegoat. Oh, I knew you would understand the case, Maître."

Dubon tried to nod wisely but sensed they were getting nowhere. The widow seemed to have only the vaguest notions of the evidence against her friend's husband.

"Did the army perhaps analyze the handwriting of the letter?" he asked, trying to remember what he had read in the press at the time.

"Yes, that's right. An expert testified, a Monsieur . . . Ber . . . Berceau . . . Bertille . . ."

"Bertillon?" She nodded at the name. "Bertillon testified! What did he say?"

"You know him, Maître? Is he very respected?"

"Yes, he's well known in legal circles. He has a system for identifying criminals—well, for identifying anybody, I guess. He goes around the jails measuring their earlobes and the like, noting any moles, that kind of thing."

"To what purpose?" The widow seemed genuinely intrigued.

"To identify them in relation to any other crimes, I guess. Suppose you had a very thorough description but no name of a culprit in one case, and then you arrested someone for another crime. If you had some kind of cross-referencing system, you might discover both crimes were committed by the same person."

"It sounds sensible."

"Yes. I always thought it seemed a bit far-fetched, the earlobes and all that, but my colleagues in criminal justice say it's revolutionizing the police courts."

"You doubt the idea that no two sets of human earlobes are alike?" she asked wryly.

"Or more to the point in this case, I doubt that everyone's handwriting is unique. I had never heard Bertillon was a handwriting expert."

"The letter does not match the captain's handwriting. No reason that it should, since he didn't write it. So, Bertillon testified that the letter did not look like the captain's handwriting because he was purposely trying to disguise his hand by mimicking that of his brother and . . ." She paused here, and swallowed as though the theory pained her. "And that of his, uh, that of his wife, too."

"And your friend and her brother-in-law find that far-fetched?"

"Yes."

"What do you think?" Dubon asked.

"What do I think?" She seemed surprised by the question and let out a small laugh. "I suppose I hadn't given it much thought because I know it's not his handwriting."

"But what of Bertillon's theory?" Dubon persisted.

"Why would anyone go to the trouble of disguising his handwriting? It's not as though the Germans would recognize the handwriting of a French officer, nor as though the culprit would expect to get caught. If he was going to sell secrets to the Germans, wouldn't they want to know his identity anyway, to verify he had the goods? Maybe Bertillon was influenced by the nature of the assignment. If you are shown two handwriting samples and asked if they could possibly have been written by the same hand, you might be more likely to reach a positive conclusion than a negative one."

"Yes, that's called leading the witness," Dubon agreed. "Phrase the question the right way, you'll get the answer you want."

"At any rate, I know the captain did not write this document, whatever it is. Anyone who knows him knows he couldn't betray his country. To prove his innocence you just need to find whoever really wrote the letter."

She smiled brightly at him now and Dubon felt his stomach flutter. He wasn't sure if it was the effect of her smile or the tenor of their conversation. Behind her girlish nervousness, she was, it turned out, highly intelligent. She just didn't know much about legal procedure or have much information about the case. It was a bad combination: if he took on this impossible assignment, she would understand precisely how he had failed her when he inevitably flubbed it. He should find her another lawyer, now.

"Let me read this file, Madame, and see what I come up with."

"Perhaps I can come and see you next week? Monday?" she asked eagerly.

"Let's say Wednesday or Thursday. Give me until Thursday," said Dubon, stalling. "I will try and have a . . . well, some ideas for you by Thursday."

FOUR

"There is no one who works in our offices by that name, Monsieur."
The newspaper clerk was polite but firm. Sitting at a discreet desk with
an even more discreet sign reading simply *La Presse*, he was stationed
beside a small door in one corner of the large marble lobby of an apartment building not far from Dubon's own offices. Many buildings in
the neighborhood gave over the ground floor to commerce, but this one
seemed slightly embarrassed that it had to share space with anything as
grubby as the press, and the effect was to make Dubon feel even more
unsure of his mission.

"But there must be," he persisted. "His name appears in the paper
all the time. Look, I found it just last week." He pulled out a folded
paper. "Here it is, Azimut Martin."

"Yes, so I see, Monsieur," said the clerk, not even bothering to turn
his head to look at the byline on the page Dubon proffered. "But there
is no one here by that name."

It was Monday and, after a visit to Madeleine on Saturday morning
since he had not seen her in three days, Dubon had spent the rest of
a rather subdued weekend going through the widow's fat clipping file.

Perhaps he would be better equipped to recommend a different lawyer if he understood the case a bit more. There were various names writing in various publications as well as many unsigned articles, most of them vigorously denouncing the traitor and congratulating the army on ferreting him out, but it was this Azimut Martin writing in *La Presse* who had a more dispassionate view. The man seemed to know a lot about the case—or knew someone in the military who did. He could tell Dubon if the captain's case was as hopeless as it looked from the outside and whether anyone had ever successfully appealed a court martial.

"If there is no one here who goes by that name, then who is he?" Dubon demanded of the clerk. "Someone here must know who writes the articles that are published in your paper."

"Really, Monsieur." The clerk was now taking umbrage. "I'm sure the editor knows. I mean, Azimut, what kind of name is that?" He snickered a little, for the astronomical term *azimuth*, meaning a path or direction, hardly seemed a likely first name. It dawned on Dubon that he had been naive; these newspaper fellows used pseudonyms, of course.

"Well," he said loudly, his embarrassment making him belligerent, "if your writers haven't the courage to use real names, why should your readers believe what you print?"

A lady entering from the street glared as she passed him on her way to a small elevator in the opposite corner of the lobby. "Journalists," she sniffed.

The clerk, who clearly did not want a scene, was now looking worried, but Dubon was not to be put off. "One way or another, I want to see the fellow, whoever he is," he said. "I insist I will see your Azimut Martin."

"And so you shall, Monsieur. Or at least, you shall see me, and I will take responsibility for whatever it is he has written that has so offended you."

Dubon turned to see a gentleman in a well-tailored gray suit who had entered from the street door and was now extending a hand.

"Who are you?" Dubon asked, shaking his hand.

The man smiled pleasantly. "My name is Chalon. I'm the editor."

He nodded at the visibly relieved clerk. "Thank you, Roger. I'll take this gentleman into my office."

"Of course, Monsieur Chalon," the clerk said in a studiously neutral tone.

Chalon led Dubon through the door into a hallway where another clerk sat at a desk. The editor greeted this second clerk and pushed through a pair of glass-paneled doors into a single large room where a dozen men sat hunched over desks surrounded by paper. Not only were their desktops covered in reams of the stuff—full sheets, half sheets, and torn scraps—but their in-baskets also overflowed, and more sheets lay at their ankles. In a corner, two figures pounded away on typewriters that produced a loud clatter, while no fewer than three telephones were ringing as they entered. Dubon was just wondering how anyone could get any work done in such mayhem when one of the seated men yelled out something unintelligible and held aloft a sheet of paper while continuing to mark up the page that lay before him on his desk. A clerk repeated the shout and came running, grabbed the sheet from his hand, and ran out the door with it, pushing past Dubon and the editor with the briefest of nods.

"You catch us at a busy time, Monsieur," Dubon's guide explained. "We go to press at two, and they still have to set the type. The typesetters and the printers are just round the corner on the rue du Croissant. I imagine that is where Perrin was galloping off to with the first pages. We share the presses at the *Figaro:* they get the early hours of the morning; we take over in the afternoon. Our deadline is eleven." It was now ten thirty.

"I'm surprised you are at leisure to see me, Monsieur," Dubon remarked.

"We can't have irate readers causing disturbances in the lobby," Chalon said cheerfully. "Normally, I would be chained to my desk at this hour, but I had to step out on a bit of business, a little political question that needed my attention."

He had, by this point, walked Dubon across the newsroom and into his office. He settled his visitor in a chair before crossing to his own desk and sitting down.

"So, how has our military correspondent angered you, Monsieur?"

He paused, and Dubon took the opportunity to introduce himself.

"My name is Dubon, Maître Dubon. I'm a lawyer on the rue Saint-Honoré. I bear Monsieur Martin, or whoever he is, no ill will. I am simply investigating a small military matter for a client of mine, and your man seems particularly well informed. I would like to meet him, that's all."

"I don't think that will be possible, Maître. Perhaps if you were to write down your questions I could relay them to our correspondent and send you any answers he could provide."

Dubon was loath to reveal the nature of his business to this newspaper editor without feeling on firmer footing in his inquiries. He had only thought to get a bit of advice from the secretive Martin that he could pass on to the widow before finding her another advocate, and he did not have a line of questioning he could summarize in a note.

"I need to know how I can contact the man so that I might meet him in person," he repeated, now more concerned with appearing in control than actually pursuing Martin.

"Maître, you must understand that in a journalist's line of work it is sometimes necessary to keep one's true identity from readers," Chalon continued pleasantly. "The correspondent writing under the name Azimut Martin has excellent connections in military circles, connections that might not wish to speak with him if they knew he was writing for *La Presse.* To some sources he may reveal his identity, to others he may prefer to remain anonymous, all the better to serve our readers by offering the most accurate accounts of military news. The man we call Monsieur Martin is not, you will have gathered, permanently in my employ; he works elsewhere and offers my editors articles as he can. We have come to rely on him over the years; he is seldom wrong. May I say, in my turn, that it is not that I do not trust you, but I would not wish to compromise his fine work. If you will leave your card with me, I will pass it on to him and suggest that he contact you."

Dubon bit his lip. It seemed he would get no further. "Might I have an envelope?" he asked.

"Certainly," Chalon replied, and after some searching through his desk drawers, he offered one inscribed with the newspaper's name and address.

Dubon, meanwhile, pulled out a business card and risked writing on it: *Wishing to speak to you about Captain Dreyfus. Please write or visit at your earliest convenience.* He wrote the name Azimut Martin on the envelope and, as an afterthought, surrounded it with large quotation marks. He slipped his card inside the envelope, sealed it, and passed it across the desk. This was the best he could do. Damn these newspaper types with their self-important games, he thought as he thanked Chalon cordially and left. The pace in the room outside the editor's office seemed if anything more frantic now, and he crossed it hurriedly, glad to leave the journalists to their cacophony.

Out on the street, he turned south toward his office, but then stopped and pulled his watch from his pocket, wondering as he did so if he might not just pop in to see Madeleine while he was in the neighborhood. It was almost eleven and he had thought, since his wife had a lunchtime engagement, to eat at a small restaurant around the corner from his office where the *patron* made a particularly good dish of tripe, but perhaps instead he might share the midday meal with Madeleine. It would cheer him up, bring his mind back to his own affairs. He expected to find her at home because she seldom left the house before noon.

He turned into the rue de Grammont with a light step and the notion of a lunchtime encounter, made all the more pleasurable for both parties by being unexpected, tingled just below the surface of his consciousness. He arrived at the narrow entrance of the small building where Madeleine lived and let himself in with his key, before walking up the three flights to her apartment and tapping gently on her door. This was their unspoken agreement: he used his key at the street door but always knocked at her apartment door to warn her of his arrival.

Today, there was no answer. He waited a minute, just in case he had caught her at her toilette. He did not keep his mistress in such style that she could afford a lady's maid to pin up her hair or tighten her corsets, and one could hardly have called her lodging large, although both of its rooms were generously proportioned. There was an alcove off the

main room where she could prepare simple meals, and a bathtub behind a curtain in the bedroom; water had to be fetched from the pump
on the landing and heated on the stove, a task performed by the daily
maid employed by the concierge who lived on the ground floor. In these
small quarters, a knock did not go unheard. Dubon knocked again. He
now thought he heard a faint rustling from within, like the swishing
sound Madeleine's skirts made as she crossed a room, but when his
third knock went unanswered, he supposed he had only imagined it,
gave up, and retreated down the stairs.

He emerged on the street in what was, for such an even-tempered
man, a sullen mood, more disappointed than he would have been if a
scheduled appointment with his mistress had been canceled. The world
was not bending itself to his will this morning, and for Dubon, a lawyer who spared himself the drama of the courtroom and a man who
had achieved what he considered a happily balanced domestic life, this
gave rise to an uncomfortable feeling of impotence.

Turning onto the boulevard, he straightened himself and breathed
in the fresh air. The wide pavements seemed full of well-dressed ladies enjoying the first fine spring day. Admiring them, Dubon felt his
good humor return and, reviewing the morning's failed business, he
reminded himself that, on the one hand, he would see Madeleine that
afternoon and that, on the other, he was not without his own contacts
in the press.

As he stepped into the office, he ignored the sheaf of messages that
Lebrun, who was now back at his post, handed him. Instead he sat
down to write a letter, which he instructed the clerk to post immediately while he went around the corner for his tripe.

The reply came promptly by midafternoon: his old school friend
and former comrade from the days of the Commune, the sports journalist Morel, was only too happy to arrange a meeting with *Le Soleil*'s
military correspondent but would be at Longchamp covering the races
the rest of the week. If Dubon was free that very evening, Morel invited
him to the Bistro des Italiens after six, when he would introduce him
to his colleagues who regularly gathered there. Dubon sighed. Events
were conspiring to keep him from Madeleine these days. No, really,
it would not do. This was not his case, after all. He responded saying

that evening was unfortunately impossible, but wondering if they could not invite the military correspondent to the races sometime in the next few days? Dubon was not a gambling man, but he might enjoy a day at Longchamp. He could always, he thought as he remembered again the fate of the unfortunate young Fiteau, set himself a strict budget.

He returned to his neglected files, and at 4:50 left the office promptly.

Letting himself into Madeleine's building a few minutes later, he inhaled appreciatively as he caught the scent of a particularly fragrant cigar smoke lingering in the lobby, and climbed the stairs with enthusiasm. This time, his knock was answered promptly.

FIVE

"I am in need, Lebrun, of a box of chocolates."

The next day, Dubon was giving a few quick instructions before he left the office for lunch. Roberge's lugubrious presence was still fresh enough in his imagination that he felt a little wave of comfort and relief every time Lebrun's face appeared at the office door.

"The five-hundred-gram with the gold bow?" Lebrun inquired.

"I was thinking the kilo today."

Dubon was feeling the need to be generous. His reunion with Madeleine the previous evening had been unusually flat, even a little awkward. When he had entered her apartment at five, he had the odd sensation that someone had preceded him; he had no rational evidence of this, no half-empty glasses on the table or a forgotten scarf trailing across the divan, just a sense that Madeleine was not the only one who had been breathing the air in those rooms or sitting on the chairs. It was not that he forbade her other companionship, but he always assumed that he was offering an easier life than the one she would have experienced had she pursued her original profession or married any of

the artists or clerks who used to hover about her. Perhaps, he thought
to himself, he was being naive.

"Pleasant afternoon?" he had asked, without mentioning to her that
he had knocked on her door earlier in the day. Was it his imagination
that she responded just a trifle too quickly, "I was out"? Their conversation proceeded listlessly from there, and what followed in the bedroom was almost perfunctory. Dubon had felt deflated as he prepared
to leave for home, and if he clasped her tightly to him as he kissed
her on his way out the door, it was to reassure himself that this little
coolness between them was an aberration, that their relations where
unchanged and unchanging.

"Very good, Maître," Lebrun replied. "I'll go around the corner
after I have closed up for lunch."

Dubon turned his attention back to his desk, but Lebrun, usually
as discreet as a ghost, lingered. He seemed to have something to say.

"I wanted to apologize again to Maître Dubon for the inconve-
nience caused by my absence last week."

"Not at all, my dear Lebrun," Dubon said, continuing to tidy his
papers.

"I know how difficult it is when you have to make do with Roberge."

Dubon looked up again. "We managed. Not as well as we do when
you are here, of course."

"I trust I always give satisfaction."

"Yes. Of course, satisfaction. Entirely. And your mother is better
now?"

"Yes, thank you, Maître. She is much improved, as much as one can
expect under the circumstances."

"Ah yes, the circumstances." Dubon hadn't a clue what the circumstances might be and wasn't at all sure he wanted to ask.

"Yes, the elderly. You know, Maître, how it is. One cannot ask that
they heal the way the young do. An elderly relative is something of a
burden. My mother is increasingly unable to care for herself. Thank-
fully, I have found an excellent housekeeper for her. The expense is
significant but familial duty makes certain demands. I do not need

to tell Maître Dubon that. I am lucky, of course, that I do not have a wife and children—that would be a great responsibility, a great financial responsibility—but nonetheless, there are costs associated with the care of an aging parent . . ."

This was about the longest speech Dubon could ever remember Lebrun making.

"Yes, well, I am sure you are a dutiful son, Lebrun," he said, as he rose from his desk to forestall the request he suspected was coming and straightened his jacket. "I must hurry home. You know how I disappoint Madame Dubon if I am late for lunch."

In fact, Geneviève was not home when he got there.

"Madame is still out," his manservant Luc informed him as he greeted him at the door.

"Out where?"

"Out visiting."

"In the morning?" Geneviève followed the convention of paying her calls in the afternoon.

"I believe she was delivering her condolences to Madame Fiteau."

"Madame Fiteau!" Dubon almost laughed. He had told his wife not to stand on ceremony, but he hadn't actually expected her to march right over there. The metallic ping of the doorbell sounded behind him, and Geneviève, who never used a key because she thought it more genteel if a servant answered the door to her, walked into the hall.

"So?" Dubon asked.

"So?" she replied, taking off her gloves and handing them to Luc.

"I hear you were visiting Madame Fiteau."

"Yes, well, you need not look at me like that. I'll tell you about it at lunch."

Indeed, once settled at the table, she was eager to recount her exploits. She had given in her card at the Fiteaus' with a small note of comfort scribbled on it and, to her surprise, had been ushered in for an audience with the general's wife.

"I think she was so relieved to see someone. Her own sisters are staying away. Can you imagine that?"

"Barbaric."

"It's hardly her fault."

"No."

"It wasn't a pleasant visit. She is in a horrible state. Part of her really can't believe it happened. She denies that the young man even gambled."

"But she must have known. Your brother said the general had refused to keep paying the debts."

"Maybe he never told her."

"Maybe. Seems a bit improbable. She's a powerful woman."

"You wouldn't have said that today. Just a shriveled old lady. A terrible thing to lose a child."

"He wasn't a child. He must have been twenty."

"For a mother they are always children. I wish you could help them, François."

"How could I help them?"

"Find out what happened . . ."

"Their son shot himself because he couldn't pay his latest debts."

"His mother doesn't believe that. Or at least, maybe part of her knows he was gaming, but she says he was inveigled, trapped somehow in some kind of plot. I told her you could try to find out what happened."

"You told her what?"

"At least, you could find out to whom it was he owed the money."

"Geneviève, if young Fiteau owed someone a lot of money, whoever it is will now make himself known to the general."

"If he dares."

SIX

Madeleine answered the door wearing an afternoon dress in a flattering shade of rose that she often favored and accepted from Dubon with half-mocking protests the box of chocolates Lebrun had procured that morning.

"Goodness, you must think I do nothing but sit at home devouring bonbons. You will make me fat, dear . . . No, no I was out this afternoon, with Lucie. We went to the gallery finally. We were entranced, the figures are so lifelike, you would almost think they'd come off the walls and talk to you. We spent so long there, we didn't even have time for tea. Shall I make us some now? I picked up a few cakes on my way home—or perhaps you would just like to eat chocolates," she concluded with a giggle.

They ate tea and cakes happily together—although Dubon himself preferred a glass of wine by that hour of the day—and proceeded to the bedroom. Later, as they lay under the covers, a seemingly sleepy Madeleine raised the topic of the chocolates again.

"You are so good to me," she sighed as she patted him gently on the thigh. "I am always grateful for your generosity."

"Um." Dubon assumed this was a reference to his sexual manners and didn't feel it required much response.

"The chocolates are a lovely treat . . ."

"Oh, the chocolates. It's nothing," he said, but Madeleine was not to be dissuaded.

"No, it's very good of you. Not every man is so attentive. The chocolates, that lovely necklace at New Year's. You are very good." She paused before adding, "But you know what they say, man cannot live by chocolate alone."

Dubon laughed. "You're becoming a wit, are you? Looking to start a salon?"

"Well, I hardly have the space here, do I?" Madeleine pointed out, gesturing around the bedroom.

"Most ladies hold their salons in the salon, not in the bedroom," Dubon replied. "I guess you might squeeze in a few poets or two next door, perhaps a duchess, hmm? A painter, you have to have a painter for it to be a true salon." Despite his joking tone, Madeleine seemed to consider the topic seriously.

"No, there's not enough space."

"Do you really want a salon?" Dubon had his first inkling that perhaps their conversation was not entirely lighthearted.

"No, of course not. I don't have such pretensions. But still, it would be nice to entertain a little, not always be locked up here alone."

"You're not locked up here alone. You were at the exhibition this afternoon with Lucie."

"I just mean it would be nice to have a little more space to invite my friends over. I get lonely during the evenings, you know."

"I know you, you are out at the cafés. You tell me you are sewing but you are probably at Montparnasse."

Madeleine laughed. "I really don't go out much, my dear. Even if I wanted to, I don't have the means."

"Why should it cost anything? Your friends will always entertain you."

"That's so typical of a man. You buy the dinner, you pay for the glass of wine, you don't realize that I have to wear a dress. And how am I to get to the café? Am I to walk alone in the dark?"

"Well, no, of course not, my sweet." He was surprised and a little hurt by her tone and responded quickly to quell any threat of discord between them. "I can give you more if that's what you need . . . a little increase . . ."

"I don't like to trouble you . . ."

"Perhaps an extra fifty? No, not enough for all these cafés and dances you are planning on attending? One hundred it is."

"No, no really. It isn't necessary."

"I'll pay a call on the bank manager tomorrow."

"Oh, don't bother. You don't need to."

Dubon looked at her. She had got her way but was now retreating, as though she did not wish to appear to have asked. Such social squeamishness was quite unlike her.

"It's no trouble," he said.

"No, my dear. Please don't bother."

Did she not want the money after all? What was her game? Angered, he persisted, "This is ridiculous, Madeleine. I will go to the bank tomorrow."

"Well, if you insist . . ."

About a quarter of an hour later, Dubon rounded the end of Madeleine's street and started down the boulevard des Italiens, thinking he would find a free cab on the busy boulevard before he got as far as the Opéra. As he passed the café on the corner of the rue Grammont, a small but tidy establishment frequented by some of the local journalists and businessmen, he saw with surprise that Masson was sitting at a table near the window. Hardly seems like his neighborhood, Dubon thought. This was the business district at the heart of the bourgeois Right Bank. Masson was a man of the Left Bank, the seat of government and learning, the home of the aristocracy. As though sensing his friend's stare, Masson looked up from his newspaper and caught Dubon's eye. He mimed a jolt of surprise and beckoned him inside. Dubon had better not be long about it; he needed to get home. Masson, on the other hand, seemed in an expansive mood.

"Greetings. Good to see you. Are you going to join me for a drink?"

Dubon pulled out his pocket watch. He could afford about ten minutes, maybe a quarter of an hour. It would be nice to have a little glass of something.

"I can't stay long. You know it's my policy never to be late for dinner. It keeps Madame Dubon happy."

"Yes, the ladies. Have to keep them happy. You have a lot more experience there than I do, Dubon. An old bachelor like me can eat whenever he wants, but in truth longs only for your cozy family dinners."

A waiter appeared at Dubon's side.

"A red wine," Dubon said. "And not any of your Beaujolais. A Bordeaux."

"What are you doing in these parts?" he inquired of Masson. "Slumming it with the press and the stockbrokers, eh?"

"I might ask the same of you." Masson laughed. "But, of course, your office is not that far away, is it. Your clients behaving themselves today?"

"Oh yes, my clients always behave themselves."

"How dull. No revolutionaries who need defending?"

"You know I gave up that stuff long ago. Nothing to report except wills and contracts, wills and contracts."

"We all rely on you, but it must be horribly technical," commiserated Masson.

His sympathy irritated Dubon. He was, after all, a moderately successful solicitor with a solid practice. If he had once entertained dreams of being a legal crusader, he was hardly the first person who could be accused of growing more sensible with age. Somebody had to look after the nuts and bolts of legal affairs.

"Well, I enjoy my work," he said a bit defensively. "And it is not all routine. I have an unusual client at the moment—rather delicate case, in fact."

Masson said nothing, only allowing a little *hmm*, which Dubon read as skepticism, to pass his lips.

"Yes, a client has come to me on behalf of friends who have some disagreement with a military court," Dubon said.

"And you know your way around the military establishment, no doubt there," Masson contributed.

Dubon registered the slight, although he knew perfectly well Masson was right and was honest enough to admit it to his face.

"I expect that's why the client chose me. The case might test some precedents if I can get to the bottom of it." Dubon, who until that moment had not the least notion of getting to the bottom of the widow's case, allowed himself a self-important shake of his head.

Masson said nothing and the silence emboldened Dubon, who was not usually a proud man but felt the sting of judgment.

"Yes, the military tribunals can be sloppy, you know, not as experienced as the real judiciary, disregarding proper procedure. It's a full court martial they want me to overturn."

"And your client doesn't need a litigator, then?" Masson inquired blandly.

"Well, yes, I am sure the client will, eventually. I am just laying the groundwork, bit of investigation as it were."

"Your client can be sure his business is in good hands. Is one permitted to ask his name?"

"She's a lady actually," Dubon said, and instantly regretted it.

"A lady? *Tout s'explique!*" said Masson grinning. "It isn't fair. You have a lovely wife, you should leave some for the rest of us."

It was as though Masson thought there was something ridiculous about Dubon's success with the opposite sex. As a youth, Dubon had casually assumed that his own easy popularity trumped Masson's aristocratic antecedents, but he now sometimes found to his surprise that his friend made him feel socially inadequate.

"She's a perfectly respectable lady, I assure you. And I would never breach the solicitor–client relationship in that way," Dubon protested with some heat, perhaps because his recent fantasies involved just such a breach.

"No, no, my friend. I was teasing you. I am jealous, that's all. Your client—I am sorry, you didn't say her name . . ." Dubon ignored the hint and Masson did not press him, saying only, "I am sure her case will prove an interesting diversion for you."

Conversations with Masson could be such slippery affairs, with insinuations of superiority so nuanced that whenever he complained to Geneviève that his friend left him feeling snubbed, she dismissed his complaint and repeated, as did everyone in their circle, "But the baron is so charming!"

"Yes, it is interesting. Interesting and difficult," Dubon said. "The charge was . . . well, let's just say it was as serious as it gets."

Masson was still for a moment, staring out beyond Dubon to the zinc countertop where the waiter was lining up clean glasses for the evening patrons now crowding the bar. He then seemed to rouse himself, to brush off a thought, and he said, heartily, "Good luck to you, Dubon. Your clients' affairs are in trusted hands. I really will get you to draft my will soon. Goodness knows, I don't have much wealth to distribute, but it is ridiculous not to have something on paper. After what we saw the other night, makes you think." He grinned, a trifle ghoulishly, Dubon thought.

"Yes, makes you think," he agreed. "Have you talked to the general since then?"

"A little. Hard to know what to say."

"Yes. Geneviève went to call on Madame Fiteau today."

"Did she? Good for her. Madame Dubon is such an admirable character."

"She said Madame Fiteau won't really believe that he gambled, or at least, she feels he was ensnared somehow."

"Aren't they all?"

"I suppose so. You don't think there's more there than meets the eye? I mean, my own brother-in-law organizes card parties, but for someone to kill himself over a debt . . ."

"Young Fiteau just got in over his head, I guess. I imagine if the debts are that large, the general will settle them now."

"Yes, that's what I told Geneviève," said Dubon, shrugging off the topic, and seeking in his pockets for change.

Masson waved off his attempts to pay. "I'll settle up when I leave."

"I'll see you Friday for dinner, then. Geneviève did say you are coming?"

"I would never miss an opportunity to sit at your table, Dubon. I am honored that you and Madame would include me."

"Oh, nonsense," said Dubon, Masson's formality somehow re-awakening in him his affection for a man who, however much he occasionally irritated him, was one of his oldest friends. "It's only a family dinner."

Perched in the back of a hansom as the driver directed his horse through the traffic around the place de l'Opéra, Dubon tried to reassure himself that he had not been indiscreet with Masson. He hadn't given him any real details of the widow's case nor revealed her name, and the man was hardly a gossip. His profession required discretion; it was in his nature. Not like the journalists, Dubon reminded himself: he had better be careful what he said when he met the military correspondent from Morel's paper.

It was only after the cab had crossed the place de la Concorde and Dubon was almost home that he recalled his recent encounter with Madeleine. He realized belatedly that two people had asked him for a raise in the space of one day. To be fair he should probably give more to Lebrun, but he would have to review his accounts and do some calculating first. He looked down at the coins in his hand as he paid the driver. Decidedly, the box of chocolates had been a bad idea from the start.

SEVEN

Dubon watched a quartet of Europe's top thoroughbreds round the final bend of the long course at Longchamp to begin their panting ascent of its notorious hill, and reflected that it was much better, in the end, to have a little female company to dilute all the horseflesh. His wife would never attend the races, which she considered a vulgar pastime fit only for the shameless, a category into which she freely cast the elder of her two brothers. She had always disapproved of gambling, even a little betting at the racecourse. Events at the Fiteaus' ball had served only to strengthen her long-held conviction. Still, she would have looked grand seated well up in the stands, studying her race card with that air of quiet remove she adopted in unfamiliar settings. Madeleine, on the other hand, would have felt perfectly at home with the boisterous ladies in the first row, cheerfully urging the horses on while leaning across the rail in a way that would have afforded Dubon a nice view down the front of her dress. She was a woman who both gave pleasure and took it with happy ease.

His companion, however, was neither his gracious wife nor his generous mistress. The widow sat tidily beside him a few rows up from the course watching the third race of the day with interest. She squinted occasionally at the horses, whether because she was puzzled by their behavior or simply nearsighted, Dubon wasn't sure, but it gave her an appealing, quizzical air. If passersby gave her black dress the occasional sidelong glance, the woman herself seemed perfectly comfortable with her surroundings. She was now discussing with Dubon exactly how the pari-mutuel system worked, having dismissed with some amusement his initial patronizing attempts to explain it.

"I don't believe you actually know. You said you never go to the races. Think about it—if everybody bet one hundred francs, and say ten thousand people are betting on the tote today . . ."

"So, the payout would be a million francs . . . What would you do with a million francs?"

"But, Maître, I wouldn't win a million francs," she pointed out, looking up at him. "Divide a million by the number of people who have correctly picked the winner."

"Of course. I wasn't thinking."

"So, say, fifty or even one hundred picked the winner, I would win ten thousand or twenty thousand francs."

She was quick with numbers, he noted, very quick.

"And how would you spend it?"

"Why, Maître, I would pay your bill!" she announced gleefully.

He smiled back but groaned inwardly. If the bill was on her mind, she definitely couldn't afford Déon. He had still vaguely been thinking of simply sending her upstairs, but he realized now he needed to find her someone young, eager, and cheap. He would start asking colleagues for names tomorrow.

She had laughed when he had, on the spur of the moment, suggested she accompany him to the races that afternoon.

"I am hardly dressed for it," she had said, indicating her mourning clothes.

"No, but I don't suppose it matters. It's a weekday: the diehards won't care what you are wearing."

"The diehards and the aristocrats . . ."

"Maybe. We can lunch there," he added expansively, supposing to himself that if she accepted he would send a note to Geneviève to tell her he was unexpectedly delayed at the office and would not be home at noon.

The truth is he hadn't known what else to suggest to the widow. She had come to see him that Thursday morning. Lebrun had been out filing documents at the Hôtel de Ville, and finding no one about, she had popped her head through his office door, calling out, "Anyone home?" He had received her gladly, but he had little to show her. The mysterious journalist, Azimut Martin, had yet to reply to Dubon's message, and his only plan was to go out to Longchamp that afternoon to meet his friend Morel and the military correspondent from his paper, a man by the name of Fournier. He had exaggerated Fournier's importance to the widow, to make the trip to the racecourse seem like some kind of action, but he had found a few of the journalist's articles in her clipping file and the man was clearly only parroting what little information the military had released officially. If Dubon wanted to find someone with an insider's view of the case so he could steer the widow toward the right lawyer, he doubted Fournier was the man.

"We will see what this journalist can tell us," he said to her brightly. "You can bat your eyelids at him. Men are susceptible to that."

She smiled, but straightened herself and smoothed her black dress with one hand. "Really, Maître, I hope that's not what you think I am doing here."

"No, of course not. My apologies, Madame. That was a thoughtless remark."

"All right, I'll come," she said, cutting short his apology. She seemed eager enough to accept the pretense she might be of some use.

"Tell me, Madame, what is Dreyfus like? What kind of man is he?" asked Dubon, as they settled together in the back of the carriage.

She looked down at her skirt as though she might find an answer in its folds.

"Noble and brave, Maître," she began.

He waited, hoping for something more revealing.

"A meticulous officer, very hardworking, and, most of all, loyal. He is always loyal."

"Meticulous, you say?" It was the only adjective that gave any hint of personality.

"Oh yes. He is scrupulous about his financial affairs and a perfectionist on the job. And very generous, to his family, to his friends. Very generous. And the children . . . he is very dedicated to his children, although of course his military duties sometimes interfere with family life. He used to work long hours. Other officers would tease him about it sometimes. It hurt him. He often said they were simply lazy. To question his commitment to the army is so unfair."

The carriage rounded a corner, jostling her against him. He gently placed a hand on her shoulder to help her right herself. Through her satin sleeve, he could feel the soft flesh of her upper arm compress ever so slightly beneath his touch.

"He sounds admirable, Madame," he said. "And your friend's family is comfortable, Madame? It is not at all possible there was some financial . . ."

"No, Monsieur, not at all. Some have speculated the captain might have stooped to spying because of financial need, and I think it is impossible. I don't know the particulars, but the family is quite wealthy, I believe. They come originally from Mulhouse, but most of the family moved to Carpentras after the war. One brother remained to run the family's businesses in Alsace—they own several textile mills, you see—and he sends the proceeds back to France. Indeed, I don't think the captain really needed the military salary. I . . . I think his wife . . . my friend . . . found it frustrating sometimes when her husband was working particularly hard. He was truly dedicated to the army; he had seen what the Germans had done. His family felt the loss of Alsace personally and he wanted to protect France. He was very eager to get his next promotion because he cared so much about the profession."

"A loyal soldier," Dubon replied soothingly, but he suspected that such a man might be rather bothersome, especially to his colleagues, an officer who didn't need the pay but showed the others up by working harder than anyone else.

"Did he have many friends in the army, then?"

"The captain is mainly a family man. He prefers to spend his time at home—even if he is distracted sometimes. I really don't know his friends . . . no, I don't think he has that many friends in the army. He was respected by his colleagues, of course, well liked . . . until this happened."

Well liked. Dubon wondered. He hesitated before beginning delicately, "You, Madame, would you be . . . that is to say . . . would you and your friends be coreligionists?"

"Yes. I am Jewish, if that is what you are asking. You are thinking we were isolated . . . It's true, the captain and his wife, many of their friends are Jewish. But it is hardly a crime to pick one's friends from among one's coreligionists."

"True, Madame."

"People seem so ready to believe a Jew would betray France, Monsieur. Yet, we felt the loss of Alsace and Lorraine every bit as much; we are as loyal citizens as any others."

"Yes, Madame, I do not doubt that."

"Do you mean that?" she asked him earnestly, her look demanding an honest answer.

"Yes, Madame, I believe religion or birth are immaterial when it comes to patriotism. Any Frenchman can be a patriot—or a traitor."

"Oh, Maître, I am so glad to hear you say that," she responded. "I did not like to ask you where you stood, but the captain's brother is convinced he has been singled out for this unfair treatment because of his religion."

"Perhaps he's right," Dubon replied thoughtfully.

This conversation with the widow had been more useful to him than her clipping file, he thought to himself, cheered by the idea he might have some skills as a detective after all. She was not, despite herself, drawing a very flattering portrait of the man: He was ambitious, serious-minded, and hardworking, that much was clear—but he also sounded stiff, even pompous perhaps, and sometimes not as devoted as his wife might have wished. He certainly had no time for military camaraderie, and his colleagues probably disliked him as a result, especially if he was rising faster than them. Did his perfectionism somehow get him into trouble? Perhaps he had been too embarrassed by some peccadillo to go to his family for money? Or had his professional success and earnest personality so angered his colleagues that one of them had framed him for espionage? His religion would have made him, quite unfairly, an all-too-easy target for a comrade with a grievance against him or perhaps a superior officer irritated by his zeal.

"That's very useful, Madame," he said as the cab pulled up outside the racetrack. "Very useful indeed."

♣

During the break after the fifth race, they ate in the public dining room, a large space on the ground floor of the racetrack's main pavilion with a good view of the course—if not the finish line—from its floor-to-ceiling windows. It was a well-appointed restaurant with white linen tablecloths and white lace curtains blowing in the breeze, as the maître d'hôtel had seen fit to open the windows despite a continuing chill in the air, but it was less than half full that weekday. Sitting at a prime table pretending it was warmer than it was, they cheerfully dined on sole and lemon mousse as though summer were truly at hand and continued their discussion of the track, content to leave the subject of the captain aside for a while.

It was as they were hypothetically debating whether they believed in backing favorites over a long shot that Dubon saw Morel signaling at him from the door of the restaurant. He excused himself and walked over to his friend.

"Morel, good to see you. Won't you come and meet . . . my companion," Dubon said, not wanting to attach the word *client* to the widow.

"No, no. I have been looking all over the place for you. I thought you would be alone and just lunching in the café. Fournier is waiting for us upstairs in the members' bar. It's men only, Dubon."

"Of course, I'll just settle the bill here and perhaps you could stay with . . ."

Morel shook his head. "Sorry, but I have to be out there doing my job. I was just going to introduce you to Fournier before I scampered. We've only got ten minutes until the sixth race." He grinned at Dubon. "Your lady friend will just have to entertain herself."

Dubon flagged the waiter, requested his bill, and went back to the widow to explain the circumstances. She was perfectly accommodating.

"You go ahead. I'll meet you in the stands later."

"Are you sure? I don't like to leave a lady alone . . ."

"I am a widow, Maître. Widows can get away with a lot."

"I'll have to remember that."

"If you're not there for the seventh race, I'll wait. But after that, I'll start betting . . ."

She waved at him reassuringly as he went back to join Morel, who was already beginning to push his way through the gathering crowds outside the restaurant, squeezing through gaps in the same sinuous manner, Dubon recalled, that he had once crawled over the Communards' barricades.

Morel never seemed to age or slow down: Dubon remembered him fondly as someone who had always been in a rush, trailing bits of paper and leaky pens as he hurried to class at the lycée, zigzagging across town with his leather satchel during the days of the Commune, or hurtling into the church but a few steps before the bride on his own wedding day. His energy was infectious and he was, Dubon gathered, wildly popular with his readers, a success based on some uncanny ability to understand sports that he was neither rich enough nor athletic enough to play himself.

"Don't know why you want to meet Fournier," Morel called over his shoulder as he hurried up the stairs to the second floor. "Don't imagine *Le Soleil* is the paper of choice in the Dubon household, and he is not exactly our brightest spark."

"Madame Dubon reads your paper regularly," Dubon reassured him, although Morel only guffawed at this. "It's just a military case Fournier has written about. A client of mine wanted his opinion. I appreciate the introduction."

"Bah. It's nothing. A day at the races is a real treat for Fournier. And me, I owe you, at the very least my livelihood—if not my life," Morel replied as he reached the top of the stairs and surged across the landing.

"It was all Maître Gaillard," Dubon said, brushing aside the compliment but warming at the memory.

"He always gave you a lot of credit," Morel said.

Dubon had retreated into his parents' house that bloody week in May when the Commune fell, slipping back safely into the new bourgeois neighborhood in the 8th, but Morel had stuck it out in the streets to the east and had been marched to the court-martials at Versailles in a parade of thousands. Nobody could find the officer who was supposed to testify against him, so he had been found not guilty—at least in theory. In practice, even those who were acquitted had a *C* stamped on their identity papers and now found schools, professions, and even Paris itself to be off-limits. Without any such stigma, Dubon was able to study law, while Morel had languished on a cousin's farm in the provinces until Dubon had asked his mentor, Maître Gaillard, what they could do for his friend. The senior lawyer was already working on the campaign for an amnesty for those in jail or in exile. He vouched for Morel with the police, brought him back to Paris, and eventually found him a job as a copy boy with the newspaper where his wife's cousin worked. Ironically, it was a monarchist publication.

Dubon now followed Morel toward the bar and over to a table where a burly man with a large black beard was waiting for them.

"You're one of the de Ronchaud Valcourts, aren't you?" Fournier inquired eagerly, once they had been introduced and Morel had escaped to the stands for the next race.

"Yes, that's right. My wife, Geneviève, is the late general's eldest daughter."

"But you aren't a military man?" Fournier sounded disappointed.

"No, I'm a lawyer. Did you serve?"

"Not more than my national service. I'm a journalist by profession. Sort of fell into the beat, you know. I used to cover police news. Grimy stuff. This is very pleasant in comparison. Talk to all sorts of fine people—like yourself. It's a larger canvas, bigger issues at stake."

"Well, your writing certainly gets at the issues. As one familiar with military life, I can say you show great sympathy for what it's really like. The straight goods," he said, hoping he didn't sound sycophantic.

Dubon had read some of Fournier's recent columns in preparation for their meeting and had found them full of sentimental stuff about the average soldier laboring to protect the motherland. The man's contacts, he gathered, were fairly low down the hierarchy, and he doubted he would have any inside information about Dreyfus, but at least Dubon could ask him where to find Azimut Martin.

"No idea," Fournier replied. "Hides behind some silly pseudonym and publishes all kinds of trash—"

A roar from outside interrupted them—the sixth race had finished—and Fournier lifted his glass and gestured toward the windows overlooking the track. The two men moved across the room and stationed themselves where they would have a clear view of the next race.

"Do you remember that story a couple of years back about a spy, fellow they caught selling stuff to the Germans?" Dubon asked. "What did you think about that one?"

"The Jew?"

"Yes, that's the one. Dreyfus. Some people say he's innocent. Any truth to it, you think?"

"Oh, nonsense. I know the man who caught him red-handed."

"Really?"

"Yes, Major Henry—"

Fournier stopped as another cheer could be heard outside the bar. The runners for the seventh race were at the starting gate. They watched them run before Dubon got another chance to speak.

"You were telling me about this major," he prompted.

"Yes, Henry. Brilliant chap. Intercepted documents going to the German embassy and got the goods on the spy, rounded up all the evidence against Dreyfus."

"What kind of evidence?"

"Well, that's a secret, isn't it. Even if I knew, I would have to be careful what I said, but Henry practically caught him in the act. Devil thought he could get away with it, passing classified documents straight to the Krauts. They court-martialed him in no time. These Jews, the nerve, they come here, make their profits, then sell us out to the highest bidder. I don't know why France lets them join the army."

Dubon glanced around him to see if any other racegoers were listening to this rant, but the next race was about to start and the buzz of excited conversation all but drowned Fournier out.

The bell for the eighth race rang and Fournier leaned over the rail to watch, leaving Dubon to consider his vehemence. Dubon and

Geneviève had no Jewish friends; her circle was resolutely Catholic and he had made no lasting friendships with the Jewish lawyers he met professionally, but the idea of doubting their loyalty to France because of their religion struck him as silly. He had heard enough patriotic talk from Geneviève's Catholic connections to know their declarations of undying love for the motherland were mainly hot air, and he instinctively distrusted the hysteria of the columnists represented in the widow's clippings. Fournier, apparently, was of their number.

He should get back to the widow. The man had not told him much, except that many believed Dreyfus guilty and that the military had assembled some kind of evidence against him.

"I should be going. Friend in the stands I agreed to meet up with," Dubon said as soon as the roar of the race was over.

"Very nice to meet you," Fournier replied. "We should get together sometime when Morel can join us properly."

"Yes, that would be pleasant," Dubon said.

"Where do you know him from?"

"Oh, we were at the lycée together," Dubon answered cautiously.

"Really?" For the first time in their conversation Fournier looked at him with what might be described as a penetrating air. "You know there is a rumor at the paper that he's an old Communard."

Dubon froze.

"I've known him for years. Not possible," he replied quickly. If Dubon stood to lose much of his bourgeois clientele were his past to become known, Morel could surely be fired. "I should be off. Interesting to hear your take on that espionage case. I'd like to meet this Major Henry someday."

"Yes, there are lots of us who would like to shake his hand, but you can't exactly walk into the Statistical Section . . ."

"The Statistical Section?" Dubon asked, but the starter's pistol had been fired and the runners were off again.

"What did he tell you? Does he know Azimut Martin?" the widow asked anxiously when he found her in the stands.

"No, doesn't know the man, doesn't know who he is. But he did provide some information."

"What?"

"I'm not sure exactly. I need to check some details with my brothers-in-law. I'll ask them on Sunday."

"Sunday? What do we do in the meantime?"

"Hmm . . . go to the public lounge for tea, I'd say, unless you have a bet on this race, of course."

She laughed lightly and accompanied him back inside, but tea was a rather deflated affair. Clearly, she had been expecting more of him.

As they left the track to find a cab in the roadway outside, they passed a group of newspaper vendors flogging the afternoon editions to racegoers on their way home. From the melee, one cry rose urgently above the rest. Somebody had a scoop.

"Traitor escapes. Exclusive: Traitor escapes!"

Dubon took three swift steps to the newsboy with the widow at his heels, searching in his pocket for a coin as he went. He pressed a franc into an outstretched hand and grabbed the paper.

The headline was the same as the cry—"Traitor Escapes"—and underneath it were the words: "Prisoner of Devil's Island ripped from shackles by his German conspirators."

Beside him the widow emitted a soft cry as her legs crumpled beneath her.

Dubon caught her just before she reached the pavement.

EIGHT

Dubon arrived home a few hours later looking forward to a quiet drink but found to his irritation that Geneviève had invited her younger brother to stay. Jean-Jean often visited on Sundays because his current posting was at Compiègne, near enough to the capital that he could easily spend his day off in town. He kept a change of clothes at their home and sometimes spent a Saturday night on the divan in the library; apparently, this week he would be spending Thursday and Friday nights there too. The man was humorless, but Dubon was fond of him in a way and had to recognize that he was certainly the more intelligent of the two brothers. Usually, he was happy enough to tolerate him; it was just that today he was looking forward to a family dinner without any stray relations and some time to catch up on his paperwork afterward.

"Valcourt. Good to see you," Dubon hailed his brother-in-law. Although he thought of him as Jean-Jean, he would never have used the childhood nickname to his face. Dubon noticed, as he shook what was usually a rather limp hand, that Jean-Jean was looking larger and firmer than before. Perhaps he had put on weight. "You look well, young man," Dubon said jovially, attempting to cover what he supposed may have been the look of disappointment on his face as he entered the room. Not that Jean-Jean was likely to notice; largely uninterested in the part of the world that was propelled by blood and guts rather than cogs and wheels, he always seemed impervious to others' feelings toward him.

"Good evening, Dubon. How is business?" he asked rather woodenly.

Dubon didn't suppose that Jean-Jean cared in the least, but still, he was pleasantly surprised by the polite question. Perhaps the man was in love; he would have to ask Geneviève. A good marriage was what Jean-Jean needed to smooth his rough edges.

"Business is good, thank you. Bit busy with a delicate case these days, might have to retire to my papers after dinner, but looking forward to a good meal now . . . So, Geneviève, what does Cook have for us?"

Geneviève took the hint and steered her family toward the table.

"How is life at camp?" Geneviève asked her brother as they settled in their places.

"Oh, camp." Jean-Jean seemed unprepared for the question. "Oh, um, it's fine. Fine . . ." Jean-Jean paused awkwardly and then straightened himself. "Don't expect I'll be there much longer."

"Why is that, dearest?" Geneviève asked in a mothering tone. "You just got there. Surely your post will run another year at least."

"Well. Yes, but there are things in the offing." Jean-Jean pulled himself even straighter and puffed out his chest a bit. The effect was not attractive. "Can't talk much about it."

Dubon began revising his judgment. This didn't seem like an affair of the heart—unless Jean-Jean was contemplating an engagement with one whose father was so well placed in the services that he could get a new son-in-law transferred to barracks in a location more suited to a spoiled daughter. Maybe that was it.

"Contemplating a change of status, are you?" he asked.

"Perhaps. One doesn't like to assume. Can't really discuss it. Premature and all that. The army, Dubon, you know. Our task is of national importance and we must remain ever vigilant . . ."

Jean-Jean launched into a self-important paean to the armed

services, one that Dubon had heard many times before, but never from his brother-in-law. This was quite out of character.

"How's your idea for that gun thing?" Dubon asked, thinking to stem the tide of platitudes.

At this, Jean-Jean looked fit almost to burst. "No, really can't say. You civilians don't understand. I mean Geneviève is different, of course. She was raised in the service, but no, I really can't say . . . but things are in the offing, things on the go, you know." He seemed torn between wanting to confide something and wanting to stress the confidentiality of all military affairs. "Yes, really can't say, but thanks for asking."

Dubon gave up trying to pull teeth on a subject that didn't interest him anyway and turned to his hitherto silent son to ask him about his day. As André happily launched into an explanation of how one tested the reflexes of a frog, Dubon applied himself to a plate of rare beef. With Geneviève in the room, the question he really wanted to ask Jean-Jean would have to wait.

About three the next day, Lebrun stepped into Dubon's office and announced, "There is a lady here who wants to see you," in a tone that suggested he might have found a dead mouse on the landing.

Dubon sprang from his desk. He had been waiting all day for the widow to reappear.

"Yes, yes, show her in, Lebrun. Show her in."

Lebrun, however, was not to be rushed through the formalities.

"She says her name is Madame Duhamel and that you have seen her before. At first, I thought she said she wanted Maître Déon, but she insisted that she is in the right office."

"Yes, it's all right, Lebrun. Show her in. She's a new client. You weren't here last week when she first came by. Roberge just let her waltz right in, and I haven't told her that we don't usually see clients in the afternoon. She was here yesterday too, when you were out at the Hôtel de Ville."

Lebrun exited and reappeared a moment later with the widow. Her eyes were red and puffy. She must have spent the night crying.

"Maître, I am so sorry to disturb you. I hadn't realized you generally see your clients in the morning. This gentleman—"

"Oh, pay no attention to Lebrun, Madame," Dubon said, as his clerk withdrew stiffly. "Sit down, do sit down. I was so anxious to see you, after yesterday. Are you feeling quite all right? You don't look yourself, Madame. Let me ask Lebrun to run to the corner and bring you some hot tea."

The widow brushed aside the offer.

"I am fine," she said quietly. "I wanted to offer you my apologies for yesterday. It was an unforgivable display."

"No, Madame, you are too hard on yourself. Perfectly understandable emotion. And you recovered yourself instantly." Indeed, the widow had only swooned and was well enough to go home from the racetrack in a barouche, unaccompanied at her own insistence.

"Thank you. You are very kind. I am beside myself, Maître," she said. "On the one hand, I think, can it possibly be true? Has he escaped? He deserves to be free."

Dubon tried to think of a gentle way to respond. He had doubted the likelihood of the story even as he read it at the racetrack, and the morning editions were full of the government's denials. The escape certainly seemed both physically and politically improbable: if the Germans had managed the impossible feat of storming Devil's Island, they would be effectively acknowledging Dreyfus as their spy. Before he could find any words, however, the widow continued, making it clear she too had been considering the implications.

"On the other hand, I think, if he has escaped, he has played into their hands, given the country grounds to think him guilty . . . I couldn't sleep last night," she added, rather unnecessarily.

He could offer her little solace but they agreed they would meet again Monday to decide how they should proceed on her file.

"I will come again Monday," she said as she rose to leave. "In the morning, now that I know your hours," she added, recovering her usual sense of humor.

"I look forward to it," he replied, and then asked, as an afterthought, "What does your friend think of this recent turn of events?"

"My friend?"

"The captain's wife . . ."

"I . . . I haven't spoken to her, haven't been able to reach her," she said. "What you must think of me, Maître! If I am upset, imagine her distress."

What Dubon pondered were her red eyes. It occurred to him that she might be a family friend a bit fonder of the captain than of his wife.

NINE

"Where were you yesterday?" Madeleine demanded, peering quizzically at Dubon over the rim of her teacup.

"At the racetrack."

"The racetrack? What were you doing there? You've never taken me to the racetrack." Her tone was increasingly querulous.

"We can go to the racetrack anytime," he replied agreeably. "Well, anytime this summer." In the summertime, his wife's absence from the city allowed him to integrate his schedule more fully with that of his mistress.

"Oh, I don't know . . . maybe . . ."

Apparently, she didn't really care about the racetrack, she just wanted to feel aggrieved by his absence the previous day. Dubon could not think why. Hadn't he just agreed to give her more money?

He wondered what time it was but did not dare look at his watch. He had arrived a bit late at Madeleine's door—his anxiety over the widow and then her appearance had delayed him finishing a letter to a client—and now he just wanted to get to the bedroom.

"Do come here, my dear," he said, taking her cup out of her hands and placing it on the table beside him.

She sat there erect and unwelcoming, but did not resist as he drew her across the divan and started to pull at a tortoiseshell clasp that held her hair. She sighed as her locks fell to her shoulders and flipped them aside with an irritated hand.

He came home that evening to find Geneviève and André sitting in the salon, waiting for dinner. "Your brother not joining us?" he asked.

"No, he's out."

"Oh. But he will be here tomorrow?"

"I don't think so. He is spending the day with Le Goff," she said, naming an old friend of Jean-Jean's.

"What about Sunday, then? Or the major, better yet, is he coming for Sunday lunch?"

His tone was brusque, and she looked surprised.

"Yes, they will all be here Sunday, the major and Mimi too."

"Good, good. I look forward to it," he said, jovial now.

"François, you don't like my brothers. Why do you care if they are coming for Sunday lunch?"

"How can you say such a thing in front of André? You know I am very fond of his uncles."

"You are polite and welcoming to them. Maman always praised you for that, for fitting in and overlooking our peculiarities. We can be overwhelming sometimes for outsiders, and you didn't grow up in a big family."

Indeed, Dubon was an only child, and his father, while successful at law, had no ambitions beyond his secure place in the bourgeoisie. Dubon sometimes resented Geneviève's insistence on the size and uniqueness of her family; his much smaller one fell well below hers on the social register and he suspected that when she remarked on the differences in their backgrounds what she was really stressing was the aristocracy of hers. Certainly, if he had earned his late mother-in-law's praise for fitting in, it was because he came unencumbered by embarrassingly bourgeois relations.

Still, Geneviève, to give her her due, was a clear-sighted woman who was not given, unlike her three sisters, to flurries of false enthusiasm for family connections she did not actually like.

"There is a difference, however, between politeness and true affection," she continued now, peering at him suspiciously.

"Do you think your uncles are peculiar, André?" Dubon asked of his son, who was picking at the braiding on a cushion, uninterested in his parents' conversation.

"Oncle le Commandant is silly," he offered promptly, "and Oncle le Capitaine is . . . well, he's silly, but not as funny. He even manages to make guns sound boring."

"But they are good chaps, all the same," Dubon replied.

"And ma Tante Mimi is just stupid."

His parents pounced.

"André, that is unnecessary," said his mother, who tolerated honesty but never rudeness.

"Really, *mon petit*," Dubon added. He should have known better than to ask the adolescent André his opinion of his relations. Goodness knows what the boy thought of his own dull, old father. Dubon's history was completely unknown to his son. He was tempted to tell him sometimes, to fill the boy up with stories that could match the tales in the adventure books he so loved, but Geneviève would be appalled if she heard him. Events that had once seemed so exciting were now forbidden territory.

"Anyway," Dubon continued, trying to take hold of the situation, "we're family, and it will be very nice to see everyone here Sunday."

"You have something up your sleeve," Geneviève remarked.

"Just a question, a little business matter. I thought one or the other of them could explain a bit of military protocol to me," Dubon replied, as Luc came into the room to announce dinner.

He had his chance to question his brothers-in-law on Sunday. He tried the younger one first because he had a moment alone with him in the salon before lunch. Jean-Jean still seemed uncharacteristically ebullient and replied enthusiastically when Dubon broached him with a question about the structure of the military.

"Fire away, Dubon. Ask whatever you like."

"Came up at work the other day. I won't bore you with the details, but there's a military department called the Statistical Section. What do they do now, eh?"

Jean-Jean looked taken aback, and then blinked hard. After a long pause during which he seemed to consider his reply, he answered, "The Statistical Section? They compile military statistics."

"What kind of statistics?"

"Um. Well, casualties and deaths, I guess, if there's a war on. Or . . . number of men needed to do X or Y; number of loaves of bread eaten; average shoe size of French soldier . . . that kind of thing."

"They need a whole section to do that?"

"Well, I guess it's a small section . . . I really don't know much about it." He seemed his own awkward self and relieved to be interrupted by the arrival of the major and his wife, she of whose intelligence André had been so scornful.

The major quickly gravitated toward the men.

"Major, I was just asking a professional question," Dubon continued. "Your brother was able to enlighten me a bit, but I'm still puzzled. There is a military department called the Statistical Section and I was wondering what kind of statistics—"

"Counterespionage, Dubon," the major replied with a grin.

"Don't tell him that," Jean-Jean said. "If it were true, it would be classified."

"Worst-kept secret in town. Everyone knows what they do over on the rue de Lille," the major replied, at which point his younger brother retorted, "I want no part of this," and stomped across the room.

The major grimaced at Dubon. "Some people never change."

"He was awfully cheerful when he arrived on Thursday. Intimated there were some changes in his life or a move in the works . . . I even thought he might be in love."

"We can only hope, eh?"

"You were telling me about the Statistical Section . . ."

"Yes, it can hardly be counted as a national secret. It's where they run the counterespionage ops."

"And what, excuse my ignorance, is counterespionage?"

"Well, you have spies, yes? Like that German and that Italian I introduced you to the other night. The military attachés, so-called." Dubon nodded to indicate he recalled having met the two foreigners the night of the disastrous ball, and the major continued. "I guess we have our own in other countries too, I would imagine. Not like we French are so pure. Anyway, then you have fellows whose job it is to root them out. That's what they actually do in the Statistical Section, try to see if they can figure out who is spying on us and stop them. You know the Jew that there has been all the fuss about in the papers this week, the spy on Devil's Island?"

Dubon nodded again, anxious to hear what came next.

"It was the Statistical Section that originally caught him," the major said. "I believe they are rather proud of it—guess that's why everyone knows who they are now."

That explained what Fournier had said at the racetrack. The Major Henry who had caught Dreyfus worked in the Statistical Section doing counterespionage. Maybe Dubon could find him.

"So the Statistical Section caught Dreyfus? How?" he asked his brother-in-law.

"Found the evidence. All pointed to one man, so off he goes to Guiana for the rest of his days, the bastard. No escaping that place, no matter what the papers say." Noting Dubon's interest, he asked, "Why? What did Jean-Jean tell you they did at the Statistical Section?"

"Something about collecting the shoe sizes of the troops."

The major laughed.

TEN

Dubon was sitting in his office that Monday morning admiring the widow's nose, or at least the bridge of it. There was a certain delicacy to the way it met her brow, creating a high arch above each eye that gave her an intelligent air when she was seriously considering an issue. She was not a woman to be trifled with, he suspected; a dalliance would be unwise.

She was restored to fighting spirit that morning and was busy plotting action. She wore a high-necked white blouse underneath a short and narrow-waisted jacket, its bottom hem descending sharply to a V just where her black skirts flared out across her body. It was a modest but flattering silhouette. Why didn't he confess then and there that he didn't have a clue how to go about uncovering a spy and pass her on to someone better qualified to help her?

She had arrived at nine, eager to discuss what she assumed would be strategy. He began gently, feeling that at least he had a better grasp of the situation since his conversations with the military correspondent Fournier and his own brother-in-law, but also knowing it did not look good for the captain.

"I am sorry to say, first of all, that most in the military seem to believe that your friend's husband is guilty. I am not sure the false rumors of the captain's escape have worked in your favor. On the one hand, they have brought the case back into the public eye, but on the other, they have allowed the press to reassure its readers that the government has the right man. I don't see any impetus in the military to look any further as long as the public is satisfied that justice has been done."

"But it hasn't been done. That is why I came to you in the first place." Her tone was disappointed. "With your reputation, Maître, I would have thought a case like this would cry out to you, but perhaps you are just not interested, perhaps . . .'"

It was a bit embarrassing the way she kept returning to his reputation, considering how long ago all that work had been. When he did not respond immediately, she made a little movement to rise from her chair.

"No, no, Madame." He reached out to forestall her. He didn't want her to leave. He liked seeing her sitting there; he liked talking to her, and, he had to confess to himself, he liked the idea that he might be about to run out and solve the captain's case—he just wished he could think how. He wanted to hand her something that would make her grateful to him.

"I have made some initial inquiries as to where the case against the captain originates. If we are going to dismantle it, it will be helpful to know how it was built. The court martial was based on certain documents that investigators intercepted indicating there was a spy in French ranks offering secrets to the Germans."

She leaned forward eagerly now, as though following his reasoning.

Encouraged, Dubon continued. "The investigation would have originated in a secret department known as the Statistical Section. It is disguised as the military's statistical research arm, but it is responsible for counterespionage." Warming to his theme, Dubon repeated to the widow all that his brother-in-law had told him of how the Statistical Section operated.

"So," he concluded, "the arrest and court martial of Captain Dreyfus were considered a great coup."

"Well, it's a fraud, Maître, a fraud. The captain is innocent, as innocent as you or me. You must go and talk to these counterespionage people and demand they review their evidence."

"I can't do that, Madame. They are a secret operation. The only way to gain access to their files would be through an appeal. Did the captain's lawyers not consider appealing?"

"We were told there was no point, unless new evidence came to light. They said court martials are very rarely appealed," the widow said. She paused a moment and then pronounced her conclusion: "You'll just have to go over there and tell them they have the wrong man."

"I can hardly march right in . . ." he remonstrated, but she was not to be swayed from direct action.

"Why not?"

"It's a strategy, I suppose. I'm just not sure it would be a productive one."

"Then we'll have to come up with something else."

"You have to remember I am not a detective, Madame. I am a lawyer."

"Yes, Maître, a good lawyer," she said with a note of apology. "You are an excellent lawyer, and the captain, well, the captain seems to have suffered some bad lawyering, wouldn't you say?"

"Certainly an innocent man convicted of a dastardly crime hasn't been well served by his lawyers," Dubon agreed.

"So approach this Statistical Section as a lawyer, as a new family lawyer preparing for an appeal."

"They would be unlikely to share the files with me."

"What about from the other side?"

"The other side?"

"If you were a government lawyer . . ."

"You mean if I were the prosecution?"

"Yes, the prosecution, preparing itself, in case the verdict is ever appealed. The family still maintains the man is innocent and the rumors of an escape have brought attention back to the case. The government must be prepared."

"I follow your thinking . . ." She was clever, and pleased with herself now, he noticed.

"So you go over there, and you say you are Maître . . . well, Maître Petit, and your superiors in the Ministry of—"

"You are suggesting I misrepresent myself?"

"Yes, I guess I am." She looked at him. "It's for a good cause, Maître."

"Yes, a good cause," he repeated, but he wondered about that, and about the pressure that built up in his chest every time she stepped into his office. It had been long enough since he had experienced the feeling that it had taken him a while to recognize it for what it was.

Love—was it really such a good cause?

ELEVEN

There were surely things much more disruptive of domestic harmony than the sight of one's brother-in-law hopping about one's library in his skivvies, but Dubon just couldn't think what they might be. Jean-Jean, who appeared to have got one leg stuck while putting on the trousers of his dress uniform, let out a yelp of surprise as Dubon entered the room and clasped his hands to his privates. This was both unnecessary—he was wearing underwear, after all—and destabilizing. He promptly fell over, landing in a pile of clothes on the floor.

"Damn it, Dubon. You startled me." Jean-Jean got to his feet, pulled on the trousers successfully this time, yanked his braces over his undershirt and began gathering up the other garments, most of them an unappealing shade of gray. "Just thought I had time before dinner to try on my new kit," he explained, although Dubon did not understand how that activity justified the man's inability to stand on his own feet. "Horrible stuff. New battledress they're experimenting with. If it works, they plan to do away with all this." He gestured vaguely at his dress uniform. He was wearing the trousers, blue with a wide red stripe down each leg, while the blue tunic with its brass buttons was hanging over a chair nearby.

"Right, well, I'll leave you to it," Dubon said, excusing himself, retreating from the room and closing the door.

He had been hoping for a nice quiet drink in his study before the guests arrived and now stood outside the room wondering where he could hide. Geneviève was in full command of both the salon and the dining room, where she had been supervising the finishing touches to her table when Dubon arrived at five. For no reason that was discernible to him, he was called upon to return home early whenever they entertained: Geneviève and Luc always had everything under control. They both loved these occasions and prepared for them like coconspirators, whispering under their breath as they adjusted the angle of a flower or a fork, and continually congratulating each other on their discernment.

Dubon made for the salon and gingerly opened the drinks cabinet. He poured himself a small glass from the decanter—he had been drinking a '91 Giscours with which he was very pleased—and placed it with great care on the table by his armchair before returning to shut the cabinet: Geneviève would be peeved if anything were out of place. He settled in the chair, took a sip, and mentally prepared himself for the evening ahead.

It wasn't that he didn't enjoy parties or that he found playing host particularly onerous, it was just that they interrupted his schedule with Madeleine, forcing him to do without her companionship for an evening. It was his old routine and one he had been sticking to rigorously all week in an attempt to build a bulwark against the new things that seemed to be happening in his heart.

Geneviève entered the room.

"Oh, good, you're home. You'll have to take that glass into the kitchen when you are finished. Luc is far too busy to be picking up after you."

He knew that Luc, who was as likely to let his employer step into the kitchen as he was to let him carry the coal, could be trusted to appear at his elbow with a tray soon enough. Dubon sank lower in his chair.

82   Kate Taylor

Two hours later he was poking some kind of molten chocolate confection about his plate with his fork—just waiting for the ladies to retire to the salon so that he could return to his wine—and growing increasingly anxious, for someone had raised the topic of Captain Dreyfus. In the weeks to come, try as he might, Dubon could never remember who had first brought it up, but the whole party had leapt upon it with glee. The government had now successfully squelched the rumors of his escape, but that week the small faction who thought the man innocent had begun once again to voice their beliefs. The press seemed to feel that swift and brutal denunciations of that position had to be made. Dubon's guests apparently agreed.

"I think it outrageous that the man tried to escape," said Madame Bataud, one of Geneviève's regulars.

"But he didn't try to escape. It was all some silly story planted by the British press." That was Jean-Jean's friend Le Goff dismissing the escape story out of hand. A lanky blond man with a sallow complexion, he had joined the service at the same time as Jean-Jean and they had trained together in Normandy. He shared Jean-Jean's intelligence but was much more worldly. Indeed, he had a certain cynical edge that had sometimes irritated Dubon, and his tone now was verging on the contemptuous.

Madame Bataud visibly bristled, but Le Goff continued forcefully, "The man can't possibly escape; he's kept in shackles."

"Well, I certainly hope they have him securely locked up," she replied, refusing to be cheated of her righteous indignation. "The man is clearly a schemer, we have proof enough of that."

Dubon leaned forward and asked, "What proof, Madame Bataud?"

"Well, he's a spy, isn't he?"

"But what proof do we have, Madame?"

"Well, they arrested him, didn't they?"

The conversation was making Dubon feel guilty. It was Friday and he had not seen the widow all week. She had kissed him on both cheeks on Monday and merely said, "Think about it. I'll come again," before leaving his office. He wanted her back but had made no decision

about her scheme to impersonate a government lawyer and realized
that he had no way of contacting her. She had simply appeared in his
office three weeks ago and now she was not appearing.

Irritated, he pressed his point: "But what, Madame, if the man were
innocent?"

Le Goff, he noticed, was leaning forward eagerly.

"He can't be innocent. He was caught spying and was court-
martialed, wasn't he?" Madame Bataud replied and, happily unaware
of the circularity of that argument, leaned back in her chair and folded
her arms with an air of having carried the day.

"But what if they were wrong?" Dubon persisted.

"But they couldn't be wrong..." The lady looked puzzled now,
while Geneviève was giving Dubon increasingly meaningful looks from
her end of the table.

It was Masson, seated across the table from Madame Bataud, who
stepped in.

"You are perfectly right, Madame. Your faith in military justice is
no doubt exceedingly well placed. Court martials may seem very harsh
to us civilians but it must be remembered that in the army, discipline
is paramount."

How suave he had become, Dubon thought, as Masson continued with a speech of appeasing generalities. A diplomat by profession, he was successfully taking charge—Dubon noticed Geneviève's
grateful glance—and rescuing the situation without ever appearing to
manipulate it. It was annoying, and because he was annoyed, Dubon
interfered.

"Is it not possible, my dear Masson, that the brass are simply preju-
diced against the man because he's Jewish?"

Masson drew himself up and gave Dubon a long look. He answered
quietly but emphatically: "Dreyfus is guilty. I am given to understand
the evidence presented to the court martial was conclusive in that respect." And then his voice grew lighter, as though he was aware he was
striking too earnest a note. He said dismissively, "All this nonsense
will blow over. You know what they say, the dogs bark and the caravan
passes."

But Dubon was not so easily put off.

"No, I don't think it's that fleeting, Masson. I believe we may yet discover the whole case against the man has been driven by anti—"

He couldn't finish his sentence because Masson interrupted him in a jocular tone: "Now, my friend, you did always sympathize with the radical element. It's got you into trouble before, you know."

The two men stared at each other. They were venturing into dangerous territory. Dubon turned away and beckoned to Luc.

"Ah yes, Luc, more of the Veuve Clicquot. We are running dry," he said, gesturing down the table. "It really is very pleasant. You know," he remarked to the assembly, "I am a Bordeaux man myself, but Geneviève and Luc know better and insist on champagne with dessert. She selects all our wine herself. Did you know that?"

"Madame has excellent taste. We always drink exceedingly well at your table, Dubon," Masson replied.

"Yes, what would I do without her?" Dubon asked, looking toward her with some pride. Geneviève, meanwhile, was making her move, rising from the table to lead the ladies to the salon. Dubon and Masson stood with the rest of the men, and Dubon watched with some relief as Madame Bataud left the room.

"Fancy a cigar, Masson?" he said expansively, as though compensating for the moment of tension between them. "I have a new one, a Brazilian that is nice and mellow . . ." He gestured toward the sideboard where Luc was busy with a tray of glasses and a bottle of brandy. "In that green case," he said.

Masson prepared to help himself, moving to the sideboard and stopping at a box covered in red velvet.

"No, no. The green one, the leather one," Dubon corrected as he came up behind him. "Those are Geneviève's chocolates. You're welcome to those, too, of course." Masson hesitated and then reached for the second box, dismissing his mistake with a light laugh.

"My old problem. Color-blind. Can't tell the two apart. Remember how you used to tease me about it when we were at school? Ah, here they are." He picked up the green box, brought it to the table to share, and began to trim and light a cigar as the other men gathered around.

Dubon, standing alone at the sideboard now, found Le Goff's tall, thin figure at his elbow.

"You're on the right track, Dubon," he said quietly. "The right track."

"In what regard?" Dubon asked, but Le Goff had melted back into the party at the table.

TWELVE

The following day, although Dubon had intended to go to the office that morning, he sat at the breakfast table long after his family had dispersed.

Jean-Jean had been up and out before they had even woken, leaving only the rumpled bedclothes on the divan in the library visible through the open door. "Early start. Off on maneuvers for the week," he had explained the night before as he headed to bed the moment the last guests had left. André had eaten in a hurry and left for his Saturday morning lessons with his mother snapping at his heels.

As soon as the door closed behind him, Geneviève settled herself at the table with a second cup of coffee and the day's mail. She had already performed her postmortem on the previous evening and shared the results with her husband. It had gone off rather well, she thought, despite that awkward little moment over dessert. Now she reviewed their commitments for the following week—Masson was taking her to a matinee Monday; Dubon still had to pay the dressmaker's bill; would he accompany her to a meeting with André's music teacher Wednesday?

"I have some shopping I want to do this morning," she said as she rose from the table. "Aren't you going to the office?"

Dubon, who was staring at the newspaper but not reading it, looked up. "Office? Yes, yes, in a minute or two. I'm just thinking."

She looked at him a little puzzled. He was not normally given to reflection.

"Is something wrong?" she asked.

"No, no, nothing wrong. Just thinking about something at work."

"Surely that would be better done at the office," she said, her tone growing firmer.

He looked at her again. The details of the law remained largely obscure to her, and she assumed that the suits, contracts, and wills that paid for her servants and her dresses would keep flowing without any need for her to express much interest in them. She used to query him about his affairs, back in their younger days when he was working for Maître Gaillard. Geneviève had rather liked the element of danger about him then. During their courtship, he could impress her with his stories of running messages across the barricades. Her conservative parents would have been appalled if they had ever found out that Dubon had been involved in the Commune, but he suspected that was actually part of the attraction for his fiancée. Still, she had never complained at the time of their marriage when he had taken over his ailing father's practice, moving easily into a less controversial and more lucrative branch of the profession. She raised an eyebrow at him now, but withdrew without further comment.

When she passed by the dining room half an hour later on her way out of the house, he was still sitting there, now doodling on the newspaper with a pen.

"Still thinking?"

He lifted his head at her voice. "Yes. Listen, Jean-Jean said he was off on maneuvers. What does that entail?"

"They go off in a field and pretend to have battles, I guess, shoot at one another. My father used to spend hours planning things on big sheets of paper before maneuvers."

"I suppose I have some idea what maneuvers are," Dubon replied with uncustomary abruptness. "But will he be gone for long? He's not likely to come back tomorrow or something?"

"I don't imagine we will see him before next Sunday," she replied coolly.

"Fine. Fine. Good. A week tomorrow, then. Right."

"Why do you care so much these days about the comings and goings of my brothers?"

"I don't really. Always glad to see them. Glad to give the captain a bed whenever he needs it. You're off, then?" He had awakened from his reverie and was now trying to get rid of her.

She gave him a long look. "You're up to something these days," she said, sounding a warning note. "Don't think I haven't noticed."

After she had gone, Dubon listened to the stillness in the house. Somewhere in the background, down at the end of the long corridor that ran from the dining room to the kitchen, he could hear the muffled sounds of cleaning and cooking. But out here, on the other side of the thick door that divided his world from that of his servants, it was quiet. He walked down to Geneviève's end of the table and rang the little handbell she kept at her place. Luc appeared instantly. He must have been standing just behind the door.

"Monsieur?"

"I will be at home a while longer. I will be busy in my study. I don't wish to be disturbed." These were much more curt instructions than the jovial Dubon usually issued, but Luc simply nodded.

Dubon went to his study and shut the door firmly before approaching the large oak armoire that stood in one corner. He opened its double doors with both hands, and stood back a little as a powerful odor of cedar and camphor enveloped him. The armoire contained several of his old suits, a greatcoat he wore only to funerals, and a rack of uniforms. It was to these last that he turned his attention, gingerly separating one from the next. This would be an old one of the general's, he concluded, examining a large garment that was worn and sagging. Geneviève must have kept it out of sentiment after her mother died and her parents' house was emptied. These slimmer, newer clothes were Jean-Jean's; here was his best parade dress, tailored by Drouet at considerable expense when he had first received his captain's stripes. It was what he had been wearing at dinner the previous night. But here also was the uniform he wore most days, with its blue tunic, matching pants, and soft cap. It was as Dubon had hoped; Jean-Jean had left most of his clothes behind and gone off on maneuvers wearing the grim, gray battledress he had tried on the previous night.

Dubon eased the uniform off its hanger. This was going to be a bit of a squeeze. He pulled the pants on and found he couldn't quite do up the top button. No matter, the tunic fit well enough and it covered the gaping waistband. He wasn't doing so badly, he congratulated himself, if he could fit into Jean-Jean's clothes. The man was at least ten years younger than he was. To complete the effect, he reached for the cap that sat on the shelf above the clothes. He surveyed himself in the mirror. The distance between the trim and authoritative figure who stood there and the fearful emptiness inside his gut made him feel faint. He drew himself taller and wondered if he could possibly go through with this.

He spent a quiet Sunday reflecting on his scheme, and on Monday slipped out to the office with a canvas suit bag under his arm. It was draped over the comfortable armchair for receiving clients when the widow stuck her head in later that morning. Lebrun had given up announcing her.

"I owe you an apology," she began. "Sometimes, I demand things of others . . ."

He sprang up nervously. He had spent the last hour at his desk doing nothing in particular, too queasy to act on the plan he had made and feeling miserable about it. Her presence did nothing to quiet him.

"Not at all, not at all. Sit down." He bolted awkwardly to the chair, trying to sweep the bag out of the way before she reached it.

"What's in it?" she asked casually.

"A uniform."

"What kind of uniform?"

"Artillery officer, actually."

"Oh, a military uniform."

"Yes, it's my brother-in-law's. An extra one—well, he doesn't need it this week."

"I see." She looked at him but did not press the point.

He lowered himself back down behind his desk. The bag now lay between them on the leather surface of the desktop.

"I just thought," he began hesitantly, "if I were to visit the Statistical Section in uniform, as a military lawyer, a military lawyer preparing in case the prisoner's family renews its efforts to win a retrial . . ."

She smiled at him. He felt the queasiness in his stomach ease.

"It doesn't fit me that well."

"Perhaps I could help."

She reached over and pulled the canvas cover off the uniform, took a look at the blue tunic, and ran a hand down it as if assessing its quality. Gently, as though the thing were very precious, she began to undo the top button.

THIRTEEN

The widow rode to the rue de Lille with him, the two of them sandwiched together on the bench of a cab that Dubon had hailed in the
street, anxious to get inside the vehicle's boxlike carriage and out of
view as quickly as possible. What if one of the other tenants in the
building saw him in this getup? What if Lebrun, who had been dispatched by speaking tube to send a message to Geneviève warning her
that her husband would not be home for lunch, came back before they
got away?

If Dubon felt horribly nervous in his new uniform with his cap
perched on his head at what felt like the most unnatural angle, the
widow seemed to regard the whole thing as a grand adventure. In the
office she had turned her back while he changed into the pants but
couldn't restrain herself while he fiddled with the waistband.

"You just need a bit of cord or something to enlarge it," she had
said as she came over to take a look. "Your brother-in-law must be a
rather scrawny fellow."

He tried to laugh at the intended compliment to his stature, but it sounded more like a croak. She helped him into the tunic and surveyed the effect.

"Spectacular, Maître Petit," she said, handing him the cap that had been sitting on the desk.

"Captain Petit," he replied. "The military title always takes precedence."

When he had finally got into the office on the Saturday morning, he had sent Lebrun to the library to hunt out the address of the Statistical Section in a government directory while he combed the widow's clipping files for the name of a lawyer he could impersonate. In the end, he decided it was safer to disguise himself as a lowly assistant and keep his fingers crossed that the Statistical Section would let him see the Dreyfus file long enough to take some notes. Its offices were located in the city's military neighborhood, across the river around the Hôtel des Invalides. The section occupied the third floor of an undistinguished building on the rue de Lille, a narrow street just one in from the river. The rue Saint-Dominique, the street that was a synonym for the military's high command, was only two blocks away, on the other side of the boulevard Saint-Germain. The spies, Dubon gathered, needed to be near headquarters but not in it. He instructed the cab to stop a few doors beyond number 113.

"I'll probably get thrown out on my ear and be back in five minutes."

"I'll wait here for you."

"But what if I manage to get a look at the file? It may take me some time."

He took out his watch, which he had carefully transferred into his new pocket, and looked at it. "It's almost eleven. If I am not back out by eleven thirty, just take the cab home, and come back to my office, oh, say, at three o'clock."

"All right, in half an hour, then . . . or at three o'clock." She took his hand and squeezed it. "Thank you, Maître. And good luck." She hesitated and then leaned closer, brushing her lips against his cheek.

He stepped out of the cab.

When he tried the door at number 113, he found it open and slipped inside the building. There was no one in the lobby, nor any sign indicating what business was conducted on the premises. Dubon noticed a small iron elevator tucked in a corner but since he had no idea to which floor he should proceed, he started up the stairs instead. The doors on the first and second floors were unmarked. He kept going, and on the third floor found a sign bearing the army's crest and the words ADMINISTRATIVE BUREAU. STATISTICAL SECTION. Stopping for a moment to catch his breath, he suppressed the panic that was rising inside him. He tentatively tried the handle of the large door in front of him and found that it turned. He swallowed. His saliva tasted foul. There was nothing for it: he had better go in.

Dubon found himself in a small foyer, facing a vacant reception desk. He waited a bit and then tried some throat clearing. When this produced no results, he went around behind the desk toward the back of the foyer and stuck his head through a door that was slightly ajar, interrupting a large man who was bent over his work.

"Excuse me, Monsieur, but there was no one at the desk. I am an assistant—"

The man cut him off. "Yes, right, well, you had better go and see the *chef.*"

"The *chef*?"

"Yes. The *chef.* I don't know anything about anything." His tone was one of umbrage, but he clearly recognized this wasn't the way to greet a visitor because he stopped and then continued in a more measured way. "We're a small outfit here and he's in charge, so he can tell you what's required."

"Ah, yes, and where might I—?"

"Across the way," the man said, nodding over his left shoulder, and then returned to his papers.

Dubon walked to the other side of the foyer to another door and knocked tentatively. A voice invited him to enter. Dubon did so and, realizing he had forgotten not only to salute the first man but also to his horror that he had called him Monsieur, took a sharp glance at the stripes on the uniform in front of him, saluted smartly, and barked out, "Mon Colonel," just the way he had seen his brothers-in-law greet superior officers.

"I am so sorry to trouble you, Colonel. I am an assistant to Colonel Aubry who worked on—"

"At last, eh? Wondered when they were going to send someone over," the colonel said. He was wearing a well-tailored tunic full of medals and sported a small, neatly trimmed mustache. Compared with his colleague, he exuded friendly competence. "Just give me one minute and we'll set you up. I'll get Major Henry to see to you."

Major Henry. It was the name Fournier had mentioned at the race-track. Dubon, whose feeling of bowel-emptying fear had receded some-what when no one had instantly seen through his disguise, now felt it all return. He was about to be introduced to the man who had built the case against Dreyfus. The colonel tidied up a file he had open, put it in a desk drawer, and locked the drawer with a key he returned to his pocket. He then led Dubon right back across the hall to the first office.

"Major. This is . . ." Dubon stood gaping at the same man he had approached a few seconds before. This disgruntled fellow was the mastermind of counterespionage? He did not match any image of a spy that Dubon had conjured for himself. The colonel, meanwhile, seemed to be repeating something.

"Your name? They didn't tell us your name."

"Dubon." He gulped, realizing too late he had abandoned his in-tended pseudonym.

"Good, Captain Dubon. This is Major Henry," the colonel said. "He'll get you started." With that, he left the room.

With barely concealed annoyance, the major now hauled himself to standing. He was not fat, Dubon realized, but bull-like, thick-set with a big head and broad face, its width exaggerated by his closely cropped hair. Heavily, he escorted Dubon back to the empty reception desk.

"There you go," he said, and lumbered back to his own office.

Dubon sat down, since that seemed to be required of him, and let out his breath. He had made it through the front door and no one had seen through his disguise; he congratulated himself, but what was he supposed to do now? They seemed to be expecting him, or at least expecting someone. The desk at which he sat was covered in paper. He sifted through it and read a few pieces at random. They were official memos of what seemed the utmost banality. "With regards to the construction taking place at rue Saint-Dominique headquarters during the month of April, note that all personnel shall henceforth use the entrance on the boulevard Saint-Germain until further notice," one advised. Another listed the dates of the various holidays for the previous calendar year. He opened a drawer. It was stuffed with more loose papers, many of them labeled *To File* or *To Copy*. He opened another drawer and found more of the same, except these were in German and labeled *To Translate*. Some were typed; some were handwritten. A few were merely ripped fragments. Dubon didn't read much German so he turned back to the other papers and leafed through them. Perhaps he was supposed to file them. There were some newspaper clippings about military affairs, but none of them mentioned the captain. Dubon almost laughed out loud when he found what appeared to be a statistical breakdown of the shoe sizes of new recruits, though his giddiness rapidly deflated as he realized that this pile of paper was completely uninformative. All that he had stumbled into was some lowly military desk job.

"Why, at last!" The front door opened and a captain burst in and smartly saluted him. He was an athletic-looking fellow, blond and well groomed, a younger version of the colonel. He was followed by a quieter sort, a small, dark man who said nothing. "And how long are you with us?" the first one asked cheerfully.

"That hasn't really been—"

"No doubt they will snatch you back the minute you get used to the place. Tessier had only been with us six months, and they sent him back to headquarters. And the last chap, can't even remember his name, he lasted a mere two weeks. No loss there. You can probably tell that from the state of the files. Anyway, welcome. I'm Captain Gingras. This is Captain Hermann." He gestured to the smaller man, who merely nodded.

"Dubon, er, Captain Dubon."

"Nice to meet you, Dubon. Artillery, eh?" he said, looking at Jean-Jean's various insignia. "Hoping to climb the ladder with some desk work? Has Major Henry got you settled? Not much to it. Just file the stuff, you know. We are drowning in paper."

"Ah. And the ones in German?"

"No trouble. Hermann is your man," he said, slapping his taciturn colleague on the back. "He's Alsatian, like the colonel. Both of them speak German like natives. You just tidy the papers and put them on his desk—you might try to put them in some sort of chronological order—and he'll work his way through them one of these years. Won't you, Hermann?"

"Undoubtedly," Hermann said, and then lapsed back into silence while Gingras prattled on.

"By the time he's got to the bottom of the pile, the Germans will probably have reached the Pyrenees and invented flying machines. And we will still be sitting here translating the ambassador's laundry list. And that's just the German. Haven't had an Italian speaker in a year." Gingras saluted and sauntered off down the one hallway that led out of the reception area, calling back over his shoulder as he pulled open an office door, "Have fun with it. See you later."

Hermann did not follow him immediately but simply stared at Dubon for a moment as though evaluating him before he too went down the hall to an office.

So this, Dubon deduced, was the mysterious world of counter-espionage. And he, apparently, had been mistaken for a temporary clerk.

It was an impression that was confirmed a few hours later when the colonel called him into his office.

"Do you take dictation?" he asked.

Dubon hesitated.

"No. Don't suppose you do. Last one didn't either. I want to send a memo, and I will speak very slowly. How's your typing? No, eh? Ask the major to show you the machine. It's quite simple, really."

Dubon left the Statistical Section shortly after five, his head spinning. It was probably too late to catch the widow at his office or to send a message to Lebrun; he could trust the man to pack up for the day on his own and usher her out. Not sure what else to do, Dubon wandered home in a haze, crossing the bridge back to the Right Bank on foot before he hailed a cab and sank onto its seat exhausted, pulling his cap off his head, undoing the top button of his tunic and wiping his brow. Like some disheveled partygoer coming home from a masquerade ball, he was thinking only of how good it would feel to change clothes and have a drink when he got home.

He alighted a few steps from his own building, remembering now that he had better take a peek through the glass in the front door to check there was no sign of the concierge in the lobby, lest he be obliged to come up with some improbable story to explain his dress. He was a few meters from the front door when a jolt of fear ran through his body, leaving his mouth dry: a neighbor who lived in the building next door was walking down the street straight toward him. He was a man to whom Dubon usually raised his hat. Dubon pulled his cap out from under his arm and jammed it on his head. Should he say hello normally? Instinctively, he put his head down and bolted toward his own door, arriving there just before the man reached him. Dubon pulled the door open and stepped into the lobby. His heart was pounding in his chest—he felt as if he had run a kilometer rather than crossed the pavement—but he risked a quick glance behind him as he pulled the door shut. His neighbor was continuing down the street completely unperturbed, without so much as breaking step. The man had just crossed paths with an army officer he did not know. The uniform in which Dubon felt so conspicuous had made him invisible.

Standing in the lobby, waiting for his breathing to return to normal, Dubon planned his next steps. He would need to sneak back into the apartment and change before Geneviève or Luc saw him. At least he had his latch key. He turned it in the lock as silently as possible and opened the door a little. Seeing no one in sight, he made for the library, slipped inside, closed the door, and pushed a chair in front of it. That way he would get some warning if either of them were going to wander in. He was about to change his clothes when he realized his own suit was back at the office. He took off the uniform's distinctive tunic, hung it back in the wardrobe, and then sprinted down the hall to his own dressing room to find another business suit. He changed as quickly as he could and then slipped Jean-Jean's pants back into the library. He straightened his own familiar tie in the mirror, took a deep breath, and attempted a saunter as he walked down the hall into the salon.

Geneviève was sitting on the sofa with Masson at her side and a tea tray on the table in front of them. She looked up at her husband in surprise and then glanced at the clock on the mantel. It was just past five thirty.

"What on earth are you doing home at this hour?"

It was only at that moment that Dubon remembered Madeleine.

FOURTEEN

"Good play?" Dubon recalled that Masson had been escorting Gene-viève to a matinee that afternoon.

"Horrible." Masson laughed. "That's why we are sitting here drink-ing tea. We left at the intermission."

"It's a good thing you weren't there, François. It was just the sort of thing you complain about. Melodramatic. I can't think why the critics recommended it," Geneviève said. Dubon's distaste for the theater was well established. His wife usually found other companions when she especially wanted to see something.

"Everyone waving their arms about, and the speeches, interminable, and that was only the first half," Masson added, and gave Dubon a rue-ful look. "Perhaps you are right about theater."

"My tastes shouldn't preclude others from enjoying themselves, but I do find it very artificial," Dubon said.

"But you still enjoy a novel, don't you?" Masson asked in a lei-surely way.

He showed no sign of rising from the sofa. Dubon supposed a more jealous husband might be offended by his lengthy tête-à-tête with

Geneviève, but he did not put much stock in his old friend's powers of seduction. Besides, whatever her social enthusiasms, he always could trust Geneviève.

"What are you reading now?" Masson continued.

"Oh, I have been rereading *Germinal*," Dubon replied, thinking of the book that had lain unopened by his bedside for several weeks.

Masson all but guffawed. "Oh yes, you and Monsieur Zola, the plight of the workers in the mines. Ever the armchair socialist, eh?"

Dubon bristled, but before he could come to the writer's defense, Geneviève interrupted.

"Now, Baron, you mustn't tease him," she said, nervously trying to smooth over any tension.

"Of course, Madame, your husband has put his radical days behind him," Masson said rather archly.

Dubon rose to the bait. "Really, Masson. I don't think I have betrayed my ideals. Many of us grow a little calmer in middle age," he said in an aggrieved tone. "I do have a family to consider."

"Oh, certainly, you would never risk your lovely wife. She is your best achievement."

"Well, I'm sorry you were both disappointed with the play," Dubon said, recognizing he had sounded inappropriately angry and trying to wrench the conversation back to a proper course. "I know Geneviève was looking forward to it."

"We will hope for better entertainment next time," Masson said genially, rising to his feet.

"There's that pianist your sister wants us to hear," he added to Geneviève. "I am looking forward to that. With your permission, I'll take my leave of you now. I have a dinner this evening and should be off home to dress." He bent to kiss Geneviève's hand, glancing at Dubon as he did so, and then followed Dubon from the room.

Dubon walked him to the front hall and, since Luc did not seem to be about, offered him his hat. He felt a creeping anxiety about what had just passed. He didn't like the implications of Masson's judgment.

"You know, Masson—"

"Yes?"

"Nothing, nothing."

"Come, my friend—"

"No, really, it was nothing—"

"You are a liberal man, Dubon. I hope you don't feel it was unduly familiar of me to stay for tea in your absence—"

"No, of course not. Geneviève enjoys your company. It's just—"

"Yes?"

"Well, there's no need to dig up old history."

"No, you are right. Your radical politics are of no import anymore."

"I actually meant the marriage contract, and the money, and all that."

Masson drew himself up and his tone was cool as he replied, "No. No need to dig up that."

Fearing he had offended him, Dubon hastened to add, "I mean, I was always very grateful to you, for your help. Our marriage would certainly never have been possible without your intervention."

"It was nothing. After what your parents had done for me, taking me into the family, I was glad to be able to repay the debt." Masson smiled at the memory. "'Dubon, a plain name, but a solid family,'" he said, quoting his own words to Geneviève's father nineteen years ago.

Masson had acted as the go-between, making Dubon's case to the general, guarding the secret of his youthful antics with the Communards, which would have ended the engagement on the spot, and negotiating the details of the nuptial contract.

"I always had the utmost respect for the general . . ." Dubon paused, and Masson finished his thought for him.

"But he could be a vicious snob. Still, the old man was genuinely fond of you," Masson continued, "and relieved, I think, too. You remember those wild-eyed types that his daughter was so interested in."

"It's true." Dubon laughed. "I was a rock of probity compared with that other fellow. What was his name?"

"I don't recall. Anyway, it was all for the best."

"Yes, Geneviève had a taste for excitement but she could never— well, look at how we live now," he said, gesturing around the front hall of his well-appointed apartment. "I think her greatest regret is that we can't afford to keep a carriage."

"You have provided well for her. Keeping her in the standard..."
He let a laugh complete the phrase for him.

The general had been prepared to accept Dubon but did not like
the look of his future. The crusading young lawyer was already making
a name for himself, the wrong kind of name. In the deal brokered by
Masson, General de Ronchaud Valcourt offered to double Geneviève's
dowry on the understanding the extra money would be invested in
Dubon's father's law practice. Dubon would move it from a cramped
building near the gare Saint-Lazare to more fashionable quarters on
the rue Saint-Honoré and give up defending workers and widows to
attend to his father's more genteel clientele. Geneviève always believed
her fiancé had taken over the practice out of a sense of duty toward
his own father, rather than to appease hers. They married in 1879, a
year before the Socialists won a majority in the National Assembly
and voted through the amnesty that would let the exiled Communards
come home and the suspected Communards in France live freely again.
Dubon's past no longer posed a threat to the young couple's security,
although it would always remain a potential impediment to their social
standing. Geneviève never breathed a word of it to friends and family.

"I would never think of betraying you to your own wife," Masson
continued. "In the future, I will be more careful." He stepped toward
the door now and grasped the handle as though to leave, but then
paused and turned back.

"Your many secrets are safe with me," he said, holding Dubon's
gaze for a moment. Then he turned and left the apartment.

FIFTEEN

The next morning Dubon did not dawdle. Some odd set of coincidences had given him an opportunity to help the widow. He needed to get back to the Statistical Section and take his chance. He helped himself to a breakfast of bread and jam before seven, waving off Luc's worried promises of coffee in just a few minutes if Monsieur would only wait, and left the house ten minutes later with a canvas garment bag under his arm. He walked briskly over to his office and let himself in with his key. Lebrun would not arrive until eight, and Dubon would have to be gone by then.

"Captain, we usually start at eight," the colonel had told him as he left the day before. "On summer schedule now, you know." The military kept up the old habit of working longer hours when there was more daylight to be had, though Dubon had noticed electric fixtures on the walls.

He opened his desk drawer and pulled out a few blank sheets of paper. He wrote a brief letter for the widow, apologizing for his absence the previous day, asking if she could possibly return to meet him at his office at five thirty, and signing his name. He then wrote a much

longer memo for Lebrun, explaining that research on a delicate new
file required him to absent himself from the office for a few days and
asking the clerk to reschedule two morning appointments and file a
dossier at the Hôtel de Ville. He added that he expected his new client,
Madame Duhamel, to stop by again that day, and that Lebrun was to
give her the attached note and, if she was at liberty later in the day,
to wait with her until he himself could return around five thirty. He
thought for a moment about the rest of his commitments, and then
pulled a *petit bleu* from the same drawer. He penned an apologetic note
to Madeleine, saying he would be absent again that evening but hoped
to attend her on Wednesday. He sealed it and left it for Lebrun to
post. Then he changed into Jean-Jean's uniform, adding his clothes
to the coatrack where his suit from the previous day was still hanging.
He tugged on Jean-Jean's tunic, put the cap on his head and locked up
the office, glancing nervously at his watch. It was twenty to eight now.
His disguise, even if it had fooled the officers of the Statistical Section
the day before, made him feel dangerously conspicuous.

He weighed the risks of running into someone he knew as he walked
or getting trapped alighting from a cab as he had the day before when
he had almost bumped into his neighbor; he decided he felt nimbler
and safer on foot. If he walked quickly, he would be at his new job on
time. He set out briskly and found there was something familiar about
this anxious walk down to the river. He was reminded of his first days
with Maître Gaillard. Every morning he would brush his one good
suit, slick back his hair, and cross the pont Neuf to an office near the
Palais de Justice, his pulse racing with excitement for the work that lay
ahead and his stomach turning at the thought of not living up to his
superior's expectations. He had a lot more reason to be nervous about
his latest assignment, but his new superior seemed a friendly enough
fellow so far.

Having crossed paths with Gingras and the silent Hermann on his
way in, Dubon was just settling at his desk when the colonel himself
arrived; Dubon sprang to his feet and saluted sharply, but the colonel
dismissed this with a wave.

"Oh, as you were, Captain . . . Dubon, isn't it? As you were. Settling
in, figuring all this out?"

"Er, yes," Dubon replied, unsure how much ignorance might be expected of a replacement clerk. "That is to say, there is a lot of paper here that needs to be filed, and I wasn't sure . . ."

"Oh yes, it's hopeless, just hopeless. My predecessor . . . I've only been here a month myself. Things were not as well organized as they might have been. We just need to straighten up the files a bit, so we know what we are working on. I'd concentrate on the German stuff, since you speak the language, and then pass those documents on to Captain Hermann for translating." Dubon's heart sank. If his new job required a knowledge of German, he would get in trouble very soon.

"Once he has done the translating he can tell you if he needs you to make copies of any of it," the colonel continued. "I trust you have a nice italic hand." He smiled as though it didn't matter much either way. "We haven't succeeded in getting much English material, but if you find anything, give it to Captain Gingras. He does the English. Do you speak some English too, Captain?"

"A very little, Colonel," Dubon said, truthfully enough. "Captain Gingras suggested chronological order was important," he added, trying to move on from the topic of languages.

"Yes, get everything in order by date. That's a start, and maybe then Hermann can get back on top of the German pile."

"And the French-language material? What do I do with that?"

"Shouldn't be much of it left, but you can just give it to me if you find any."

"There seem mainly to be a lot of memos here addressed to the Statistical Section or addressed to headquarters."

"Oh, you mean the shoe sizes and the loaves of bread?" The colonel laughed. "Got to keep up our cover. There are files of that stuff over there." He indicated a filing cabinet behind Dubon. "There is some sort of system to it, if you take a look. I'm sure you'll figure it out. You found the glue, did you? You'll want to work quite carefully with it."

"Oh yes, of course," Dubon replied, unsure as to what he was supposed to be gluing.

Later, as he was organizing the German material into chronological order, he noticed some of it had been ripped into pieces. He uncovered a glue pot in the desk and soon understood why the colonel had suggested care. It was tricky finding which pieces went with which and Dubon had to rely almost entirely on the shapes since he couldn't read the foreign words. It was like assembling a jigsaw puzzle, he thought to himself as he tried to glue the pieces carefully enough that he did not obscure the writing. After some messy attempts, he decided that if the paper had been used on only one side he could best reassemble it by gluing the pieces down on a new, clean sheet. He came across a few pages in French that were also ripped and pieced them together more quickly. The documents seemed of little import to him. Some were pages from a personal letter; another was a *petit bleu* addressed to some Hungarian nobleman requesting details on a business proposal. Dubon dutifully put them in a separate pile from the military memos so that he could pass them on to the colonel.

By ten, he was making good progress and was sufficiently engrossed in the job that the fear in the pit of his stomach had receded enough to let him concentrate. He sensed some movement to his right and looked up to find a rather fat lady in a worn blue raincoat standing in the corridor that led down to Gingras's and Hermann's offices. Dubon wasn't sure how she had got there, since she had not come through the front door, but she must have come from outside: her coat was wet.

"Raining is it, now?" he asked as she walked up to his desk, seeming quite at home in the place.

"Just started to drizzle. So, you're new." She stopped in front of him, opened the clasp of a large leather purse that was shaped like a doctor's bag but oversized and dumped the contents onto the desktop. "There you go. Until next time." She waved and walked back toward the head of the corridor, which was located on the same side of the reception area as the colonel's office. Gingras's and Hermann's doors were at the end of it, but she stopped before that, opened a smaller door—perhaps it was that of a water closet—and disappeared.

Dubon looked down at the desktop, now littered with more scraps of paper. He took a breath and started sorting again. Some were in German; some were in French. There were typed memos and a few handwritten notes. Many appeared to be rough drafts that ended in midsentence or had words crossed out. Some were ripped, like the papers on which he had been working. Some were crunched into balls. One was badly stained with the telltale ring of a wineglass. The fat lady had simply emptied the contents of a wastepaper basket onto his desk, Dubon concluded.

He spent the morning organizing these latest contributions to the section's intelligence, smoothing out the crumpled ones and reassembling the ripped ones. None of them mentioned Dreyfus. Some of the papers bore dates, especially the drafts of letters and memos, but some did not or if they did, the fragment bearing the date happened to be missing. He had noticed that in his previous piles the dates were often added by a different hand, and that the same dates appeared again and again: these must reflect not the date of the document, which could not be known, but the date it had come into the section. Accordingly, he began to scribble the date—*Tuesday, May 11, 1897*—on each of the undated sheets that the fat lady had brought him that morning.

He was getting to the end when he came to a piece of paper that made him stop. The sheet had a large ink blot in the middle, which explained why the writer had thrown it out, but a tidy signature was visible at the bottom of the page: *Schwarzkoppen.*

Dubon felt his mouth go dry. That was the name of the military attaché he had met at the Fiteaus' ball.

He swallowed and began to read. The letter was in French but the hand was small and difficult to decipher in places. The text started in midsentence: ". . . events, of which you have no doubt heard, were not in fact the . . ."—here there was a word Dubon could not make out— ". . . of the evening. The boy was silly and if his father was once a highly effective general, he was already in decline before he was dealt this great personal blow." Dubon ran his tongue over his teeth. His saliva tasted oddly bitter. The attaché was describing the ball. "The interesting part," the letter continued, "happened earlier when there was much attempt to silence that young Captain Valcourt, who was discussing the hydraulics on the field guns within our hearing. I don't think he knows what he is talking about, but it's an indication the French are still hard at work on the problem. You should have seen—" At this point the ink blot obliterated the rest of the sentence, leaving only a lengthy salutation visible before the signature.

Major de Ronchaud Valcourt had been perfectly right to silence his brother, Dubon thought: Schwarzkoppen *was* a spy. And the Statistical Section was spying on him in its turn.

The idea of Schwarzkoppen's proximity was terrifying: a German spy was hardly likely to walk through the front door of the Statistical Section, but it reminded Dubon that any number of his brother-in-laws' colleagues might appear on the premises and recognize him. He doubted he could count on the casual inattention his neighbor had shown the previous day if an officer who knew him walked up to the reception desk. He had to find the prosecution's file on Dreyfus and get out of this place fast.

SIXTEEN

"Hold the fort, won't you, Dubon?"

It was the colonel, calling out as he went off to lunch. "I'll be back before three."

Moments after he left, Major Henry, who had spent the morning in his office behind Dubon with the door closed, emerged and stood at the desk. He puffed out his already significant chest and glared down at Dubon, who belatedly realized he was supposed to salute.

"Major!" he said, scrambling to his feet.

Henry looked at the pile of papers Dubon had been working on.

"There was a delivery this morning?"

"Yes."

"Good. I will expect them on my desk this afternoon."

"Major." Dubon saluted again, since Henry seemed to expect it, and watched as the man marched forcefully from the office. The whole exchange struck him as unnecessary. Henry seemed to be an officer who relished authority for its own sake.

A few minutes later the ebullient Gingras poked his head into the foyer, as though he had been waiting for the coast to clear.

"Plans for lunch? The colonel and the major always go home—very loyal husbands, you know." He laughed. "I usually go over to the mess. You're welcome to join me."

"The mess?" Dubon could barely contain his horror. A whole room full of military officers. What if he saw someone he knew?

But Gingras took his reaction for incomprehension. "The headquarters mess. Doesn't take two minutes to walk over to the rue Saint-Dominique. We'll be back long before the colonel and the major."

"Oh. Thank you, thank you. I'll just stay here, I think. So much to do and the colonel did seem to think I would stay."

"Picquart won't care."

"Picquart?"

"The colonel, Colonel Picquart. Didn't they tell you at headquarters who you would be reporting to?" Gingras looked puzzled, and now peered at Dubon as though he were noticing him for the first time.

"Ah, well, I guess they just mentioned Major Henry," Dubon improvised, only now realizing he had not caught the colonel's name.

"Shows where their allegiances lie," Gingras said, satisfied with the explanation. "Anyway, if you want to come for lunch, we do usually shut the office. We all have keys, so whoever is back first can get in."

"Maybe I'll pop out to the corner later, when you get back, or something."

He left, and Dubon slumped back in his chair in relief. He had avoided the mess hall and was now safely alone. For the first time since he had arrived that morning he could relax and stop pretending he knew what he was doing with all these bits of paper. Relief, however, brought hunger; he would have liked lunch, having had nothing to eat since the bread and jam at seven. He was just rising to get a drink of water from a jug kept on a small table beside the exterior door, when he sensed rather than saw a presence in the corridor leading back to the offices. He turned to see a disheveled man standing there. He was wearing drab clothing and badly needed a shave. His face was worn, but his age was hard to calculate; he could have been thirty-five or fifty-five. He carried an old leather satchel under one arm.

"Have I missed Henry?" the man asked.

"The major?" Dubon replied. "Just left for lunch."

"Damn. Thought I'd catch him." The man turned and began walking back down the corridor.

"May I tell Major Henry who called?" Dubon asked.

The man turned and stared back at him with an amused expression. "Tell him who called? Uh, no, I don't think so."

He walked down the hall to the same closet door the fat woman had used and disappeared, leaving Dubon cursing his own stupidity. The man was clearly a spy and Dubon's ignorance of the mere etiquette of espionage might have given him away.

He should be profiting from the others' absence by riffling through the files to see if he could find what he needed, but he had no idea where to start and he felt paralyzed, dreading the idea that someone might return from lunch and catch him in the middle of it. Instead, he sat at the desk with a rather sick feeling in his stomach, sifting purposelessly through the loose paper. Frustrated with himself, he got up. He had to show some initiative. He would go poke his head in that closet to see where the mysterious visitors came from. He stood still for a moment, listening for the sound of the others returning and hearing only the ever-so-faint rumbling of a train somewhere in the distance. He drew himself up, walked swiftly down the corridor, and was just reaching for a door handle when a voice barked at him: "Not that one!"

Dubon started violently and let out an involuntary cry. Steadying himself, he turned to see Hermann standing on the other side of the corridor, at the door to his office. He had forgotten all about the studious Captain Hermann; he had not gone out to lunch.

"I don't know what you are up to, Dubon," he said in a cold voice, "but if you are looking for the water closet, we use the one on the landing. The one here is only for the colonel and the major."

"Oh, very sorry. Didn't realize," Dubon mumbled as he retreated hurriedly, bumping into a wall.

Hermann just stared at him and then asked, "Where did you go to school, Dubon?"

"Ah. Saint-Cyr," Dubon replied, and instantly regretted it. In Jean-Jean's case it was the truth, but the elite military academy created a tight cadre. He assumed an Alsatian like Hermann had probably risen through the ranks, but it would not be hard for him or anyone else in the section to start asking around.

"Saint-Cyr? And you are still a captain?" Hermann asked dubiously.

Of course, that was another point. Jean-Jean was ten years younger than he was. Any graduate of Saint-Cyr would have been expected to rise higher than the rank of captain by his midforties.

"I am only thirty-five," Dubon said, shaving eight years off his age. Hermann, he supposed, was around that age himself so might be more comfortable with the idea that captain was an acceptable rank at that point in life.

"Really? You look at least forty," Hermann said gracelessly.

"No, thirty-five, and still hoping for promotion."

"Well, if you want to get ahead around here, don't use the senior officers' closet," Hermann said. "The colonel may not care about these things, but the major is a stickler for rank."

"Right. Very good. I'll just go out to the landing, then," Dubon responded, glad of a reason to end the conversation.

As he relieved himself in the correct closet, which he had already visited that morning but felt it was important to revisit in case Hermann was watching, he felt the fear that had rushed into his body slowly ebbing, only to be replaced by ferocious hunger. He left the building and hurried across the street to an unsavory establishment he had noticed on his way in that morning. He estimated he was less likely to run into anyone he knew in such a place and found it empty except for a few local deliverymen washing down their meal with tumblers of red wine. He gnawed his way through the daily special, a particularly unappetizing piece of tongue, paid his bill, and carefully scanned the street before pushing open the door and leaving. He hung back in the doorway of the café for a moment looking about him and then, seeing no familiar faces, he sprinted back to number 113.

There were no more mysterious apparitions in the corridor that afternoon, but a visitor did walk through the front door. He was a scrawny young lieutenant who tried to close the door behind him while simultaneously saluting and then, when Dubon waved him in, stood in front of the desk shifting awkwardly from one leg to the other.

"I am Lieutenant Laurent. From headquarters. I was supposed to be here this morning but there was a mix-up at the rue Saint-Dominique. I had to go back to get the papers signed." At this he held up an envelope. "I know I was supposed to start this morning. I'm very sorry."

Dubon felt his skin crawl. This surely was the temporary clerk, the *real* temporary clerk. Could he dare send the man about his business?

"Really, I mean, I'm not sure, you are . . ." He stalled for time as he rose to his feet.

At this point, the colonel returned from lunch and stopped at Dubon's desk. The lieutenant saluted.

"Who are you?" the colonel asked incuriously.

"Laurent, sir. Reporting for duty. Sent over from the rue Saint-Dominique."

"Isn't that just typical." The colonel laughed. "My predecessor put in the request for a clerk in January, they send us two in May."

"I know I was supposed to be here this morning—"

"You were supposed to be here four months ago. Anyway, we don't need you now. They already sent over this fellow yesterday. Off you go, back to headquarters. They'll find something else for you to do, I'm sure."

"But, Colonel—"

"Off you go now," the colonel repeated, moving in the direction of his own office.

The lieutenant saluted and left, backing away without turning around, as though the colonel were some royal personage to whom one might never turn one's back.

The colonel watched him leave and caught Dubon's glance as he did so. He rolled his eyes and, as soon as the lieutenant disappeared through the front door, said to Dubon, "Well, guess we got the better end of that deal, eh?"

Dubon saluted him smartly and sat back down at his desk, feeling warmed by the compliment. He savored it for a moment until he realized how idiotic it was to be flattered that someone would judge him to be the better clerk. What if Laurent's superiors called on Picquart to explain why he had been returned to them? Dubon would be exposed and sent packing, to his great humiliation, if not much worse. He supposed there were severe penalties for impersonating a military officer, although the government might be embarrassed enough he had got inside that it would not risk prosecuting him. Could they actually accuse him of being a spy? He would have to count on the evidently glacial bureaucracy of the rue Saint-Dominique and Statistical Section's low standards of administration to keep him safe for another day or two while he hunted for the Dreyfus file. In the meantime, the colonel and the major were less likely to question his credentials if they wanted to keep him; he needed to do the clerical work correctly, and he couldn't help feeling a little pleased with what he had pulled off so far. He had insinuated himself into the place and discovered the French were somehow getting hold of papers the Germans had discarded; now he needed to find the ones that had led Henry to finger Dreyfus.

Three hours later he had made no progress but had at least tidied the desktop before he left for the day. As he walked down the rue de Lille, his huge relief at being out of the place for a few hours gave way to a sense of exhilaration and adventure. He hadn't felt this giddy since he first made plans to rent an apartment for Madeleine. He tucked his cap under his arm and walked briskly, scanning the crowds. They were heavy enough at this time of day that he could easily enough sidestep any approaching acquaintance. Still, he was happy to get through the doors of his own familiar office, where he found Lebrun, tidying up for the day.

"Ah, Lebrun."

Lebrun looked puzzled; Dubon could not for an instant think why, and then remembered the uniform. Goodness, what had he been thinking?

"Ah yes, well, a family uniform, of course . . . bit of playacting on my part . . . uh . . . for a rather delicate case."

"That would be the widow Duhamel's case, Maître?"

"Yes, yes. Of course. Did she come today?" he asked eagerly.

"She's waiting in your office now, Maître."

"I'll just go in, then," he said, moving toward the inner office.

"Very good, Maître," Lebrun said coolly.

Dubon turned back to him. "This case may take some time, Lebrun. I'll need you to handle the office during my absence. Perhaps another week or so. I'll try to get here every evening by six, and if you would stay a bit later, we can review the day's business then. Of course, I'll, er, compensate you for the extra work. Was, uh, thinking of raising your pay in September, in any case. I had been meaning to tell you, but I have been a bit busy."

"Thank you, Maître. That is most appreciated, Maître, most appreciated. There were some messages today. And I will need to know how I should proceed with the Montcharnet file. We have yet to hear from his lawyer and it has been a month."

"Right. I'll leave you a note with instructions. You'll want to go home now," he said as he turned the handle on his office door.

He found the widow waiting for him inside, studying, as far as he could judge, his bookshelves. At the sight of her, he felt suffused with a sense of triumph. She turned to him with a vague look on her face and squinted a bit as though to bring him into focus. He hurried across the room to her, caught at her sleeve, and pulled her toward him, holding on to her arm in a posture that would have been awkward for both of them were it not for his excitement.

"You'll never guess," he said, "who they think I am."

SEVENTEEN

The next day, Dubon was sitting at what he was coming to think of as his desk, puzzling over what a biblical prophet might have to do with a Russian anarchist or a German gun with the château of Vaux-le-Vicomte. At the start of the day he had walked down the corridor to where Gingras and Hermann had small offices, little more than cubbyholes, and deposited his bulging file of German-language documents on the latter's already overflowing desk, trying to smile politely at the man's curt "Thank you." He then walked back to his own desk and turned his attention to the metal cabinets that surrounded it. His goal was to parse the filing system and discover Captain Dreyfus's documents as quickly as possible before someone at the rue Saint-Dominique asked why the young Laurent had been returned to sender.

As he hunted, he kept a folder with him on top of the cabinet filled with pages and pages that he remained unable to file. If the colonel, the major, or either of the other two officers passed through, he would occasionally slip a page into the cabinet, and then take it out again as soon as they had gone, not wishing to appear incompetent or stymied.

Not that they paid him much attention; they seemed to have accepted his presence in their midst.

If he had hoped that he had simply to look under *D* and there discover the file on the Captain Dreyfus whose case increasingly consumed the newspaper pages, he had been naive. There seemed neither rhyme nor reason to the names of the files, although they were organized alphabetically. The *C*'s included *Canute, Chartres,* and *Crystal;* the *E*'s included *Emerald, Etretat,* and *Elephant;* the *R*'s included *Rouen* and *Rhinoceros*.

Organizing the names by theme, Dubon found some patterns: there was a series of Old Testament names—Ezekiel, Habakkuk, Joshua, Jeremiah—most of which seemed to contain files pertaining to Russian subjects, except one that was full of information from Belgium and listed payments to a certain Rousseau. The great châteaux and cathedrals of France—Chartres, Senlis, Versailles, Rouen—appeared to be used as file names for intelligence from Germany. But again, the system wasn't consistent, since some of the German files were named after gemstones. At this rate, Dubon figured he would have to go through every file in the cabinets—there had to be hundreds—to find the one he wanted, and he was brought to the point of despair when he found several pages about uniform reform sandwiched in a report on fortifications in northern France in a file labeled *Zebra*. This was some devilishly encoded filing system, and was he, as a temporary clerk, expected to know the code?

He was working away on this puzzle when Hermann came quietly into the reception area carrying a file folder and stuck his head in Colonel Picquart's door.

"Colonel. A moment if you please," he said, and closed the door behind him.

He was inside a good ten minutes or quarter hour. When he came out, he crossed to the filing cabinet and addressed Dubon in an undertone.

"Captain. These documents—" He opened the file to show the papers Dubon had given him that morning. Was it Dubon's fearful imagination, or was Hermann's quiet voice purposefully threatening. "You glued them together?"

"Yes, Captain," Dubon replied in what he hoped was an even voice.

"Why did you do that?"

"Well, that was my understanding from the colonel. That is, he—he gave me the glue pot."

Hermann stared at him. "Do you actually speak German?" he asked.

A nasty hole opened in Dubon's stomach. He must have made some mistake gluing the pieces back together that revealed he couldn't read the language. Should he confess to his ignorance? If he pretended otherwise, Hermann, the German speaker, would uncover him in no time.

"It's rather rusty, I am afraid."

Hermann was silent for a long moment.

"We requested a German-speaking clerk," he finally said. "That was why we had to wait so long."

Dubon squirmed inwardly.

"There aren't that many about who really do speak good German. You are a rare commodity, Captain Hermann," Dubon said, trying a bit of flattery. Hermann's expression did not change. "And I guess since the section already has you, my superior did not feel the request . . . Perhaps I overstated how much German I've studied . . ." He broke off, silenced by Hermann's implacable stare.

"So, how did you manage to piece together a German text?"

"I did it by the shapes."

"Well, don't. It's too easy to make a mistake. In future, leave that to me." He turned to go and then, as he reached the corridor, added as an afterthought: "So you haven't read through any of the documents you gave me this morning?"

"No."

"Neither the German nor the French?"

"No, Captain. I just sorted them."

Hermann nodded and disappeared into his office.

Dubon sat down heavily at his desk and pondered the encounter. He seemed to have escaped with a warning, as long as Hermann didn't complain to the colonel about his lack of German. And why had Hermann asked him if he had read French documents? He thought he had given all those to the colonel; there had been Schwarzkoppen's letter about the ball, that *petit bleu* addressed to the Hungarian, a few memos.

Dubon sat worrying for a while about how bad his slip might have been before he eventually returned to his ineffectual browsing through the filing cabinets. The only interesting thing he learned was that the Statistical Section was keeping copious files on French citizens, including its own military officers. He scanned those he came across but did not recognize any of the names. Most of these files seem banal, little more than personnel reports on the various officer's postings, specializations, and medals.

Nobody disturbed him any further in his searching, although at two the major, dressed in civilian clothing, walked down the corridor to the mysterious closet without any comment or explanation and disappeared inside it. He did not reappear in the corridor until an hour later, leaving Dubon to wonder where exactly the closet led. When the major left the office through the front door shortly before five, he was back in uniform and this time nodded curtly on his way past as Dubon saluted.

Back at his desk, Dubon began tidying away the mysteriously named files. *Emerald, Pearl, Topaz.* Each exotic word couldn't represent an individual code; they were groups that must somehow have been applied sequentially as disguises to the real file names. Somewhere there had to be a master list.

Ten minutes later, he reached the river to find an omnibus marked MADELEINE—ST-LAZARE stopping on the quay, so he jumped on, confident that few of his acquaintances would be found riding a bus. He inquired as to the fare, paid the conductor, and sandwiched himself in among the other passengers. The bus drove across the bridge and up the place de la Concorde, depositing him at the corner of the rue Saint-Honoré. He tucked his cap under his arm, scanned the street for anyone he knew, and set out rapidly for his own office, covering the ground with long strides.

"You just missed the lady," Lebrun informed him as he came through the door.

"The widow?" Dubon asked eagerly. "But we had agreed she would come tomorrow."

"Yes, she said she would come again Thursday as arranged but happened to be in the neighborhood today and hoped to catch you. She asked if you had any news for her."

"I wish I had." He turned to his desk and the papers Lebrun had organized into neat piles.

"It's that captain, Maître, isn't it?" Lebrun asked.

"Excuse me?"

"Her case. It has something to do with that captain who was court-martialed for spying. That Captain Dreyfus."

"How do you divine that, Lebrun?"

His tone must have sounded a little chilly for Lebrun defended himself, "I won't usually ask, Maître. I certainly don't wish to pry. But I seem to be taking charge of the office all week and, well, if she comes again when you are not here, it is easier if I know her business."

"She is a friend of the Dreyfus family. They believe he is innocent— not surprising, I suppose—and are working to exonerate him."

"Very good, Maître. You then are working to exonerate the captain too?"

Lebrun's tone was neutral, but Dubon considered the question more than rhetorical and pondered it seriously.

"Do you think it wrong? To be working to free a convicted spy?"

"Maître, I have worked for you long enough to know that every man, whatever he may have done, has the right to a good lawyer."

They turned to the day's business, sorting through the messages and files that had accumulated. Most were routine, but at the bottom of one pile was a telegram that had arrived that morning and caught Dubon by surprise.

Can we meet to discuss the case in which you are interested? I will be at the Café des Artistes on the boulevard du Montparnasse this evening from 6 p.m.

The signature, in quotation marks, was Azimut Martin.

Dubon had almost forgotten about the pseudonymous journalist.

Now he had finally made contact. He looked over at the clock; it was past five thirty; it would probably be six thirty before he made it out to Montparnasse, and he'd have to forgo his visit to Madeleine. It would be the third night this week he had stood her up. He sighed; this was getting complicated. Perhaps those who signed up for the telephone were right; it might make business easier. He scribbled a message to Madeleine, and Lebrun left with it as Dubon rapidly changed out of the uniform and made for the river, hoping he might catch a cab on the way.

It had been warm and rainy all week, and the windows of the café were steamed over with the moist heat when he arrived, later than he had hoped. He pushed through the door and looked about. How would he recognize his contact? How would Monsieur Martin recognize him? He noticed someone waving discreetly from a table in the middle of the room. At first he thought it might be his man, but he realized it was that friend of Jean-Jean's, Le Goff. He hadn't recognized him at first because he wasn't in uniform. Damn him. The last thing Dubon needed now was to waste a quarter of an hour exchanging pleasantries. He tried a vague gesture of recognition without approaching Le Goff's table, but the man persisted with his waving.

It was then that Dubon heard a voice in his head, repeating words spoken at the dinner party the previous week. *You're on the right track, Dubon,* Le Goff had said.

He approached Le Goff's table and extended his hand.

The man took it. "Azimut Martin, at your service."

EIGHTEEN

"Well, I never dreamed..." Dubon stared at Le Goff, not sure what to make of this revelation. Around them the café buzzed with other conversations; it was a good meeting place, too busy for anyone to notice them and too noisy for anyone to overhear them. Le Goff seemed pleased with the effect he was having on Dubon.

"You'll notice I left my uniform at home," he said, leaning back in his chair and showing off his suit jacket.

Civilian dress suited his thin frame better, Dubon thought as he sat down across from Le Goff, and in this setting, he appeared both larger and more relaxed than the brittle character he knew through Jean-Jean.

"You write all those articles? But, Le Goff, surely this is a breach of military discipline. I mean..."

"I have never revealed classified information. All my military informants speak to me freely, well aware they are talking to the press, as it were."

"Still, surely, if you were ever discovered..."

"Yes, perhaps. Although, it's not as if I actually write every word of it. I give them a first draft, but then the editors get to work. I'm often surprised when I read in the paper what they wind up with. Azimut Martin is a fictional character, a composite created with my contacts' information and several different pens."

He seemed perfectly at ease with this arrangement.

"So, why take the risk? Is there really so much satisfaction in seeing your . . . well, it's not even your name . . . but your ideas in print?"

"A question asked by a man with family wealth. I do it for the money, Dubon. What else?"

Dubon felt compelled to defend himself. "I haven't a centime I don't earn myself, and my wife's income is hardly lavish."

"Still, it's a cushion, isn't it? That little bit extra. I can't even afford to marry." His voice was hard but without evident bitterness. "I'm thirty-two. I'll be thirty-five or older before I can contemplate taking a wife. I'll have to find some nice young thing whose family is impressed by a splashy uniform but whose tastes are not too extravagant."

He paused, perhaps embarrassed now by his candor. Dubon got the impression that perhaps he already had his eye on a nice young thing. Or perhaps she was not so young, and she couldn't wait much longer.

"I hope they pay you well, your editors," Dubon said, trying to lighten the tone. "You took a while to reply. It's been two weeks since I left that letter with Chalon."

"I hesitated because I knew you. I could not contact you without revealing my identity and I didn't know what your interest might be. Then at dinner last week—so kind of you to include me; you and Madame Dubon have always been most kind—well, at dinner I got the impression that you . . . that you were asking yourself, as I do, whether it's possible that Dreyfus might be innocent. Or at least thinking that there is something not right about the whole case."

"You've thought it over carefully."

"I'll be honest with you. Since the rumors of the escape—the false rumors—my editors have been pressing me. 'Who is this Dreyfus?' they keep asking me. 'What grounds do you have to question the court martial?'"

"And what do you reply?"

"First, I have to ask you, Maître, what your interest is. If we are both of one mind on this affair, I am happy to share information.

Indeed, that is why I finally contacted you. But I have been totally honest with you about my motives."

"Yes, of course. I represent . . . that is to say I have a client who believes fervently in the captain's innocence. Close friend of the Dreyfus family. Swears the man is incapable of such a betrayal of his motherland. I gather there are differences of opinion within the Dreyfus family as to how their relative's case is best treated, and I have been approached on the side, apart from the main effort that the brother is making. My assignment from my client is quite simple and quite impossible: I am to find the real spy."

"So they believe there is a spy out there, still at large?"

"Yes, the client has suggested the evidence of espionage is incontrovertible. There is a spy in the ranks—they court-martialed the wrong man."

"How much do you know about the case?"

"Le Goff, I'll tell you. I am painfully ill equipped. I know only what the client tells me and what I have read in the press. I have not even seen the actual court evidence against the captain, and the press accounts are thin. The reporters seem to have just taken the military's explanation that it had caught a spy and punished him accordingly. They've done nothing but denounce the traitor and cheer on his prosecutors. Except you, of course. That's why I approached you; your articles were the most measured."

"Thank you, but I don't know how much I can help. The trial was closed to the press, but I have had the evidence described to me. They call it the bordereau, the list. It's a scrap of paper our intelligence services somehow obtained from the German embassy and it lists various types of information Dreyfus was allegedly offering for sale."

"A spy's catalog of wares?"

"That's right. Documents about troop movements, maneuvers, and that sort of thing, and also possibly about armaments. We are testing various new guns, you know."

Dubon nodded, thinking of the document he had read in the Statistical Section in which Schwarzkoppen had noted Jean-Jean's interest in developing better artillery.

"That's why the intelligence services concluded the writer was an artillery officer with certain credentials," Le Goff continued. "They fingered Captain Dreyfus and, as you will have gathered from the papers, the fact that he is Jewish or that his family comes from Alsace is proof enough to them that he is willing to betray his country to the Germans."

"You distrust that argument?" Dubon asked.

"It's circular. Jews are spies because Jews aren't loyal to France. Where's the proof in that? What proof do we have that Jews or Alsatians are less loyal than the rest of us? And anyway, a hypothetical predisposition to betrayal is hardly enough to convict Dreyfus."

"My client said the memo was unsigned but that Bertillon, the criminologist, testified at the court martial. His theory was an elaborate one—that the captain had disguised his own hand to write the list."

"Yes. I heard about that, too."

"You don't trust Bertillon's testimony?"

"You're a lawyer. You know a lot more about him than I do. But it all sounded too convenient to me. Handwriting doesn't match? Why it's because the man was disguising his own writing. What reason would he have to do that? He had no reason to believe the letter would be read by anyone other than the person to whom it was addressed. None of my informants seemed to know whether the letter was unsigned or whether the signature was simply missing. The Germans would need some assurances as to the identity of their would-be spy. The whole thing seemed flimsy to me, but when I questioned it, I was continually assured the generals had their proofs. Indeed, there's a rumor that there's more evidence."

"More evidence?"

"Yes. A secret file that was shown to the judges on the side."

"Not shared with the defense? That's a violation of all legal principles." Here Dubon's tone grew firm as he moved from the world of spies and military secrets back into his own realm. "How can an accused respond to charges if his legal representation is not privy to the evidence? It is the most basic right, Le Goff."

"In a civilian court, perhaps, but this was a court martial."

"The law as it applies to court martial is the same. If a military court can incarcerate the guilty, not just dismiss someone from his post but actually jail him, it must follow the same procedures as a civilian court. The judges in the captain's case should never have permitted the prosecution to present evidence on such terms."

"But surely the nation—"

Dubon cut Le Goff short. "No. We are talking about rights of which no French citizen may be deprived." His voice was rising with his rhetoric, causing the patrons at the next table to look up from their drinks. "If it's true the captain was convicted on secret evidence, that itself is a miscarriage of justice and grounds for declaring a mistrial."

"Yes, yes," Le Goff agreed in a low voice, restraining Dubon by cocking his head in the direction of their neighbors. "If you can prove that the secret evidence exists."

"True," Dubon said, more quietly now. "Find the secret file, and exonerate the captain."

"Or at least get him a second trial where they can find him guilty fair and square."

"But do you think he's guilty, Le Goff?"

"No. I don't. For two reasons. First, I can't see the motive. I wouldn't make the assumption that his religion predisposes him to treachery. So, what am I left with? Money? The family is wealthy; he could live quite comfortably without working at all, I'd say."

"Yes, my client gave me that impression."

"Political conviction? Seems an odd way to go about it."

"And your second reason?"

"I never met the man, but I know several who have. He hasn't got it in his personality to go adventuring. He's too rigid, annoyingly so, I gather. He is exceedingly hardworking. To be frank, he's a rather boring character, not very popular with his colleagues. I did wonder if that might have something to do with his conviction. Convenient scapegoat, that sort of thing."

"You confirm my own impressions," Dubon said. He had reached similar conclusions with much less evidence at his disposal. His powers of deduction weren't half bad for a dull old solicitor.

"What else do you know?" Le Goff asked.

"Not much. I gather the case against him originates in an obscure department known as the Statistical Section, which is actually a cover for counterespionage."

"Oh yes. They are quite famous now—the clever fellows who caught the spy."

"I am not sure they are that clever," Dubon said, thinking of the disastrous backlog of paper on his desk and the affable Colonel Picquart, the authoritarian Major Henry, and the gleeful Captain Gingras. Thus far only Captain Hermann had shown the skepticism one might have expected from a spy.

"Why do you say that?"

Dubon paused. "I . . . uh . . . I have a contact there."

"You have a contact inside the Statistical Section?"

"Yes, a reliable contact, I'd say."

Le Goff leaned across the café table and gripped Dubon's arm.

"Then, Dubon, all you have to do is get him, somehow or other, to let you see the secret evidence."

NINETEEN

The following day, Dubon began his lunch hour skulking around the boulevard Saint-Germain in his uniform looking for a florist who would deliver. He continually scanned the crowd ahead of him to make sure he was not about to bump into anyone he knew, and his progress was slow. It took him about ten minutes walking down the boulevard in fits and starts before he found a little shop hidden behind big buckets of roses and lilies set out on the pavement. He went in and ordered a large bouquet of red roses to be sent to Madeleine before the end of the day and scribbled a small note apologizing for his absence the previous evenings and saying he eagerly anticipated a belated reunion the next night.

It had been well past seven when he said good-bye to Le Goff, promising to report back any more information he could find from his "contact" at the Statistical Section. And it was fifteen minutes past the appointed dinner hour of seven thirty when he finally arrived home to find Geneviève and André already eating. It was the second night in a row that he was late, and if his wife had been largely uninterested in his apology the night before, she was now even less understanding and more alert to his unusually excited behavior.

"Oh dear. I'm late again. Awfully busy at the office at the moment." He found himself babbling as she watched him with a disapproving eye, letting a long pause draw attention to his lapse. He felt like a schoolboy whose ominously silent teacher would not speak until he settled down. He glanced across at André to see if he might try raising a joke with him to escape the situation, but his son was staring intently at the meat he was cutting.

"This is most unlike you, François," Geneviève finally said. "You are usually so punctual. It disrupts the dinner hour when you are late. How are the servants supposed to plan a meal if they don't know when you will arrive? I can't have you behaving like Claude. He drives my poor sister to distraction with his lateness. I rely on you, you know." She looked at him sternly and remained standoffish for the rest of the evening.

Her sister's husband was not merely tardy; he was also a well-known philanderer whose indiscretions were always causing his wife grief. Geneviève was hardly going to mention that in her son's presence, but Dubon was being warned. He had long suspected that his wife was not completely unaware of Madeleine's existence and accepted it as long as her routines and her household were not disrupted. How ironic, Dubon thought, if Geneviève were to stop tolerating his extracurricular activities only because the widow's case was now causing him to neglect both his wife *and* his mistress!

Standing inside the humid florist's shop, surrounded by a pleasantly earthy smell, Dubon paused. He couldn't remember when he had last given Geneviève flowers. Her previous birthday, perhaps? Would this second bouquet be an admission of guilt?

"Was there anything else, Monsieur le Capitaine?" the clerk asked.

"Yes, another bouquet. Not roses, I don't think."

"Perhaps the Dutch tulips, Captain, lovely at this time of year. Or we have several colors of lilies now. The pink, a little unusual . . ."

"Yes, the lilies. The pink ones. No, no, just the yellow ones," he said, recalling that pink was more Madeleine's color than Geneviève's. "They will go well with, uh, with the salon."

Dubon sent off this second bouquet, with a second apology, this one to his wife, but still lingered. He would dearly have loved to send a third bouquet—he made a mental note to get the widow's address from Lebrun's files for future reference—but he would be seeing his client that afternoon anyway. He was now bursting to tell her Le Goff's news about the secret evidence.

Dubon turned and walked back out to the street. A few doors farther up the boulevard, he passed a baker's stall where he stopped and ducked his head under the green-and-gray-striped awning to buy himself a pastry. The awning hung low, blocking his peripheral vision, and it was just as he was finishing his transaction and emerging from underneath it that he found his path blocked by a wall of dark clothing. He looked up to find himself face-to-face with the large forms of General Fiteau and his wife. At least, he presumed it was Madame Fiteau at the general's side, although he could not see anything of the lady's face for the black veil wrapped around her hat.

The general was staring straight at him. Dubon felt his innards seized by panic and the adrenaline flowing into his legs, tightening his muscles as they prepared to run. He fought the instinct and rocked back on his heels to compensate for the way he had pitched forward. The general had recognized him; a look of puzzlement spread across his face. There was nothing to do but to play along.

"Mon Générale!" Dubon barked, saluting sharply with one hand, while the other surreptitiously nudged the twist of paper containing his pastry back onto the edge of the baker's table.

The general returned his salute and there was a moment of silence. Dubon could hear his own pulse beating inside his ears. Was the general not going to say something at least? Dubon, belatedly remembering himself, bowed to Madame Fiteau.

"Madame."

There was a murmur of reply from beneath the veil.

This was doubly difficult, Dubon thought. He had to dream up some explanation for his uniform—maybe he could suggest some silly family joke was being played on Jean-Jean—and he had to offer condolences.

"May I say, Madame, how very sorry Madame Dubon and I, that

is, how very sad we were to hear of your loss . . ." Goodness, he was babbling. He and Geneviève had hardly needed to hear of the Fiteaus' loss; they had been standing right there when it happened. He tried again. "That is, how very sorry we are for your loss." There he had said it. There was no point dwelling on it. Singing the praises of the young Fiteau would only sound insincere under the circumstances. Again there was but a faint murmur from underneath the veil. The general pressed his wife's arm closer to his side and patted it with his free hand.

"Thank you, Dubon. Kind of you. Just out taking the air, you know. Told Marthe we must get out," he said awkwardly, before changing the topic. "I have never seen you in uniform before. I did not know you were in the reserves."

"Uh, no." What did he mean? The reserves . . .

"It's much appreciated, Dubon," the general said, drawing himself taller. "It's so hard to attract good officers to the reserves. Well, I am sure I don't need to tell you that."

Of course, the reserves. Amateurs. Playing at being soldiers a few weeks a year and then returning to their regular jobs. Thank God. The general had just handed him an excellent excuse.

"One does like to do one's duty," Dubon mumbled.

"But we never see you in your uniform. You should be proud of it. We certainly encourage wearing it on official occasions."

"Of course, of course. It's just, you know, with my wife's family. I am an amateur among professionals. I prefer to maintain my civilian identity. Don't want my brothers to think I am competing."

"I see, I see," the general said, but his tone was skeptical.

Their conversation felt stilted, but Dubon couldn't tell if this was his own nerves, their grief, or the general's puzzlement over his uniform. The man maintained his hand on his wife's arm but what had looked at first like affection now appeared more and more to Dubon like physical restraint, as though he were keeping her from bolting or falling down. There was a slight but persistent sound from under the veil, a quiet sort of gulping, and Dubon realized that the woman was crying.

"I must take Madame Fiteau home now. Good day," the general said abruptly.

"Madame." Dubon bowed slightly, and then saluted the general again, standing aside to let them pass.

As he did so, Madame Fiteau pitched herself at him, clutching Dubon with her free arm. Her voice was a desperate whisper from under the veil.

"Geneviève said you could help. Please. Find out who killed him."

"Marthe!" The General pulled her back toward him. "Good day to you, Dubon," he said almost fiercely as he hurried her away.

Dubon turned back to the baker's table and picked up his pastry. He unwrapped it and bit into it as he started walking back down the boulevard in the opposite direction, but he barely noticed what he was chewing, and by the time he got to the door of the Statistical Section he discovered that the whole thing had vanished without his having registered its taste.

TWENTY

With a pleasant sensation of familiarity, Dubon dusted off the cover of a large leather ledger. Here, at least, was something he knew. He was trying to banish the anxious question that was nagging at him—what would happen when the general mentioned to some friend or family member that good old Dubon had a secret career as a reservist?—by returning to the mysterious files. He should have examined this ledger on top of the filing cabinet first, for he quickly recognized its function. It was a file log; some larger law firms used the system too. Every file that was removed had to be signed out by an officer, with the date recorded; the clerk signed it back in when it was returned. The arrival or creation of new files was also dutifully noted.

The log showed the comings and goings of exotic animals, gemstones, and monuments, but the main thing it revealed to Dubon was that the Statistical Section seemed to do very little work. There had been no entries since he arrived and the entries that preceded his arrival showed little activity from one month's end to the next. In the previous months of 1897, perhaps two dozen files—including monkeys, camels, diamonds, rubies, Saint-Denis, and Saint-Michel—had been consulted. The year of 1896 did not look as though it had been any busier. Did the main business of the Statistical Section lie elsewhere? He noted that the German documents he had given to Hermann never returned to him to be filed, nor did the French ones.

He was standing at the cabinet puzzling over this when Gingras came back, whistling to himself as he sauntered through the door. He paused at the desk, always ready to chat, and Dubon decided he would risk asking. Surely as a new clerk he could pretend ignorance of the code.

"Gingras, I've been meaning to ask you—this filing system . . ."

"Major gave you a copy of the book, did he?" Gingras asked, nodding in the direction of Henry's office door.

"No, actually," Dubon said, lowering his voice.

Gingras laughed. "What have you been doing for the past three days if you can't file all the junk?"

"I . . . well, I didn't like to ask the major," Dubon said, more quietly still. "He was rather preoccupied the day I arrived."

"More like ferocious, but it's all bluster, you know," Gingras replied as loudly as ever, ignoring Dubon's attempts at discretion. "Anyway, you can always ask me. Back in a minute," he added over his shoulder as he now headed down the corridor toward his office.

He reemerged moments later with a small notebook in his hand.

"Ever seen one of these before?" He handed the notebook to Dubon.

"No, I don't believe I have."

Dubon skimmed through it. It contained a list of dates with a word beside each one. He recognized the words as the file names, following broad categories—monuments of France, biblical names, animals, flowers. Scribbled in pencil beside each one was what appeared to be a legitimate file name, so that Chartres was *Germany—Armaments* and Rouen was *Germany—Berlin Agents*.

"What is it?"

"It's an old codebook, from the war. Those are keywords. I use them to provide code names for these files."

"Ah." Dubon turned the little book over in his hand.

"How much do you know about ciphers?" Gingras asked.

Dubon hesitated. How much might he be expected to know about ciphers?

"Not really my area," he tried.

"We've got even more sophisticated ones now, but during the war they were still using the Vigenère cipher."

"Of course," said Dubon, who hadn't the least notion what the Vigenère cipher might be. As he hoped, Gingras was all too happy to explain.

"It's a multiple alphabetic cipher. Each letter of a message is encoded using a different letter of a keyword. In a simple alphabetic cipher you just use a displacement to give an alternative letter for each letter you want to encode: *A* is *B*, *B* is *C*, *C* is *D*, and so on until you get back to *Z*, which is *A*.

"But the Vigenère system uses the letters of a keyword to provide multiple alternatives. So, if you use the keyword *Rouen*, for example, the first letter of your message is encoded using an alphabet in which *A* is *R*, so *B* would be *S*, and so on, but the second letter of the message is encoded in another alphabet in which *A* is *O*, and the third letter in a third alphabet in which *A* is *U*.

"It's ingenious, very complicated to crack, although the Germans supposedly have. We don't use it anymore—not considered secure. But during the war, it was still the thing, and in those days there were books like this issued every six months, full of the next set of code words. This one covers the first half of 1870. It's basically a list of about 175 words, one word signifying the cipher for each day. I got five copies of the book from one of your fellows in the rue Saint-Dominique. Just gave them to me for a laugh, bit of a curiosity.

"And then I had the idea of using it. The colonel's predecessor, Sandherr, was trying to impose a bit of order on the files that came over from the rue Saint-Dominique. He liked word games, so I suggested to him that we encode the file names simply using the old keywords. It was sort of a tribute to the old cipher clerks, you know. I distributed my copies around the office and just penciled in our file names in alphabetical order. Anybody who wants a file just looks up the real name alphabetically in the book to discover the code name. Then look up the code name alphabetically in the files, and there you have it."

"So all you need is the codebook?" asked Dubon.

"Yes, that's right. I'll leave you to get some filing done," he added with a snicker and walked back to his office.

The system struck Dubon as cumbersome and unnecessary. Surely it would have been easier to keep the files under lock and key? He suspected Gingras had merely dreamed up the ciphers to amuse himself, but the minute the man was gone he sat down and started looking through the codebook under any names or subject headings that might be significant. Then he went back to the beginning and read the whole alphabetical list. There was no reference to Dreyfus anywhere.

He clearly wasn't cut out to be a spy and just wanted to see the widow again. She would be waiting for him that evening and he felt nothing but relief when, a few minutes after five, Picquart came out of his office and dismissed him. Shaken by his encounter with the general and his wife, he decided he could no longer risk walking about in public in uniform. He crossed the rue de Lille, walked up to the quay, and slipped inside a small green kiosk he had spotted on previous mornings. The stench was appalling. Dubon preferred never to use public urinals, but today he was thankful for them. He pulled off his tunic and cap, bundled them into a tight roll under his arm, and reemerged on the street. It was mid-May now, warm enough to wear shirtsleeves, and if this dishabille shocked any acquaintance he happened to meet as he walked back to the rue Saint-Honoré, he judged it would be easier to explain than a uniform. Some story about a jacket soiled in a nasty encounter with a careless cab driver would be all that was required.

When Dubon arrived back at his own office, Lebrun looked disapprovingly at his shirtsleeves but said nothing, simply indicating with a nod of his head that the widow was waiting inside.

"I left the day's messages on your desk, Maître. Something from Chaudière again; otherwise nothing that can't wait. I'll see you tomorrow evening."

"Yes. Thank you, Lebrun," he said, as he unrolled the tunic, shook it out, and hung it and the cap on the coatrack before walking with anticipation into the inner office.

The widow turned to him eagerly as he entered. "Maître, I am so relieved to see you."

"Madame." Dubon gave her a little, half-mocking bow, moved to her, and took both her hands. "I have all sorts of things to tell you, but most of all I have good news."

"Good news?"

"Yes, good news. There exists in the Statistical Section a secret file of evidence against the captain."

"Secret evidence?" She pulled back and dropped one of his hands. "Why is that good news?"

"Ah, Madame . . ." he said as he took back the hand she had pulled away. "I am a lawyer, and you were right to come to a lawyer. It's good news because whatever it contains, it was kept secret. It was not shown to the defense."

"That's not fair," she protested, gripping at his hands.

"Not fair, Madame, and not legal. It is, in and of itself, grounds for an appeal. There will be a new trial. There *must* be a new trial."

"Oh . . ." She gulped and did not resist as he moved toward her, drawing her into an embrace.

At first, as he kissed her, she seemed to melt into him as though wanting the contact as much as he did, and he could feel the weight of her chest pressing against him through his thin shirt. Then they quickly pulled away from each other, simultaneously realizing the implications of their kiss.

Dubon was the first to recover his composure.

"Madame. My sincere apologies. I forgot myself. That was unforgivable. I assure you it will not—"

"No, no, Maître. You don't need—"

"Really, I . . . if you wish to change counsel . . ."

"Maître, please. Just find this secret file."

TWENTY-ONE

Dubon stretched and his hand encountered soft flesh. In that luxurious state halfway to waking, he explored a thigh that seemed to go on forever, until a slight movement on the other side of the bed startled him.

"What time is it?"

"It's almost half past seven, dear," Madeleine replied, pushing herself up on one elbow.

He sat up abruptly, now fully awake.

"I have to go," he said, reaching for his clothes. He had blundered over here from his own office, arriving after six and dragging Madeleine into the bedroom for the encounter he could not have with the widow. He had meant to leave immediately afterward. He would be late for dinner a third night in a row. "Why didn't you wake me?"

"You haven't been here all week, you arrive late. How am I supposed to know your schedule?" she asked.

Dubon sighed as he buttoned his shirt. He was expecting an argument when he arrived home, but Madeleine was usually genial. He tried smiling at her, but she was busy admiring the line of her naked ankle and arched foot as they protruded from under the sheets. He supposed she wanted to talk about something, women usually did, but he simply did not have the time.

"Hope to see you tomorrow," he said as he pulled on his jacket. He kissed her quickly on the cheek and was gone.

The next afternoon was spent fruitlessly sifting through the files, an exercise that felt especially deflating after his encounter with the widow the previous evening. Sitting at his desk or standing at the filing cabinet, where he now could put the occasional piece of paper in its proper place, he would stop and replay their kiss in his mind's eye before remembering that he had both promised her it would never happen again and assured her he would find the secret file. At that point, his fantasies would evaporate to be replaced by a growing sense of panic: he needed to find something fast to satisfy her and allow him to end his dangerous impersonation.

"Twice in one week, eh? Your lucky day."

It was the fat lady in the raincoat, appearing at his elbow and interrupting his increasingly desperate thoughts. Again she dumped the contents of her bag onto his desktop and waved cheerfully before turning on her heel, going back down the corridor, and disappearing through the small door.

As he sat there trying to sort these latest offerings, the colonel emerged from his office.

"Another delivery from the usual route, Dubon?" he asked.

"Yes, Colonel. I will tidy it up before I go home."

"Too late to start piecing things together now. Just put it in a file as it is and bring it to me; I'll lock it in my office for the night and you can get it again tomorrow."

"Yes, Colonel."

Dubon found a fresh file folder, tidied up the paper as best he could, and brought it to the colonel's office.

"Off you go, then."

And he did, but not out the front door. If he could not find the secret file, at least he could discover how it was documents were coming into the Statistical Section and people were going out. Slipping past the major's office, where the man could be seen sucking on his pencil as though laboring over some composition, Dubon walked quietly toward the hallway and started down it, trying to look as though he knew exactly what he was doing. At the end of it, both Gingras's and Hermann's doors also stood open and he could just glimpse Hermann's foot beneath his desk but could not see his face. Dubon stopped at the small door, gently turned the handle, and stepped quickly inside.

He found himself in utter darkness, and even after waiting what seemed to be a long moment for his eyes to get used to it, there was precious little light to see by. Only the faintest line on the floor showed him the door he had just come through. He ran his hand around the walls on either side of it but couldn't find any light switch. He must be inside some kind of closet; the air felt close and stale. He put his hand up toward where he supposed the ceiling would be and waved it to and fro; sure enough, it connected with a string and he gave a tug. An odd orangey-yellow light came on, but it didn't feel like that much of an improvement, only partially illuminating the room.

Despite the dimness, he noticed a second bulb with a second string; he pulled that and was rewarded with better light. He appeared to be standing in a laboratory. There was a wooden counter on which various bottles and vials sat alongside several shallow pans. At the end of the counter stood a mysterious machine, a large black box, about the size of a big cooking pot, which ended in an accordion-like sleeve and was mounted on a flat wooden rod. Dubon carefully tried the round handle located on its side and found that the rod was notched and the handle moved the box slowly up and down it. He then raised the box high enough that he could look into the bottom: it was outfitted with a round glass—a lens, he supposed. The thing looked like a giant camera suspended upside down, and Dubon realized that was precisely what it was. He was standing in a darkroom.

Most of the material he had seen in the files had been copied out by hand, but there were a few photographic copies too. This must be where the section was doing its photography; it saved sending files over to headquarters. Dubon wiped his brow—he was now sweating profusely—and began hunting as quietly as he could through the few drawers beneath the counter. He found various metal instruments that looked like tongs and clips, and a heavy leather pouch. He opened the pouch but the only thing it contained was a stack of blank paper. He put the pouch back and closed the drawer.

He looked around the rest of the tiny room but could find nothing else of interest, nor any exit, except the door he had come through. If the fat lady and the major were using this as a route out to the street, they must be magicians, he concluded.

"Good-bye, then. See you tomorrow."

The voice made him jump before he realized it was coming through the wall from Picquart's office. The colonel was bidding one of the others good night.

He waited a few minutes and then opened the small door again very gingerly and, hearing no one moving on the other side, stepped back into the corridor. He looked to his right, back toward the colonel's office, and then to his left, realizing there was a second, even smaller door a few paces farther down. He opened it and slipped inside.

This time, he had no problem identifying where he was. He had walked into the forbidden water closet. There was a flush toilet in one corner, operated by a large cistern suspended well above it on the ceiling, and a very small sink with a single tap. A rather grubby towel hung to one side. He didn't think he had seen either the colonel or the major enter the water closet and emerge in an amount of time that would suggest they were using it for the purpose it seemed intended. In fact, the only officer he had seen go down the corridor and disappear was the major, but he could not imagine him or the fat lady climbing out the one, small, high window to the left of the toilet.

He gently tapped on the linoleum-covered walls to discover if they concealed a door. He found one panel that sounded different from the others, directly under the window, but no amount of pushing seemed to open it and he could find no catch or handle. He was feeling in his pockets for something he could use to pry at it when he noticed a short wooden ruler on the floor under the sink. He slipped it into the crack where the panel ended and, sure enough, it sprang open like a door. He looked out and found he was standing at the top of a metal fire escape leading into an alley below. He replaced the ruler under the sink and walked onto the fire escape, pulling the small door closed behind him.

It had a regular handle on the outside, but when he tried it, he found it had locked automatically. He was now locked out of the building on a fire escape three floors above the ground! The fat lady, the major, and even the disheveled visitor of the other day must have keys, he concluded. Or the visitors warned the major in advance and he left the door ajar for them. Either way, the logistics of how they got through the door did not trouble Dubon much until he climbed down the fire escape to the ground and realized the alleyway was without exit.

At one end, a high brick wall cut it off from a property on the street behind, and at the other end, it acted merely as a light well between the two buildings whose facades were joined together on the rue de Lille. He paused to think: surely those who used this exit were not climbing over high walls. He began trying the several doors that gave onto the alleyway, starting with the one on the ground floor of the building he had just exited. It was locked. He tried three doors on the ground floor of the building across the way; one opened easily and he found himself in a warm corridor; a din of conversation and clinking glasses came from the room beyond. There was a telephone cabin on his left and a door marked wc on his right. He was standing at the back of the next-door café.

He took a breath, squared his shoulders, and walked forward, preparing to sit down at the first table he could find and order a drink, as though he were merely a patron who had used the toilets before taking a seat. As he squeezed himself into a chair at the back of the room, congratulating himself on his sangfroid and looking about for a waiter, he noticed the fat lady. She was sitting at a table in the front window, nursing a short glass of wine.

Dubon slunk down in his chair and stared at the tabletop, believing, whether rightly or wrongly, that if he did not look at her, she would be less likely to see him. He sat there for what felt like a long while, occasionally sneaking a glance across the room to her table. Eventually, a waiter appeared at his elbow.

"My apologies, Captain," said the waiter, looking at the stripes on Dubon's uniform. "I didn't see you come in."

Dubon ordered a dry sherry—he seldom drank the stuff but wanted something he could either linger over, or gulp down if that proved

necessary—and asked for the bill when it arrived. He was only halfway
through his drink when the fat lady hailed the waiter and called for
her bill. She gave Dubon plenty of time to decide on his next move as
she fiddled with her bag, extracting a money purse from its depths.
He quickly crossed the room and paid the cashier with the coins he
had ready. He nodded curtly and left through the front door. Out in
the street, he slipped into the next doorway, a stationery store that was
closing for the evening; the manager gesticulated broadly through the
glass that he was shut and Dubon waved him away.

The fat lady soon emerged from the café and turned up the rue
de Lille, moving toward its intersection with the boulevard Saint-
Germain and the quay. She walked briskly for a heavy person; she was
not unhealthy, Dubon judged, and he found that his usual pace kept
up with her nicely. He was not sure why he was following her, or what
exactly he hoped to find out, so when she joined the crowd waiting for
the omnibus at the top of the boulevard, he decided he would keep
going in his own direction, cross the river, and walk back to his real office. He reminded himself he was no detective and had no idea how you
tailed someone in the closed quarters of a horse-drawn public conveyance. But just as he was turning toward the bridge, the bus pulled up,
and as he watched his quarry board at the back with a clutch of other
passengers, he realized that if he climbed to the upper deck, known affectionately as l'Impériale, he could get on without her seeing him. He
bought a ticket as he boarded and settled himself in a seat toward the
back. The omnibus began its slow progress down the boulevard Saint-
Germain. To his surprise, they had gone only a few hundred meters
when the fat lady came out to the conductor's platform at the back
of the bus. Could she really be getting off so soon? Dubon prepared
himself to disembark too.

"Whew. It's close in there," she remarked to the conductor. "I'll just
go up and join the gentlemen."

Dubon froze in his seat. He had never expected a lady to climb
those stairs. He had miscalculated severely: his quarry was not, of
course, a lady. Geneviève had never ridden an omnibus in her life and
certainly never would have climbed to l'Impériale, while Madeleine
had once recounted to him as a great adventure the time she was forced

upstairs by the crowd of men sheltering from the rain below. The fat lady was now reaching the top of the steps. Dubon looked in the opposite direction, over the rail, turning his head as far to the side as he could, hoping his cap would hide his face and feeling increasingly ridiculous. He felt someone settle a weight in the empty seat beside him and a voice rang out.

"Good evening, Captain. Did you enjoy your drink?"

TWENTY-TWO

"I noticed you in the bar," the lady explained. If she was aware that he was following her, she did not show it. Her approach seemed genuinely friendly.

"Is this your usual route home?"

"Well, no. I . . . um . . . I am on my way to a friend's," Dubon stumbled.

"I see. I'm off home for supper. I live out near the place Monge. Have to turn around and come straight back again to go to work, but the major pays me handsomely for my time, so I don't mind. Not a bit."

She seemed to assume all this would make sense to Dubon.

"And, uh, where do you work?" he ventured. At this, she looked askance.

"Don't tell you much there, do they. I work just down the street," she said, nodding in the direction they had come from.

"On the rue Saint-Dominique?" he asked.

"No, on the rue de Lille, at the German embassy, of course." Dubon had forgotten the Germany embassy was so close by, in the midst of the government quarter along with that of several other nations. All very cozy.

"And what do you do there?"

"I am the cleaning lady. Where did you think I get the papers?"

So, this lowly cleaner was the source of the section's intelligence on German activity in France. She emptied the Germans' trash and delivered it to French counterintelligence down the street. No wonder they needed a secret door.

"I've worked there for years," she continued. "And with the major too. Can't think how long now, at least six, oh, it would be seven now. They call me 'the usual route'—did you know that?" She smiled, evidently pleased with the notion she was valuable enough to have earned a nickname.

Dubon recalled the colonel had used exactly that phrase that afternoon.

"So were you involved in catching that Jewish spy?" he hazarded.

"Oh yes," she agreed proudly. "Major gave me a bit extra that month."

"I understand that it was some sort of . . ."

Dubon hoped to prompt her into revealing what exactly the evidence was, but she wasn't helpful in that regard.

"No idea. No idea what was in the packet."

"I suppose it was in German . . ."

"No, the papers were in French. I can read, you know." She said this somewhat defensively. "Don't think I am illiterate. That's what the Germans think, just some old lady who doesn't know her *ABC*'s, and I let them believe it. But I can read perfectly well, French at least."

This disdain for their cleaning lady perhaps explained why the German diplomats were so lackadaisical about the wastepaper, Dubon thought, as the woman continued.

"But I haven't got time to go reading all that I sweep up. Besides, the major always says I must leave the papers as they are, not to even uncrumple them, you know, or try to glue the ripped bits together. Just bring them over to the office as soon as possible—usually that's the next day since I don't finish up at the embassy until past midnight—and that's what I do. I used to meet the major off the premises, all hush-hush like, but since they caught that spy, he wants me to bring everything over right away. Lets me use that back door, so nobody knows what I am about. Two deliveries this week."

Dubon wondered why, if he had caught the real spy, Major Henry was in such a rush for German documents: did he think there was another spy at work, or was he looking for more evidence against Dreyfus? Meanwhile, the fat lady, who clearly liked an audience, kept talking, boasting of her importance without revealing much more to Dubon about the contents of the German wastepaper baskets. He finally decided he had better get off the omnibus before he was forced to travel all the way to the place Monge, and as they approached the boulevard Saint-Michel, he saw his opportunity.

"My stop, here. So nice to talk with you, Madame."

"Why, we have never even been properly introduced, have we, Captain."

"Er, Dubon, Captain Dubon, Madame."

"And I am Madame Bastian. I'll see you next week, I'm sure."

"Good-bye, Madame. Until next week, then," Dubon said as he walked toward the stairs.

Hopping off the bus, he turned toward the river, crossed the Île de la Cité on foot, and soon found himself on the Right Bank, now waiting on the quay for the electric tram that would take him back the distance he had traveled on the Saint-Germain omnibus.

One showed up soon enough and he got on. As he rode along he found himself turning the encounter into a story he could tell the widow.

When he arrived at his office, still in full uniform because he had not happened to pass any urinals after following Madame Bastian, he found Lebrun at his post with the week's files.

"Will I see you tomorrow morning, Maître? Perhaps we can review things then."

"No. I won't be here tomorrow morning—I'll leave you to hold the fort again, I'm afraid."

The next day was Saturday; Dubon assumed the Statistical Section would not keep working much past noon and that he would at least be able to get home for lunch on time. His absence from Saturday lunch would not be appreciated; it was a cheerful meal that marked the end of the working week for both him and André, and Geneviève always tried to ensure there was some treat for them both, his favorite Roquefort or cream puffs for his son.

"Perhaps I'll come in sometime tomorrow afternoon, so I'll catch up on things if you just leave them for me."

In fact, after their surprising kiss, he and the widow had agreed, in as businesslike a manner as possible, that they would meet again Saturday afternoon—but there was no particular need to tell Lebrun of this.

"Very good, Maître. I will see you Monday, then . . . in the evening? Same routine as this week?"

"Maybe so. I'm not quite sure how long this will take me. Another day or two, I guess."

After Lebrun left for the day, Dubon changed back into his civilian clothing. It was past six thirty when he finally locked up, so he went straight home without making his promised stop at Madeleine's. He really must see her on Monday, Dubon thought to himself, but in truth he was already fantasizing about the next day's meeting with the widow as he walked home looking forward to another glass of the Giscours, a good meal, and time alone with his thoughts in his study.

The excitements of his day, however, were far from over. He pushed open the door of the apartment to find his household in crisis: Jean-Jean stood in the front hall in muddy battledress expostulating as Geneviève and Luc circled him making pacifying noises. For a moment, Dubon could not think what the matter might be.

"You're sure you didn't take it with you?" Geneviève was asking, but Jean-Jean was adamant.

"I tell you I left it in the armoire right beside the other one. And now it's gone!"

TWENTY-THREE

That Saturday morning did not begin well. The colonel, usually affable, was in a foul mood. He was there already when Dubon arrived at eight, working at his desk, and when he heard his clerk enter he got up and pointedly shut his office door. About half an hour later, he stuck his head out and called for Captain Gingras, who had not arrived yet. When Dubon informed him of this, he swore, muttered under his breath about lack of discipline, and asked that Gingras be sent to him immediately upon his arrival. When Gingras did arrive at nine, Dubon sent him in. Gingras left the door to the colonel's office partly open, and Dubon could hear the senior officer harshly asking his underling where the papers might be.

"Pages seem to be missing, Captain. This can't be all there is. I came in early Saturday morning to get a bit of quiet to work on the file, and I find it contains nothing more than these!"

"Yes, sir."

"Where do you think the rest of it might be, Captain?" His tone now sounded sarcastic.

"It's really the major's file, sir. I haven't had much occasion to use it. Perhaps you should ask the major."

"So, all this is the major's problem, is it? Well, he isn't here this morning, so that's convenient."

"He doesn't usually come in on Saturday morning, Colonel."

"No, I am aware of that, Captain Gingras."

"Perhaps if you consult the log," suggested Gingras, who sounded uncharacteristically subdued.

"I *have* consulted the log. The last date I could find was two years ago. Do you think these papers have been missing for two years?"

"I really don't know, Colonel. It's always possible that pages, well, that pages got mixed in with other files. I have known that to happen."

At this, the colonel shouted for Dubon and informed him he would need files.

Dubon entered the office, saluted sharply and replied, "Yes, Colonel. Which files?"

The Colonel pulled a ledger toward him; it was similar to the one Dubon had found on top of the filing cabinets by his desk, and apparently served the same purpose, for the colonel produced a string of dates covering almost three years.

"November 12, 13, 14, 15, and 16, 1894, and December 3 through 8. Write that down. Goodness, man, do you not have a pencil on you?"

"Ah no, Colonel, er . . . yes, Colonel . . ." Dubon ran back to his desk, grabbed pencil and paper, and starting jotting down the long list of dates Picquart read out to him. The file the colonel was looking up in his log had been used practically every day in the fall of 1894.

"Look up in your log all the files that were used on those dates, and pull them out and bring them to me. Now."

"Colonel." Dubon saluted, since Picquart's tone seemed to demand it, and returned to his desk. He was standing at the filing cabinets pulling the ledger toward him when Gingras left Picquart's office, closing the door behind him.

"Get to it, Dubon," he hissed as he walked by.

"I don't really understand what we are doing," Dubon confessed. "Why are there two logs? What are we cross-checking?"

Gingras laughed. "You don't think we keep our files out here in the front office just hidden away behind *Elephant* and *Hippopotamus*, do you? My code is just a lark, really. These are only the intelligence files, and you'll have to forgive us a little joke at the expense of your service, Captain."

"My service?"

"The intelligence service."

Dubon still wasn't following, but Gingras continued.

"Maybe we feel the rivalry more acutely than you fellows over at headquarters. These are the intelligence files from the rue Saint-Dominique, or at least those files that the intelligence branch sees fit to share with us. To be honest, we don't take this stuff too seriously. We're in the business of counterintelligence, Dubon."

"Of course, of course." Dubon tried to sound jovially aware of the rivalry between the two sections. "Thought we were all working for the same nation. My mistake."

"And the counterintelligence files are locked up in the colonel's office," Gingras went on. "Nobody signs them out without his permission."

"So he is looking up dates in a counterintelligence log and..." Dubon's voice trailed off, and he waited for Gingras to fill in the blanks.

"He has got a file on his desk that he believes may be missing pages. The dates he has given you are dates that his log, the *counterintelligence* log, shows that the file was used. Look up those same dates in your log, the *intelligence* log," he said, mockingly stressing the words, "and pull the files that were used on the same dates. Maybe we'll find the missing pages were tucked into the wrong file . . . or maybe not."

"You don't think we'll find them?"

"He's got the Dreyfus file on his desk. It was always, in my opinion, a bit slim. But don't ever tell anyone I said so, especially the major."

And with those cryptic remarks, Gingras saluted jauntily and returned to his office, leaving Dubon with the same kind of jittery feeling in his stomach that he got when he suspected he was holding a winning hand in bridge. He had finally figured out where the section kept the Dreyfus file.

Trying to suppress his excitement, he sat down with the intelligence log, dutifully looking up the dates the colonel had given him and jotting down the files that had been used those days. They had been in heavy use in those weeks in 1894. After a quarter hour's work, he had a list of about fifty files, which he began to pull from the cabinets and accumulate in cumbersome piles. In the space of another quarter hour, his desk was covered, and he had pulled only half the list. To clear some space, he walked down the hall to the colonel's office with a first load.

"Ah, Dubon. Well, that's not too bad," he said, looking at Dubon's armload.

"This is only about a quarter, Colonel," Dubon said, and stood there waiting for instructions. "There are more on my desk, and I haven't finished pulling all the ones that were used on those dates."

The colonel, whose desk was already littered with stacks, sighed deeply. "Only a quarter? I've only just started on the counterintelligence files; there must have been several hundred used during those weeks. Paper. We drown in it, Dubon. You join the army to fight battles and win wars, and instead you find yourself stuck at a desk." He sighed again, looking at the heap in front of him. "I suppose you were hoping to leave in time for a nice Saturday lunch, eh, Dubon?" he asked.

"Yes, Colonel," Dubon said.

"Me too. You're going to have to help me search. I haven't seen your orders, but obviously you are at least cleared for your own intelligence files." He looked up, waiting for confirmation.

Dubon grasped for the right response.

"Yes, Colonel," he said as blandly as he could manage. "Clearance for the intelligence section's classified documents."

"Right. Take those back to your desk and start on them. Once you've gone through all of them, you can refile them and go home."

"What am I looking for, Colonel?" Dubon asked.

"Bit of a sensitive file here. It seems to be missing documents. It's the file on the Dreyfus case—the spy, you know. You're looking for any documents relevant to the case or that bear his name. Not the court-martial transcripts or the official exhibits from the trial. I've got those. But I have another file of extra evidence. That is what seems to be missing paper. So just see if you spot anything that got tucked into the intelligence files by mistake."

"Very good, Colonel," Dubon said, trying to keep any emotion out of his voice.

Extra evidence not submitted as an exhibit? The colonel had the secret file, and the key to getting Dreyfus an appeal, sitting right on his desk. Dubon just had to figure out some way of getting at it.

He took his load of files back to his desk, pulled the remainder of the list, organized all the folders in piles on the floor, and began the laborious process of scanning every document in each one. Much of the material was handwritten and Dubon often had to read a page at length to decipher its contents and eliminate it. After some time he glanced up at the wall clock. It was already ten and he needed to get home on time for Saturday lunch. First, though, he had to get back across the river to his own office, where he could change out of his uniform before he headed to the apartment. There, he needed somehow to sneak the uniform back into the armoire in his study, so that it could be conveniently discovered for Jean-Jean, whose outrage of the previous evening had been caused by returning from maneuvers to find it missing. Jean-Jean had gone out for dinner wearing his dress uniform, with Geneviève assuring him the other one would show up before it was needed on Monday. And then Dubon was due back at his office for a three o'clock meeting with the widow.

God knows what I'll do for a uniform on Monday, he thought as he discarded one file and moved to the next, if I'm still here. One thing at a time, he reminded himself as he began skimming intelligence reports on the activities of a Russian ballerina, hunting for any bit of paper that mentioned the captain.

As he replaced the ballerina's folder and turned to the next pile, he brushed against it with his sleeve, scattering classified documents all over the floor. He was scrambling to retrieve them when he looked up and found Hermann staring at it all in disapproval.

"Oh, Hermann," Dubon gasped. "You surprised me."

The man made no response but just kept looking at the papers without bending down to help. Finally he asked, "What are you doing, Dubon?"

Dubon found his presence so disconcerting, he had to remind himself that he had, in this instance, nothing to hide.

"I am looking for some papers for the colonel. He thinks they might have been misfiled."

"Ah." Hermann, who was carrying a single sheet of paper himself, turned and went into Picquart's office.

"Thought you might want to see this, Colonel," Dubon heard him say, before Hermann went back to his own office.

Shortly after eleven, the colonel emerged again. "Any luck?"

"No, Colonel."

"I haven't found anything either." He stood there for a moment, looking at Dubon, who looked back at him, guessing his thoughts.

"Perhaps, Colonel," Dubon ventured, "there aren't any missing pages?"

"No, Captain. Perhaps not."

The colonel paused and then added, "Finish up the job, then, and get home." He started back to his office and then stopped, turning toward Dubon. "Don't tell the major how we spent Saturday morning, will you, Captain? I will ask him about the state of the file in due course."

An hour later, as he hurried back to his own office, it occurred to Dubon that the colonel had specifically chosen to hunt for the papers on a morning when he knew the major would be absent. Apparently, Colonel Picquart did not trust the major any more than Gingras did. Dubon changed outfits, smoothed out the wrinkles in Jean-Jean's uniform as best he could—it was getting rather creased from crossing the river every day bundled under his arm—and headed home with his canvas bag.

He could hear noises from the dining room as he arrived but he slipped down the hall to his study. He hid the uniform in the opposite corner of the armoire from where it had been hanging, sandwiching it between two of Geneviève's ball gowns in hopes this would provide sufficient explanation as to why Jean-Jean had been unable to find it earlier.

But that did not solve the problem of what he was to wear to the Statistical Section on Monday. Even if he could be sure his brother-in-law would now leave his fancy clothes behind, Dubon hardly wanted to draw attention to himself by showing up at the office in Jean-Jean's best parade dress with the red braid down the pants, nor did he want to give up the chase. He was tantalizing close to the file on Captain Dreyfus and had not felt this potent combination of fear and excitement twisting his innards since his best days with Maître Gaillard. He took a breath to calm himself and began sorting through the contents of the closet more carefully, examining the various outfits hanging there, and stopping at a slimmer navy tunic, so insignificant compared to the general's old greatcoat that hung beside it that he must have passed it by before.

"*Dieu, merci.*" He pulled the hanger from the closet. There were the captain's stripes on the tunic's sleeve and the blue pants with the blue braid down the sides. Jean-Jean's summer clothes. Cotton instead of wool. Jean-Jean had made no mention of changing over to summer wear yet. Dubon could probably count on getting a few days out of it, long enough to make some kind of plan to get hold of the secret file. He tucked the uniform right inside the greatcoat to be certain no one found it, and then surveyed the closet. Reaching for the wool tunic he had been wearing that morning, he tweaked a bit of it forward so that it could be seen peeking around a ballgown. Satisfied with the effect, he hurried back across the apartment.

To his relief he heard Geneviève announcing, "We are going to have one more good hunt in that armoire," as he pushed open the dining room door. "Lost things are often where you would expect them to be—you just haven't looked quite hard enough," she continued. "François, where in heaven's name have you been? At twelve thirty we simply gave up and went to the table."

"Busy at the office these days," he mumbled as he sat down, knowing the excuse and her patience were wearing thin but that Geneviève would not want a showdown in front of Masson, who was seated at the table with Jean-Jean and André. Dubon had forgotten his friend was coming for lunch, if he had ever known. He supposed Geneviève had told him.

"He has some very mysterious client at the moment whose case is keeping him horribly busy," Geneviève explained to Masson, an uncharacteristic note of sarcasm audible in her voice. "This is the first day this week he has been here for lunch, and in the evening he arrives home at the most outlandish hours." She glared at Dubon.

"Madame, if I were lucky enough to have a wife, I fear I would make her very unhappy," Masson said. "I am often not home from the office before eight."

"Well, of course, Monsieur. The affairs of government . . ."

"No, no. Nothing as important as that, I assure you," he replied.

"I hope you are not implying my work is not important, Geneviève," Dubon contributed as he lowered his soup spoon into the clear broth Luc had just set in front of him. "It may be dull, but it's our bread and butter." Dubon was feeling a little defensive on the subject of his professional achievements. He had built up an enviable practice and clearly he still had much to give the profession. He itched to tell somebody of his recent exploits, even if they represented unconventional behavior for a member of the bar.

"Of course it's important, my dear. Somebody has to tend to all the paper in the world and you do an excellent job. Papa was always so grateful that time you cleared up his disagreement with the Grillets. But you aren't keeping France safe from her enemies," she continued, turning again to Masson.

"Madame, you greatly overestimate my role in the government," he replied.

"No, you are just being modest, Baron," Geneviève insisted. "My brother, the major," she added, "was telling me how you are known to have the minister's ear on—"

Masson, who seemed decidedly embarrassed by this line of talk, cut her off. "No, really, Madame. With all due respect, your brother knows little of the inner workings of the quai d'Orsay. I am a bit player; it's very flattering when I am called on to consult the minister on a few of my special areas, our relations with Russia," he said. "But the government is really only interested in the German question."

Masson clearly wanted to change the subject, and Dubon suspected

Geneviève, for all that she seemed eager to flatter the man, had hit a sore point. His career must be stalled.

The conversation moved on and settled on what was, it seemed to Dubon, the increasingly inevitable topic in the capital these days: the certain guilt of the inmate of Devil's Island. It was Jean-Jean who launched into a rather pompous explanation of the rightness of military justice. Geneviève kept blinking her eyes at her brother to catch his attention, and tilting her head in André's direction to indicate she did not consider this a suitable topic to be discussing in front of a child.

Suave as always, Masson eased the conversation along, asking Dubon if he had been following the case in the papers. Dubon, who had barely had time to read a newspaper all week, could honestly confess he had not.

"The family maintains the man is innocent," Masson said dismissively. "The brother actually gave an interview this week to that effect. With *La Presse*. Appeared with the wife, all injured innocence. The woman insists on wearing only black." Masson all but snickered.

"Black?" Dubon asked.

"Yes, as though she were a widow, don't you see, in mourning for her lost husband."

Dubon stared down at his plate, wondering how he could have been such a fool.

TWENTY-FOUR

It probably would have been an awkward meeting anyway. After their kiss on Thursday, they would have been circling each other with embarrassment, simultaneously wanting the conversation to turn intimate yet knowing they should not go down that road. Now, instead of feeling embarrassed, he was angry, more probably because he felt stupid than because she had really practiced some great deception. After all, he had been suspicious of her story about her friend and had noticed she seemed unemotional about her supposed bereavement. He should have seen right through it; Maître Gaillard's practice used to receive numerous clients whose initial approach concerned "a friend." Perhaps he hadn't come to the obvious conclusion about her real identity because he didn't want to; he enjoyed her present identity too much, her energy, her intelligence, her sense of fun. And the mission she had given him. For all its perils, he felt excited about work for the first time in years. He knew it was inappropriate, dangerous even, but he had wanted her, had fantasized that as soon as he managed to pull a rabbit out of a hat in the Statistical Section and she had paid his bill . . .

"I think, Madame, we had better put an end to this charade," he said sternly, dragging his thoughts back to the present.

"Charade?" She looked puzzled.

"Really, Madame Dreyfus. I think it would have been easier if you had told me from the start whom I was representing and the family's real position on the case."

She appeared shocked and at first just looked down at her hands.

"Oh, I see. Yes, I see. I am sorry," she finally said without glancing up. "I should have been direct with you. How did you conclude—?"

"You are described in the newspapers, Madame. The loyal wife who dresses as a widow."

"Oh, of course. That interview . . ."

"Madame, I don't see how I can be of much use to you. The captain's lawyers—"

"Maître. I may not have been honest about my identity, but I have not misrepresented the situation. I do not agree with the approach the captain's brother is taking; it is not yielding results. You must understand it is very important not to show any chink in the family's armor. So, I approached you privately, hoping you might succeed where others have failed. Maître Dubon, who else would have done what you have done this week? Who would have dared?"

She stared at him now, silently willing him to agree. Her expectant face seemed so familiar to him. Once word had got out that the lawyer was defending the Communards, Maître Gaillard's office had been swamped with pleading women. Their husbands were in jail or in exile; their sons could not pursue their trades because they had been labeled as sympathizers. It was Dubon's own idea to sign them all up; file every petition, appeal every conviction, grieve every outrage, swamp the ministry with paper—and ultimately the bureaucrats would have to realize there was something in the radicals' idea of an amnesty. He had left the firm in 1883, eleven months before the Socialists had taken office and finally passed the amnesty into law, but grateful clients remembered him to this day. He had helped get them justice. He would do the same for the captain's wife.

"I have to confess," said Dubon, trying to keep his voice light, "that

I was starting to enjoy myself this week, until my brother-in-law came home Friday night and discovered that his uniform was missing."

They laughed together and reclaimed a bit of their old footing.

"I do have more news for you too."

"Yes?"

"The secret file does exist. The colonel in the Statistical Section is currently reviewing it."

"So . . ."

"He finds it suspiciously slim."

"Something's missing?" she asked.

"No, I would say the issue is whether there was anything there in the first place."

"What do you think?"

"Don't know until I see it . . ."

"Yes, you need to get a good look at it," she agreed.

They smiled at each other, enjoying how she was playing him.

"You, Madame," he replied, "are always full of impossible assignments for me."

"And what are you going to do about your brother-in-law's uniform?"

"Start using his summer kit."

"So you will continue working on my case?"

"Apparently so."

In the end, Picquart simply pushed the secret file across the desk to him.

It was the Monday morning and when Dubon came in, the colonel was sitting at his desk as though he had not moved since Saturday. Dubon, entering his commander's office to see if he had further instructions on the files, saluted.

"Did you sleep here, Colonel?"

Picquart looked up distractedly. "What? Eh, oh yes, yes. No, I did go home Saturday afternoon." He smiled, realizing Dubon's purport. He looked down at his papers and then back at Dubon.

"Sit down. You're an intelligent man, Dubon. Can't think why you are still a captain, at your age, in fact. Read that. Tell me what you think." He slid a ten-page document across the desk.

Dubon looked at him to assure himself he was supposed to read it then and there, and dutifully began. It was a report on the character and biography of the accused, assembled from various of Dreyfus's former commanding officers, many of them complaining he was cold, officious, did not socialize with his colleagues and, surprisingly considering these were reports from his superiors, was overly keen. Dubon gathered the accused was given to boasting of his expertise in military matters and not above mentioning his family wealth. One officer suggested that his work ethic was suspicious; another said he was not surprised the man was a spy. There was an account of an incident that occurred during his training, years before—a charred piece of an instruction manual had been found. The report alleged the accused had copied out the manual by hand and tried to get rid of the original by burning it. No proof was given to support this thesis.

"Was this presented as evidence at the court martial?" Dubon asked.

"It was shown to the judges. Privately, I believe."

Dubon found both anger and excitement rising inside him. Picquart seemed no more concerned than Le Goff that evidence had been kept from the defense.

"It's of no value," Dubon said decisively. "It's all hearsay."

"Hearsay?"

"Secondhand evidence . . . Uh, I believe that is what the lawyers would call it, no, Colonel?" The last thing he wanted was to draw attention to himself by offering specialized knowledge.

"Read that, then." The colonel pushed a single tattered sheet across the desk and, as Dubon read, drew his attention to a particular line by placing his finger beside it.

The letter itself was of the kind Dubon was now very used to seeing. It had been ripped into half a dozen pieces that someone in the section had then glued back together, although the signature was missing. The hand looked the same as that on some documents Madame Bastian had delivered from Schwarzkoppen's wastepaper basket the previous week and the letter was addressed to the German military attaché. In French, the correspondent wrote that he was sharing some information that he had acquired recently, twelve plans of the military installations at Nice, which "that bastard D" had sold him. It was this phrase that Picquart was pointing out.

"D?"

"Yes. D."

"Just an initial. The same as the accused's . . . as the prisoner's."

"Yes, the same initial." Picquart stared at the page as though lost in thought.

"So." Dubon spoke slowly, wanting to know the man's thoughts. "The judges were shown some bad character references and speculative reports on suspicious activities along with a letter that, while damning, only incriminates someone with the initial *D*. Quite a common initial. Dupont. Durand. Delmas."

"Or Dubon, eh?" Picquart laughed brittlely. "I take it you are not the bastard in question?"

"No, Colonel."

"So, that's their file," the colonel concluded, drawing the papers back. "On top of it all, the bastard letter has no date. Who knows how long it has been kicking around here. The minister wants to see some explanation of Dreyfus's motive for spying. It nags at him, and all I can show him is the slightest circumstantial evidence of guilt, let alone motive."

"But what of the original evidence, Colonel?" Dubon could no longer remember whether, as a junior intelligence clerk, he could have known of its existence or not, but the colonel seemed unsuspicious.

"Oh yes. The bordereau. The list of the spy's information. It's anonymous, of course, but evidence of treachery, to be sure. Somebody was offering secrets to the Germans. The question is: Did we get the right man?"

"Indeed, Colonel," Dubon said as neutrally as he could manage.

"You had better get back to your desk," Picquart said. "Our hunt has produced nothing."

Dubon retreated to his own desk and sat thinking about what he had seen. The very existence of the secret file, if it became known, was reason enough to grant the captain a new trial. Furthermore, nothing he had seen in the file suggested the captain would have difficulty winning an acquittal. The evidence was circumstantial, speculative, secondhand, or nonexistent. Indeed, it was so scant, he suspected it had been withheld from the defense not for reasons of national security but because the captain's lawyer could have demolished it in a minute.

The question was how to get an appeal. If Dubon was really going to help the widow—for that was how he continued to think of her—he would have to find a way to make the secret file public. Perhaps Le Goff could help him there, publish some speculation, and explain that secret evidence invalidated the trial; rattle the original military judges enough to get an investigation going. That seemed a long shot. He was thinking like a lawyer not a detective. The lady had given him his assignment from the start: the coup de grâce was to uncover the identity of the real spy. He still hadn't got a look at the bordereau, the original evidence that had convicted the captain. The colonel must have it—or at least a copy of it.

As he was puzzling over how he could possibly get into the colonel's files, Picquart himself emerged from his office, crossed behind Dubon's desk, and called abruptly to the major, who was working with his door ajar.

"A word, Major, if you please."

"Yes, Colonel," Henry replied as he strode back to his superior's office and, at some indication from Picquart, shut the door behind him.

"Someone's in trouble." Gingras had just come into the hall in time to see Henry summoned and was now smiling maliciously at the closed door.

"The colonel is unimpressed with the file on the Dreyfus case," Dubon ventured.

"Yes, and Henry is its chief architect. He put it together before they went to trial. And his good name—I guess more than his good name—rides on the captain's guilt."

"Why is that?"

"He testified at the court martial that he had received warning of a spy in the ranks and he swore up and down it was Captain Dreyfus."

"Did he say how he knew it was the captain?"

"No, he wouldn't reveal that."

Again, Dubon was appalled at what the judges had permitted.

"But he was convinced it was the captain?"

"Well," said Gingras slyly, "he was convinced his superior officers needed a conviction." He turned to the filing cabinets and threw his next words over his shoulder. "Can't have spies wandering about, can we?"

Dubon made no response and sat there gazing vacantly into the air, pondering the nasty implications of what Gingras had just said. Not only should the judges have rejected Henry's testimony as hearsay, but also Gingras was now implying that Henry had knowingly perjured himself. If that was the case, Major Henry had more than professional reasons for needing Dreyfus to remain guilty. If his lies were exposed, Henry himself could be court-martialed.

Gingras was still rummaging around pulling files when Major Henry emerged from Picquart's office a few minutes later looking angry or worried, Dubon wasn't quite sure which. Henry ignored both of them, went back into his office, and shut the door firmly.

He emerged just before lunch with a *petit bleu* in his hand and gave it to Dubon.

"Send this at once, Captain," he barked.

"From a post office, Major?" Dubon asked. Most of the section's correspondence was carried over to the rue Saint-Dominique by a young lieutenant who showed up daily with a leather pouch over his shoulder.

Henry looked at Dubon as though he were particularly stupid and enunciated slowly. "Yes, Captain. The post office. On the boulevard Saint-Germain."

Dubon saluted and put on the jacket of his uniform, pocketed the telegram, and set off.

Once inside the post office, he took a good look at the addressee, a Monsieur Leblanc, who lived at number 35 rue de Bretagne, and trusted it to memory before approaching the counter, paying his coin, and posting the message.

At the end of the day, the unshaven character he had seen the previous week again appeared in the corridor that led to the water closet and the darkroom.

"Monsieur Leblanc?" Dubon hazarded.

The man stopped on his way toward the major's office and smiled. Without knocking, he slipped through the major's open door and closed it behind him.

TWENTY-FIVE

At six o'clock that evening, Dubon found himself undoing an inordinately long series of tiny pearl buttons.

"So, tell me about the great mystery," Madeleine said.

"What mystery?" he asked disingenuously as he slipped a delicate little loop sewn from a twist of blush-colored linen off one button before proceeding to the next, located just south of her left breast.

This dress, her spring afternoon dress, was something of a standing joke between the lovers. It was her own design and she was particularly proud of it: the buttons began on the far right side of a high Chinese collar and continued in a slow spiral downward, between her breasts, across her left side and down her left hip before tailing off in the folds of the skirt. Another dressmaker, she explained to Dubon, would have been content to hold the form-fitting outfit together with invisible metal hooks and eyes down the back that required a lady's maid to help her fasten. Madeleine had made a virtue of necessity and spent many hours twisting the pink linen into a fabric cord to hold the buttons just so. A seamstress's delicate fingers could undo the dress in no time. Dubon still fumbled about, but they tacitly agreed it was his job, not hers.

"François," she replied. "This is the first evening you have been here in a week. You send telegrams, you send flowers, you promise you'll come tomorrow, you don't show up. What are you up to?" She sounded aggrieved.

"I've got a tricky case on the go at the moment."

"A case that requires you to go about in disguise?"

He dropped his hands from her chest and rose up off the divan in alarm. Had she somehow seen him?

"You didn't wear these clothes to work today. The shirt is smooth and the collar is perfectly fresh. You don't usually bother putting on a clean collar to come here." Indeed, Dubon had changed into a fresh shirt and collar on his way over because the anxiety of his new assignment was leaving him sweaty. "Besides, you smell different from usual. Perhaps you were disguised as a policeman? Or an artist? No, no, a gypsy . . ." Her tone was sarcastic but made him laugh all the same.

"You aren't far off the mark," he said as he sat back down and began to tell her of his current assignment. It felt comforting and safe to talk.

"You remember a case, a few years ago, of a spy, a military officer who was caught selling secrets to the Germans?"

"That one there's so much fuss about in the papers? The one who tried to escape?"

"He didn't really try to escape. Anyway, that's the man. And it's his case I am working on. I have a client who has an interest in proving his innocence."

"Who's the client?"

"A relation of the family who believes in the man and wants to see him exonerated."

"But why did he come to you?"

"I do have a certain reputation and I was recommended to the client. Uh, the client, well, this client is . . ."

Madeleine sensed he was avoiding a pronoun and pounced. "Is the client a woman? François, it's always about women with you. Don't think I don't notice. Anytime we are on the street together, your eyes are all over the place. Goodness knows what you get up to when you aren't here. You say you are somewhere with your wife, but for all I know—"

"No, no. Mazou. I have eyes only for you," he reassured her, return-ing his hands to her dress, which now flapped open to reveal her lace camisole. "The client is quite ugly, as a matter of fact. An old aunt of the accused. It's about the case," he said, and, as he fingered a button just above her waist, he began to explain his increasingly firm convic-tion that the captain was innocent of all charges against him.

Pacified, Madeleine allowed him to proceed.

❦

Later, as he was putting his own clothes back on, she returned to the topic.

"You never told me why you need to wear different clothes to work on this case."

Dubon, flush with both his sexual prowess and his success that day in getting sight of the secret file, was only too relieved to come clean. With both his wife and his mistress, he liked to maintain a well-ordered life that, as long as neither asked too many questions, never required him actually to lie.

"I am working undercover, Mazou."

"Undercover?"

"Yes, I have got myself a job as a filing clerk with military intel-ligence so that I can poke around in their files, and I go in every day wearing a spare uniform of my brother-in-law's."

"They don't know who you are?"

"Not yet. Think I am just the temporary clerk, filling in for an absence."

"How much longer do you expect you'll be at it?"

"Oh, just another day or two. Then we'll be back to normal, my dear."

"Well, I hope so," she said petulantly. "Will I see you tomorrow?"

Dubon recalled he had sent a message to Le Goff, asking to meet him the following day at six. "Now that I think of it . . ."

"Too busy? More secret missions for your lady client?" She sounded angry now. "You know if you aren't interested anymore, I have other things I could—"

"Of course I am interested. Wednesday, I will be here Wednesday."

❧

On the sidewalk across the street from Madeleine's building, a man lingered, smoking a cigar. As Dubon stepped onto the street, the man stubbed it out on the ground, consulted his watch, and began walking away. Dubon might not have noticed him, but it was a short and narrow street that ran only one block down from the boulevard des Italiens before it ended at the next boulevard, and there were never many pedestrians on it. The man kept looking straight ahead and walking with a gait of studied leisure. Dubon crossed to where the fellow had been standing and looked down at his cigar butt. He had smelled cigar smoke before around the entrance of Madeleine's building. Was it possible someone was shadowing him?

Alarmed, Dubon started after him and for the rest of the block he and his quarry pretended they were two men who happened to be walking the same way. Before the man reached the next boulevard, he passed a narrow curving street that opened on their left. He stopped, as though pondering his next move. He started up again and turned into this street, which Dubon knew came to a dead end just around the bend. The man would be forced to double back and run smack into him—which is exactly what happened.

"Excuse me, Monsieur. You seem lost," Dubon said.

The man looked back at him pleasantly enough and spoke with an excruciating English accent.

"I was trying to get back to the . . . the boulevard des Italiens," he said, pronouncing the *d* on *boulevard* and simply substituting the English "Italians" for *Italiens*.

Who was this Englishman and why was he following him?

"It's that way, Monsieur," he said, gesturing back the way they had come, toward the busy boulevard at the top of Madeleine's street. "Just what exactly is your game?"

The man replied with the same painfully accented French, "I might ask the same of you, Maître Dubon."

TWENTY-SIX

"You're following me," Dubon cried in indignation, surprised the Englishman knew his name.

The man smiled. "No, Monsieur. I believe you were following me."

"Only because I wondered what you meant by following me," Dubon replied.

The conversation was growing childish. The two men stood in the street eyeing each other and feeling increasingly ridiculous. Dubon considered some way around the impasse.

"Perhaps we share an interest?"

"Yes, perhaps we do . . ."

"In a woman?" Dubon asked dubiously. He supposed he had given Geneviève grounds for suspicion lately, but surely she would not stoop to such a stratagem.

"No. The women are your business," the man replied.

"Ah." Dubon was initially relieved, but when he came to think about it, he liked the alternatives even less. He hesitated, looking for a safe way to phrase the next question.

"So perhaps we share an interest in a certain army captain?"

"Yes, that might be closer to the mark," the man agreed.

Dubon considered this for a moment. The French military was unlikely to be using a foreigner as an agent; perhaps the man was an English spy. Other nations were increasingly following the case since the rumors of Dreyfus's escape, and the English were said to favor the theory that the captain was innocent. It occurred to Dubon that really there were only two sides to this matter. Some believed Dreyfus had never received a fair trial; others believed he was guilty and justly punished.

"Monsieur," Dubon ventured. "We need only tell each other our beliefs."

"What do you mean?"

"The man is a spy."

"Is he?"

"If he isn't, tell me what *you* think."

"No, no, you first."

Dubon, frustrated, took the plunge: "I increasingly believe Dreyfus is innocent."

"My client would be glad to hear that."

"Your client? Who is your client?"

"I cannot identify him."

"Are you a lawyer?"

"No, Monsieur, *you* are a lawyer."

"Yes, well, I also represent a client who would be glad to know of the captain's innocence. That is my interest. Now tell me yours."

The man looked sheepish. "I am a detective, a private detective. I work for a client who wishes to prove the captain's innocence."

"You are one of the brother's schemes, aren't you? The captain's brother hired you."

"And who hired you?"

"Another . . . let's say a friend of the captain's, a friend of the family."

"His brother doesn't know of this. Or at least I was never told about it."

"So you admit you work for the brother. An English detective . . ." Dubon paused as he remembered how her brother-in-law's strategies had so disappointed the captain's wife. "It wasn't you who planted

those outlandish stories about the escape in the British press, was it?"
He took the man's silence and an abashed look as a yes. "Well, that
really backfired. Have you seen the reaction? The French papers are
virulently insisting on his guilt."

"Nonetheless, I would point out that the captain's case is now
talked about in every newspaper and in every drawing room, and that
was our goal," the man replied huffily. "He won't get any justice as long
as he's been forgotten."

"True enough. We both seem to want the same thing here. So why
are you following me?"

"I have been looking for an entrée into the Statistical Section and
suddenly a new recruit appeared," he said.

Dubon felt his mouth go dry.

"I thought it might be possible to approach him, that he might be
less, let us say, imbued with the section's esprit de corps," he continued.
"I followed him and, lo and behold, I discover he is a prominent Paris
lawyer in disguise."

This was alarming. They might be on the same side, but if this incompetent character had succeeded in tying Maître Dubon to Captain
Dubon, he did not like to think what a quicker sort like Picquart or
Hermann might achieve if suspicious. He needed to find out how much
this detective really knew about him and about the case.

"We should be working together," he suggested.

"Indeed. Perhaps we could share some information," the detective
replied.

This was tricky, Dubon thought; he did not really want to share
information; he wanted to extract it.

"You place me in an awkward situation, Monsieur. My client has
given me express instructions that the captain's brother is not to know
of my work."

"You represent the wife, do you? I thought as much."

"No, a friend of hers. This lady is not satisfied with the progress
and wants to make her own inquiries."

"Women, eh? Well, as I said, I leave the women to you. But at least
we can compare notes."

"Yes. Perhaps we could," Dubon replied as he puzzled for a moment over this last remark. "Do you know the purpose of my business here?" he asked, gesturing with his head back to Madeleine's street.

The detective smirked, pulled out his pocket watch, and checked the time. "Home for dinner by seven? I can guess the nature of your business."

TWENTY-SEVEN

"Sherlock Holmes, I presume."

"No, actually, his name is Brown."

"With an *E* or without?"

"I have no idea," Dubon replied with irritation.

For some reason, Le Goff was in a playful mood. Dubon, on the other hand, was feeling inadequate and anxious after two unprofitable days at the Statistical Section and another missed evening with Madeleine. He had postponed his drink with Le Goff by a day to meet the English detective, but their exchange of information had not proved fruitful, while Brown's ability to link him with the section continued to gnaw at him. He was an amateur in the world of espionage who might be disastrously exposed at any minute. He wanted to get Le Goff's advice on strategy and get home on time.

"How did Mr. Brown know you were on the case?" Le Goff asked.

"He followed me from the Statistical Section one day."

"You meet your contact at his office in the section?" he said in surprise, and Dubon remembered belatedly that Le Goff did not know the extent to which he had penetrated the Statistical Section and that there was no reason to tell him.

"I . . . I went there once, just the one time, and Brown trailed me back to my office. I guess when he discovered I was a lawyer, he thought I was worth pursuing. He doesn't know about the secret file, either."

"So, there definitely is a secret file?"

"Yes, yes. That's why I wanted to talk to you. I was shown the file."

"Your contact showed you the documents?"

"He snuck it out of the office. I got a quick look at it. Anyway, the point is, evidence was withheld from the defense, clear grounds for an appeal. And it gets better: the evidence in the file is slight, monstrously slight, in fact."

In his enthusiasm over what he had found, Dubon shook off his ill temper and brought Le Goff up to date.

"There are only two documents," he said, moving a wineglass out of the path of his gesticulating hands as he began first to describe the letter referring to "that bastard D."

"So who was it written by?" Le Goff asked when he had finished.

"I don't know. It's a fragment without a signature or a date, though the hand looked familiar to my contact. He said he thought he had seen other documents in their files written by the same person."

"Probably Panizzardi, Schwarzkoppen's counterpart at the Italian embassy," Le Goff offered. "The two go everywhere together."

"The Italian fellow? He was at the Fiteaus' ball with Schwarzkoppen."

"Yes. That's him."

"So, Schwarzkoppen and Panizzardi must know whether they used Dreyfus or not," Dubon reasoned. "Would the Germans not try to tell the French if they had the wrong man?"

"Couldn't do that," Le Goff pointed out. "They would have to admit they use spies. What's the second document in the file?"

"A report about the captain's character and professional history, all speculative stuff. Some hoary old story from his training days about somebody finding a charred piece of an instruction manual in one of the classrooms."

"Ah, last day of school; the boys were burning the books." Le Goff laughed.

"Really?"

"Used to happen at my school. Why not in training camp?"

"Hadn't thought of that. Anyway, the report offers this wild theory that Dreyfus had copied out a manual to sell to the Germans and then destroyed the original."

"Why would you bother destroying the original? Why not just pass the original to the Germans?"

"It made no sense to me, and the rest is just character assassination by superior officers who happened to dislike him."

"And who put this secret file together?"

"A Major Henry," Dubon said. "Authoritarian and plodding. Very loyal to the higher-ups."

"I've heard of him: he was the hero who provided evidence at the court martial."

"Yes, he swore they had the right man."

"But does he believe that?" Le Goff asked.

"What do you mean?"

"The Statistical Section fingers Dreyfus; Dreyfus goes to court martial and Henry helpfully puts together this extra file of evidence. Because he believes they have the real culprit and he wants to secure a conviction? Or because he knows he has fingered the wrong culprit and wants to hide his section's incompetence?"

"Dreyfus was a convenient scapegoat," Dubon agreed. "But as to whether they knowingly framed an innocent man . . ."

"Ah, falls into one of my two categories. Venal or stupid . . ."

"Venal or stupid?"

"Yes, covers most of the foul-ups in life. Is the perpetrator venal or merely stupid? Never underestimate the stupidity of the military, Dubon. I speak from personal experience. The Statistical Section wasn't smart enough to find the real spy so they picked someone who fit the broad description and happened to be unpopular, and they handed him over."

"Certainly if somebody was framing him, you would expect them to do a better job."

"And yet, however flimsy, the evidence was enough to secure a conviction," Le Goff mused. "Who does Henry report to?"

"Colonel Picquart. But he's new. Indeed, I suspect Major Henry feels he was passed over for the promotion."

"Probably working on his own initiative, then."

"Why do you say that?" Dubon asked.

"If someone had ordered him to compile that file or swear at the court martial that Dreyfus was guilty, he would have got his reward, not been left where he was. So, maybe the higher-ups don't realize how flimsy his evidence was. What is Picquart's attitude? He has a good reputation."

"Probably deserved," Dubon replied. "He's reviewing the evidence and he isn't impressed. He's called Henry into his office several times."

"And where did Henry get his evidence in the first place?"

Dubon explained about Madame Bastian and the wastepaper baskets.

"Those stupid Germans!" Le Goff guffawed.

"Apart from the cleaning lady, Henry seems to have various unsavory contacts," Dubon continued. "Scruffy characters who come and go from his office. I suspect they sell him information."

"There is a veritable network of these so-called spies," Le Goff explained. "Pretty low level; I wouldn't know how much to trust them. They'd lie and fabricate stuff if they thought they could sell it. Occasionally, they offer it to the newspapers; nobody with any professional integrity would print it."

"Integrity among journalists? Didn't know there was such a thing."

"Ha ha. Still, Henry's spies might know something. They would be able to tell us whether or not they believe in the case against the captain."

"Should I try to talk to one? My man has the address of one of these characters."

"No harm in it. You could start by asking him how many colleagues he has whose names begin with *D*."

Dubon looked at his watch. It was past seven.

"I must be going," he said, glancing about for the waiter.

"But we haven't talked about my story yet. My editors are getting impatient. I'd like to give them a piece about the secret file—that would certainly get people's attention. Can you give me more details about the documents? You did actually see them?"

Dubon drew back in some alarm. The last thing he wanted right now was somebody hunting around for a leak in the Statistical Section.

"You'll have to wait, Le Goff. Just wait a bit. I need more information from my contact before we risk exposing him. Maybe we could meet again Saturday afternoon?"

"No, tomorrow evening. If I'm going to make Saturday's paper, I need Friday to write it up. And I warn you I'll be trying to get the existence of the secret file confirmed by other sources in the meantime."

TWENTY-EIGHT

Dubon was late for dinner—again. He found Geneviève eating a solitary meal at the dining room table.

"I held dinner half an hour," she said coldly as he seated himself.

"I'm very sorry, my dear. Very sorry. Where's André?"

"He is at Pierre's house working on his recitation." She continued eating without looking up, and Luc appeared beside him with a plate.

Dubon put a fork in the food and found it was cold. Clearly, his household was united in its disapproval of his tardiness.

"Luc," he called out before his servant could leave the room. "My apologies for my lateness. I know it inconveniences the kitchen. This, however, is cold."

"Yes, Monsieur," Luc said impassively as he took back the plate.

"It's work," he said to Geneviève as soon as Luc had left, "and my work covers Luc's salary and just about everything else around here." It was a harsh reminder, but Dubon felt his authority slipping.

"Well, you *say* you are working—"

"I *am* working, very hard as a matter of fact."

"That's not what Madame de la Roche says. I met her at my sister's this afternoon and she complained that you are not attending to her business."

Dubon scowled. Madame de la Roche was a client of long-standing, a young widow engaged in a lengthy dispute over the division of her late husband's estate with his children from a previous marriage. She had left a message the week before, though Dubon had already advised her she was unlikely to get any more money.

"I will make time to see her next week," he said.

"One hardly wants to discuss one's husband's business at a party," Geneviève continued. "It was already most embarrassing that she brought it up, and then the baron piped in with some remark about how I should advise you to attend to your knitting."

"Masson was there?" Dubon asked in surprise. "His career must really be suffering if he has time to take afternoon tea with the ladies."

"It wasn't afternoon tea. I told you we were going to my sister's to hear that young pianist. She wanted the baron's opinion. He has serious cultural interests, you know."

Geneviève glared at him, from which he concluded she did not consider his cultural interests sufficiently serious.

"I did say I would go to that art show with you. And I read novels . . ." he replied to her unspoken criticism.

"I never suggested you were illiterate."

They sat in silence until Luc returned with the food, which looked as though it had been baked onto its plate. Dubon pushed aside some dry-looking beef with his fork and tried piercing a potato croquette; it released a little funnel of steam.

Geneviève waited until the servant had withdrawn and then asked in a more conciliatory tone, "What is this case you are working on?"

He could hardly tell her the details, let alone where he was spending his days.

"You wouldn't be interested. Let's talk about something else."

"No, I am interested. I'm always interested in your work."

This was not, Dubon knew, particularly true but perhaps he kept too many secrets from her. She was his wife; if he couldn't trust her, whom could he trust?

"You know the case that has been in the papers recently, that man who was accused of spying. We were talking about it at lunch Sunday."

"That Jew?"

"That's right. I have been approached by a client who is interested in proving his innocence. I am doing some preliminary research into the court martial to see if it can be appealed."

Geneviève looked stunned. "But you can't do that."

"Why not?" He hadn't expected her to like the idea of his taking on such a file, but he hadn't expected blanket condemnation either.

"You can't appeal a court martial. That's not your area. You can't just change the kind of law you practice."

"Well, I am not a litigator, but there is no rule that says I can't undertake some preliminary investigation for a client. If I found evidence—and, I have to say, I am finding some evidence—"

She interrupted him. "François, you have got to drop it. You have to stop."

"Really, my dear, I can take on what cases I see fit." Dubon was starting to feel aggrieved.

"Not this case. What would our friends say? What would my family think? You haven't made any effort to help the Fiteaus, but you can take on—"

"Dreyfus is innocent, Geneviève."

"François, the man is a spy. The newspapers say so. The baron has told you he is guilty. He said so at dinner the other night. You can't defend a traitor. Do you think the Fiteaus or Madame de la Roche, or the baron, for that matter, would ever come through that door again"—at this she gestured toward the front hall—"if they knew you had taken on a traitor to France as a client?"

"Calm yourself, Geneviève. Everyone has a right to a lawyer."

"He *had* a lawyer and he was found guilty and that's the end of it. We don't need to go poking about in something that doesn't concern us."

She paused and then started up again, her tone sounding less angry and more worried now. "Is the client offering you a lot of money? Is that what this is about? I noticed you still haven't paid the couturier for my new dress. The bill is sitting on the hall table. Can't you find some other case that would pay well?"

For a moment, Dubon saw in her uncharacteristically troubled face the young woman he had married, the convent girl half terrified by her own rebellious streak. The naive enthusiasms that had once so charmed him had now given way to mere stubbornness and her idealism had evaporated. He loved her in his way; he provided for her; he supposed he had also promised to protect her—he must have said something to that effect in their wedding vows, but she never seemed to require much protection these days. Suddenly she looked vulnerable and he realized that, for all her snobbery, she was as fearful for their security as for anything else.

"My dear . . ." he said tenderly. She looked at him with some puzzlement, waiting for reassurance. "I am not taking the case for the money. I have no idea when or how much the client might pay."

"Then why are you taking it? You are all riled up about it. It's unsettling the household."

"When you met me I did work like this—"

"Oh, for heaven's sake, François," she said, her anxiety swiftly giving way to exasperation. "That was years ago. You aren't a teenager playing at revolution anymore. I will not tolerate you gambling with our social position. You are to give this case up. Drop the client. I insist."

She scraped back her chair and left the room.

He slept the night on the divan in his library and awoke the next morning feeling anxious, and then heartsick as the memory of Geneviève's reaction the previous evening came back to him. In the adjacent bathroom, he washed and shaved as quietly as he could. Once dressed, he tiptoed to the dining room, where breakfast was waiting. Luc had noticed Dubon's early departures and now made sure the coffee was ready and some bread was on the table as soon as it was delivered to the kitchen, often still warm from the baker's oven. Dubon had actually started to savor these early meals; they were the only moments in the day when he did not have a knot of fear in his stomach.

But now he had come under attack at home. Geneviève might be wrong about the captain's guilt, but she was right about one thing: this wasn't his kind of law. He was sticking his nose into business where he had no place, and he could all too easily be exposed. And what would Geneviève do if she discovered just how deeply he had become embroiled? He was not merely risking his career with this escapade but also his marriage.

When he arrived at the Statistical Section just after eight, the front door was unlocked but no one seemed to be about. He sidled up to the door of Picquart's office. He needed to get his hands on the secret file somehow, just long enough to make a copy for the widow, and then he could happily return to his former life.

He was reaching for the handle when he heard low voices inside. Hurrying back to his desk, he busied himself with the stack of paper there, the delivery Madame Bastian had made the Friday before. He set aside several pieces of a letter in German, but finished gluing together a page that had been ripped in two and bore only a few words in French. Next, he pulled out a complete page, a letterhead with an ornate coat of arms supported by two lions. Dubon did not recognize the crest, but the hand was Panizzardi's again, and this time his signature appeared at the bottom. As he read what the Italian diplomat had to say, he stopped cold. He sat there for a moment as the implications gripped him.

It had been Dreyfus all along.

He had better leave now. He rose to his feet and reached for his tunic, hanging off the back of the chair.

Suddenly, Picquart's office door burst open and Major Henry barged out.

"Dubon!" he yelled. "Just who the hell do you think you are?"

"I . . . uh . . ."

"They may be all chummy over on the rue Saint-Dominique, but we run a tight ship around here. You never presented your orders to the colonel when you arrived. In the colonel's office. With your order papers. *Now.*"

TWENTY-NINE

Typically, Colonel Picquart was more polite about the lapse in paper-work. Dubon suspected that Major Henry's rage was not caused by an underling's supposed insubordination but rather by the major's guilty conscience. In his sulky mood on the day Dubon arrived, the major had failed to ask for his papers.

"Sorry, Dubon," Picquart said, as Dubon entered the office. "Henry thought I had seen your orders and I thought he had. We were just dis-cussing your clearance level. You did say on Saturday, didn't you, when we were going through all those files, that you were cleared up to your own section?"

"Yes, Colonel," Dubon said, trying to keep his voice even.

"Well, the thing is, those documents you are gluing together, that's *counter*intelligence. And if you aren't cleared for counterintelligence . . . Anyway, just go and get your letter from the rue Saint-Dominique so I can see what they said in your orders."

Dubon paused, unsure what to do next. Picquart mistook the rea-son for his hesitation.

"Look, I don't want to have to get a new clerk. You are working out very well. If you are cleared only for your own section's material, we will work something out with the rue Saint-Dominique. We'll get you higher clearance. But first of all, I need to see your papers."

"Yes, sir. Immediately, sir."

Dubon left Picquart's office, turned back to his desk, and sat there, rummaging through drawers as though looking for something, all the while thinking frantically. He had come to the end of the line. He couldn't stay any longer—and he no longer had any reason to do so. After a few minutes, he simply picked up the sheet that he had just found and walked back toward Picquart's office. It wasn't his order papers but it was a piece of paper that would stop Picquart in his tracks just as surely as it had stopped Dubon. After all, he thought to himself, he really had a duty as a French citizen to show this to the colonel.

"Colonel," he began, making up his excuse as he went, "I realize this is stupid . . . but I left the order papers at home. I've changed into my summer kit, and I'm afraid I've left them in my other uniform."

"That's no excuse, Dubon." His voice was less friendly now.

"No, Colonel, but I think, I think there's something you should see right away . . ." Dubon placed the sheet of paper on Picquart's desk. "I found this paper this morning."

Picquart looked sharply at Dubon and turned the sheet so he could read it.

"It was in the batch Madame Bastian delivered last week. It's addressed to Schwarzkoppen and signed by Panizzardi. It's pretty damning, Colonel."

"Shh."

It *was* damning. The letter began with some pleasantries and suggested a future meeting before coming to the point: "I have learned that questions are to be raised about Dreyfus in the National Assembly. If asked by Rome, I will deny I ever had any traffic with that Jew. You must do the same; no one must know what happened with him."

There was a pause as Picquart read the letter twice over, considering the implications. If the Italian military attaché was instructing his German counterpart to deny to their own governments that the pair had ever had contact with Dreyfus, it could only be because they had both used him as their agent. The colonel looked up at Dubon.

"We were wrong ever to doubt the evidence," he said slowly. He opened his desk drawer and slid the sheet inside. "They got the right man. The generals will be very pleased. That will be all, Dubon."

"Yes, Colonel. I will just go home now and get those papers. I live, um, at some distance. I may be gone awhile."

Dubon saluted, turned on his heel, and walked back to his desk, defeated. Dreyfus was a spy and he himself was a fraud. He slipped his arms into his tunic and walked out the door, knowing he would never return.

THIRTY

Dubon crossed the river slowly, berating himself as he went. Dreyfus had been guilty all along and he had been wasting his time. Really, it made sense when he stopped to think about it. The military prosecutors were unlikely to have made as gross an error as the secret file suggested; they must have known they had the right man. The judges had bent the rules of judicial procedure—no, broken them altogether—but in the name of a good cause: they were protecting France from a spy. What game exactly did he think he had been playing—a barrister turned undercover detective? It was silly, schoolboy stuff. Geneviève had been right. He wasn't a teenager anymore, nor was he the legal crusader of his youth. What a fool he had made of himself. At least now he could honestly tell Geneviève that he had abandoned the case.

The truth was that he had been seduced not only by nostalgia for his days with Maître Gaillard but also by the widow's eyes. Well, the eyes of the captain's wife, he thought bitterly. Pretty women had always been his weakness. He couldn't blame her for wanting to save her husband; all the same, he was going to stick her with a bill large enough to do more than pay for Geneviève's new blue dress. He had devoted hours to a wild-goose chase; he had been at the Statistical Section for more than a week. If he had been caught, he might have been charged himself or at the very least been barred from his profession.

God, he would be glad to be rid of the uniform. The cotton was stiff and chafed at his skin.

As he pushed open the door to his office, he found Lebrun had allowed a visitor to wait for him: the captain's wife was sitting in the armchair across from his desk and rose to greet him eagerly. She was the last person he wanted to see.

"I am sorry to keep bothering you, Maître," she began in a subdued tone, sensing his displeasure.

"If you have come today looking for more news, I'm afraid I have little and what I have is not good."

"Oh." She looked crestfallen and sank back down into the chair.

"Today, I have seen with my own eyes clear evidence of the captain's guilt."

"That is impossible," she said indignantly.

"It is a letter written to the military attaché at the German embassy in which his Italian counterpart names the captain as a contact they have both used."

"It is a lie." She was growing more agitated. Clenching her hands into two fists, she chopped the air in frustration as she spoke. "Anyone who knows the captain, I mean *really* knows him . . ." At this, she stopped and gave up, unclenching her fists and wiping angry tears from her eyes.

Dubon remained unmoved.

"Madame Dreyfus," he said, placing a hard insistence on the name so as to assure himself he was breaking free from any fantasy he had about her. "Perhaps you are misled by your wifely devotion."

"I am not such an innocent, Maître. I know I must appear ridiculous to you, but I am quite capable of sound judgment. The captain's heart is true."

The woman seemed restored to fighting spirit by her tears.

"Maître, last time I visited here, you told me you knew the secret file existed and you believed it was very scant. Have you made any progress in confirming its existence?"

"Yes, it does exist. I have seen it."

"And what does it contain?"

"Madame, a day ago I would have told you it contained nothing much, some scraps of circumstantial evidence, but coupled with this more recent letter, it is incriminating."

"Whatever the nature of the evidence, it was withheld from the defense. You said that alone was grounds for appeal."

"Yes."

"So we know for certain there is evidence that was withheld from the defense. I will launch an appeal, then. You see, you do have good news, Maître."

"Madame, the captain's lawyers may launch an appeal," he said, "but what point is there to launching an appeal if the new evidence is against the captain?"

"A second trial will prove his innocence."

"Even to win that trial you have to get the authorities to admit there is a secret file . . ."

"Yes. Well, how should we proceed in that regard?"

"I have no plans to proceed. I resign from your file."

"But you did have a plan, Maître. Before you saw this latest evidence, you had a plan. You always do."

Dubon considered how he might best disentangle himself. He could let Le Goff publish his article on the secret file and then stand back and watch the captain's lawyers deal with the rest, including the new evidence.

"I did finally hear word from Azimut Martin and he's, um, sympathetic," he said. "He could publish a story affirming the existence of the secret file. I think from there, you could trust the captain's lawyers to press for an appeal."

"Yes. Maître. Thank you. Contact your journalist friend. But I still want you to keep looking for the real spy."

"No, Madame, you must realize—"

"You have achieved far more than the captain's lawyers already—"

"But I do not wish to continue . . . and, well, there is the question of my bill."

"Oh, don't worry about the money. I will pay, Maître, whatever it is."

It appeared the stories about family wealth had not been exaggerated.

"I also have other clients who need my attention."

To this the woman made no response. She simply sat looking at Dubon, waiting patiently for him to acquiesce.

"I will contact the journalist about publication. To what address can I send the bill?"

The woman seemed knocked off balance by this simple request.

"Oh. Oh yes . . . my apologies. I will leave my address on your clerk's desk on my way out. In the meantime, I have a little gift for you."

She eyed him with that deceptively girlish air she sometimes conveyed and Dubon could not help but smile back.

She leaned down beside the chair and picked up a loose bag he had not noticed lying there. It was similar to the canvas garment bag he had used to tote Jean-Jean's clothes about, and as she pulled it up, it revealed a summerweight uniform with its captain's stripes in place.

"I thought you might find this useful," she said.

THIRTY-ONE

Waiting in a café that evening, Dubon was of two minds as to how much he should tell Le Goff, but the journalist slid into the seat across from him before he had made any decision.

"What news?"

"Nothing much. I haven't made any more headway, and my client cannot keep paying my fee forever without seeing more results. We have agreed that you can publish and see what response your story brings. At the very least, it will bolster demands for an appeal."

"Good, good. My editors are hungry as ever. I'll give them something tomorrow and they can publish it Saturday. So, you described two documents . . ."

Dubon discussed the contents of the secret file with Le Goff for half an hour, describing in as precise detail as he could the report on the captain's history and character and the letter with the phrase "that bastard D," and trying yet again to impress upon him the injustice of withholding evidence from the defense.

"I wouldn't tell you how to do your job, Le Goff. But the fact that evidence was withheld should be your emphasis, not the nature of the evidence. Whether he's innocent or guilty, it wasn't a fair trial."

"But we know he's innocent, don't we?"

Dubon gave no response and Le Goff now sensed his reluctance.

"You've gone cold on me. Do you know something more?"

Dubon hesitated, and then plunged forward, describing the new letter from Panizzardi to Schwarzkoppen.

"Clearly, both attachés had been using Dreyfus as an agent," he concluded.

"Very convenient timing," Le Goff said. "Ever since the story of the escape, people are starting to look at the case, question it. The original evidence is very weak and now, presto, here's the bloodstained dagger?"

"Well, it couldn't have surfaced any earlier. It didn't exist until a few days ago. It's a damning document."

"You haven't actually seen the thing, have you?"

"Er, no. But my contact described it to me in detail. It is hand-written on letterhead, the Italian crest. It's one page . . ." Dubon's voice trailed off as he pictured in his mind's eye the letter he had found that morning.

He saw the ornate coat of arms with the lions, Schwarzkoppen's name written tidily at the top, Panizzardi's flowery signature at the bottom. It was one page, one single sheet that had been ripped across the middle and glued back together again. But who had glued it? Not Dubon. If the major or Gingras or Hermann had for some rea-son gone through the file on Dubon's desk, found the two pieces and assembled them, surely they would have alerted Picquart instantly rather than replace the thing. The document couldn't have come into the office with Madame Bastian's scraps. It must have been planted on Dubon's desk.

"Dubon?" Le Goff was waiting for him to continue.

"That letter is a fraud," Dubon exclaimed, awaking from his rev-erie. Order papers be damned, he would just have to go straight back into the section the next day.

Dubon arrived there at eight to find the door locked. The others had keys, but he had not been given one and had not had the nerve to ask. He waited, rehearsing his excuse about his lost papers in his head and nervously anticipating Picquart's arrival, but Hermann was the first to show up a few minutes later.

Dubon saluted smartly and said, "Good morning, Captain."

"Captain," Hermann said blankly. He fiddled with his keys in silence but finally, as he opened the door, asked in his graceless manner: "And when will you be leaving us, Dubon?"

"Uh, that hasn't been determined precisely," he replied. "I don't expect to be here that long."

"Oh, stick around, Dubon. We missed you yesterday afternoon. You're invaluable."

The man's tone was so cold, Dubon wondered if he was being sarcastic.

Hermann walked off to his office and Dubon settled at his desk. Gingras hailed him gaily when he arrived a few minutes later, followed by Major Henry, who said, "As you were, Captain," when Dubon saluted. The major headed to his office and closed the door firmly.

Dubon wished Picquart would come and yet fervently hoped he wouldn't. He needed the colonel to accept his story for a day at least—and let him see the Italian letter again so he could confirm his suspicions—but he didn't suppose there was anything to stop the man from marching over to the rue Saint-Dominique and demanding to see Captain Dubon's file.

It was past nine and still the colonel had not arrived. To distract himself, he took out the little codebook Gingras had given him and began looking up the names of people he knew. He noted there were files on his late father-in-law and on both his brothers-in-law. Were they merely personnel reports or something more nefarious? Knowing both the Statistical Section's mania for collecting paper and his wife's family, he rather suspected the former. He was about to hunt them out, when another thought came to him and he looked up General Fiteau. There he was, *Gen. L. Fiteau,* but the next name on the list made Dubon stop.

It was simply *L. Fiteau.* The file was code-named *Anemone,* and Dubon rapidly turned to the first filing cabinet.

The file on Louis Fiteau was one page, noting the basics of his biography and education, his relationship with his father, and his gambling habit. Dubon wondered if it was assessing him as a risk, weighing the likelihood that he was privy to any information through his father that he could sell. One thing was certain—no one was filing these intelligence reports swiftly: the one page on Louis Fiteau failed to record his death.

Dubon was just slipping the page back and thinking of hunting out General Fiteau's file when the colonel finally arrived, looking grim.

"Colonel." Dubon saluted. "Can I present—?"

"Not now, Dubon. Oh, it's your papers, is it? Finally. Well, clear that up with the major," he said, walking into his office and closing his door behind him.

Dubon sat down, swallowed, and felt the welcome sensation of saliva flooding back into his mouth. He was safe—for now. Picquart seemed distracted by other matters. But how could he ask him to take a second look at the Italian letter?

A few minutes later, Picquart emerged from his office and called sharply for Major Henry. The major's door was still shut, so Dubon knocked lightly. The door was flung open with some force.

"What?"

"The colonel wishes to see you, Major."

"Oh." The major looked disconcerted now, and he pushed past Dubon without another word, entered the colonel's office, and shut the door.

Gingras, who must have overheard their exchange from the corridor, came into the reception area and, smiling, perched himself on Dubon's desk.

"I'd love to be a fly on the wall for that one," he said, inclining his head in the direction of the closed door.

He reminded Dubon of a cat, or perhaps a malicious child, hovering on the sidelines gleefully to observe others getting into trouble.

"I guess Henry thought he could satisfy the colonel with his decisive new evidence, whatever it was."

"A letter. I found it in the pile that Madame Bastian brought in last Friday. Pretty conclusive. Mentions Dreyfus by name."

"Oh, I am sure it was conclusive. Henry never fails to please in that regard."

Dubon did not reply. He was too busy considering what Gingras had just said: he was equally suspicious of the convenient new Italian letter. But how could Henry get such a thing? Was he possibly in collusion with the Italians himself?

"My guess," Gingras continued, "is that Picquart is now after Henry about the second spy."

"The second spy?"

Gingras leaned in closer and lowered his voice. "There's evidence of another spy in the ranks. I think that's why Picquart reopened the Dreyfus file in the first place. A telegram came in through 'the usual route' that showed the Germans are still in touch with a source inside the army."

Dubon felt a surge of adrenaline in his gut. Someone else had been offering secrets to the Germans. Was this the real spy?

"Hermann showed me the telegram last week," Gingras said. "He was annoyed because it was in French, and he's only supposed to do German. Maybe you put it in his pile by mistake. Anyway, he thought I was trying to slough off work and pass it over to him. Then we both read the thing and he grabbed it back quick enough when he realized he could be the one to march it into the colonel's office. Innocent little *petit bleu*, unless you happened to notice it was written by the German military attaché to a French officer. I guess it was never posted, since it was found in the trash."

This explained Hermann's questions the previous week about whether Dubon had read either the German or French documents. Dubon tried to remember what bit of paper in French he might mistakenly have passed on to Hermann. There had been a telegram, but it had been addressed to a Hungarian count.

"Hermann took it in to Picquart," Gingras continued, "and Picquart must have taken it to the rue Saint-Dominique. I don't suppose he likes his orders from that quarter."

"What orders?"

"To cover it up, I imagine. Find the second spy as quickly as possible and discharge him quietly. After the fuss over Dreyfus, the army can't possibly withstand another court martial. The public would lose confidence."

"Yes," Dubon agreed, "the place would seem to be crawling with spies."

THIRTY-TWO

The rue de Bretagne was bustling with Saturday morning shoppers when Dubon arrived there. Against the backdrop of the jewelers' windows that lined the old street, a market was in full swing; women with bulging straw baskets were assessing their potential purchases, weighing vegetables in their hands or nibbling on slivers of cheese proffered on the blade of the cheese merchant's knife.

Dubon passed a fishmonger bellowing out his prices and a butcher's shop festooned with rabbits, their bodies skinned to reveal the fresh meat but their heads and paws still covered in fur, before he found the address he was looking for. Number 35 was a small building on the corner with a narrow exterior door leading through to a courtyard. Apartment 3, a small sign indicated, could be reached by an exterior staircase leading up to the second floor.

Dubon was making a delivery for Major Henry. About eleven that morning, Henry had come out of his office with three letters and asked Dubon to mail them before the post office shut at noon, grandly allowing that the clerk could then leave for the day.

In the queue in the post office on the boulevard Saint-Germain,

Dubon looked down at the envelopes in his hand. All three bore civilian names and local addresses. He did not recognize the first two, but the third letter was addressed to a Monsieur Dubois on the rue de Bretagne. He had seen the address before; it was the one where Monsieur Leblanc lived. The ridiculously common names must be aliases, he decided, for the same shifty fellow who had, now that he thought of it, eyed him ironically when Dubon addressed him as Leblanc. He stepped up to the wicket and posted the other two letters; this last one he would deliver by hand.

He didn't really know what he was going to ask the mysterious Leblanc/Dubois if he answered his door, but Le Goff had suggested all these shady characters were for sale. He would use the delivery of the major's letter as an entrée and sound the man out; suggest that if he had information for sale, Dubon might be able to get him a better price. Perhaps ask him if he knew who "D" might be.

A lengthy silence greeted his knock, but eventually there were sounds from inside and the scruffy man from his earlier encounters in the Statistical Section stuck his head out.

"Yes? What do you want?"

"I . . . I don't know if you recognize me—"

"Yeah, I recognize you. What do you want?"

"Can I come in for a moment? I have a message . . ."

The man begrudgingly opened the door and Dubon found himself in a generous room that overlooked the street corner. It had the feel of a studio with large windows on two sides letting in the north light and a big standing desk, like a draftsman's table, pushed up against them. The rest of the room was in chaos, with discarded clothes lying on chairs, a tangle of blankets decorating the one couch, and a plate of congealed food on the floor, but the desktop was perfectly ordered, with a series of ink pots lined up across the back beside a jam jar filled with a variety of pens.

"What's the message?"

Leblanc/Dubois did not seem in any mood for chitchat, so Dubon made a show of shuffling through his pockets and finally pulled out the envelope the major had given him to post. As the man opened it, Dubon stepped aside, so as not to seem inquisitive, and fell to examining the only picture on the walls, a small document tidily mounted in a frame. It was a brief letter, or perhaps a page torn from a longer letter, in which the writer swore undying devotion to his beautiful correspondent and promised an imminent reunion. It was signed with a flourish: *Napoléon.*

"Humph . . . Very nice. Very prompt," Leblanc/Dubois said. He looked up from the envelope, from which Dubon could just glimpse the corner of a banknote protruding, and asked, "Why the special delivery? The major normally uses the mail."

Dubon thought it best to invent an excuse. "I confess that the major entrusted the letter to me to post last night, saying I was to catch the five o'clock so that it would be delivered today and you wouldn't have to wait until Monday. Unfortunately, I was a bit delayed getting out of the office . . ."

"Stopped for a drink and missed the post, did you?" The man sneered. "Well, thank you."

"Not at all. I must be going now. Just wanted to make sure that it was in safe hands," Dubon said.

He took his leave promptly, without attempting any further conversation. He had found all the information that he needed on the man's wall.

He had to restrain himself from running down the two flights of stairs and dancing his way up the rue Réamur and across the boulevard de Sébastopol. The two-kilometer walk over to Madeleine's apartment seemed to take only two minutes and he twitched with impatience as he waited for her to answer the door. He was bursting to tell someone what he had just discovered and guessed that his mistress, always a late riser, would be happy to receive a surprise Saturday visit after another week of absences. She had called out "Coming!" at his knock, but it took her a while to appear sleepily in her peignoir.

"Oh, it's you."

It wasn't exactly the enthusiastic welcome he had hoped for.

"Expecting someone else?" he joked, taking her into his arms. She pulled away.

"No, of course not. It's just that you haven't been here all week and now you wake me up on a Saturday morning."

"Mazou . . . you're still half asleep. Let's have coffee. I have a story to tell you."

Once she had made the coffee and they were settled on the divan, she seemed to recover herself, and listened as Dubon recounted his morning.

"Napoléon. Plain as day. Signed with a big sloping *N* and then a series of squiggles. A love letter to Josephine."

"That was true love," Madeleine sighed. "The emperor would have done anything for her."

Dubon refrained from noting that the emperor had eventually divorced his true love for the sake of his crown. He was too eager to produce his discovery: "So, where would he have got such a thing?"

"I have no idea. From an antiques dealer? Lots of people would pay handsomely to have one of Napoléon's love letters. Imagine having such a thing to hang on your wall—"

"That's the whole point, you see," Dubon said impatiently. "The man I was visiting didn't buy it, he *made* it. He's a forger. He's got a nice large desk with the most lovely selection of inkpots and pen nibs. The army is employing a forger in the case against Captain Dreyfus."

He knew now that the fresh evidence against the captain was fake. It had not been written by Panizzardi at the Italian embassy but by a weaselly forger in the rue de Bretagne. He himself had just delivered payment for the job. Picquart had complained the evidence against Dreyfus wasn't strong enough, and Henry, the loyal facilitator, the original architect of the case against the captain, had obliged by producing something better. The major simply slipped the forgery into the file that Madame Bastian had brought the previous week. It was proof of deceit on the part of the captain's prosecutors. Dubon would have to find some way to expose the forgery to Picquart so he would reopen the Dreyfus case. He might not find the real spy, but he could at least help the captain's wife obtain the appeal her husband deserved.

Dubon was jubilant, and a week's absence from Madeleine's apartment had inflamed his passions. His coffee drunk, his secrets spilled, he practically dragged her to the bedroom.

❧

Afterward, as he dressed hurriedly, she did not linger either, but pulled a clean pair of white stockings from her top drawer and arranged fresh underthings. As she removed her fabulous pink linen dress from the closet, it dawned on him that she was going out.

"Lunch date?"

"Yes."

"Who with?"

"Just the old gang."

"Fancy dress for the old gang. You look good enough to lunch on yourself. Wish I could go with you."

"You wouldn't be interested."

As he pulled on his own clothes, she tidied her hair and then affixed a hat and veil over her chignon.

"New hat?" It was a large, sloping affair dyed a shade of green just as pale as the pink of her dress. It seemed an unusual color combination—but what did he know of fashion? Certainly, with the hat sitting at the jaunty angle at which Madeleine managed to make it cling to her head, the effect was very dashing, and he felt a tingle of arousal as they walked to the end of her street together arm in arm before parting company on the boulevard.

THIRTY-THREE

"You're jumping to conclusions, Dubon."

He and Le Goff were sitting in an outdoor café in the park at the bottom of the Champs Élysée the next day, sheltering under the shade of a flowering chestnut tree and drinking glasses of beer to fend off an early heat wave that had descended unexpectedly on the city. Dubon was in a hurry and had grown tired of hiking all the way to Montparnasse to meet. Le Goff, meanwhile, was disappointing him; he was much less excited by the Napoléon discovery than Dubon had been and was now putting a damper on his whole theory.

"The man's a forger, I tell you."

"I don't doubt he's a forger, but that isn't proof that letter is a forgery."

"Why else would Henry have contact with a forger?"

"I can think of other reasons why the Statistical Section might use forgeries. They are in the business of counterintelligence, after all. They may be trying to pass information back to the enemy."

"Why would they want to do that?"

"Disinformation, they call it. False information. Troops are to move left when actually you plan them to move right; tests of a new gun show it has failed miserably, no threat to you there, Monsieur Boche. You can go back to sleep. Or it might be true information that you want the enemy to have but that diplomacy prevents you from releasing officially. Tests of a new gun show it performs exceedingly well; we are now in a position to blow your brains out one hundred times over."

"And this information is forged?" Dubon asked peevishly. Le Goff's sense of humor was wearing on him.

"You are hardly going to ask the generals to sign false troop orders or release their actual gun reports to the enemy."

"Why not?"

"Too embarrassing if they got caught. Plus you don't want to disturb them. Never bother the superior officers: rule number one of a successful career in the military."

Dubon wondered if the military bred such cynicism in all its young officers. Le Goff's position was so totally different from that of his brothers-in-law, the younger so earnest in his attitude to the army, the older so affectionate.

"Your Major Henry is certainly a familiar type in that regard. Mr. Fix-It," Le Goff continued. "Colonel wants stronger evidence; stronger evidence miraculously appears."

"But I thought you said the evidence wasn't forged," Dubon protested. His head was starting to swim trying to understand Le Goff's take on the machinations of intelligence.

"I'm not saying it isn't a forgery," Le Goff said. "I am just cautioning you that Major Henry may have perfectly legitimate, well, perhaps not legitimate, but perfectly professional reasons for doing business with a forger. You're the lawyer; what do you have proof of? That some suspicious man with whom Henry has had some kind of transaction likes to amuse himself by re-creating Napoleonic memorabilia. Not much to go on."

"I need to prove he forged that letter . . . I'll go and talk to him again. And I'll ask Picquart to take another look at the letter."

"Picquart is your contact?"

"Well, yes. I . . . that is . . ." He had tried to hide the extent of his activities from Le Goff, but the man now guessed what was up.

"Dubon, are you inside the place?"

"Yes, actually. I have taken a post as a temporary clerk in the Statistical Section. I showed up wearing Jean-Jean's second-best uniform."

"Impersonating a military officer! Daring stuff, Dubon," Le Goff said with a note of sarcasm. "But just think what it will do to Dreyfus if you are caught: he's going to have a hard time proving he's not a spy if he's got spies working for him."

Dubon had not thought of that. He wasn't just risking his own career; if he was exposed, he would jeopardize the captain's cause. He was being foolhardy—foolhardy and stupid. He reached for his beer.

"Does Picquart believe the captain is innocent?" Le Goff persisted.

"He did, or at least he was very suspicious, until that letter came in. If I can get him to examine it, maybe he'll realize it's phony and take it to the higher-ups," Dubon said, trying to bolster his own confidence.

"I wouldn't bank on it. He wanted to see stronger evidence. He may be rather pleased."

"I'll just wait and see what signals he is sending out on Monday," Dubon replied, deflated. "If he can't be trusted to expose the forgery, I'll find some other way. Maybe you could print something?"

"Not without some proof," Le Goff replied. "What I want is the stuff about the secret file. You were supposed to let me run with it yesterday. The other papers have nothing new, but that doesn't stop them from rehashing tales of the captain's perfidy. He's news now, like it or not."

"Give me a week. I'll expose the forgery and then you can expose the secret file."

"I can't promise you that, Dubon. My editors want copy, and frankly, I need the money. I'll give you a couple of days but if you are not in touch by Wednesday, I'll just write up what I already know and publish that."

Four hours later, Dubon was gazing at a half-naked woman and trying to find some comment to make other than to remark on the shape of her breasts.

"Yes, very touching . . ."

It was a biblical scene, Susanna spied on by the elders as she bathed. Geneviève gave it a perfunctory ten seconds and then looked up, carefully scanning the press of gallerygoers before she moved on to the next painting. Dubon followed her with some amusement. He had always suspected that she attended these occasions not to see art but to see people. He did not enjoy galleries but felt it was only politic to accompany her. He had arrived home in good time for dinner Friday night and for lunch Saturday. And he had spent an hour after lunch reviewing her guest list for the following Tuesday. It was her big spring dinner party, an occasion that marked the end of her social season and imminent departure for the coast, and there would be a few new acquaintances she would seek to impress alongside her old reliables.

She had not asked Dubon about the Dreyfus case again, and he was hoping he could somehow expose the forgery to the colonel on Monday and get out of the Statistical Section for good so that the next time she challenged him about it he could say, more or less honestly, that he was finished.

"That's Madame du Châtel," she whispered at him, cocking a head across the room. "We should work our way over to her."

But as they approached the next painting, the last in a row, they were interrupted by the appearance of Masson in the doorway.

"Baron!" Geneviève called out with overenthusiastic delight.

"Madame, Dubon . . ." He took Geneviève's hand and kissed it.

"Will you join us, Baron?" she asked, and then paused. "But perhaps you haven't seen this room yet. We were just finishing," she said, keeping up the pretense they were all there to see paintings.

Dubon noted her excited face and it dawned on him that she had set up this meeting.

"Oh, I can come back to it," Masson replied coyly. "I seem to be going through backward. No matter. You, Madame, are more beautiful company than any painting."

Dubon had to bite his lip to stop himself from laughing out loud—Masson could be so unctuous—but Geneviève smiled in apparently genuine appreciation, and the three of them moved on to the next room, which was devoted entirely to landscapes. Masson and Geneviève agreed they particularly liked an Italian sunset and spent some time analyzing its merits, although Dubon wondered if Masson were not completely color-blind to the lurid effect of its glowing red sky.

They were about halfway around the room when they came face-to-face with Madame du Châtel, whom Geneviève now seemed less interested in meeting, even though that lady professed delight at being introduced to Masson. She joined their party for the rest of the exhibition and as she chatted with Geneviève, Masson drew back to make polite conversation with Dubon.

"Madame Dubon tells me you are still busy defending the indefensible," he said.

His tone was lighthearted but the remark made Dubon pause: had Geneviève told Masson that he was working on the Dreyfus case? He didn't ask, but replied instead, "It's a lawyer's job—defending whoever needs a defense."

"Remember what I told you, Dubon," Masson said. "The caravan will move on, and you will have associated yourself with another lost cause."

"That's my business, I guess," Dubon said as he stepped forward to join the ladies.

THIRTY-FOUR

"Dubon. In here. Now."

Dubon hurried into the colonel's office and saluted sharply. As he raised his hand, he could feel a slight tearing under his armpit—stitching giving way. The uniform Madame Dreyfus had provided was of a fine serge, a much more comfortable fabric than that of Jean-Jean's summer kit, but the tunic was too short and pressed on his shoulders, leaving him feeling as hunched over as an orangutan.

"What is *this*?" the Colonel demanded, gesturing at the front page of a newspaper sitting on his desk.

It was the Monday morning edition of *Le Soleil*, his friend Morel's paper. Dubon hadn't read it, he seldom did, but as he turned the folded broadsheet to face him he saw that the article the colonel was pointing at was written by one J. Fournier, the military correspondent whom Dubon had met at the racetrack.

"Shut the door, Dubon."

He obeyed and returned to stand in front of the colonel's desk.

"You don't know this story?"

"No, Colonel."

"It says that the military holds a file of conclusive evidence proving the guilt of Captain Dreyfus, including a letter from an Italian diplomat that speaks of buying information from 'that bastard Dreyfus.'"

"Not 'that bastard D'?"

"No, 'that bastard Dreyfus,' all spelled out, nice and clear."

Somebody was leaking stuff to Fournier. Probably Henry, Dubon guessed. He must think the case against Dreyfus needed some fuel in the press. Le Goff was going to be furious he had been scooped.

"Dubon, what do you have to say for yourself?"

"For myself, Colonel?"

"This is classified information. Sharing it with a newspaper is a serious offense, subject to immediate discipline, if not court martial."

"Colonel, you don't think it was me who leaked this to the press," Dubon protested. He had, of course, been about to do that very thing, but his surprise that someone had beaten him to it—and embroidered on the information—added sincerity to his tone of injured innocence.

"Yes, I do, Dubon. Temporary clerk. New to the section. None of my regular staff would ever betray our work in this way. They are too loyal."

"Perhaps that is your problem, Colonel," Dubon suggested gently. "Someone feels the section's work needs to be defended in the press, that the questions being raised need to be quashed. Perhaps someone is *too* loyal . . ."

"Henry. He wouldn't . . ." Picquart picked up the paper as though to weigh this conclusion and began smacking the desk with it. "The fool, the fool . . . Didn't he realize . . ."

He did not finish his sentence, but Dubon could guess what line of reasoning Picquart was now following. In his attempt to bolster the case against Dreyfus, Henry had just handed the prisoner's lawyers exactly the material they needed to launch an appeal: reason to believe evidence had been withheld from the defense at the time of the court martial. All they had to do was come forward and say this "bastard" letter had never been shown to them.

Now another thought came to Picquart as he stared at the paper again.

"Why do you suppose the name is spelled out? If it's Henry, he certainly knows that only an initial appears in the 'bastard' letter. And why not tell the paper about the newer letter, the second Italian letter that does name Dreyfus? It's much harder evidence."

"Maybe the journalist confused the two," Dubon said. Fournier wasn't particularly bright, he recalled, and he would have been dealing with a lot of information.

"Or maybe," Picquart speculated, "his source led him to think the original evidence actually named Dreyfus ... Maybe his source ..." He opened a desk drawer, pulled out a bunch of keys, selected one, and turned with urgency to the filing cabinet behind his desk.

He laid his hands on the necessary file instantly; Dubon supposed he had been consulting it often of late. He put it on his desk and then pulled out the letter that he and Dubon had examined together before, and gestured to Dubon to sit down. The sentence that ended with the words "that bastard D" was at the close of a paragraph and it now clearly read "that bastard Dreyfus."

"Someone has tampered with it," Picquart said. He looked back at Dubon.

"Colonel, there is a man who comes to see the major occasionally. A rather seedy character, seems to be called Leblanc ..."

"You mean Rivaud, the forger. This is his handiwork?"

"He has been here several times recently."

"Henry is the only other person who has a key to that filing cabinet," Picquart said, shaking his head.

The two men looked down at the letter. It was a hugely risky move, Dubon thought to himself. The original judges at the court martial had been shown in secret a letter with only an initial. If it ever came to a second trial and the improved letter became part of the public record, the inconsistency would be glaring. Henry was relying on the judges' silence. Evidently, he felt his superiors would agree that the end justified the means.

Picquart, meanwhile, had been doing his own thinking and now came to the conclusion Dubon had reached so joyfully on Saturday. "And the new letter. It must be a forgery too," he said almost sadly.

He opened the file again and pulled out the Italian's letter, and then produced another sheet in the same hand. Its content was banal, a letter of thanks after some kind of party, but Picquart must have dug it out of the files for comparison. He and Dubon studied the two at length; both were written on onionskin paper faintly lined in blue, and the handwriting on the thank-you note looked identical to that of the incriminating letter of warning.

"Well, if it's a forgery, it will take sharper eyes than ours to unmask it," Picquart finally said. "What a mess."

"Yes, Colonel."

"Headquarters wants this file closed once and for all. I have orders to find both motive and stronger evidence. And last week the evidence showed up through 'the usual route.' My superiors were pleased. I can't go back to headquarters now and say I suspect the authenticity of the letter, not unless I can really prove it's a fraud. And if I am not going to help them build their case against Dreyfus, then I had better be able to hand them another spy."

"Another spy, Colonel?"

"The *real* spy, Dubon. I increasingly think we are talking of the real spy, who may still be at work. I'll work on finding the spy; you can start by putting together a file to exonerate Dreyfus."

"Me, Colonel?"

"Yes, you, Dubon. The rue Saint-Dominique is not going to believe the second man is guilty unless we show the first is innocent. The generals are obsessed with Dreyfus, just like Henry. I am giving you a chance to prove yourself now. You do the job."

"Yes, of course, Colonel. And where would you suggest I start?"

"Start with this," Picquart said, indicating the new letter. "We have to prove it's a forgery. Go directly to Rivaud. Get him to confess. He doesn't need to name Henry; indeed, I would prefer if he didn't. Just get him to explain how he did it, so I have grounds to burn the pestilent thing. Here, take it with you," he said, pulling an envelope from his desk and slipping the paper inside.

"Yes, Colonel." Dubon reached for the envelope. He now had the Italian letter in his hands. Dare he ask for more? "But if I am going to work to exonerate the captain, I do need to see the original evidence too. I need to see the bordereau."

Picquart hesitated but then turned again to the filing cabinet and pulled out a second file.

"It's the original. There is a photograph over at the rue Saint-Dominique, I believe, but this is all I have. Here you go."

He passed it across his desk and Dubon began reading the piece of paper that had started it all. It bore no place line, date, or signature and ran as follows:

I am still waiting for any word that you wish to see me, Monsieur, nevertheless I am forwarding you several interesting pieces of information:

1. A note on the hydraulic brake on the 120 and the way in which it behaves.
2. A note on covering troops (several changes will be made under the new plan).
3. A note on a modification to the artillery formations.
4. A note on Madagascar.
5. The preliminary Firing Manual of the Field Artillery (14 March 1894).

The latter is extremely difficult to come by and I can only have it for a few days. The War Ministry sent a fixed number to the Corps and the Corps is responsible for them. Each officer has to remit his copy after maneuvers. So, if you wish to take from it what interests you and then keep it for me, I will come to retrieve it. Unless you would like me to have it copied in its entirety and just send you the copy.

I am just off to maneuvers.

"So, an artillery officer about to depart on maneuvers..." Dubon said as he finished reading.

"Yes, that's why they fingered Dreyfus initially. He fit the bill."

"But others must have fit the bill too."

"That's what I intend to find out," the colonel replied.

"Can I make a copy of this, Colonel?"

"You mean photograph it? Henry's shown you our darkroom, has he?" Picquart paused again, but then made up his mind. "No, Captain. We have had far too much copying going on. If you feel the need to consult it again, you can always ask me. Work on the forgery angle and get that Italian's letter back to me as soon as possible. I want to be able to seek permission to destroy it by the end of the week, before somebody leaks *it* to the press."

Dubon was rising to leave when the colonel asked, almost as an afterthought: "And I think now I should see your order papers, Captain."

Dubon froze and said nothing.

"Did you ever show those papers to Henry last week?" Picquart asked in a tone that suggested he knew the answer was no.

"Colonel, I am very sorry, but the thing is, my papers have been destroyed," he replied.

"Destroyed? Dubon, you told me your papers were in your winter uniform. Were you lying to me?"

"No, no, Colonel. My papers were in my winter uniform when you asked for them last week. And then I went home and my wife . . ." Was it realistic to think he could afford a wife on a captain's pay? "My wife had sent the uniform to the cleaner's and the trouble, you see, well, the papers went through the wash. Illegible. Just a pulp."

The colonel now gave him a long, appraising look.

"You are a good officer, Dubon. I think you want to know the truth about this case as much as I do." He pulled a sheet of blank paper toward him. "I am now going to write a letter to the rue Saint-Dominique. Under the circumstances, I will ask Personnel for your entire file, and for a new copy of your orders. And . . ." He paused for a moment to let his next words sink in. ". . . you will deliver this letter yourself."

Picquart was testing him.

"We should get an answer tomorrow, Wednesday at the outside," the colonel concluded as he began to write.

He was giving Dubon forty-eight hours to expose the forgery before he had to prove his identity—or disappear.

Dubon returned to his desk, pulled his tunic on, and was just putting his cap on his head when he found Hermann at his side. Startled, Dubon stepped back. The man always seemed to appear from nowhere.

"Are you leaving, Dubon?" he asked.

"Yes."

"You are gone, then?"

"I'll be back later."

"Oh, I thought perhaps you were going for good."

THIRTY-FIVE

The next day Dubon was sitting at his own desk in his real office, trying on false beards and asking Lebrun to judge which was the most effective, when the English detective walked through the door.

"And just who exactly are you dressing up as now?"

The accent was heavy, but the sarcasm came through loud and clear.

"You, actually. I am dressing up as you. *I am dressing up as you . . .*" Dubon said a second time, trying to copy the English detective's accent. Dubon had not seen him since their exchange of notes the previous week.

"You don't look the least bit like me," the detective protested. "And why would you want to, anyway?"

"I am not trying to look like you specifically. I am going to visit a witness disguised as an English detective in the pay of the Dreyfus family."

"Why can't you just visit your witness dressed as a French lawyer in the pay of a friend of the family?" Brown asked.

"You mean dressed as myself? Can't do that because the man already knows me as a military clerk."

"Ah, yes, your other costume."

"I asked Lebrun if he would do the job for me, but he declined."

"I have my professional ethics to consider," Lebrun explained rather haughtily.

"You're a clerk, Lebrun. You can't be disbarred for impersonating somebody."

"No, but I'll never be called to the bar if I am caught impersonating a lawyer before I have even started."

"Do you plan to become a lawyer? I had no idea." The notion that Lebrun might have professional ambitions was so novel that Dubon turned his head sharply to look up at his clerk and found the beard slipping. "Damn this thing."

He had concocted his scheme the day before at the Statistical Section and run a much-edited version by Picquart that morning before he had gone back to his own apartment to change. The trick was not to approach Rivaud from the side of his paymasters but to offer him more pay from new masters.

It was simple enough, or so it had seemed to him as he walked confidently up the rue Saint-Honoré in a rumpled linen suit he had pulled from the back of his closet. It was a good beginning. Next he needed something transforming—like a beard.

"Where did you get it? It's horrible," the detective said.

"I bought it in the costume department at Galeries Lafayette. Cost me two francs."

"I'll make you a deal. I will outfit you with a professional disguise that may actually fool your quarry and you can tell me what you are up to."

The detective opened the briefcase he was carrying, took out a small wooden box, and, sweeping Dubon's selection of beards out of the way, unfolded it on the desk. It contained a few tiny bottles, thick colored crayons of face paint, and various strands of hair. The detective pulled out one of the bottles and held it up.

"Spirit gum. We'll give you some whiskers that stay in place and look real."

"All right," said Dubon, and, waving Lebrun out of the office, he began to explain the conundrum of the new Italian letter.

"Things are moving fast," Brown said once he had finished. "You saw *Le Soleil*."

"Yes. Your client must be well pleased, despite the tone of it." Le Goff, on the other hand, was angry. Dubon had just replied to his resentful telegram, promising better and truer information soon.

"Very good news," the detective agreed. "Grounds for appeal. Monsieur Dreyfus is going to petition for one this week."

Dubon smiled to himself. The captain's brother might be able to take credit for getting an appeal after all. "That's good. But if there is going to be a second trial, we don't want some bit of paper floating around that affirms the captain was spying for both the Germans and the Italians."

"Better yet, we want to find the real spy," Brown replied.

"I am working on that. So is the head of the section. He's one of the few who has kept an open mind about the case. And in the meantime, I am going to visit a forger."

"The forger of this document that names the captain?"

"Yes. I am going to suggest to him that the document is known to be false and that the Dreyfus family will pay handsomely for proof that it's a forgery. I'd also like to know if he's responsible for tampering with any other evidence."

"You plan to buy him?" the detective asked.

"He's not a savory character. That's why I am disguised as you: I thought he would feel more at home with a private detective than a barrister."

"Thanks very much. And the clothes? You thought they were appropriate for an English detective?"

Dubon looked down at his old suit. "This is mine actually. An old favorite. My wife wouldn't let me wear it anymore, but I refuse to throw it out."

"I would never wear such a garment on assignment," Brown said, as he began spreading spirit gum over Dubon's chin. "It wouldn't appear professional."

"I am aiming for a much lower type of detective, I assure you, Monsieur Brown," Dubon replied.

"Stop talking. I'm going to start applying hair now."

✤

A half hour later, when Brown held up a small mirror he also kept in his case, Dubon saw himself transformed. The detective had scattered a few tufts of long whiskers across Dubon's face; the effect was aging and very unattractive. He had also parted Dubon's hair right down the middle and slicked it flat on either side of his head. Dubon was proud of the continuing abundance of his hair, but the detective had somehow managed to make it look thin and greasy. Finally, he produced a pair of glasses from his kit.

"The lenses are just plain glass; they won't affect your sight. But the man will notice them, which will put him off noticing other things about your appearance, things he might recognize. Let's get your clerk back in here."

Lebrun entered and, to the detective's gratification, was impressed. "Unrecognizable, Maître. Your own mother, were she still alive . . ."

"Yes, Lebrun, yes. Very good," Dubon said, still trying to effect the English accent.

"Skip the accent," Brown recommended. "It will only slip. Try something simpler. Can you lower your voice a little?"

"Like this . . . Like this," Dubon tried. "André, I have told you often enough there is to be no ball playing in the house. Yes, that's it, the voice of authority. Sounds a bit different from my own, no?"

"Yes, that's good."

"Right. I'll be off, then," said Dubon, looking at his watch. It was almost five o'clock.

"How do you know he'll be home?" Brown asked reasonably enough.

"I don't."

THIRTY-SIX

Dubon arrived at Rivaud's apartment about half an hour later to find the door slightly ajar. He knocked, waited, and, unsure whether the muffled voice he heard was inviting him inside, pushed the door open slowly, calling out, "Monsieur Rivaud?" as he did so. He was greeted by a blinding flash of light. It seemed not only to illuminate the ghastly scene inside but also to brand the image on his retina with the permanence of a photograph. Rivaud's body lay sprawled on the studio floor, his head snapped over at an angle so close to his shoulder that his ear was touching it and his eyes wide open as though his death had taken him by surprise.

"You kill him?" asked a voice, as a large figure in a black suit stepped away from Rivaud's big desk, where the ink bottles still stood in their tidy line.

"*Mon Dieu, non,*" Dubon replied.

"Friend of yours?"

"No, no, not really. No, not a friend."

"Business associate?"

"No. Who are you?"

"That's just what I was going to ask you, Monsieur," replied the man. "But I don't mind going first. Inspector Maury of the Sureté. This is Pons." He indicated the man who was the source of the flash of light—a police photographer, to judge from his tripod and camera. He seemed to be busy setting up for another shot and, having fiddled with his camera for the duration of Dubon's exchange with the inspector, was now carefully spooning some kind of powder into a short metal trough. He put a match to it, lit it, and, while he held it aloft, pushed a button on the camera. The room was once again illuminated.

The inspector ignored the light and asked Dubon, "And you are?"

Dubon paused. The inspector was investigating a murder, and Dubon was a member in good standing of the Paris bar. Probably best not to lie.

"Maître François Dubon. A barrister," he explained.

"Really?" The inspector raised an eyebrow at Dubon and kept it raised as he stared at him. Perhaps this was how he got suspects to confess. "You don't look like any kind of lawyer I would hire."

Dubon put a hand up to the fake whiskers.

"I don't usually dress like this. I confess I was not going to reveal my true profession to, er, um . . ." Dubon looked back down at the forger's dead body. This was the second violent death he had witnessed in the space of a month. It was not a pleasant feeling. He felt his stomach churning, and he turned away, struggling to quell his nausea.

The inspector waited a moment and continued.

"So, you weren't planning to tell the gentleman who you really are. But you know who *he* is?"

"Yes, his real name is Rivaud, although I believe he goes by various aliases. He's a forger by trade."

"Ah yes," replied the inspector, "and known to the Paris police, Monsieur—Dubon, you said it was, I believe." His tone suggested he thought Dubon was probably an alias too. "And why would a lawyer be visiting a forger in disguise?"

"I have a client who is working to exonerate a man we believe to have been the victim of a miscarriage of justice," Dubon said, as succinctly as he could. "I think Rivaud forged some of the evidence against the man, and I was going to attempt—"

"You were going to wring a confession out of him, were you?"

"Yes, well, something like that."

"And when you couldn't wring a confession out of him, you wrung his neck instead, did you? And you just came back now because . . . perhaps you forgot something or you realized you had missed an opportunity to riffle through his files . . ."

"That is preposterous, Inspector." The accusation made Dubon recover himself in a hurry. "If I had killed the man and then been stupid enough to return to the scene of my crime, I certainly wouldn't have pushed open the door when I heard a voice inside."

"Maybe you are a lawyer, after all." The inspector laughed. The man seemed quite unmoved by the dead body on the floor.

"Maître." He used the title with ironic emphasis. "Sit there for a moment while we finish up our work. Another detective will be along in a bit and he can take you into the commissariat to make a statement."

Dubon knew he could insist on the presence of a lawyer before he answered any questions, but he decided it wasn't wise to argue. He began pushing aside some of the clothes, newspapers, and debris that covered the divan to make a place for himself.

"Not there! We haven't photographed that yet," the inspector shouted at him.

Dubon found himself a chair and perched on it as the photographer turned his attention to the room.

"Interesting, the killer ransacked the room but left the desk," the inspector remarked to his colleague as he began to take pictures of the divan.

"I think it was always like this," Dubon said.

"What?"

"The room . . . I visited Monsieur Rivaud once before. On that occasion, he was very much alive, and his desk was the only thing in the room that was tidy." Dubon gestured at the ink bottles and brushes. "I guess he took pride in his, er, his craft, if you want to call it that."

Dubon kept to himself the one thing he had noticed that was different about the room. Napoléon's love letter had been removed from the wall. There was a barely discernible rectangular patch where it had hung, faintly lighter than the surrounding plaster and marked with one small black hole where a nail had been.

THIRTY-SEVEN

Dubon returned home in a police wagon. The inspector had kept him waiting an hour in the forger's studio until a constable finally showed up and was dispatched to find the boss. The chief inspector arrived promptly, full of apologies for detaining a busy man like Maître Dubon.

"Nasty business, these underworld characters," he said to Dubon, genially dismissing Rivaud's murder. "It will be some deal that has gone awry, you can count on it—another criminal type." He asked Dubon to accompany the constable to the commissariat, where Dubon dutifully answered the few questions that were put to him and signed a statement. After the inspector's hard approach, it felt perfunctory to say the least.

As the constable drove him home in the wagon, he hoped Geneviève and the servants would not spot him alighting from such a notorious conveyance—and puzzled over who had vouched for his identity with the chief inspector.

It was only as he walked into the foyer of his own home and saw the look on Luc's face that he remembered: it was the night of Geneviève's dinner party. It had been called for seven. He pulled out his pocket watch: it was eight thirty.

"Madame held dinner for half an hour, Maître," Luc said in a tone carefully scrubbed of judgment. "She decided she could wait no longer. They have just sat down: Major de Valcourt Ronchaud took the head of the table."

"Oh good, good. That's fine, I'll just pop in and sit at his place."

"Would you not prefer to change, Maître? And perhaps . . . shave?"

Dubon was reminded of his disguise; he had abandoned the glasses Brown had offered him, but the whiskers were still in place.

"Yes, yes. I'll go and change and get these things off my face." He gave a good tug to one tuft of hair and bits came off in his hand. He laughed, but Luc just looked a little sick. "I'll be as quick as I can. Is my evening suit ready?"

"Yes, Maître. I had laid it out on the bed for you. Madame had expected you at six."

Of course Geneviève had spoken to him about the dinner the previous evening, but he had been too busy considering how to expose the forgery to listen. He had been out of the house before anyone else had woken that morning but he had come back to get his old suit around eleven. He should have remembered the party—there had been two bouquets of flowers in the hall and sounds of activity in the kitchen, he now recalled—but by then all he could think of was what he was going to say to the forger.

There would be hell to pay, he thought to himself as he made his way into the bathroom and started pulling at the whiskers; they came off erratically, leaving patches of skin that were both sticky and flaming red. The result looked worse than when he had started and he surveyed himself in the mirror with rising panic.

"What are you doing?"

The voice made him jump. It was André at the bathroom door.

"Removing a false beard," Dubon replied testily. At least with children you did not have to explain yourself.

"For the school play, we used face cream," André offered helpfully.

"Maybe Maman has some." He turned to his mother's dressing table in the bedroom behind him and rummaged about before returning with a jar in his hand.

Dubon applied the stuff and found it melted the gum and took off the whiskers with a lot less yanking. He achieved an effect that made him look clean-shaven but ruddy-faced, as though perhaps he had spent the day outdoors. The cream had a flowery perfume that he rather liked; it conjured up images of cozy family dinners or Geneviève rising from the breakfast table to plan her morning. It was her scent, he now realized, hoping it would not smell as strong to his dinner companions as it did to him.

"Not bad," he said to André, who followed him back into the bedroom. There he pulled on evening dress and began knotting his evening tie in the mirror.

"Why were you wearing a beard?" André asked.

"For work. I wanted to talk to someone without his knowing who I was." He fumbled with the tie; Luc would have done a firmer job.

"That's clever," André said in a tone of uncharacteristic awe. "Do you get to wear any other disguises at work?"

"No, not usually," Dubon replied, thinking of his borrowed uniform. "I must go to the table or your mother will be furious."

"She already is," André said, as Dubon hurried to the dining room.

But of course Geneviève was not going to show her displeasure in front of her guests. She would take a jovial tone of wifely forbearance with the major and Masson providing backup. As he slid into the chair originally intended for his brother-in-law, Dubon recognized that the storm would wait for later.

"Hope you don't mind my taking the head of the table, *mon vieux*," the major greeted him.

"No, no, not at all. Best thing to do under the circumstances. My apologies, Mesdames," he said, smiling at the female guests with what he intended to be captivating charm but he suspected looked merely smarmy. Certainly the Comtesse de Chambort, from whom, he now recalled, Geneviève was hoping for more regular invitations, did not look impressed.

"I was unavoidably detained at the office. I am sure that Geneviève has complained already this evening about a particularly onerous case I am working on at the moment. It has been most inconvenient, and I am so sorry it has disrupted my duties as your host."

"Work, work, it is all the gentlemen ever talk about these days," the comtesse offered. "It is a wonder we can get to the table at eight, the men are all so busy at their offices. When I was a girl, we ate at six, and not just *en famille*. Six even if we had guests, well, six unless we had a ball, and of course, then we had a late supper after the dancing too. Did I tell you, my dear"—she turned to Geneviève now—"that the count has taken an office? I don't believe he really does anything there, but he feels it necessary. He wants to return home at seven o'clock, like a working man. I tell him all this socialism is an affectation, but it makes no difference. He insists he go there every day. At least it keeps him out of my way."

Dubon gathered that the count himself was not present, but couldn't recall why.

"Oh, I don't deny the power of a profession, Comtesse," Geneviève replied. "In my family, of course, my cousin, the Comte de Ronchaud Valcourt, never took a profession, just lived on the estate, but my father always had a vocation for the military. Both the major and my younger brother, Captain de Ronchaud Valcourt—I don't believe you have met him, Comtesse—both of them follow in the family tradition in that regard. No, I never begrudge François his work, certainly I don't."

Nor my income, Dubon thought to himself, inured to Geneviève's efforts to present his law practice as little more than an interesting hobby.

"You have a forgiving wife, Dubon. You are blessed," Masson said.

"Baron, you are always envying our domestic harmony, but now you see what I have to put up with, a husband who comes home for dinner two hours late," Geneviève continued.

"We missed his company, but here he is, safe among us now."

"You are taking his side only because you were late yourself, Baron," Geneviève said, all but wagging her finger at him.

Here, Masson looked nonplussed and wasn't as eager as usual to continue their bantering.

"My apologies again, Madame," he said in a low voice. "Called back to the office just as I was dressing for dinner."

Now that the men had humbled themselves, the dinner party continued happily enough, although Dubon found his thoughts drifting away. Comfortably settled at his own table with a good glass of wine but unable to banish the image of Rivaud's body sprawled amid the chaos of the studio, he began to question the import of what he had seen. Who had killed Rivaud? Was it really some criminal dissatisfied with a deal? Or was his death related to the captain's case?

Dubon was at sea here and thought with some relief about returning to the Statistical Section the next morning. He could tell Picquart what he had stumbled across, hand the problem over to him. The colonel's reaction would give him some idea of what was afoot.

Once the guests had left, Geneviève initially pursued her restrained tone, albeit on a cooler note than she had affected at the table. Her party had been a success; she was flush with the pleasure of it and several hours removed from the tense moments between six thirty and seven.

Settled at her dressing table and unpinning her hair, she eyed her husband reflected in her mirror and asked calmly, "You haven't given up that case, have you?"

"Well, not quite yet. There were some dramatic developments this evening, and I do hope I am reaching an end."

She dismissed this answer with a wave of her hairbrush, so uninterested in his work that its dramatic developments were of no import to her.

"Tomorrow, François. I insist," she said. His failure to arrive in time for dinner had been a significant breach; she had the high ground here and she was going to use it. She began brushing her hair with fierce strokes, each one culminating in a sharp flick of the wrist. "You need to send the client a message tomorrow saying you are passing the file to someone else."

"No, I can't simply abandon a client like that. I am almost finished, but it will take another few days."

She banged the hairbrush down on the table and swung around to confront him. "I don't understand you. Do you not read the papers? What is going to happen if our friends find out you are defending this fellow?"

"There are more important issues at stake here than your invitations," Dubon retorted, and as soon as the words were spoken he knew he had made a mistake.

"It's not the invitations; it's the income," she spat back. "You think I am so trivial, and you so above it all. Where do your clients come from? Who has provided you with all those contacts over the years? Where will your practice be if our friends desert us?"

Dubon was still for a moment. She had a point. Why was he taking such a risk? Because he believed captain Dreyfus was innocent? Because the captain's wife had beautiful eyes? Because he felt happier than he had in years?

"Geneviève." He tried a gentle tone. "I would never call you trivial. I have always admired your wit and your spirit, but we cannot lose sight of what is important to us. Of course we need money to live, and I have worked hard to provide us with a good life in that regard. You have helped by introducing me into your family's circle, but our friends would not continue to use my services if I did not give satisfaction. And surely they don't matter to us only as business connections but as those who provide us with warmth and companionship. At the end of the day, we have to stand for something or we are not worthy of their affection. Friendship matters—but what of justice? I will pursue this case because I believe it is the right thing to do."

They stared at each other.

"I do apologize for my tardiness," he added. "I know how much you wanted the dinner to go smoothly and I wasn't here to help you."

"The major was happy to step in." She turned back to her mirror.

He couldn't tell if she had acquiesced or was just saving her ammunition for another day.

"Good, good," he said, and retreated to the bathroom.

A few minutes later, he heard a sharp cry from the bedroom.

"What on earth has happened to my cream?"

THIRTY-EIGHT

Dubon entered Picquart's office the following morning, gave the colonel a perfunctory salute, and sat down in the chair across from him.

"Rivaud is dead," he announced without preamble.

"Dead?"

"Murdered."

"Murdered? Who killed him?"

"I don't know, but Chief Inspector Remy of the Sureté is happy to embrace the theory that some ruffian probably already known to police wrung his neck in a dispute over what we can safely assume was a criminal activity."

"A thug kills a minor criminal, nobody much cares, and the whole matter can be swept aside," said Picquart, following Dubon's lead. "How did you find this all out?"

"I walked in on the police investigation in progress."

"Ah. So you missed your opportunity to talk to Rivaud?"

Dubon nodded.

"But how did you explain your presence to the inspector?"

"Luckily I wasn't in uniform, since my idea had been to pose as a representative from the Dreyfus camp. I just told the police I represented a client who hoped to make Rivaud an offer for a confession to forging evidence."

"So you didn't mention the Dreyfus case or the section?"

"No, I thought it wiser not to. They seemed satisfied and let me go about my business."

"Good, good. You handled yourself well, Dubon." Picquart paused, the implications of Rivaud's death just sinking in. "So, now we can't get Rivaud to confess he improved the bastard letter *or* to expose the new letter."

"No," Dubon said. "I should give it back to you." He held up the envelope with the Italian letter in it, the one that Picquart had allowed him to take away the previous day.

Picquart accepted it, slipped the page out of the envelope, and put it on his desk.

"I could consult one of the graphologists, privately, ask if it would stand up in court . . ."

The two men looked at the page again, Dubon turning his head at an awkward angle to read it. The office was full of spring sunlight, but Picquart switched on his desk lamp to further illuminate the lined paper with its ornate letterhead. It stared back at them, unwilling to release its secrets. Picquart sighed and lifted the page, ready to return it to the envelope. Dubon could see the dust dancing in the sunlight coming in from the window to Picquart's right, and the beam now shone briefly on the paper.

"Wait!" he commanded. Picquart looked at him, startled. "Hold it up to the window."

Picquart turned his body in his chair and held up the paper with both hands. Both of them could see it clearly now. The stationery was a translucent writing paper with fine blue lines to guide the writer's hand; in any regular light the colors looked identical, but with the sun shining through the paper it was clear that at the bottom of the page the lines weren't blue but rather a dark burgundy.

"The top and bottom don't match," Picquart said. "There's the tear . . ." There was a tear through the middle of the page as though the recipient had ripped the letter before discarding it.

"It arrived on my desk in one piece," Dubon explained. "Someone had already glued it together."

"The letterhead is the genuine article...the crest..." Picquart said. "The first lines..."

"But the reference to the captain is in the bottom half. Someone has ripped a blank area off another sheet, stuck it on the top of a real letter, and just added the forgery at the bottom."

"Daring, considering the forger has got to match the handwriting that's already on the page," Picquart noted.

"Rivaud was nothing if not daring," Dubon said, thinking of Napoléon's signature hanging on the forger's wall. "I am surprised he didn't notice the lines, though. His studio had good light."

"Perhaps someone gave him the paper already assembled. You and Henry and Gingras, well, you all do a lot of gluing, and none of you has much light in your office," Picquart said.

"So Henry assembled the page for Rivaud here, and then gave him his assignment: add one paragraph at the bottom of the page. Rivaud did it, and then Henry slipped the letter into the latest file from the usual route."

"I don't want to implicate the major in anything," Picquart said. "Perhaps he has been overzealous, but I have no evidence he ordered the forgery. I wish I had never shown it to headquarters. I'll have to retract it, tell them I am investigating how it came to be created, and get permission to destroy it. The generals will just have to understand that if the Dreyfus family gets an appeal, we will have no conclusive evidence to present at a second trial."

"And you think they will accept that?"

"Why shouldn't they?" Picquart asked in a defensive tone.

"Because," Dubon replied. "Somebody just killed Rivaud to make sure the conclusive evidence stays that way."

THIRTY-NINE

Henry reappeared late in the morning and passed Dubon's desk with the briefest of nods. He didn't look guilt-stricken, Dubon thought, swiveling around in his chair as quietly as he could to watch the man's back as he walked to his office. Was this the demeanor of a murderer? Dubon had no idea.

Picquart must have heard him come in, for he appeared at his door a few minutes later and simply raised an inquiring eyebrow at Dubon while tilting his head toward Henry's closed door. Dubon nodded. Picquart crossed the reception area and knocked.

"Colonel."

"Major. If you would be so good as to step into my office."

Henry followed Picquart back across the room and the two entered Picquart's office and shut the door behind them.

What I would give, Dubon thought to himself, recalling Gingras's phrase of the previous week, to be a fly on the wall. He stood up now, looked about, and quickly set off down the corridor, moving as quietly as he could so as not to draw the attention of Gingras and Hermann, both working in their offices. He could hear the rumble of Picquart's

voice even as he stepped inside the darkroom. He looked about hope-
fully. Geneviève had always said that when they were children, the de
Ronchaud Valcourts used a water glass to eavesdrop on the nursemaid's
conversations with their father's valet. There were various beakers sitting on the counter and Dubon gingerly picked up the smallest and put
it to the wall. Geneviève was right. It did work. He could hear almost
every word now. Picquart was, as he had expected, confronting Henry
with his handiwork.

"So you found the pieces in the file, matched them up, and applied
the glue?"

"Yes, Colonel."

"Do you think we ever make mistakes with our gluing, Major? Get
the wrong pieces . . ."

"Well, maybe with something that was ripped into tiny fragments."
Even through the wall, Dubon could hear the hesitancy in Henry's
voice. "But not with a letter like that; it's only two pieces."

"Why did you not bring it to me at once when you saw the contents?"

"I often work on the files after the others have gone for the day, to
speed the work along, Colonel. I certainly planned to bring it to your
attention the next morning."

"Very well, Major. So you are sure the two pieces you glued both
came from the same file?"

"I guess it's possible I could have made an error, and that one of the
pieces was in some previous file . . ."

"Major, are you telling me you cobbled this letter together from
two pieces from two different time periods?"

"I . . . I don't know what you want me to say, Colonel . . ." Henry
sounded increasingly miserable.

"I want you to tell me the truth, Henry. Did you tamper with this
letter?"

"Well, perhaps I added a few words that were difficult to read.
Sometimes the ink is smeared and—"

"The ink is perfectly clear here, Major. Are you in the habit of
improving documents?"

"We sometimes pencil in missing words . . ."

"So, you are saying words have been added to this document?"

"Colonel ... I really don't know what you expect ... I have done what my superiors needed me to do."

"What they needed, Major, or what they ordered?"

"Colonel. I have done my duty."

"So you felt you had some duty to improve upon this letter?"

"Colonel, I really—"

At this point, Picquart must have grown exasperated. Dubon could hear a chair scraping back, and he pictured the colonel moving to the window.

"You see the lines, Major? Blue. Burgundy. Two separate sheets of paper."

There was a long silence now, then Henry finally spoke: "Colonel, you yourself told me the generals needed conclusive evidence. I did what my country required."

"I think it is best left up to our superiors, Major, to decide precisely what one's country might require. You put me in a very awkward position. I have affirmed to the rue Saint-Dominique that this letter is legitimate. I must now go back and seek permission to destroy it. The situation is extremely delicate. You are aware there have already been press reports of documents naming Dreyfus."

It was a tactful phrasing, Dubon thought; Picquart was not pursuing the issue of the leak.

"Imagine," Picquart continued, "if it were discovered that at least one of these documents, one piece of this supposedly conclusive evidence, is a fraud. What then would happen to the government's case against the man?"

"I only thought, Colonel ..." Henry was trying to recover himself and was now growing defensive. "The generals have always appreciated my work. They appreciated my testimony at the court martial."

"Yes, Henry, but now I must go to the same generals and tell them about this forged letter. It throws all your testimony into question."

"I can go to the generals, too, Colonel. I have friends, good friends in the rue Saint-Dominique."

"Is that a threat, Major?"

Dubon could hear movements in the room but could not make out Henry's reply. No doubt he was moving toward the door.

Picquart, he noted, had not named Rivaud. He wasn't accusing Henry of using the forger, and he certainly wasn't accusing him of murder. And when Dubon came to think of it, would Henry murder Rivaud?

Dubon could hear footsteps now. It was Henry's heavy tread proceeding back to his office and closing the door. He waited a bit before cautiously opening the darkroom door and peeking out. Seeing no one, he slipped back to his desk and busied himself with the papers strewn across it.

Neither Henry nor Picquart spoke another word to him that day, although the colonel nodded as he left the office at lunchtime. He was gone for most of the afternoon and reappeared with a particularly grim expression on his face. Dubon guessed the rue Saint-Dominique had not received the news of the forgery well. He himself packed up soon after and hurried back to his real office.

He sorted through business with Lebrun as quickly as he could because he was determined to see Madeleine on his way home. When he had time to think of her these days, a sense of unease nagged at him. He suspected his absences were increasingly forcing her back into the arms of her old circle. Perhaps there was some new recruit with enough money to keep her in style. Some young fellow who wasn't married yet and who wanted the company of a woman of the world. Dubon should be at his mistress's hearth, asserting his claim, but he also could not risk being late for dinner.

He arrived on the landing outside her rooms to find her just pulling her door closed. She was dressed to go out and surprised by his appearance.

"You weren't expecting me?" he asked.

"It's well past five. I assumed you weren't coming."

"My apologies. I should have sent a message." There was an uncomfortable pause before Dubon cocked his head toward her door and said, "Well, I guess you can keep Lucie and Carl waiting a few minutes."

"I don't see them anymore," she replied, without budging.

"Ah. New friends?"

"None that would interest you," she replied.

"I *am* interested. Why else would I ask?" He moved to her and took her hands. She did not grip back, and when he tried to tug her gently toward the door, she resisted.

"There's only one thing you are interested in," she said. "You don't care about me, you only care about—"

"Madeleine. You know my feelings for you, love in all its dimensions."

"Yes, but one dimension in particular." She pulled a key from her purse and stepped to the door. "All right, then. Shall we?"

Now Dubon stood still. He was not in the habit of forcing himself on reluctant partners.

"No. Thank you," he said as calmly as he could, and turned to walk down the stairs. "I'll come back someday when you're in a better mood."

Dubon spent the next day miserably sitting at his impostor's desk trying to banish his unhappy doubts about Madeleine, wondering if the rue Saint-Dominique would really just ignore the news of the forgery, and if it did, what he should do about it. He got an answer of some kind around three when two officers he had never seen before walked through the front door. He scrambled to his feet and saluted, noting that the senior of the two was a colonel.

"Is Colonel Picquart here?" the man asked.

"In his office, Colonel. I'll just get him," Dubon said, moving toward Picquart's door, which had remained shut all day.

"Don't bother," the colonel said, and walked over to the door followed by his companion, a captain. As the colonel stood aside, the captain knocked and, without waiting for a reply, opened the door for his superior and stood back to let him step inside.

They shut the door behind them, but emerged only a few minutes later with Picquart following them.

"I'll be gone for the rest of the day, Dubon," he said as he walked by, following the colonel but with the captain at his heels. To Dubon, the image was reminiscent of an arrest.

The following day, to Dubon's relief, Picquart was back at his post. He could be seen through his open door bustling about, arranging something. After lunch, he called Dubon into his office, where he was packing files into a leather box that sat on his desk. There were several empty crates on the floor.

"I am leaving, Dubon. Won't be in tomorrow."

"Leaving, Colonel? Why?"

"I am needed for an assignment in Algeria. I am being seconded to a detachment there immediately."

"Algeria, Colonel? What on earth could you possibly have to do in Algeria?"

The colonel stood back from his boxes and drew himself up. "It's not your place to ask such a question, Dubon. I have my orders. I obey them. As should you."

"Yes, Colonel," Dubon, recalled to military discipline, replied as briskly as he could.

"Major Henry will be taking over during my absence."

"How long will you be gone, sir?"

"Indefinitely."

"So, Major Henry will be in charge of all files, Colonel?"

"Yes, Dubon, exactly," Picquart said in a neutral tone.

Dubon's heart sank. Clearly, the higher-ups were not interested in hearing that the case against the captain was flimsy and that a second trial might end in an acquittal. They weren't exactly shooting the messenger, just replacing him with one who delivered the news they wanted to hear.

"I think you should be leaving too, Dubon," Picquart said.

"Me, sir?"

"Yes, Dubon, before Major Henry finally decides to march over to the rue Saint-Dominique and pull your personnel file himself." Picquart now gave him a long look that froze Dubon in his shoes. "In fact, I have told Henry that you have been recalled to the rue

Saint-Dominique as of Monday morning and that he needs to reapply to headquarters for a temporary clerk. Whoever you are, Dubon, it's time you moved on."

Dubon's reply was only a croak. He swallowed and tried again. "Yes, Colonel."

"I expect to be here late this evening, Dubon. I have arranged with Major Henry that I will drop my keys off at his lodging tonight. I am spending next week with my family in Alsace before I leave for Marseille. My ship sails a week Monday. Henry won't be in tomorrow morning. Gingras will open and lock up for you. You can say your good-byes to him."

"Yes, Colonel. So I will come in tomorrow morning, but then return to the rue Saint-Dominique on Monday."

"Yes, Dubon." Picquart paused. "Tomorrow morning you may find that in my haste I have forgotten to lock all my file drawers, but Major Henry can tidy everything up next week. He may curse my absent-mindedness, but I am sure he wouldn't find anything missing. You understand me, Dubon?"

"Yes, Colonel. Perfectly. May I say what a privilege it has been working for an officer as honorable as yourself and I wish you the best of success in Algeria in the hopes you will be returned to France very soon."

"Thank you, Dubon. I certainly hope my assignment will not last long. It may depend a bit on the . . . well, on the climate."

"Yes, Colonel. Good-bye, Colonel."

Dubon saluted and left Picquart's office. He had his orders. He was to continue the work Picquart could not. For a brief period on Saturday morning he would have access to the captain's file and the bordereau. Somehow he had to get them out of the Statistical Section and into Le Goff's hands.

FORTY

Le Goff's response was instantaneous. "We need a photograph of the bordereau," he said when he met Dubon at his office that evening. "Come on. If we hurry, we'll catch one of the photographers at *La Presse*, and he can lend you a camera."

"But how am I to photograph it? At best, I'll be able to sneak another look tomorrow morning. I was thinking I could transcribe the file."

"We need to be able to identify the hand," Le Goff replied as he bounded down the stairs ahead of Dubon. "That must be what Picquart hopes you will do. It's the key to the whole thing. Whoever wrote that list is a spy. The paper will publish it. 'The handwriting of a traitor ... Does anyone know this handwriting?' It will be a coup!"

Le Goff practically dragged him through the lobby of the building that housed *La Presse*. The unhelpful clerk whom Dubon had met that very first day when he had come looking for Azimut Martin was just closing up for the evening, but Le Goff brushed past him with a nod, pushed through the doors into the office, and was soon clattering down a tiny staircase that led to the basement. He made his

way through a labyrinth of cupboards and storage rooms and found
a photographer still working away in a darkroom that was larger than
the one at the Statistical Section but seemed to feature the same chemistry set. The man was only too happy to stop what he was doing and
produce a camera for Dubon, if it meant he could deliver a lecture on
the fundamentals of photography. After unlocking a metal cabinet and
removing a large leather suitcase that held the camera, he began with a
long lesson about light and chemistry, before finally coming around to
the basics: how exactly Dubon was to hold the thing and operate the
shutter.

"I just need to load some film for you," he concluded, pulling a
leather pouch toward him and waving it at them. Then he lined up a
stack of flat metal cases about the size of postcards on the counter in
front of him and snapped off the lights. In the darkness, they could
hear the cases clicking open and shut. In a minute, he had the lights
back on.

"Each one of these now contains a piece of film," he said, holding
up one of the metal cases. "I've loaded a dozen so you can take twelve
pictures without having to worry about reloading them. You get used
to doing it, but it's finicky for a beginner, doing it in total darkness. So,
you slip the film in like this," he continued, pushing one case into a slot
on the side of the camera and then withdrawing it. "The case protects
the film from the light. It pops out again but leaves the film in there. It
unloads the same way."

"What would happen if it wasn't protected?"

"But that's what I've been explaining," he said with some exasperation. "If you simply expose the film to light, you'll just get a fogged bit
of film, worthless."

"Is the paper like that too?" Dubon asked, remembering with guilt
that he had pulled a stack of paper out of another leather pouch in the
darkroom he had discovered at the Statistical Section.

"Yes, except it doesn't see light across the entire spectrum. That's
how the safe light works."

"The safe light?"

"The amber light. When you are working with the film, I mean
loading the plates or developing it, you have to work in total darkness.

When you are making prints you can use the safe light, because the paper doesn't read that amber light."

"Ah," said Dubon. That explained the odd orange light in the Statistical Section darkroom. "What did you do before you had electricity?" he asked, indicating the gas nipple that had not been removed from the wall.

"Oh, we muddled through in the dark or used a candle. The old glass plates were much less sensitive so you could let a bit of light in under the door in those days. So, what's your subject?" he asked.

"A document."

"Ah, well, that's easy, then—it's stationary. What's the light like?"

"Depends a bit on tomorrow's weather, I suppose."

"You are photographing a document outdoors?"

"Oh no. In an office, but there's a window with good light."

"Be careful about that. If you shoot looking toward the window, the sunlight will overwhelm the image. Stand with your back to it, so its light is cast on to your subject. But look out for shadows. Our eyes tend not to read shadows; we know to ignore them. The camera, on the other hand, reproduces them faithfully. You'll probably have better luck if it's overcast; the light will be consistent. I'd try a few shots without the flash, and a few with."

"The flash?"

The photographer produced a metal trough of the type that Dubon had seen the police officer use to take the pictures of Rivaud's body and began to explain how the powder was lit. Dubon didn't like the idea; the flash of light might alert someone outside to his presence, and the trough seemed cumbersome.

"Do I have to use it?"

"Well, not if you've got a tripod; then the camera is so steady you can risk a long exposure. In fact, if you are shooting a document, that's probably your best route."

The photographer produced his tripod; Dubon paused when he saw the size of the thing. How was he going to be able to sneak all this equipment into the Statistical Section the following day without someone noticing? But the photographer also produced a leather suitcase; inside, it was cleverly outfitted with a series of straps to anchor the camera, the flash, and the tripod, which collapsed down to a quarter of its full height. It wasn't a bad size. If anyone asked, he could say he was on his way to visit a cousin in the country right after work.

No one was about when he arrived at the Statistical Section and slipped the heavy case under his desk. Peeking down the corridor, Dubon saw that the doors to both Gingras's and Hermann's offices were open, and he sat there in an agony of uncertainty, wondering whether he could risk going into Picquart's office, shutting the door, and getting to work. He was still debating the wisdom of this move when Major Henry pushed through the front door and marched past Dubon's desk on his way into the colonel's office.

Dubon sprang to his feet and offered a salute. "I wasn't expecting you this morning, Major."

"Just thought I would pop in and sort a few things out now that the colonel has gone," Henry said as he passed.

About ten minutes later he called for Gingras and questioned him about various files. The conversation seemed of little consequence, but Gingras kept repeating "Yes, Major," in a tone so obsequious that Dubon was surprised Henry had not found him guilty of insubordination.

A few minutes after Gingras left, Henry called in Hermann for the same kind of talk, before finally summoning Dubon. The major was sitting behind his desk with his beefy arms stretched across its width and a satisfied expression on his face. He tapped the fingers of each hand lightly on the desk surface as though he were exploring the boundaries of his new territory. He had come in that morning only for the pleasure of feeling his new authority, Dubon realized.

"I am told you are leaving us, Captain."

"Regrettably so, Major. Recalled to headquarters on Monday."

"They need you in intelligence, do they? Got some hot work they need to set you on right away?"

"Apparently so, Major."

"The colonel tells me I have to do all the bloody paperwork again, is that right? Ask for a replacement for you?"

"Yes, Major. The rue Saint-Dominique requires an entirely new request for a temporary clerk."

"Perhaps they will even send us a permanent clerk this time."

"Yes, Major. I have done my best to understand the operation, but you really need a permanent person who you can spend some time training."

Henry bristled. "Are you suggesting we didn't train you, Captain?"

"Not at all, Major. You and the colonel were most helpful."

Henry peered at him as though he detected sarcasm.

"We shouldn't have that much trouble replacing you," he said with a dismissive wave of his hand.

"Major." Dubon saluted and left the room.

The major left the office a short time later, having spent less than an hour there. As soon as he was gone, Gingras emerged and said exactly what Dubon had been thinking.

"So, the major just popped in to remind us all that he is now boss before he goes home to a good lunch. What happened to the colonel, do you figure, Dubon? You were getting very chummy with him. Did he tell you what was going on at headquarters?"

"Only that he was needed for some special mission in Algeria."

Gingras snorted. "Special mission in Algeria. How convenient these colonial enterprises are. I suspect that the colonel has been asking awkward questions about the Dreyfus file, and nobody on the rue Saint-Dominique wants to hear them. The captain was found guilty and he's going to stay that way."

"But what if he isn't guilty? What if he didn't do it?" Dubon asked.

"That's dangerous talk, Dubon. It has become increasingly important that he remain guilty. France's honor demands it." Gingras said these last words with some note of irony. "The major understands that. He will protect the Statistical Section. He will protect the military and he will protect France."

"And who will protect us from the real spy?" Dubon asked.

"I don't know but I'll tell you one thing; if there is another spy, he will be dealt with a lot more quietly than the captain was. The higher-ups can't stand the way this has got into the press. I don't know if you have been reading *Le Figaro* or *Le Soleil* lately . . ."

Gingras was in one of his talkative moods and now seemed prepared to spend the rest of the morning gossiping. Unusually, the taciturn Hermann emerged from his office too and joined them, listening intently as Gingras speculated on the reasons for Picquart's sudden removal. There was something of a holiday atmosphere in the absence of both the colonel and the major, and Gingras grew increasingly boisterous, offering more and more outlandish suggestions.

"I hear the Socialists have hooked up with the captain's family," he said, as Dubon wondered if he was trying to goad Hermann into some kind of response. "Maybe Picquart is in their camp and was leaking information to them to launch an appeal."

"No," Hermann replied in a disapproving tone. "The colonel would never do that."

"How do you know, Hermann? I mean, it's clear he doesn't believe in Dreyfus's guilt anymore."

"The evidence at the court martial was conclusive," Hermann replied quietly but emphatically. "Dreyfus is guilty. Speculation otherwise is unwise."

"Conclusive! Don't you read the papers, Hermann? They are full of speculation. Did you read *La Presse*—"

"It's all just talk," Hermann interrupted him, showing an uncharacteristic bit of choler. "It will pass. The dogs bark but the caravan moves on."

The old proverb echoed in Dubon's ears. It was the same one Masson had used. *The dogs bark and the caravan passes.* And the same argument, for that matter. Masson had said Dreyfus was guilty; the evidence was definitive. This would all blow over. He had repeated it at the art gallery on Sunday. How could Masson be so sure? And how could a low-level officer like Hermann, who reported only to Picquart, know anything about it at all? Just how far did this shadowy world of counterintelligence extend?

Dubon had to get into Picquart's office, photograph the bordereau and get out of this hall of mirrors. Gingras was still prattling. Would he never stop? Eventually, although it was not yet eleven, Gingras suggested he'd lock up and the three of them would go for lunch. Hermann begged off, as did Dubon. Since nobody had seen his suitcase under his desk, he now invented a demanding wife waiting with his Saturday dinner.

"All right. On my own, I guess," said Gingras. "I'll go over to the mess on the rue Saint-Dominique and see if I can scare up some better company." He laughed and tossed the keys to the section's front door up in the air and caught them again.

Dubon felt his stomach turning with anxiety; Gingras was about to usher them all out of the office. As the three men moved toward the front door, his gastrointestinal distress provided inspiration and, clutching at his stomach, he said, "I just have to go to the wc before we leave." He hurried down the corridor.

Out of sight of both Gingras and Hermann, he passed the darkroom and opened the door of the wc. He picked up the wooden ruler that was sitting in the same place beneath the sink and slid it into the panel that he had opened before. The outside door sprang open and Dubon looked back around the small room. There was nothing on the washstand that might help, but behind the radiator he noticed a short plank of wood, probably used as a doorstop. He pulled it out and jammed it in place. The door held. He left the water closet and hurried down the corridor to rejoin Gingras and Hermann, his stomach troubles forgotten.

Hermann looked at him oddly. "I told you never to use that closet," he said under his breath, as Gingras led them out the door.

FORTY-ONE

It took Dubon another half an hour to get rid of Gingras, who insisted it was not yet lunchtime and the two could surely share a good-bye drink in the café next door to the section before Dubon had to get home to his wife.

Inside the café, Dubon found himself in a quandary. He was sitting exactly where he needed to be to make his next move—to the toilets at the back of the establishment and then out into the alley and back into the Statistical Section through the door he had propped open. But he couldn't go until Gingras did, and the man seemed to have no inclination to leave. Finally, Dubon pulled out his watch and made noises preparatory to departure, saying he hoped he and Gingras would cross paths again.

"Sure to," said Gingras. "Surprised I didn't know you already. I know most of the other fellows in intelligence."

"I have to run. Saturday lunch. Sacrosanct, you know."

"I'll come with you. Which direction are you walking?"

Dubon indicated his usual path toward the quai d'Orsay, knowing it was the opposite direction from the one Gingras would take to reach the rue Saint-Dominique mess, and after they had paid the bill and emerged on the street, with great relief he parted company from his sometime colleague.

Dubon walked slowly up the rue de Bellechasse, away from the rue Saint-Dominique and toward the river, looking back occasionally to see if Gingras was still in sight. When the other man finally disappeared from view, Dubon retraced his steps to the café, and as the barman looked up at him, waved a vague hand toward the toilets, indicating he had forgotten to relieve himself. There was no one in the back corridor of the café, and he slipped easily out into the alleyway. At the top of the fire escape, his doorstop was still in place; he pushed open the door, kicked the plank of wood ahead of him, and stepped back into the wc. He closed the panel behind him and then pushed the real door open, sticking his head out into the corridor before he moved forward. There was no sound of anyone about. Dubon took a deep breath to steady himself and walked firmly down the corridor to his desk. He pulled out the leather suitcase, carried it into Picquart's office, and shut the door.

Picquart had always pulled the captain's files from the first drawer in his filing cabinet. Dubon tried the drawer, praying Henry had not already discovered it and locked it, but it was open, and Dubon found what he was looking for soon enough: the document in which an officer offered his correspondent various military documents.

Arranging the sheet on the desk in the path of what light was coming through the window was simple enough; remembering how to unfold the tripod was another matter, and it took several minutes of fussing before Dubon had it in place. He mounted the camera on it and tried to calm himself enough to remember what the photographer had said about apertures and exposure times—one let more light in, the other less, or something like that. He settled on a combination and depressed the shutter, and then made a second attempt with a longer exposure, before he realized he had not even loaded film into the camera.

He got one of the metal plates out of the case, slipped it into the camera as the photographer had shown him and began again, remembering now to reload film each time he depressed the shutter. In the end, he tried every combination of apertures and exposure times he could think of and, finally, he pulled out the flash. It was the last thing he would attempt. The windows in the building across the street were at the same level and he did not want to draw attention to himself with a burst of light. Certainly, the flash Dubon had seen the police photographer use was startling in its intensity.

Dubon pulled a small packet out of the suitcase and ripped it open with his teeth. He placed the trough on the desk and poured the powder into it, careful not to spill a grain. The photographer had warned him that once he had lit the powder, he had about one second before the flash would erupt. He had to be ready for it and depress the shutter in time. To make the job easier, the photographer had given him a cord that attached to the camera so that you didn't have to lean over it to depress the shutter.

Dubon tested the pose: left hand with the trough of powder held aloft; right hand with the shutter cord. He put the trough back down on the desk and let the cord dangle while he readied his light. He lit the powder, grabbed the cord, and raised the trough above the desk just as the flash went off. Stunned, he missed his opportunity altogether; by the time he was ready to press the shutter button, the flash was over.

He would try again, but first he had to get rid of the used powder. He needed a bag—or an envelope. He opened the middle drawer of Picquart's desk. It was empty, save for some paper clips. He tried the other drawers and found them bare but for a few scraps of paper. The colonel had cleaned things out. Dubon returned to his own desk, pulled out a document envelope, and returned to Picquart's office. He disposed of the powder and then opened a new packet to fill the trough again. This time, he was ready for the flash and managed to depress the shutter just as it illuminated the room.

There was a third packet of powder in the suitcase, and he used that, too, before he set about cleaning up. He wasn't sure how to get some spilled powder off the floor and finally resorted to licking his finger, daubing at it and then wiping his finger off on his handkerchief. Inevitably, he tasted some of the stuff; it had a bitter, metallic flavor. Probably deadly poisonous, Dubon thought to himself as he put his envelope of used powder away in the suitcase. Now that he had made his best efforts to photograph the bordereau and still had several unexposed film cases left, he could not pass up the opportunity to photograph the secret file too. It would not do the captain much good if it were published as it was; indeed, with Rivaud's improvements it was incriminating, but photographs of it might help him prove its very existence. He turned back to the top drawer of the filing cabinet but couldn't see the file. He hunted through the entire top drawer, file by file, and then turned to the other drawers, but couldn't find anything.

Perhaps Picquart had removed the secret file on orders. Perhaps it was now in Henry's possession. At any rate, it was gone.

Just as he started to pack the camera back into the photographer's suitcase, he heard the sound of the front door opening. Panicking, Dubon threw the tripod into the suitcase. Without bothering to strap anything down or lock the case, he tucked it under his arm and bolted down the corridor beyond Picquart's office, slipping into the first door he came to. He was back inside the darkroom and would have laughed at the irony of it if his heart had not been pounding in his chest.

"Is someone there?"

It was Major Henry. He had heard the darkroom door close. Dubon paused, holding his breath in the dark and hoping Henry would assume it was just a door banging by itself and give up. But the major seemed to know where he had heard the sound, for a moment later he knocked on the darkroom door.

"Is someone in there?"

"It's Captain Dubon, Major. Don't open the door!"

"Why not?"

"I am . . . I am developing film, Major," said Dubon, improvising madly. "You'll expose it if you open the door."

"Film of what?"

"Well. Well, of, of documents, of course, Major."

"What documents? You're photographing documents?"

"Yes, Major. That's my job, Major. Standard procedure on the rue Saint-Dominique. Photograph every new document that comes in. I thought before I leave the section, I had better finish up all the recent stuff and develop the film for you."

There was a pause. "I see," said the major. "You have photographed all the files that have come in during the month you have been here, is that right?"

"Yes, Major. Just finishing up. May take me a bit to do the developing, though. Have to work in the dark, you know." Surely, he would not stand outside the door forever.

"Don't bother with the developing, Captain. Just leave the film with me. The next fellow can do it. I'll take care of it."

I bet you will, thought Dubon.

"Very well," he answered. "I'll just have to slip them all back into their covers. May take me a few moments here. There are a fair number. Don't want to inadvertently expose anything."

There was a pause. Dubon could hear the major's heavy breathing through the door.

"Is this going to take long, Captain?" he asked after a few minutes. "I do have some other business to attend to."

"You have to appreciate, Major, the work must be done entirely in the dark. Perhaps if you have work you need to do, you can give me a few moments here, and I'll come and get you when it's safe to turn the light on."

"Very well. Come and see me as soon as you are done."

Dubon waited until the footsteps had retreated and turned on the light. He took his last four unused metal cases out of the suitcase and put them in a pile before rifling through the drawers of the darkroom and scrounging up another dozen cases, as well as a leather pouch of a similar size. He thought about the situation for a moment and then snapped off the light. He reached his hand into the pouch to pull out a thin stack of film before carefully closing it again. Then he turned the light back on and started quickly loading a piece of film into each metal case. All the film would be exposed, worthless and foggy if anyone tried to develop it, but at least Dubon would not be presenting Henry with empty cases. He suspected that Henry would open each one to the light anyway, destroying every image in case any of them included his handiwork.

Dubon put the plates on the countertop, packed up the suitcase, and listened carefully for any sound of Henry. As quietly as he could, he opened the door to the darkroom and, taking his precious suitcase with him, slipped into the water closet next door. His arms were full and grasping the door handle was awkward. He missed it, and the door made a *smack* as it swung shut.

Dubon heard rapid footsteps coming down the corridor.

The door was yanked open and the major stood there full of aggression.

"Just what exactly, Dubon, is your business?"

FORTY-TWO

"Just the usual business, Major," Dubon replied as calmly as he could, buttoning up his fly and leaning over to pull the toilet chain. "I'll get you those plates. Be careful with them, won't you? No light, right?" He slipped by the major's bulk before the man had time to ask more questions and opened the darkroom door again.

"Here you go. That's the lot. Three weeks' work."

"Good. Thank you, Captain."

"Thank you, Major. May I say what an honor it has been to work for you. I regret having to leave so soon. I do hope they send you—"

"Yes, yes, Captain. Off you go."

The major saw him out the front door and watched as he started down the stairs.

"Good-bye, Major."

"Good day to you, Captain."

Out on the street, Dubon did not wait. The major had come in the front door, but if for any reason he chose to leave through the water closet, Dubon was sunk. He hurried into the café and slunk past the barman and out the back door. From the ground, he could see the photographer's suitcase was still where he had left it, perched up on the fire escape outside the water closet door. He climbed the iron staircase as swiftly and silently as he could, reclaimed the case, and descended. Carrying his suitcase, he left the café as rapidly as he had arrived, glad to be gone. For good or for ill, he was done. His brief career as Captain François Dubon, temporary file clerk in the Statistical Section of the Administrative Bureau of the French Army, had now come to an end.

He made his way toward the river and gratefully hailed a passing hansom as he got to the bridge. Less than an hour later, he was inside *La Presse*'s darkroom.

"Uh...uh...uh...uh..." The photographer uttered a little series of encouraging sounds as though teasing images out of the pans of chemicals.

Looking over his shoulder, Dubon, his nerves finally settling, could barely contain himself. "Did I get it? Can you see it?"

"Ahh...there we go...yes, yes, looks nice and sharp. Congratulations, Monsieur Dubon. Perhaps you should consider a new career."

Dubon leaned forward eagerly to see the image appearing. "It doesn't look like much. Are you sure it's clear?"

"Just wait until we've fixed it and can turn the light on," the photographer replied. "Then we'll see what we've got."

Dubon was alone with him in the darkroom because Le Goff had no desire to be seen coming in and out of *La Presse*'s offices any more than necessary. Assuming he had the goods, Dubon was to meet Le Goff at his own office by three.

The photographer transferred the photo to another bath and after a few minutes announced, "You can turn on the light."

Dubon found the switch and the orange glow of the darkroom light was replaced with the full power of a regular electric bulb.

"Damn." The photographer prodded the image with a pair of tongs.

"What is it?"

"Did you use the tripod?"

"Yes, yes. I used the tripod. What is it?"

"It's fuzzy. Something must have moved. I didn't notice it on the negative, it's so subtle. It's much worse at the bottom than at the top. Maybe there were air currents in the room wafting the paper. Or vibration? Any trains nearby?"

"Don't think so. There's construction on the quay. Is it usable?"

The photographer squinted at the image. "You are trying to identify the hand, is that right?"

"Yes."

"Well, the first few lines are clear, so you have a good sample of the handwriting, but you can't read the bottom half. Monsieur Martin will have to talk to the boys upstairs, I guess."

"Monsieur Martin?"

"Our correspondent."

"Oh yes, of course," Dubon said, realizing he was referring to Le Goff's nom de plume.

"I wonder if there isn't anything better here," said the photographer, going back to the parade of negatives that hung on a washing line farther down the room. He got out a little magnifying glass, like a jeweler's glass, and peered at them one by one. Earlier, when Dubon had looked at them he found it impossible to read these images in which dark was light and light was dark, but he was beginning to understand the process.

"Ah yes, you've done it. Good man," the photographer said.

"What is it?"

"The ones you took with the flash. There are two images here; your shutter speed was so much faster, it didn't have time to register whatever it was that was vibrating the paper. Let's give these a try."

Dubon sneaked a look at his pocket watch. He would soon be late for Le Goff.

By the time the photographer handed him a dry print, twenty minutes later, he had no time to admire it, only to register that he did indeed have a legible copy of the bordereau and stick it in an envelope. He approached the washing line and began to unclip the negatives.

"Hey there, what are you doing?" the photographer demanded.

"I'm sorry but this material is highly sensitive. Monsieur Martin will return to the paper soon with his copy of the document, the one that will be printed. But I have to take all other copies."

"But I'll need the negatives to make another print tomorrow if we are going to publish Monday."

"What's wrong with this print?" Dubon asked, indicating the envelope.

"Well, it's fine, but I'll tinker some more to get a better contrast."

"You can tinker tomorrow. Martin or I will bring the negatives back to you then. I am releasing the image to the paper for one purpose and one purpose only, and that is to print on the front page of Monday's paper."

"By the time they print it on the front page of Monday's paper there will be thousands of copies throughout France," the photographer pointed out.

Now there was a wonderful idea, Dubon thought to himself as he tucked the negatives into the envelope with the print.

He hurried back to his office and found Le Goff waiting outside the locked door.

"I've got it," said Dubon, flourishing the envelope.

They went inside and settled at Dubon's desk as he pulled out the one good print.

"Thank goodness for that flash, in the end. I was very nervous using it, thought I might set fire to the place, and then where would I be?"

Dubon's excitement was making him voluble, but Le Goff wasn't listening. He was poring over the document.

"So, as you described it, a sample of wares," he said, looking up.

"Yes."

"I tell you one thing. I don't think an artillery officer wrote this."

"Why not?"

"Look at this phrase. The author offers information on how the new 120 behaves."

"Yes?"

"A gun doesn't 'behave.' At least that's not what a gunner would say. He would simply say how the gun works."

"It's a small difference."

"Still, the lingo is wrong."

"When the army went hunting for the author of the bordereau, they looked only in the artillery . . ."

Le Goff completed his thought for him: ". . . so, they didn't find the right man."

Le Goff and Dubon then turned to a discussion of Monday's publication, debating how the paper should play the document.

"I make no promises, Dubon," Le Goff said. "My editors always have their own ideas."

There was a quiet knock at the office's exterior door. Both men stopped and looked at each other. Le Goff quickly slipped the bordereau back into the envelope while Dubon, reminding himself he had every right to be in his own office, crossed to the outer door and opened it.

The captain's wife stood there. She looked as though she had spent the week in tears.

He ushered her gently into the inner room and hesitantly introduced her to Le Goff.

"Madame, may I present Captain Le Goff," he said. "Captain, this is, er, this is Madame Duhamel." No need to tell Le Goff the real identity of his client.

"I'm so sorry to interrupt you, Maître."

"Not at all, Madame. Le Goff was just leaving." Dubon picked up the envelope off his desk and handed it to Le Goff, who smirked in amusement at his haste.

"So we are agreed at least on what we would like your editors to say, yes?" Dubon said as he shepherded him back to the outer office. "The negatives are in here too. The photographer wants to make a better print, but I told him I want them back, all prints and the negatives. We don't want anyone else to have the opportunity to publish, eh?"

"All right. You'll be here next week?"

"Yes, back at my post, finally."

"I'll be in touch, end of day Tuesday, I imagine, if not before." He leaned around Dubon and called back to the captain's wife, "Good afternoon, Madame."

She inclined her head politely.

After Le Goff left, Dubon said to her, in an attempt to dismiss the subject quickly, "Captain Le Goff is in the artillery but he sometimes supplies military news to *La Presse*."

"You mean he's Azimut Martin?" She seemed to perk up at this news.

"Yes, that's right, but just forget that, won't you?" Dubon said, belatedly realizing he should have introduced Le Goff only by his alias. "Better for both of you that you not know each other. I have a lot to tell you," he continued, but paused as he looked at her face.

"What is wrong, Madame? You look unhappy."

"I had news of the captain this week. He is now kept shackled at night."

"Shackled? Didn't they say he was always shackled? When there were those reports about his escape, a month ago . . ."

"Yes, the government's reply was that he was kept in a walled compound and shackled at night. It wasn't really true. He could see the sea from his prison, and he wasn't ever shackled. Anyway, I found out this week, they made it true retroactively. Since the reports a wall has been built, and he is now shackled to his cot at night. He can't get comfortable; he's barely sleeping. Maître, he has been prone to despair from the start; I fear for his sanity, I really do."

"He won't be there much longer, Madame, I promise you. I am glad you are here so I can warn you what to expect on Monday. You are in for a surprise."

"You have found the spy?"

"Not quite, but let me explain. I have got a copy of the bordereau, the original evidence against the captain. I have a good photograph of it, and the promise from our Azimut Martin that the paper will publish it Monday morning. Our idea is that widespread publication of the handwriting will bring forward someone who can identify the true spy in time for the appeal."

"That's wonderful, Maître."

"Yes. It is wonderful, although you should prepare yourself. I imagine there will be quite a reaction on Monday, some backlash. You can't have enjoyed the publication of the . . . that is . . . that letter." Dubon felt awkward repeating a word as foul as *bastard* in front of a lady. "Even if it did give you grounds for the appeal."

"There have been difficult moments."

"I should tell you, Madame, that we also now have clear evidence that the second letter, the one that named the captain, is a forgery, which in turn throws suspicion on the veracity of the first one."

She nodded, seeming to take this news for granted.

"You aren't surprised?"

"Well, no. Any letter that names the captain as a spy is a fabrication. It seems there was a conspiracy against him from the start."

"No, Madame. I think perhaps it's worse than that. At first, there was just a stupid mistake made out of laziness, prejudice, and convenience. But in the intervening years, the military has broken more and more laws to avoid ever admitting it, and now a conspiracy has blossomed."

"Will Monsieur Martin expose the forgery, too?"

"One step at a time, Madame. We don't want to tip our hand. We find the real spy and we should be able to ensure the captain is granted an appeal. He gets another trial and, if the prosecution is dim enough to introduce the forged letter, we discredit it then. We have to wait for the new trial."

"The captain cannot wait any longer, Maître," she said, her voice growing strained.

He moved closer to her and brushed a hand across her cheek, then quickly let it drop.

"Madame, you have been exceedingly patient, but it is only six weeks since you first came to me. Let's see what happens next week. I have finished my little stint of fancy dress, you know, and now that I am back at my regular desk my schedule is my own. Perhaps you could come and see me some morning. I will send you a message as soon as I hear any news. And I must return that uniform to you," he said, gesturing down at the pants he was still wearing. "I would do so now, but I would like to have it cleaned first." In fact, Dubon had rent the tunic under both arms and wanted to have the tears repaired before he gave it back to her.

"There's no hurry about the uniform, Maître."

"Still, I should return it. And I'll send you a message as soon as we catch our spy."

As he packed up after she had left, he realized he was exhausted. He looked at his watch and was surprised to find it was not yet five. He felt as though he had crossed continents and moved mountains today, yet he would still be home in plenty of time for dinner. Geneviève would be pleased. Or perhaps not. He had sent her a message the previous afternoon telling her not to expect him home for dinner that night or any meal on Saturday. Maybe he should just drop the uniform off at a tailor's establishment on the rue de Rivoli on the way home so he could pick it up again the following week. He certainly did not want to ask Luc to repair it.

He crossed to the coatrack in the outer office to get his own pants, taking the tunic off the hanger and buttoning it up before slipping it into the canvas bag in which the captain's wife had brought it. As he did so, he idly tweaked at the tailor's label sewn on the inside under the collar. Beneath it was a faded tag and if he looked closely he could just make out the name of the uniform's owner: Dreyfus.

FORTY-THREE

"I can't believe you read that rag."

Geneviève was looking up from her preferred daily—which was, in Dubon's opinion, one of the more offensive of the Catholic papers—and frowning down the breakfast table at his copy of *La Presse*.

"Why do you call it a rag?" he asked innocently. The bordereau was splashed all over the front page; the headline was exactly what he would have chosen. "The hand of a spy: do you know this writing?" And then underneath: "Doubts cast on guilt of Captain Dreyfus. The editors of *La Presse* invite the public to identify true author of document that sent unfortunate officer to Devil's Island."

"Look at it. It's irresponsible, inflaming the public like that. It just invites disorder. The army knows what it is doing; we have to trust the high command when they tell us they have the right man."

"Perhaps, my dear, but there really is compelling evidence to the contrary." They had not spoken about his work on the Dreyfus case since the night of the dinner party, when he had held his ground and insisted he would not give it up. Geneviève was ready for a second assault. "Besides which," Dubon added mildly, "the man, guilty or innocent, never got a fair trial."

"Well, really, François, he's a Jew."

"And what," Dubon asked, trying to keep his tone calm, "is wrong with that?"

"Nothing, nothing, but these people ... Would you accord him the same rights as a Frenchman?"

"That is a very dangerous argument, and one not worthy of your intellect. What is worth defending about France? Red wine? Sunday lunch? The Napoleonic Code? Liberty, equality, and fraternity? Surely one thing worth fighting for is the notion that all citizens are equal before the law."

"But in a case such as this, when the very security of the nation is at stake," Geneviève interrupted him with passion, "the army must be allowed some latitude in dealing with a spy."

"He hasn't been proven to be a spy. And until he has been given a fair trial, he has the same right to the presumption of innocence—"

"You underestimate what damage this case is doing to the military, François. What is the life of one man, in the end, when the safety of all France is at stake?"

"Ah, now you are starting to argue like a German," he said. "He's probably guilty, and even if he isn't, the honor of our military is too important for us ever to admit we might have made a mistake."

"You forget my family has served France—"

"Yes, Geneviève, your family has served France honorably." His tone was conciliatory, but he couldn't help noting sadly that she sided with her family's view of the matter rather than his.

"However," he continued, "the men who consigned the captain to Devil's Island on evidence that was both circumstantial and withheld from his defense are not honorable. And their inability to admit to their mistakes and rectify the situation makes them more dishonorable. Thank goodness the press is pursuing them."

"Don't think I don't know those newspaper stories have something to do with you," she replied fiercely.

"My dear, I—"

"Don't tell me," she said, raising her hand to silence him. "I don't want to know. I have warned you, you can't say anything about this to our friends. They'll cut us dead if they believe you are now siding with these ghastly Dreyfusards. And don't you dare say anything about it to my family."

"What's he not supposed to say to your family?"

Jean-Jean appeared at the dining room door and took a place at the table. He was to be in town all week, checking in with headquarters. Something about this new assignment they kept promising him, Dubon supposed.

"Nothing, dear. Did you sleep well?" Geneviève said to him in a motherly tone designed to close the previous conversation.

Dubon refused to be so easily silenced.

"She doesn't want me to discuss the Dreyfus case with you—or anyone else."

"Oh. Why not? Anything new?"

"This." Dubon handed him *La Presse*, despite a glare from his wife.

Jean-Jean began to read intently, barely glancing up as Luc poured him coffee.

After a while, he looked back at Dubon.

"This is the evidence?"

"That's it."

"Oh" was all Jean-Jean replied, before putting his head back down. He frowned and sighed as he read but said nothing more.

Geneviève decided it was best to ignore the situation, and, after announcing she had letters to write, left the room, while Dubon set out on his walk to the office, wondering when it was that Jean-Jean had become so interested in Dreyfus.

There was no word from Le Goff and after a day spent catching up on other business, Dubon returned to find that Jean-Jean was still sitting at the dining room table as though he hadn't moved all day. He was just passing by the room on his way to his study to get a book when he noticed his brother-in-law and stopped in, thinking it a rather odd place for him to be stationed.

"You look like you haven't moved since breakfast."

"What? Oh. No, I went out for a bit this morning, I think. Yes, this morning, after breakfast. Or maybe it was after lunch."

"Didn't you have to stop in at headquarters today?"

"I am supposed to go in tomorrow, I think. Tuesday. Tomorrow's Tuesday, isn't it? Or maybe it's Wednesday I go in. Wednesday would be better." He sounded confused and looked unpleasantly pale.

"Why don't you come out of the dining room, Jean-Jean," Dubon said gently. "Luc needs to get in to set the table for dinner. Geneviève must be in the salon by now. Come and keep us company."

"I guess I'll just go to my room for a while."

"We'll call you for dinner. You'll want dinner? You aren't feeling sick, are you?"

"No, no. I'm not sick," Jean-Jean said in the same vacant tone. "At least, no more so than everyone else in the world."

Dubon puzzled over this new philosophical streak as he followed Jean-Jean to his study to get his book. He then left his distracted brother-in-law and went to find Geneviève.

"What on earth is wrong with your brother?"

"I have no idea; I haven't seen him all day. Is he home now?"

"Yes, I found him in the dining room, just staring into space. He seems completely distracted."

"Well, I imagine he's worried about this new assignment, whatever it is. All rather hush-hush. I do hope it's something good. He has certainly earned a promotion."

"Hmm, no doubt." Dubon sounded unconvinced, and Geneviève, on the alert for perceived slights to her family since their recent disagreements, persisted.

"He does deserve a great career, you know. He is really clever about artillery and he should be allowed to use his talents. Because he is shy, people underestimate him. He looks up to you, you know, thinks you are a man of the world, but you never take him seriously."

"I don't know if that's fair, dear. I am fond of him and, of course, he's highly intelligent in his way," Dubon responded. "It's just that he can be so awkward sometimes. The state he is in currently, you are going to have to remind him when it's Wednesday."

"Fine," Geneviève replied curtly. "I will remind him to go to his meeting. He may be upset about his new assignment, but at least I can trust *he* isn't up to something silly."

Dubon bit his lip and said nothing.

By the following day, however, Jean-Jean's absentmindedness seemed to have cleared and he appeared for all three meals, although he remained monosyllabic.

The bordereau was the talk of the town, but there was no word from any quarter as to who its author might be. Le Goff sent a telegram to Dubon's office and it said only, "Powerful reaction to your best work. No further news at present."

That afternoon, Dubon approached Madeleine's door with an unusual sense of trepidation. It had been a week since he had walked away and, distracted by developments in the Statistical Section, he had waited several days before sending a bouquet to her address with the suggestion he return that Tuesday. Though he had never had a disagreement with Madeleine before, his experience with Geneviève had taught him it was best not to dwell on who was in the wrong but simply to express regret and move on. Madeleine had replied by telegram that she looked forward to his visit, but she was uncharacteristically subdued when she answered his knock.

"Thank you for the flowers," she said without much enthusiasm, gesturing toward a bouquet of red roses sitting on a small table.

"You are very welcome."

"Would you like a glass of wine?"

"Please."

She pulled out one of the bottles he kept there and watched while he uncorked it.

Their conversation proceeded in this stilted manner as though they were newly introduced strangers trying to find something to say, but when they moved to the bedroom, their new tentativeness struck Dubon as touching. As he rose from her bed, he leaned over and gently ran his hand down her cheek.

"Shall I come again tomorrow?" he asked.

"If you like."

"I finished my undercover assignment, so no more disruptions."

"You will be here every day?"

He had thought she would welcome the news, but her tone sounded anxious.

"Does that not suit you?"

"I have an engagement Friday."

"Really, with whom?"

"With Claudine. I thought I was safe to see her Friday afternoon."

"Of course, of course, my dear. You make whatever arrangements you like. I'll come again tomorrow and Thursday, then. And perhaps I'll even manage Saturday this week. You'll be home in the morning?"

"Yes, Saturday is fine, just not Friday. And not next Monday, I don't think. I have made some plans . . ."

"So, let me get this straight. You will be at home Thursday and Saturday, but not Friday or Monday." Dubon's tone was slightly arch— he was still footing the bill, after all—but his heart sank. Clearly, his fears about some handsome young man were not out of place.

Wednesday brought more developments in the press and Dubon came in to breakfast to find Geneviève looking triumphant.

"Read this," she said, holding out her newspaper.

Dubon began reading. Increasingly, questions were being asked in the National Assembly about the Dreyfus case, and on Tuesday the minister of war, Godefroy Cavaignac, had risen to reply to them, affirming the government's position that the captain was rightly condemned. He cited overwhelming proof, including a letter that he read out to the deputies in which a foreign diplomat, whom he carefully did not name, warned a colleague that no one must know of their contacts with Dreyfus. It was the Italian's letter, Dubon thought. Cavaignac stood by this evidence and the assembly voted overwhelming in favor of his right as a deputy to *affichage:* his speech was to be posted in every commune in the country.

Dubon nearly laughed out loud. So that was why Picquart had been banished so swiftly. The rue Saint-Dominique had already passed on the Italian letter to their minister and weren't going to have any-one question its authenticity. Now, in his ignorance, Cavaignac had made public a document that Dubon could show was a forgery. The case against Dreyfus was doomed. What would happen to Major Henry when his superiors realized their loyal soldier had exposed them to accusations of fraud?

He smiled as he put down the paper. Geneviève glared back at him, expecting more contrition on his part, but instead Dubon said, "Dreyfus has won, my dear. He's won."

FORTY-FOUR

"We've got him!"

It was Le Goff, bursting into Dubon's office on Friday morning.

"You can come with me. He can see us this morning; he's at his office now."

Dubon had yet to see Le Goff so gleeful about the case.

"Who are you talking about?"

"A stockbroker by the name of Castro."

"He's the spy?"

"No, no. He has identified the handwriting. Belongs to a client of his. He sent the paper a message yesterday. He said he would be in his office this morning and was happy to speak with a correspondent from *La Presse*. We have to go now, Dubon; we don't want to miss him."

Le Goff, he noticed, was in civilian dress.

"You'll be posing as a journalist?"

"I will be myself, Azimut Martin," he said with gusto. "You can be a news photographer."

"I don't have a camera."

"You won't need one. He's not going to want his picture taken."

"What newspaper photographer would go out without a camera?"

"Can't you just bring some old suitcase or something and pretend it's got your camera in it?" Le Goff replied, looking about the room.

"No. What if he agrees to a photo—*the man who identified the spy!*—he might want the publicity. We'd better stop at the paper and see if your photographer can lend me his kit again."

"All right, but hurry up."

They took a cab back to *La Presse* and while Le Goff paid the driver off and waited in the street, Dubon went inside and found the same photographer poking away in his darkroom. The fellow agreed to the loan without hesitation; he had been impressed by the reaction the previous assignment had garnered.

"More documents?"

"Maybe a person," Dubon replied.

"Trickier, trickier. People move, you know," the photographer said, and he proceeded to issue a few pointers.

The rue du Croissant, the street where much of the Parisian press had its offices, was right in the heart of the financial district, just to the east of the stock exchange in the place de la Bourse. With the heavy camera case in hand, Dubon followed Le Goff as they made their way on foot to the stockbroker's office. A small man with thinning hair and a nervous demeanor, he reacted with some alarm when Le Goff introduced Dubon as a news photographer.

"Oh, I don't want my picture taken. I don't want you to use my name at all. I'll just tell you what I know."

"Not to worry. Old Bernard will just sit in a corner while we talk," Le Goff replied amiably.

Amused at his new pseudonym, Dubon put down the camera case and sank into a chair at some distance from the stockbroker's desk.

"I recognized the handwriting right away, you know, but I didn't really want to get involved," the man began. "It was my wife who persuaded me. I was worried about it and she said if an innocent man had been condemned, I had a duty to speak up. And it's not as though I owe the chap any favors. He still owes me three thousand francs."

"What for?" Le Goff asked.

"Some stock trades. Highly speculative stuff," the man said.

He looked miserable, Dubon thought, completely unlike the few self-confident and prosperous brokers he knew. Maybe Castro wasn't much good at the job.

"I made the mistake of lending him the money to make the buy," Castro added, confirming the impression. "Should never have trusted him; he's not good for it. The stocks he bought plummeted. I'll never get my money back. I suppose that's why he was trying to peddle secrets to the Germans. Desperate for cash."

"And his name?"

"He always called himself Count Walsin-Esterhazy, but I doubt that he's really a count."

Esterhazy. It was the name of the Hungarian on the *petit bleu* that Dubon had seen in the Statistical Section.

"Esterhazy. I might have known it!" Le Goff exclaimed as soon as they were out on the street again.

"You know him?" Dubon was surprised.

"I saw him at a party last week, in fact. He's a notorious man about town. Little work and much play. You know the type. He was at that horrible ball too, the night young Fiteau shot himself."

"He was there?"

"Yes. I guess the general knows him. His wife's from an old family. But I think Castro is right and his own title is pure fabrication. Bastard descendant was what I always heard. Very remote connection to the great name."

"He's French?" Dubon asked. Le Goff was painting a very different picture from the faint outlines of some Hungarian nobleman that Dubon had created for himself when he had dismissed the *petit bleu* as unimportant. He had been damn lucky in the Statistical Section; his detecting skills were laughable.

"Oh yes. Born here, lived here all his life," Le Goff answered. "He's been hanging around the papers for years. Always trying to peddle something to somebody. *La Presse* won't use him. Says it doesn't pay for information, but I think some of the other papers have bought stuff from him."

"*La Presse* pays you for information," Dubon pointed out.

"I am a correspondent," Le Goff replied, drawing himself up. "I research my stuff and I write it up, or at least I make a stab at writing it up. Anyway, the papers aren't going to print anything they think is too sensitive—don't want to get in trouble with the government."

"Did Esterhazy have that kind of stuff?"

"Hard to know. The list he sent to Schwarzkoppen promised a lot, but who knows what he actually delivered. There was a firing manual. There are probably lots of copies of that floating around, but it might be very useful to the German artillery, if they don't know the French guns. He offered information on Madagascar—could be totally banal. Then he promised them a note on the 120; that's a new gun. I'm sure the Germans would love to know how it works, but I don't think Esterhazy was the man to tell them."

"Why not?"

"As I suspected, that document wasn't written by an artillery officer. Esterhazy's a staff officer. I would be surprised if he knew enough about the functioning of the gun to inform anybody about it. You should talk to your brother-in-law about that, though. He knows a lot more about the 120s than I do."

"Jean-Jean?"

"Yes."

There was a pause before Dubon asked what was on his mind.

"So, Le Goff, would you write up the kind of information that Esterhazy was selling for the paper?"

"Let's get this straight, Dubon. I make a little money on the side getting the army's point of view into print in ways that the generals might love to but can't. I know my stuff, but I am not selling secrets. Esterhazy is a traitor."

"Of course, of course. I wasn't implying anything. Just trying to get the lay of the land."

They walked in silence for a bit, Dubon lugging the heavy camera case. It had proved useful in the end because Castro had produced a sample of Esterhazy's hand, a letter written to him with various stock orders. It did indeed look like the same handwriting as in the bordereau and Le Goff had asked if Dubon could take a picture of it. The stockbroker had agreed, on the condition his own name and address were blacked out.

"But we can keep Esterhazy's signature?"

"Oh yes. As I say, I don't owe the scoundrel anything. He owes me."

Dubon had set up the camera again, trying to remember all the photographer's instructions. Now, under circumstances where the result mattered less and he didn't have that awful sensation that he was about to be caught trespassing, his sangfroid abandoned him and he fumbled badly with the tripod. Then he fussed and fiddled with the camera, unable to remember which button or dial was which. He finally managed to get some shots but didn't bother with the flash. He hoped the stockbroker knew nothing about photography but suspected his own amateur status was all too apparent.

Now, out on the street, he set the case down beside a bench.

"I have to stop a minute," he said to Le Goff.

"I'll carry it the rest of the way."

"Yes, you can carry it, but I'm going to rest for a minute first," Dubon replied, settling himself on bench.

Le Goff perched beside him, his posture betraying his haste. "I'll want to file by the end of the day if they are going to get this in tomorrow's paper, and it will take me all afternoon to work up my piece. I'm not a quick writer," he complained.

Dubon ignored him and sat looking at his shoes for a minute.

"There's something else," he eventually said, now voicing the thoughts he had had when the stockbroker first uttered the name. "I've heard of Esterhazy before . . . or at least, I have heard of *an* Esterhazy. It must be the same man."

Le Goff turned to look at him and slid a bit farther back onto the bench.

"It was during my first week in the Statistical Section. I had to clear the desk of all these bits of paper that the cleaning lady had brought in from the German embassy's wastepaper baskets, what those wags dubbed 'the usual route.' A lot of it is in pieces, you know, ripped down the middle like the bordereau. I pieced together a telegram from the military attaché Schwarzkoppen addressed to a Count Esterhazy. At the time, I thought nothing of it. Well, just that all these bits of paper were so insignificant. Here was a communication between the German embassy and some Hungarian, some business meeting or party or something. But now I wonder if that's not what alerted Picquart to the existence of the second spy."

"The second spy?"

"While I was there, there was talk of a second spy, that they had—to their embarrassment—uncovered yet another one. Dreyfus's accomplice, they thought. It would explain why Picquart opened up the captain's file again."

"And gradually realized..." Le Goff prompted him.

"...that there is only one spy—that Esterhazy is the man who wrote the bordereau, that Dreyfus is innocent, and that documents suggesting otherwise are forgeries."

"Picquart goes to headquarters with his suspicions..."

"...and discovers he is needed in Algeria," Dubon concluded bitterly.

"So, in the space of a few days, your colonel finds himself on a slow boat to Africa while Esterhazy is still honoring Parisian hostesses with his presence after, what...?"

"A month. The rue Saint-Dominique has known he's the real spy for at least a month. If the generals are planning to take any action, they are moving awfully slowly."

"Admitting to a second spy is bad enough," Le Goff said. "Admitting they not only have the wrong man but have let the real culprit go about his treacherous business for two years completely unmolested..."

"So they don't take any immediate action against Esterhazy and provide the minister of war with enough falsified evidence against Dreyfus that he will confidently stand up in the National Assembly and swear to the guilt of an innocent man!" Dubon's voice rose in outrage with these last words.

He got to his feet, his anger now fueling him. Grabbing the camera case, he started running down the street, lugging it awkwardly behind him.

"Come on, Le Goff. You've got to start writing."

FORTY-FIVE

Dubon dropped both the camera and Le Goff at the paper, leaving the secretive Azimut Martin to make a rare personal appearance to confer with his editors, while he hurried home for his lunch. When he arrived, no one was about, so he settled himself in the salon with a glass of wine, noting with some surprise that it was almost noon. After a few minutes, Luc appeared.

"Did Monsieur wish to dine?" he asked, a shade anxiously, as though an affirmative answer might come as an unwelcome surprise.

"Well, yes, eventually. I was hoping to," Dubon replied.

Luc simply nodded. Irony, Dubon had often noted, was completely lost on him.

"Where is Madame?" Dubon asked, suspecting his wife's whereabouts were the source of the problem. If Madame had been sitting in the salon, lunch would have been served immediately. "She is in the study, helping Captain de Ronchaud Valcourt with his packing."

"Oh, is he off today, already?"

"Yes, Maître. To Algeria."

"To Algeria!" Jean-Jean had never mentioned going abroad. "All right, Luc. I will see if I can extract Madame from the study so that we can have lunch."

Dubon entered his study to find Jean-Jean standing against the mantelpiece looking grim while Geneviève busied herself with the packing. There were two open trunks on the floor and heaps of clothes on the divan and all the chairs.

"Captain. Congratulations, I hear you have your new assignment. Algeria, is it? How exciting!"

"That's what I keep telling him," Geneviève said, looking up from one of the trunks. "It's a horrible rush, but I'm sure he'll have a great time when he gets there."

"When do you leave?"

"I take the train to Marseille tomorrow; I sail Monday."

Same boat as Picquart, Dubon thought to himself. Something wasn't right about Jean-Jean's posting.

"Was this the assignment you had been hoping for?"

"One goes where one is needed. I have my orders."

"Well, yes, Valcourt, but it's not the Church, for heaven's sake. You can at least tell us if it's not what you wanted."

"No, it is not what I wanted. I had hoped for a special assignment here at headquarters."

"Ah, well, still . . . Algeria. Might be exciting . . . Good to get some foreign service under the belt."

Luc appeared at the door now, reminding Dubon why it was he had come into the study.

"Yes, yes. Geneviève, poor Luc has been waiting to serve lunch for ages. Can't we finish the packing this afternoon? Come, Valcourt. You'll tell us about Algeria over lunch."

Dubon returned to the office after lunch, sent the captain's wife a *petit bleu* telling her he had news he wanted to share, and began eagerly rehearsing their meeting in his head. She had said "find the spy" and he had done it. He noted with some amusement that the only address she had been willing to leave with Lebrun was *poste restante* with a post office in the 8th arrondissement. She must have been checking the box regularly, though, for she appeared in his office before the end of the day, looking excited, her eyes sparkling and her cheeks flushed. Dubon took a long appreciative look at her. Perhaps, when this whole thing was over . . . He interrupted his own thoughts: when this whole thing was over, her husband would be returned to her and that would be that.

"News? You've caught the man?" she asked.

"Sit down, Madame, do sit down." Dubon settled her in a chair and sat back down at his own desk, pausing before he spoke—for effect, he had to admit to himself.

"Madame."

"Yes?"

"Madame, almost two months ago now, it was in April, and now here we are in June already."

"Yes, Maître." She directed a quietly expectant gaze at him.

"Madame," he began again, trying to get his announcement right. "Two months ago you came to me and said, 'The captain is innocent; find the real spy.'"

"Yes."

"And so far, I have found you evidence not so much of the captain's innocence as of the abuse of his rights; I have given you sufficient cause to launch an appeal, which you have done. Today, however, I have more than that: I have for you the name of the real spy." He paused again.

"Yes. Maître, do go on."

"The spy, the man who wrote the bordereau providing the Germans with French military documents, is a staff officer by the name of Major Esterhazy. He also goes by a title, although I believe he has no particular right to it. He is known as the Count Walsin-Esterhazy."

"And who is he?"

"A man of some notoriety," Dubon said, and proceeded to relay Le Goff's description of Esterhazy's personality.

"He has motive, then?"

"Yes. Probably debt."

"Still, it is shocking, is it not, Maître, that an officer would betray his country?"

"The man's clearly a scoundrel, Madame."

"They should have suspected him from the first."

"Perhaps, Madame. I don't wish to defend the military, but because the original list included an artillery manual and information about a new gun, those who investigated it assumed the culprit was an artillery officer. They were looking in the wrong place, as it turns out."

"And do you have proof that this Esterhazy is the right man?"

"Yes, Madame. There is a stockbroker named Castro—I will give you his particulars—who is ready to swear that the handwriting on the bordereau is that of his client, Major Esterhazy. The man is a speculator, an unsuccessful one. He owes Castro money."

"More motive, Maître. This is excellent; I can pass on this information to the captain's brother. Perhaps we will not even need to appeal; surely once the army knows who the real culprit is, they will simply release the captain."

"Certainly that is how it should be, Madame. Unfortunately, I increasingly believe the army will go to some lengths to avoid admitting the mistake. You need to tell the captain's brother that his lawyers must continue to pursue their fight with vigor; the name of the real culprit will fortify his claim."

She sighed and looked down at her hands without speaking.

"I know it is not fair, Madame . . ."

"Nothing has been fair about this from the start. I get my hopes up, that we will see justice, but it is so slow coming."

"The press may prove more of a friend in this regard than the military."

"The press? Maître, do you not read what they write in the papers? It's foul; I have to turn my head every time I pass a newsstand."

"Most of the press, yes. But there are papers, like *La Presse*, that doubt the captain's guilt. I think once Esterhazy's name becomes public—it is my hope *La Presse* will publish it tomorrow—you will find your case taken up by certain journalists. The court of public opinion is a powerful one, Madame."

"We'll see. Nonetheless, I am very grateful to you. You have done all I asked."

"I will write up a report for you; the captain's lawyers will surely find it useful in pursuing the appeal. In the meantime, you can pass on Esterhazy's name to them immediately, and see where they get with that. It will take me a few days to get my report ready; perhaps we can meet again next week. Indeed, I was hoping you would do me the honor of dining with me, to toast our success." Her husband would not be back for months; there was nothing to prevent him from at least enjoying a meal with her.

"Dining?"

"Yes, Madame. I know a very pleasant restaurant near here . . ."

"Dinner in a restaurant! Goodness, I don't know how long it has been . . ."

"Could we say Saturday evening?" he asked, picking a day when he would not be depriving himself of Madeleine's company at the beginning of the evening.

"Yes, dinner in a restaurant," the captain's wife agreed. "Why not? Why shouldn't I, for once?"

Dubon got home early, since Friday was one of the days Madeleine had said she was busy, but Geneviève and André were not about. He poured himself an aperitif and sank into his armchair. He was not entirely satisfied with the resolution of this business; he had little faith that the military would actually pursue Esterhazy, but he had performed his client's commission faithfully and rapidly and certainly surpassed his own expectations in that regard. He was greatly relieved to be out of the Statistical Section, and if justice for the captain might still be a long way off, let some more prominent lawyer fight for it, a social activist like Déon or one of the great minds in criminal law. Dubon was finished playing detective.

He picked up the newspaper and, purposely avoiding the story on the captain that now seemed a daily feature of the front page, turned to the sporting news. He was just reading an article about the latest in bicycle racing when Jean-Jean appeared in the doorway.

"All packed?"

"Yes. I am ready. I have something to give you, Dubon."

"Ah." Dubon held out his hand to accept the large envelope Jean-Jean placed in it.

"What is it?"

"My will."

"Oh yes, well, I suppose that is sensible under the circumstances. Algeria is a long way off and all . . . Is it a new will?"

"No, it's the one you drafted, after my father died. Same one."

"Fine, fine. I do believe I have a copy at the office, but good to have another one."

"There are some other papers in there, Dubon. Important papers. I entrust them to you, in case anything happens to me." He stared down at Dubon with solemnity. Really, Jean-Jean did dramatize his own importance sometimes.

"Right, of course," Dubon said, rising to his feet reluctantly. He supposed he was required to tuck the envelope away in the desk in his study now. "I'm sure you'll be home again in a year, safe with us."

"Just in case, Dubon, just in case."

FORTY-SIX

By Monday *La Presse* still had not published Esterhazy's name, but Dubon thought little of it until he returned to the office after lunch to find a disgruntled Le Goff waiting for him.

"They won't print anything more," Le Goff said, as soon as Lebrun had shut the door behind him. "The readers know that the captain is guilty and don't want to hear otherwise. Ten thousand of them have canceled their subscriptions. Imagine, Dubon, the power I have. I have unsettled ten thousand people, introduced a tiny shadow of doubt into their self-righteous conviction that when looking for a traitor one need look no further than the Jew."

"What are you going to do?"

"Not much I can do. Chalon was very sympathetic. He knows where the truth lies. He's not going to cut me off altogether. He'll take my articles on other subjects, but nothing on Dreyfus."

"And what about Esterhazy? How do we get his name into print?"

"Take it to Clemenceau, I guess."

"Clemenceau, at *L'Aurore*?"

"Waging a campaign, from what I read. He'll print anything."

"Well, it's your article. Why don't you take it to him?"

"Because he's the competition. *La Presse* is still paying me for a weekly column on other military affairs; I don't want to lose that income."

"You could let Clemenceau have it under another pseudonym."

"Chalon would know."

"So, in the end, nobody is willing to take the loss."

"That's not fair, Dubon. I am one man. What can I do?"

"I don't know, Le Goff. I don't know. But I guess at least I can go to Clemenceau and tell him about Castro."

After Le Goff left, Dubon kept working away on the mass of paper that had accumulated on his desk, but he gave up at five o'clock to turn to a different assignment. To his surprise, Lebrun had come to him that morning and asked for a letter of reference.

"You are leaving me, Lebrun? Are you not happy? I had no idea—"

"No, no, Maître. It is not like that; let me explain. The letter is for my application."

"Your application?"

"Yes. I am applying to the faculty of law for the fall term."

"You are applying to the university? Lebrun, really, do you think—?"

"I had excellent marks at the lycée, Maître."

"But that was some years ago, Lebrun. I mean, if you don't mind my asking, how old are you?"

"I'm thirty-four, Maître. Not so old I cannot consider a change."

"Still, Lebrun. I mean. It's very hard work, the law, very demanding; the course of training is long, arduous ... a young man with a certain, well, a certain background, such a young man might consider ... How will you be able to keep yourself while you are studying, if I may ask?"

"I have been saving. I have enough."

"That's very good, Lebrun. Very forward looking of you. You just want to be sure that the law suits you. That you are not wasting your savings or your time."

"Maître, I have just run your office for the better part of a month. I am well aware what the law entails."

"That's true. That's true," Dubon conceded. "Still, it also requires family support. That's really very important; especially when it comes time to set up a practice, one needs the kind of family—" Dubon heard what he was saying and pulled himself up short. He had the right family. He had inherited his father's practice and improved it with Geneviève's father's money. He had never been independent; he had abandoned a crusade for justice so that he could marry and live well. If Lebrun were to succeed in getting through law school on his own money, he already would have achieved more than Dubon ever had.

"I will support you," he said to his clerk. "Tell me what kind of letter you need."

It was six thirty before he finished the letter and started for home, but he had no reason to leave the office earlier because Madeleine was not free that evening. He entered the front hall of the apartment to find Geneviève readying herself and André to go out.

"Where have you been?" she asked coolly.

"I was at the office."

"You forgot we were having dinner early. I did mention it to you at lunch. I'm taking André to a concert." She paused. There was only so far she would go in the presence of their son. "You had assured me that at the very least your lateness was going to stop."

"Oh yes. I am sorry. I . . ." Dubon paused, realizing that lying to his wife had become something of a habit but that there was no reason he should not tell her of this particular development. "I was busy writing a letter for Lebrun. It's the most amazing thing. He has decided to apply to the faculty of law."

"Silly man. He's far too old. André, pass me my gloves, will you, dear? You'll go to law school, darling. Unless you want to follow your grandfather and your uncles and go into the army. You'll have to start thinking about it soon, eh?"

"Law school," André replied emphatically. "More interesting."

Dubon beamed at his son—he had never expressed any enthusiasm for law before—as the boy turned to fetch Geneviève a pair of black gloves that were sitting on the credenza.

"Not those, dear. Look at me. Do I look like someone who is about to put on a pair of black gloves?" She laughed, indicating her skirt and matching jacket, which were a rich shade of navy blue. André clearly did not know what his mother was talking about, so Dubon reached for the blue gloves that were also sitting there and passed them over. Mother and son set off, leaving Dubon standing in the middle of the hall staring blindly at the door that had just closed after them. He stood there for a long moment without moving before Luc appeared.

"Shall I put dinner on the table, Maître?" Luc asked.

"No, Luc. Thank you."

"Is Monsieur not dining at home this evening?" Luc asked tentatively.

"No," said Dubon, making up his mind. "No, Luc. I am going out. I won't need dinner."

He rushed down his street and out onto the quay, toward the place de la Concorde. He was not retracing his path to the office but rather his more common evening route, the one that led from Madeleine's apartment off the boulevard des Italiens to his own front door. He might have hailed a cab but he was too distracted to look about for one. As he walked at a furious pace, he thought about his wife, a woman who would never wear a pair of black gloves with a navy suit, and his mistress, a woman who would surely never wear a pale green hat with a pink dress—unless, of course, she had been given it by someone she wanted to please, someone she could not afford to displease, a new lover perhaps, or a man who was readying himself to become her lover. And Dubon thought also about the one man he knew who might mistake a pale green for a pale red.

FORTY-SEVEN

Masson was sitting on Madeleine's divan smoking a cigar when Dubon opened the door to her apartment. Madeleine rose in surprise at the intrusion.

"François—"

"Yes." Dubon just stood there.

"I don't want a scene, François."

"Am I making a scene?"

"I don't expect you to barge in without knocking, even if you do have a key."

"I don't think it's my manners that are at issue here."

Masson stubbed his cigar in a dish on a table at his elbow, rose calmly to his feet, and smiled wryly at Dubon.

"I was just on my way. I will leave you, my dear. I'm sure that you have things to discuss." He ran his hand delicately down her arm and then walked slowly toward the door.

"Good-bye, Dubon," he said easily as he slipped from the room.

Madeleine waited a moment, perhaps to be sure Masson was out of earshot, and then started in defensively.

"You have barely been here in weeks . . ."

"I am not sure that is reason to take a lover—"

"He's not my lover."

"But soon will be, I imagine."

"I wanted to talk to you—"

"Organize a smooth transition . . ."

"There's no need to be sarcastic about it. I have to earn my keep, François."

"Ah, he's going to pay better, is he?"

Madeleine drew herself up with injured pride; Dubon could see he had hit the mark.

"He's promised me an apartment in a building on the rue du Bac."

"Lovely."

She put a hand up behind her head as though to fluff her chignon. "And a lady's maid . . ."

"Ah, a lady's maid . . . And what am I to do? Is there to be bidding, is that what I am to understand?"

"François. That's horrible of you. You know how fond—"

"Yes, fond, but at the end of the day, it is not fondness that binds us, is it."

"I have to look to the future. I have always supported myself. I am not your wife who doesn't have to worry about whether you still find her attractive, whether you will keep paying the bills."

"How long has he been coming here? How did you meet him?"

"You introduced us."

"I did?"

"Last summer. At lunch. When your wife was on holiday."

It had been one of those wonderfully leisurely Sunday lunches in which he and Madeleine indulged themselves during the two months when Geneviève took her holidays, first at a hotel on the coast and then with her sisters at the family house in the country. He had felt contented, expansive, so expansive that when his friend Masson had happened by their table, he had hailed him, introduced him to Madeleine without much thought of the implications. His relationship with Madeleine was not a secret from his male friends; there was always an understanding that they would not discuss it with their own wives, let alone with Geneviève. They had their own secrets to keep.

"So when were you planning to tell me about this?"

"Soon, very soon. I was just waiting, well, until . . ."

"Until you had finalized all the details?"

"Until he signs the lease on the apartment."

"Get him to sign a contract with you. If he'll steal his best friend's mistress, what loyalty do you think he will have when he tires of you?" Dubon said. He barely knew Masson, he thought. Was this man who had betrayed him the same sad and lonely character to whom his parents had given a home? Was it the same helpful comrade who had kept the story of Dubon's days on the barricades from the general so that he could marry Geneviève, the intimate friend who had sat at their table for all these years, charming Dubon's wife?

"Why did you come here this evening?" Madeleine demanded.

"Because I guessed," Dubon replied. Her appointments and her distraction, the sense he sometimes had that someone else had preceded him into the room—those had only made him suspicious. A whiff of cigar smoke in the vicinity of her building he had attributed to the English detective. But it was not Brown but rather Masson who had been there before Dubon and stopped to light up as he left. The image of his rival smoking a postcoital cigar as he sauntered away jabbed at him.

"It was your hat that gave him away—the green hat. It doesn't match your pink dress."

"Well, it's an unusual choice, but chic, I think . . ."

"No, Madeleine, he's color-blind. Always has been, since we were schoolboys. We used to tease him about it. He can't distinguish reds from greens. He thought he was buying you a pink hat."

"Yes, perhaps, but it's a gift. He is so generous. He has promised to take me to Deauville for a few days and . . ."

They were standing at the door, but her eyes slid over to the table beside the divan where Masson had butted his cigar in a dish. There was a package lying beside it, unwrapped but sitting in its paper. Dubon had interrupted another bit of gift-giving.

"What has he bought you this time?"

Madeleine stood there silent and unhappy, her lips pursed.

Dubon crossed over to the table and flicked back the wrapping paper. He stared down at the gift, a chill of fear passing over his body while his brain whirred.

To decorate her new apartment, Masson had given Madeleine, mounted in a small gilt frame, a love letter signed by Napoléon.

FORTY-EIGHT

Dubon spent most of the following day in his office, alternating between bitter grief and fearful bafflement. When he thought of Madeleine, a great howl of pain rose up within him, and it was all he could do to remember Lebrun's presence in the outer office and not lash out in anger at the furniture. When he thought of her thighs and her easy laugh, he ached at the idea she would no longer share them with him. At other moments, he silently delivered bitter speeches of recrimination in his head. In passing, he might admit that his brief dalliance with the captain's wife suggested his relationship with Madeleine was on the wane—that he was bored or that they were growing apart—but it did nothing to mitigate his current pain. There is nothing like losing something you take for granted, to make you recognize its value.

When he thought of Masson, he only felt worse, tumbling into a pit of confusion and fear. Why did his friend—his former friend, that much was clear—have the Napoléon letter? Did he know who had killed the forger? Dubon realized he had no idea exactly what Masson did. He worked for the Foreign Ministry—at least, Dubon supposed he worked for the Foreign Ministry—but he also seemed awfully friendly with the military brass. Was he perhaps some kind of arranger or fixer? The army did not want Henry's forgery exposed. Had *Masson* killed the forger?

Then a worse thought occurred to Dubon: he had told Madeleine about the forger; he had even told her about the Napoléon letter. She had been intrigued by the thing. Had she told Masson? Had Dubon unwittingly brought about the forger's death? And why would Masson take the letter and give it to Madeleine? Did the man actually want Dubon to see it in her apartment? Was he thumbing his nose at his rival?

These questions only made him more miserable, and he was sitting at his desk stabbing a blank sheet of paper with a pen nib when Lebrun announced a Mr. Brown. In strolled the English detective.

"I stopped in to say good-bye. I'm heading back to London on the boat-train tomorrow."

"Good-bye, then," Dubon mumbled.

"How did your little deception work out?"

"Which little deception?"

"The whiskers, the glasses . . ."

"Oh yes. Wasn't needed in the end. The man I was attempting to deceive was dead when I arrived."

"Dead! My goodness."

"Murdered, actually."

"Dubon, really, you are dabbling in some nasty stuff here."

"Yes, perhaps I am. I should return these to you . . ." He fished around in his desk drawer and found the blank glasses the Englishman had lent him.

"So, I have been discharged by the client," Brown said. "Not needed anymore. The family has somehow discovered the name of the real spy."

"Really?" For the first time since he had left Madeleine's the evening before, Dubon permitted himself a smile.

"Yes, some contact passed it on to them."

"And what is the spy's name?"

"I'm not sure I am at liberty to divulge that, although it will probably become public soon enough."

"It isn't Esterhazy, is it?" Dubon asked, feeling like a character in a fairy tale who miraculously guesses the villain's strange name.

"The rumor is out there already, then? It all seems to be on the right track now."

"Wish I could share your optimism . . ."

"Surely, the army will be forced to admit its mistake and the captain will be exonerated," Brown said earnestly.

"I wouldn't underestimate how far the army will go to cover up the mistake and shield Esterhazy—"

"You're in a bad temper today, my friend. I could see it when I came through the door."

"My mistress is leaving me."

"Ah yes. Your French domestic arrangements." Brown paused a moment. "He'd be a tall fellow, this other man? Black hair, big man but elegant? Very good suit?"

"Yes, that's him," Dubon said, recognizing the description but surprised to hear anyone describe the once awkward Masson as elegant.

"I saw him outside the building near the boulevard des Italiens," Brown explained. "That day I followed you there. He arrived about an hour after you and waited outside for a bit. He kept looking up at the windows of the building and at his watch. I wondered if he was waiting for you or for someone else in the building to appear, but then after a while he cleared off.

"I suppose I could have told you," the detective offered sympathetically. "Perhaps you'll have some luck with that other beauty."

"Which other beauty?"

"That lady who comes here. Sorry, I was shadowing your office for a few days before we, uh, met, so to speak. That client of yours . . . she's something, you have to admit, despite the black dress."

Dubon pulled himself up straight. "Listen, Brown, I would never indulge in any kind of improper relations with a client. That's Dreyfus's wife."

"No, it's not."

"What do you mean?"

"That lady is not Madame Dreyfus."

A surge of excitement rose through Dubon's body and into his mouth.

"I have met Madame Dreyfus," Brown said. "It was the first time the captain's brother gave me my assignment. Your client is not the captain's wife."

"My God," said Dubon, his head now swimming with new romantic possibilities. There could hardly be two women running around town dressed as widows when they were actually married to living men. "Then who *is* she?"

He and the detective took a drink together in the quartier before he returned home at seven thirty, late for dinner, but in his current state of heartache, confusion, and anticipation he hardly cared.

"Madame is in the salon, Monsieur," Luc informed him in a hushed tone. "Major de Ronchaud Valcourt is with her."

"Is something wrong?"

"I think you had better go in to Madame."

Dubon raised an eyebrow. "All right."

He found Geneviève sitting on the sofa crying, while the older of her two brothers, the usually affable major, paced the room with a grim expression of paternal authority on his face. He had started to look like his father, Dubon thought fleetingly—his father on some occasion when one of the children had done something especially naughty.

"Where have you been?" he asked in an accusatory tone, as Dubon entered. "We sent a message to your office to come home immediately and your clerk said you had left hours ago."

"I was having a drink with a colleague," he said as he hurried over to Geneviève. "What is wrong, my dear, whatever is wrong?" He got down on his knees in front of her and took her hands in his.

"It's Jean-Jean," she sobbed, but couldn't say more.

"We got a telegram this afternoon. There has been an accident," his brother-in-law explained.

"An accident? What kind of accident? Is he all right?"

"No, Dubon. He's dead."

"Dead?" Dubon felt a fog of fearful incomprehension descending on him.

"Yes. He got to Marseille. He got the boat, boarded it Sunday because they were sailing at dawn. There was some kind of accident during the night. They think he may have got up in his sleep and been disoriented."

"What happened?"

"We don't know exactly. He fell overboard somehow and drowned in the harbor. His body . . . his body washed up yesterday. It's being sent back to us tomorrow for burial."

Dubon was too shocked to accept what he was being told. "He can't have just fallen off a boat. How is that possible?"

"I don't know, Dubon. I don't know how it happened. They performed an"—here he turned away from his sister and lowered his voice—"an autopsy. The doctor said it was death by drowning."

"An autopsy?"

"His superiors are really being very good about this. They know we won't want to wait for a funeral. The body comes home tomorrow."

"The body . . . I see."

Geneviève, who had been sitting with her eyes shut and her hand across her pursed mouth throughout this exchange, began to cry again.

"Saturday. He was just here on Saturday. I helped him pack on Friday. All those clothes, his uniforms . . ."

Dubon leapt up. "I'll be right back."

He sprinted to his study, opened the desk drawer, and pulled out the envelope Jean-Jean had given him the day before he left. Inside, he found the will he himself had drafted a few years before, and a second envelope, addressed, to his surprise, to him. There was a letter inside.

"Dear brother," it read. Dubon was touched by the salutation; perhaps Geneviève was right and he had never done Jean-Jean justice.

"I believe you have taken some interest in the case of Captain Dreyfus. I have heard you on one or two occasions questioning those who assume his guilt. Perhaps, like some of us junior officers, you have been increasingly suspicious of the evidence against him and want to see revision. Hoping this is so, I want to share with you some information.

"I hope I will not try your patience if I begin by explaining some of my thoughts on French artillery technology." There followed several dense paragraphs of technical explanation that Dubon plodded through, stifling his annoyance and reminding himself this was his brother-in-law's last word on any subject.

His point addressed the problem of recoil. In the case of even the new, lighter models of field guns, the force of the bullet created an opposing reaction so strong that the jolt of the machine frightened the horses, ground the surrounding earth to mud and forced gunners to waste precious minutes in battle repositioning the gun before they could take aim again.

"In theory, the solution is obvious," Jean-Jean wrote. "Our guns need better brakes. In practice, this will require some technical advances in the use of hydraulics. I have personally been working on this problem for some time as a hobbyist, and I had developed some ideas I felt it was worth sharing with my superiors. I did not find them particularly receptive and perhaps I was indiscreet in discussing the topic when I felt I was among friends.

"In April I was called into headquarters for a meeting with a general, who I will not name, and two officers who, I gathered from their highly technical questions, were themselves working on developing new hydraulic brakes. They were very interested in my concept for a floating piston. They did not inform me of how far they had come in their work, but after they left, the general promised me a reassignment to the team that was developing a new 75 mm gun. I was warned that the work was top secret and that I was never to mention the nature of my assignment, even to brother officers, nor to discuss the operation of artillery with anyone.

"I waited a month, but my new assignment never materialized. I never saw the general in question again. I now believe the point of our meeting was to ascertain how much information I had about hydraulics and to warn me to keep my mouth shut. Perhaps the team was advanced enough in their development of the 75 mm gun that my services were considered redundant.

"I was disappointed, but I had no choice but to continue in my post at Compiègne and wait for some future reassignment. I stopped thinking about the issue until last week, when I was in town visiting headquarters and read in the papers the text of the bordereau that the artillery officer Captain Dreyfus was believed to have written to the

Germans. I was shocked: that document could not have been written by a gunner. The writer offers a note on the functioning of the hydraulic buffer on the new 120, but in fact the new 120 has a *pneumatic* buffer.

"I also note that the writer offers a copy of the artillery manual, suggesting it is very hard to get. The manual is as common as mud—extra copies can be purchased for two centimes each in my unit—and the writer also has the title of the manual wrong. Whoever wrote the bordereau is clearly not an artillery officer and also not a very effective spy. All the information he is offering is wrong, out of date, or widely available.

"After I read the bordereau, I struggled mightily with my conscience for I found it hard to believe that the generals could have been so slapdash in their investigation of the case and sent Dreyfus to Devil's Island on such scant evidence. Torn between my duty toward my superiors and my conviction that they must reopen the case because they have the wrong man, I felt compelled to speak out. I asked for a second meeting with the general. I was not able to obtain an audience with him but was taken in to see another. I presented all my evidence, as a result of which I was accused of insubordination and sent on my way again. The next day, I received my new assignment: I was to be posted immediately to a detachment in Algeria.

"I have been naive. The generals are not interested in knowing of Dreyfus's innocence. They will go to any lengths to protect another man who, whatever his identity, was an exceedingly bad spy.

"I hope you can put this information to some use, brother, and will have the courage to express unpopular opinions. I have often noted your wisdom and discretion, and I know you will be able to counter our family's inflexible views on this subject. My own insistence on Dreyfus's innocence can no longer be a danger to me: if you are reading this letter, it is because I have died in Algeria. I hope I have not contracted the fever, but have fallen for France."

FORTY-NINE

Exhausted from crying, Geneviève finally fell asleep in her husband's arms at three in the morning, but not before she had asked Dubon in a plaintive voice, "You won't leave, will you?"

"I'll stay here all night."

"Not just tonight. I mean forever. You won't ever leave me."

"No, Geneviève, I would never leave you. Try to go to sleep now."

"I know you have other interests . . ."

"I've been busy with this case, but I am almost through with it. I just have to write up a report and deliver it to the client, and then it will be over, and we won't have to argue about it anymore."

"I don't just mean work. I know you have always had other interests, since André was a baby."

Dubon wasn't sure what to say. He had often suspected that she knew something of Madeleine's existence, but they seemed to have a tacit agreement that these things were best left unspoken as long as he remained affectionate and polite, paid the bills on time, and showed up for dinner.

"That doesn't matter as long . . ." She seemed now to want to spell out the terms of their arrangement openly. Either his behavior or Jean-Jean's death had made her more bold. "... as long as we respect our bond and don't break it. You will stay?"

"Of course, Geneviève," he said, appalled at her suggestion that he might simply leave. "I know I have not always been the best husband. I will try to do better." He stroked her hair.

A few minutes later she spoke again. "You really believe Dreyfus is innocent, don't you."

"Yes. I really do."

"Jean-Jean agreed with you."

"How do you know?"

"He told me when we were packing his bags. I was complaining that you were taking an interest in the case and he just said, 'He's right.' When I reminded him where our family loyalties must lie, he said ... well, it surprised me, coming from him. He said, 'It's not about loyalty, it's about justice. The second must trump the first.'"

Jean-Jean's letter saved Dubon. As Geneviève mourned his death, and Dubon mourned his rupture with Madeleine while puzzling over the widow's true identity, the letter gave him something tangible on which he could concentrate. He read it over and over, examining Jean-Jean's conclusions and wondering about the conclusions his brother-in-law had not reached. By Thursday, he had not only written up his report for the widow, but also had prepared another statement about the case. He called Lebrun into his office that morning.

"How many copies can you do on the machine at once, Lebrun? Three, is it?"

"No, Maître. The original and one carbon. You are never satisfied with the quality of the second copy when I try using two sheets of carbon paper."

"Right. Well, I need four of this. So you are going to have to type it up twice. And this letter too. Four copies of it as well."

"Very good, Maître."

Lebrun was a slow typist who had never really embraced this part of his job description, but by lunchtime he had produced the four copies of Dubon's statement and Jean-Jean's letter, Dubon sealed a pair of each in four separate envelopes, addressing two of them to Le Goff and two to Clemenceau at *L'Aurore*. He took one of each of these to his bank, where he left them in his safety deposit box; he placed the other two in his own desk drawer and called Lebrun back into his office before he went home that evening.

"I have taken some precautions, Lebrun, of which I wanted to inform you. My brother-in-law's death has reminded me that one must always be ready. I would never wish to leave Madame Dubon in an awkward position. You know I keep my will at the bank, in the safety deposit box. Madame has one key; the other is in my desk drawer, should you ever need it. If anything happens, simply look here."

"I certainly hope that day is a very long way off, Maître."

"Of course, Lebrun. A very long way off. It will be your successor who has to deal with it. You'll have your own office by then."

"I hope so, Maître."

Dubon then took the original handwritten versions of his statement and of Jean-Jean's letter and put them in an envelope, which he addressed to Geneviève. This he took home and placed in the drawer of the desk in his study.

On Friday, the day of the funeral, Esterhazy's story began to appear in the papers. *La Presse* remained curiously silent on what the press had dubbed "The Dreyfus Affair," but *Le Siècle*, to which Dubon subscribed, reported government sources who said it was well known the real spy was still at large and that he was a titled officer stationed at a garrison just outside the capital. Dubon supposed that the Dreyfus family had now gone to the government with Esterhazy's identity and that it was someone with a sympathetic ear inside the government who had told the papers where to look.

The funeral service was at ten and the family was to gather at the apartment at nine to ready themselves to follow a military cortège to the church. After breakfast, before his wife's family descended on his home en masse, Dubon went out for a brief walk to clear his head.

Passing a newsstand, he picked up a copy of *L'Aurore*. Le Goff was right; the editor Clemenceau was waging a campaign; his lead article went so far as to name Esterhazy. Clemenceau was willing to risk a libel action.

But it was as he read on that Dubon got a real surprise: Clemenceau somehow knew that the Italian diplomat's letter that Cavaignac had read out in the National Assembly was a fake. Perhaps it was merely bravado on his part, but he denounced the letter as a forgery created by the military to bolster a feeble case.

The paper denounced the perfidy of the military in continuing to pursue the case against Dreyfus and went on to remind readers of the human cost of the affair, describing in the most pitiable language Dreyfus's plight, festering in a tin shack on Devil's Island, and that of his family, mourning his absence in Paris. The writer expounded at length on the loyalty and perseverance of Dreyfus's wife, Lucie, who had never abandoned hope and never allowed herself or others to forget the injustice done her husband, going so far as to wear mourning dress ever since the day, two and a half years before, when he was shipped in shackles to Devil's Island. The front page article continued on an inside page, and there was a photo that, according to the caption, showed the captain's wife caught by the photographer the previous month on her way to register her appeal against her husband's conviction. It wasn't a very clear photo, but Dubon could see the English detective was right. The woman in the newspaper was not his client.

I wonder if the lady will actually show up for dinner tomorrow night, Dubon thought to himself. He also wondered whether the mysterious lady for whom he had been working since April was going to pay his bill.

L'Aurore was not a newspaper he would ever have expected his brother-in-law to read, so he was surprised at lunch after the burial when the major, obviously looking for some topic to distract himself from Jean-Jean's death, observed to him: "Have you seen the papers? Seems Dreyfus must have had an accomplice, because they are saying that fellow Esterhazy is also a spy."

"Have you been reading *L'Aurore*?"

"Goodness no. I never read that trash. It was in *Le Siècle*. We get it as well as *Le Matin*, just for some balance. They called him a titled officer stationed at a garrison just outside Paris. Well, not hard to identify who they mean if you know the man."

"You know Esterhazy?"

"He's come to my card parties once or twice. Bit of a cad. Didn't invite him back after a small problem with losses that were never paid."

It seemed to Dubon all Paris should have known that Esterhazy was the spy.

"Someone told me he was at the Fiteaus' ball the night young Fiteau killed himself."

"Really? I don't remember seeing him," the major said.

"What's he look like?"

"Insignificant character. Slinks about. You wouldn't notice him if it weren't for the mustache. Great walrus thing, all white . . ."

A shrunken man with a huge mustache. It was the man who had pushed his way past them all after young Fiteau's body had fallen into their midst. It was the man who had said, "My God, I thought he was joking."

"I saw him," Dubon said. "He was in the same room when Fiteau shot himself. They must have been playing cards." He hesitated, unsure how to ask his next question. "Valcourt . . . When you have your card parties, how much money . . . ?"

"Oh, little parties. Not high stakes. We would never let someone get into that kind of trouble."

"How would you stop him?"

"Well, like we did with Esterhazy. Just not invite him if his losses were mounting. It's only a social thing, after all, a game between friends."

"But what if it's not a social thing, if they aren't friends?"

"You mean if there's a house? You think Esterhazy was running a game?"

"I don't know the vocabulary . . ."

"Taking a cut. Organizing the game, and then taking a cut of the winnings."

"I assume you don't do that, when you organize your games?"

"Goodness, no, Dubon. That's not legal. Mine are gentlemen's parties."

"But Esterhazy is clearly not a gentleman."

"No, clearly. His debts mounting, he tries his hand at spying. Maybe that doesn't pay enough, so he starts running a game. It's possible, I guess. Might explain why young Fiteau was in so deep."

"Why?"

"Some of them can't do without it. It's like an intoxication, a mania. They need to bet every night and they don't live in Monte Carlo. You can't find a gentlemen's party every night. So, you'll find a game. Someone will put you in touch. But they are ruthless. If you don't pay your debts, they'll come after you. If that was the kind of card game young Fiteau was playing, it's little wonder he killed himself."

So, Madame Fiteau was right, Dubon thought to himself. Esterhazy had entrapped her son. He wondered if she would want to know.

FIFTY

Geneviève glanced up from the mail and remarked, "How kind. You should read this, François. It's really a beautiful letter, from General Fiteau and Madame. After all their pain..." She proceeded to the second page and then stopped.

"The general says something about how they hope to see you in uniform more often, and a reservist should be equally proud of the service. What can he mean?" she asked.

"Oh, it's just a conversation we were having. We were talking about the reserves the last time...uh, at the ball, you know before every-thing..."

Geneviève began to blink back tears at the memory of another death.

It was the day after the funeral and they were sitting in the sa-lon after a brief and subdued Saturday lunch. André had removed himself to his room while Geneviève was working her way through the many letters of condolence that had arrived in the morning post. Dubon had not said anything to her about his conviction that it was the now-notorious Esterhazy who had got the young Fiteau hooked on gaming. It was probably much better the Fiteaus not know; he didn't suppose it would help them recover any faster. He scanned the two pages quickly: apart from the general's leading remark about wearing uniform, his letter, it turned out, expressed nothing more than the predictable sentiments.

Dubon was just replacing it in Geneviève's pile when the front door-bell rang. She looked up in surprise; despite her own forwardness in visiting Madame Fiteau, one did not expect anyone to disturb a house of mourning. They could hear the sounds of Luc emerging from the kitchen and going to the door, followed by a brief conference in hushed voices. Luc then appeared in the room.

"It is Captain Le Goff, Monsieur."

"Really, Luc, I don't think—" Geneviève began.

"I'll see him in my study. Thank you, Luc," Dubon said, adding to his wife, "I'll just go and see what he wants, dear. He was very close to Jean-Jean. We mustn't stand on ceremony with him."

He met Le Goff in the hall and showed him down the corridor to the study.

"I'm sorry to show up like this, Dubon. My apologies to Madame, and my condolences, of course. I should send her a letter. I just"—he waited until the door was closed behind them to continue—"found out something I think you need to know."

"Yes."

"I have a source who knows the superintendent of the Mont-Valérian prison. Major Henry was taken there last night."

"Goodness. So he's going to take the fall. They will no longer try to use the forged letters as evidence." It was good news, Dubon thought, although at any new trial, the unmasking of forged evidence would have been an ace up the defense's sleeve.

"Let me finish, Dubon," Le Goff said. "He was found dead in his cell this morning."

"Dead?"

"Slit his own throat with his razor."

"He was allowed a razor?"

"Apparently so. Allowed a razor to shave himself and did the honorable thing. Wherever the affair ends, the generals are desperate to distance themselves from Henry's antics."

Poor Henry, Dubon thought. The loyal Mr. Fix-It to the end.

"And *La Presse*? Will it publish this at least?"

"Saw my editor this morning. He is panting to get it into print and curses that he doesn't publish on Sundays."

"So, it will be public knowledge by Monday?" Dubon asked, thinking to himself that he now had another piece of news to tell his client if she did show up for dinner that evening.

"Yes. I imagine other papers will have it on Monday too; I am keeping my fingers crossed that none of the Sunday papers get a hold of it."

"Well, it will be all over town soon enough. Henry's suicide is tantamount to a confession to his perjury and forgeries. Revision is inevitable now."

"I hope you're right, Dubon, but I wouldn't underestimate how stubborn the anti-Dreyfusards may be. They may try to turn Henry into some kind of martyr: persecuted by his superiors for a little tweaking of the evidence against a man everyone knows is guilty. Unorthodox, perhaps, but all in the best interests of France."

"The wind is shifting," Dubon answered. "Even my wife is re-examining her position. She had complained to Jean-Jean that my support of the captain might cost us socially, but he told her that I was right."

"Your brother-in-law was . . ." Le Goff began, but his voice cracked. "I am sorry. It's only the day after the funeral, and here I am barging in with my news. He was a dear friend. Many found him annoying, so earnest. We were very different people, but I really valued him. His death seems so odd. Ironic, and irony is not something I ever associated with him. A military man succumbing to a stupid accident. He deserved a more heroic death. He was a hero in his way, the kind of quiet hero on whom the military depends."

Not for the first time since his brother-in-law's death, Dubon felt a pang of guilt. He had undervalued Jean-Jean. It was not merely the sentiment that follows death, the eulogies that canonize the most ordinary people. Dubon could not imagine anyone calling Jean-Jean's older brother, the ever-genial major, a quiet hero. Others saw something in Jean-Jean that he had missed, a clarity of purpose, a willingness to risk unpopularity to pursue his goals. Jean-Jean's letter to Dubon proved as much.

"There was something else I was meaning to ask you," Dubon said, returning to a previous line of thought.

"Yes?"

"Was it you who told Clemenceau that the diplomat's letter was a forgery?"

"Well—"

"How else could he have known? Aside from Picquart, only Henry and the generals knew and they weren't about to tell the editor of *L'Aurore*."

"After what you said when *La Presse* wouldn't publish Esterhazy's name . . . I felt like a coward. I went to Clemenceau. I told him it was Esterhazy and I told him the letter was a forgery. I decided to risk my column. It seemed more important to get the news out."

"So, Henry's suicide . . ."

"He made his choices."

"Oh, indeed. Never bother your superior officers. It was a lesson he had learned well."

He thanked Le Goff for all his help and promised to keep in touch before going back to Geneviève in the salon.

"What did he want?"

"What did he want? Well, to share his grief, I guess. He's lost a friend. He wanted to tell me how much Jean-Jean had mattered to him."

"Oh," said Geneviève, and then, after a pause, "I never liked that man."

"He has a hard edge to him."

"Intelligent, but always making you feel stupid . . . well, not so much stupid, but naive, as though he knows how the world works and you are just an infant in it. Do you know what I mean?"

"Oh, precisely, my dear. He's a cynic. Rare in the military, I would have thought. Or perhaps not. Perhaps in wartime, the exigencies of battle and the generals' foul-ups make all the lower ranks cynical, but these days there seems to be such emphasis on esprit de corps, never questioning the brass . . ."

"You mean because of this affair, no one is allowed to question?"

"Yes. But Le Goff questions. It doesn't make him likable, but it does, I think, make him admirable."

"No doubt you are right. Perhaps I should try harder to like him."

"You are under no obligation, my dear. No obligation at all."

Geneviève returned to the pile of letters in her lap, and they sat companionably as occasionally she laughed, or sighed, or tut-tutted and said at various points, "Madame la Baronne . . ." or "Monsieur Lavallé . . ." or "les Archembaults . . ." as if by way of explanation. After about twenty minutes of reading, she remarked, "A lovely letter from Masson."

At the mention of the name, Dubon looked up sharply from his book.

"He says he's sorry he couldn't be at the funeral," Geneviève said, "but he was out of town on business and he's only getting back today. It's not like him to miss something like that. He is always so gracious. Such a fine man."

"You used to be rather dismissive of him when we were younger," Dubon couldn't help observing.

"Was I?"

"You were scathing when he took his father's title. Baron . . . just some Napoleonic invention, you said. You used to have trouble getting the word out of your mouth whenever we saw him." Dubon, as a childhood friend, had simply stuck with "Masson," but his wife, who had previously called him "Monsieur," had little choice but to address a baron by his title.

"Well . . . I . . ." She hesitated. "His mother's family is an ancient one."

"She was crazy, that woman."

"Yes, so everyone said. Ran in the family, they used to say, although he never shows any sign of it. Anyway, we should judge the man, not his lineage."

Yes, Dubon thought to himself, we should judge the man.

"May I read his letter?" he asked, reaching across and pulling it off the top of her pile.

It was a model letter of condolence, containing a few telling observations about the fine personality in which the deceased rejoiced and one fond anecdote about him, before observing how proper it was for his correspondent to be grief-stricken over the loss of such a relative. Perhaps he had a form in his drawer to which he just added the appropriate adjectives and stories that a particular death demanded. Dubon had planned to confront Masson soon. If the man had played some part in the forger's death, Dubon did not expect he would ever pay the price, but the very least he could do, since he had come this far, was make sure that Masson, whoever he was, did not stand in the way of the captain's appeal. Dubon rose to his feet.

"I am afraid I must go out," he said.

"Where are you going?"

"I need to . . . well, to go to the office for a bit."

"Will you be back before you go out to dinner?" she asked. Dubon had already gently paved the way for his absence that evening.

"I'm not sure. Probably just in time to change. You'll be all right? You and André will go over to your sister's soon?"

"Yes. I'll be fine. Maybe we'll walk out with you."

"I'll take you to Anne-Marie's and go on from there."

"But it's in the opposite direction. You don't want to have to go all the way to the Left Bank and back."

"No matter."

Dubon went to warn André they were leaving and returned to the front hall to find Geneviève preparing herself to go out. She was wearing the same plain black suit in which she had attended the funeral the previous day, hidden beneath a black veil that she now unpinned from her large hat, ready to appear in the street without it. He knew she would discuss with her sisters that day what form their mourning would take and how long it should last, but it would be months before any of them might venture out wearing a white collar let alone a gray suit. He was wearing a black armband himself, as was André, who appeared now, pulling on his jacket.

"Where is Papa going? Can't I go with him instead?" André asked.

"He is just going to the office for a bit, darling. You come with me to your aunt's."

"But I want to be with Papa. I won't bother you," André said, turning to his father.

"Not today, André," Dubon said, smiling gently at his son. "Soon, though. When school's out you can come to the office and I'll show you what we do all day, me and Lebrun."

In fact, the youngest of Geneviève's three sisters lived in the right direction for Dubon's purposes. After he dropped his family there, he proceeded to Masson's apartment off the rue de Varenne—very convenient, now that he thought of it, to Madeleine's promised rooms in the rue du Bac.

His manservant said he was out, but suggested Dubon return around five.

"Monsieur le Baron made a brief trip to Deauville Thursday. I do not expect him back until four at the earliest."

It was only half past three, so Dubon spent the next hour and a half wandering the streets, rehearsing in his head what he would say to Masson. He did not want to talk to him about Madeleine; he did not even want to think about her, although he realized that Masson's business in Deauville must have been their little honeymoon by the seaside.

When he returned to the apartment, Masson still was not back but his servant showed Dubon into Masson's study to wait. A few minutes later, the doorbell rang. Dubon supposed it was Masson and that the man didn't bother with a key, but after a moment, the servant reappeared in the room with a telegram that he placed on the desk.

"A telegram for Monsieur le Baron. I'm sure he won't be long,

Maître. He has a dinner engagement, so I expect him very soon." The servant shut the door and left him again.

Dubon crossed over to the desk, picked up the telegram, and tore it open. He read it twice over, surprised that Masson did not already know the message it contained, and was just stuffing it into his pocket when the doorbell rang again.

FIFTY-ONE

"So, my old friend, we are to have the inevitable confrontation. I had hoped to avoid anything so melodramatic," Masson said as he settled himself in a chair across from Dubon.

"About Madeleine, you mean?"

"Yes." Masson looked at him quizzically. "If not about Madeleine, well, you tell me . . ."

Dubon said nothing. Masson let the silence sit for a while and then offered his condolences. "How is Madame Dubon? Not taking it too hard, I hope."

"She is managing, thank you. She was touched by your letter." Despite himself Dubon found the conventional niceties issuing from his lips.

"You have a very lovely wife, Dubon. I have always envied you Geneviève."

Dubon noted with annoyance that Masson took the liberty of using her first name.

"You should pay her more attention. You wouldn't want to lose her . . ."

"... too," Dubon added sharply. It occurred to Dubon that perhaps Masson had stolen his mistress because he couldn't steal his wife. The man had wanted something and had taken what he could.

"Madeleine is a businesswoman," Masson said. "I made her a better offer. That's fair."

"Well, I wish you the joy of it, my friend, but if you look on your relationship with her solely as a business transaction, you are unlikely to be satisfied."

Masson just smiled a superior smile.

"I didn't come to talk about Madeleine," Dubon said. "I have a question I need to ask you. You gave Madeleine a letter signed by Napoléon. Where did you get it?"

"She showed it to you?"

"It was still sitting there on the table when I arrived."

"Lovely thing, isn't it? Not real, of course," Masson said lightly, but his body betrayed some irritation as he rose from his chair and went over to stand by his desk.

"Where did you get it?"

"Friend of mine in the police passed it on to me. Something of a joke, really. He knew the man who, well, who created it, shall we say."

"Don't toy with me, Masson," Dubon said angrily. "Madeleine told you I had seen it at Rivaud's, and you took it to give it to her. What, to prove to her you had more power, more contacts, than I? Or were you hoping I would see it and guess at your scope? You had Rivaud murdered to protect Major Henry's evidence against Dreyfus."

"Goodness, Dubon. What an accusation. What kind of power do you think I have?"

"I don't know, but I know you have been fixing the case against the captain."

"I fix many things for my masters in government," he said as he perched himself on the edge of the desk. "France needs Dreyfus to be guilty."

"But you and I know he isn't guilty. Why can't France be satisfied with a guilty Esterhazy instead?"

Masson paused, as though reevaluating the situation.

"Ah, you've heard that name," he said as though to himself.

He hadn't seen Friday's papers, Dubon realized, thinking bitterly that he must have been too busy in bed with Madeleine in a Deauville hotel room to read the Paris press.

Masson pushed himself away from the desk now and walked around behind it to sit down. He looked at Dubon across its large expanse and said, "I underestimated you, my friend. Did you root out Esterhazy in your little escapade at the Statistical Section?"

It was Dubon's turn to be surprised, although he realized he should have guessed that Masson knew about his undercover work. "So, Madeleine told you all about it," he said.

"No. She didn't betray you. She told me about the Napoléon letter. She seemed impressed by it, so I got it for her. But it was you who told me you were working to reverse a court martial. Do you remember? That time we bumped into each other in that café around the corner from her place. I was waiting for you to clear out of the way actually. Madeleine did tell me you were working on some special assignment that made it impossible for you to visit her, but I also have my contacts in the Statistical Section. When I heard of an odd new clerk who did not speak as much German as required, well, I began to have my suspicions."

Hermann. The colleague who had questioned Dubon's German and always seemed to be popping up without warning. He was Masson's eyes and ears in the section.

"If you knew I had infiltrated the Statistical Section, why did you leave me there?" Dubon asked.

"At first I thought we had better rope you in before you got into trouble. But then you were getting along very well with Picquart. So, I left you there to see what you would find out," Masson answered, looking pleased with his own cleverness. "If you could discover ways of proving Dreyfus innocent, I needed to know them."

Dubon gasped at the man's vanity. "So I was working for you, was I? Your unwitting spy in the Dreyfusard camp?"

"Over the years, I have found that is the best way," he replied. "Spies are unlikely to betray their masters if they don't know who they are working for. It's a little technique I developed after my experiences in Russia, where we always had trouble recruiting local agents."

"But how do you get the information out of them?"

"People invariably talk. I think that you, for example, have things to tell me about the case against Dreyfus. I'll find them out, eventually. I was going to suggest we have a good, long dinner sometime, but now you have saved me the trouble." Masson leaned across the desktop, looming toward Dubon with a smirk on his face. "We can just keep chatting and you'll betray yourself," he said.

If the effect was supposed to be menacing, it failed: Dubon was only reminded of the awkwardly unctuous schoolboy Masson had been.

"Spies are an unreliable breed. We have agents in foreign countries reporting on the activities of their own governments, but you can never fully trust them. What kind of man betrays his country for money? It's no better at home. Various criminal types offer information. All these characters can be bought by either side. They are, like your Madeleine, for sale to the highest bidder."

Dubon reared up at this last insult. "Stop!"

"I am sorry, my friend. Perhaps my work has made me cynical. There was some disinformation we needed to plant with the Germans," he continued, "but they were always ferreting out our agents; they were naturally suspicious of any Frenchman who approached them. Thinking on the problem, I realized that if a double agent doesn't know he is a double agent—if he actually believes he is working for the enemy— then his mission can never be uncovered."

"Esterhazy . . . the incompetent spy . . ." That was why Dreyfus had to be guilty, Dubon thought, to protect Esterhazy's cover.

"Oh yes, horrible fellow, all puffed up with his own importance, hawking instruction manuals that half the artillery officers in France are using as doorstops. He served our purposes very nicely. He was already trying to sell information to the newspapers. All we had to do was instruct a few of our less reputable contacts to whisper in his ear how the next level of the business worked, then leave a few documents within his reach, and watch him scamper off to the Germans. It was all going swimmingly—"

"Until the Statistical Section uncovered evidence of his treachery."

"Luckily, those fools could be counted on to get the wrong man. They sent Dreyfus to Devil's Island, leaving my project to continue."

"You know Dreyfus is innocent. You left him to rot."

Masson's expression was impassive. "There are larger issues at stake here than the life of one small man," he said grandly.

"There are. Justice, for one. If the Republic does not—"

"Spare me, Dubon. I have worked all my life for the good of the nation."

"And the disinformation that it was so important to plant with the Germans? It was the material about the artillery, wasn't it? Tell the enemy all about the new brakes on the 120, convince them they are on to the latest developments in French artillery. It was all a ruse to protect the secrecy of the 75 mm, the gun with the braking system that really works. The 75 mm will decide the next war, and only France will have it."

"So, you can see I have the nation's interests at heart," Masson replied smoothly. "Was it your brother-in-law who told you about the new gun?"

"No," Dubon said, not wishing to draw Jean-Jean into it. His brother-in-law had seen the mistakes in the bordereau's description of the 120 but had not realized how close he was to the truth when he told his superiors that all this incompetent spy had done was help the French cause by misleading the Germans.

"Well, you are cleverer than your brothers-in-law. Silly men, both of them, in their different ways—the younger one running about town telling anyone who will listen that he has invented hydraulic brakes and the floating piston in his broom closet. And there's the major, inviting foreign military attachés to his little card parties."

"What's wrong with that?" Dubon asked.

"Oh, you know, situations just ripe for the kind of indiscretions that can lead to blackmail."

"Blackmail." Dubon said the last word very slowly as a nasty thought blossomed in his mind. It wasn't the major's parties that might lead to blackmail. It was other parties, more serious parties, the kind young Fiteau had attended. He remembered Masson sitting on the sidelines with the general the evening of the ball . . .

"Why does all Paris know that General Fiteau refused to keep paying his son's debts?" he asked. "*You* put that story out there."

"It was hardly a story. It was true. The general asked my advice—"

"You were setting the young man up, so somebody could blackmail him. Turn him into another of your unwitting agents." The Germans were unlikely to doubt the quality of information they were getting from the son of a general, particularly a son with secret gambling debts to pay.

Dubon looked at his former friend with dawning horror. He was as blank as the bedsheet on to which the pictures from a magic lantern are projected. He would reflect whatever image you wanted, take on whatever role you needed and then hold your reliance and your gratitude over your head. He could play piteous orphan to Dubon's charitably minded parents or generous patron to Madeleine's ambitious desires; he could be the silent street sweeper who would come in the night and clean away the generals' great big mess or the garrulous go-between who arranged everything for the young Dubon and his fiancée.

"You might as well have killed Fiteau!"

"That's a monstrous accusation," said Masson. He pulled open a drawer in his desk and began fiddling with something inside it. "I had no idea the young man was so lacking in courage. Perhaps he wouldn't have been a good agent after all."

"Have you no conscience? Have you seen his mother since his death? That lady who invited you into her home, at whose table you ate? How many other people have you killed, Masson? Was it you who arranged Jean-Jean's mysterious accident? His superiors had told him to be more discreet, but that wasn't the problem, was it. No, the real problem was that yet another person could show exactly why Dreyfus was innocent."

"Your brother-in-law's accident was sad, very sad." He paused, removed a small vial from his drawer and placed it on the desktop. Then he reached into the desk again and pulled out a syringe. As Dubon watched in confusion and mounting fear, he loaded the contents of the vial into the chamber of the syringe. "It will be especially hard on Geneviève if she is to suffer another bereavement so soon after her brother's death," he said as he held up the needle. "I am bigger than you, always have been. The needle is filled with prussic acid, Dubon, and there is no point calling for help. Mathieu has gone home for the evening and the upstairs neighbors are in the country."

The man was serious. Masson would kill him. Dubon couldn't imagine his own death and felt instead an odd calm that enabled him to think.

"What will you do with my body?"

"I'll call a doctor I know," Masson explained cheerfully. "A heart attack fells a prominent Paris lawyer. Very sudden. But perhaps not so surprising. Overworking lately. Even his wife will say so." He paused, and when he spoke again his voice seemed distant, almost dreamy.

"Poor Geneviève. I'll comfort her, of course. We'll be drawn closer inevitably. They say if widows or widowers are going to remarry, they usually make a new match within a year. No old parents to block us now, no fanciful worries about hereditary conditions, madness in my family that might be passed on to children . . ."

He looked up and his tone hardened. "You were always so sure you could have what you wanted, Dubon. It was only natural Geneviève would fall in love with you. You were the handsome one. I was just that ugly, stringy Masson. You were grateful enough for my help convincing her family of your worth. Did you ever think what it might feel like to be the one on the outside looking in?"

Dubon cried out, but the noise served only to awaken Masson to his purpose. With a swift step, Masson crossed the room with the syringe in his hand and grabbed him.

FIFTY-TWO

Dubon could feel the tip of the needle grazing his neck. One quick jab and a push on the plunger and he would be dead. Masson had his arm twisted painfully behind his back and had shoved him up against a wall and pinned him in place with his knee. Dubon dared not move for fear the needle would hit its mark.

"What's the point, Masson?" he asked, trying to speak as neutrally as possible, willing himself to breathe slowly despite his pounding heart. "You can't kill everyone who is demanding the truth." He tried to lean away from the needle a little by sliding his head along the wall, but Masson tightened the grip on his arm.

"I should warn you that I have left accounts of my conclusions about the captain's innocence with several prominent journalists. They will print them. It's too late. Revision is inevitable." Dubon thought he felt Masson's grip on his arm slacken a little, but he replied in an unrelenting voice.

"They won't print anything, Dubon. There can be devastating penalties for a newspaper that endangers national security. And nobody will be able to refute the government's evidence. The caravan will move on."

So I keep hearing, Dubon thought to himself, and might have laughed were it not for Masson twisting his arm yet more tightly. Dubon felt the tip of the needle push ever so slightly into his skin.

He tried to swallow and then blurted out, "Your evidence is a piece of paper that Henry cobbled together from different sheets. The lines are blue at the top and purple at the bottom."

Masson let Dubon's arm drop down his back but did not let go. "Ah," he said reflectively. "Hermann thought you had discovered something, something about the Italian letter." Masson laughed lightly. "I told you that you would betray yourself. You just gave me the key."

Clearly, Picquart had not had the time or inclination, as he was packed off to Algeria, to explain to the generals how he knew the new evidence against Dreyfus was a forgery.

"But what good is it to you?" Dubon asked. "The letter can be exposed as a fraud by anyone who holds it up to good light. It's too late, Masson. It's over." As Masson hesitated, Dubon pressed his advantage home. "If you don't believe me, believe your own kind. Look in my pocket." He gestured with his head to his right pant leg.

"If you are trying to trick me into letting go—"

"Don't let go. Just put the needle down, or at least back it away a bit."

Masson withdrew the needle a few centimeters and released his knee from Dubon's lower back so that his captive could reach awkwardly around his own body with his one free arm. Dubon pulled the crumpled telegram from his pocket and tossed it onto a small table. Masson now had to make a choice. He let go of Dubon's arm but kept the needle, holding it aloft as a threat. Stooping to the table, he used his left hand to smooth out the paper. Dubon shook out the arm that had been twisted behind his back and stepped gingerly away from the wall, watching as Masson read the news of Henry's arrest and suicide.

"The idiots! I told them to stay the course," he said, his arm holding the needle now falling to his side.

They had reached an impasse. Masson slumped down in one of

the chairs, leaving Dubon standing. Faced with the reality that Henry had fallen on his sword and that the generals' cover-up was unraveling, Masson could no longer deny Dreyfus's innocence even if he could still try to protect Esterhazy, his unwitting double agent.

"Let me go and I will forget this episode," Dubon said, desperately thinking how to extricate himself from their encounter. "I will not pursue you. Nor urge the journalists to ask how high the cover-up extends. Rivaud's murder can languish at the back of some police file for eternity."

At this Masson snorted and drew himself straighter in his chair. Dubon backed away a small distance, moving closer to the door.

"I will not tell anyone what I know of your involvement; most especially I will not tell Madeleine what kind of man you are. She can find that out for herself. And, of course, I will never mention to Geneviève what fantasies you might have about her, nor will I tell her the real reason you are not welcome at our table anymore. I will never show her the letter that her brother left me when he set off for Algeria, a letter in which he reports how he went to his superiors with his suspicions about the bordereau only a few weeks before his mysterious death. But you must promise me two things."

Masson stared at him, the syringe in his hand, waiting to assess the deal: Dubon's life for Masson's invisibility. He was wary now, but at least he no longer seemed murderous.

"First, you will never see Geneviève again, and you will never accept any invitation she might extend to you." It was the ban he had been rehearsing in his head since he had walked in on Masson and Madeleine.

"And the second thing?"

"You will no longer stand in the way of revision. Do what you want with Esterhazy—I can't imagine the Germans will still buy information from him now that his name is public—but don't block those who will prove Dreyfus's innocence. Let justice take its course. Do I have your word?"

Masson paused and took a breath.

Dubon waited, not daring to move.

"Ah, my word. Yes, my old friend, you have my word." If he was vexed by his defeat, he did not show it. He stood and crossed back to his desk, dropping the syringe into the open drawer and sliding it silently shut.

Dubon backed away quickly now, reached the door, and fumbled for the handle.

"There is just one other thing, Dubon. One thing that has puzzled me. Who exactly is your client?"

Dubon almost laughed as he maneuvered his body out the door. "I can tell you with all honesty that I really don't know."

FIFTY-THREE

Dubon did not stop running until he reached the Seine. He crossed the pont Solférino and walked the rest of the way home in a haze. He had stared down a man who had planned to kill him. He had won justice for the wrongfully convicted. He badly wanted a drink. He contemplated opening that '75 Margaux. It had been a spectacular vintage in an outstanding decade. The seventies—they had been his glory years too.

It was just as he pushed open the door of his apartment, deciding that the wine would be wasted on him in his current condition, that he remembered he didn't have time for a drink. He had to dress for dinner with his client, whoever she might be. He looked at his watch and discovered that the appointed time was half an hour away; he was going to be late.

When he arrived at the restaurant, he found to his embarrassment that the lady was already waiting for him at a table on the far side of the room. She looked around as though expecting someone but did not appear to see him. The maître d'hôtel, who knew Dubon slightly, appeared at his side.

"I showed the lady to a table, Maître Dubon. That was her preference."

"Good. I'll join her."

Dubon followed him across the room, moving eagerly toward the lady, whose beauty, he had to note, was somewhat marred by the way she squinted as he approached. He was just launching into his apologies when he stopped himself.

"I don't know how to address you, Madame. All I know is that you are not Madame Dreyfus."

She looked down at her lap. "I am not the captain's wife . . ." She hesitated, perhaps too embarrassed to continue.

"But you are someone who loves him just as much," Dubon said. "Someone who keeps one of his old uniforms in her closet." The kind of woman, he thought to himself but did not add, who will agree to meet a man in a public restaurant.

"Yes. I'm the captain's mistress." She said it sadly, as though the status demeaned her.

"Why did you let me believe otherwise?" he asked.

"I never told you I was Madame Dreyfus."

"No, but you are something much closer than a family friend."

"I really am a widow, although my husband has been dead more than eight years now. I don't usually dress in black, but I do find it convenient sometimes, when I want to pass unnoticed. People don't pay much attention to a middle-aged lady in a black dress."

"People would always pay attention to you, Madame."

She acknowledged the compliment with a wave of her hand. "So, we have both made mistakes, Maître Dubon, but things seem to have worked out for the best."

"What was your mistake?" he asked.

"Well . . ." She grimaced. "On the day I came to you, I actually entered your building looking for the famous Maître Déon." She fumbled in the soft bag in her lap for a few seconds and pulled out a pair of glasses. "Can't abide them, although I do have to wear them for shopping. Otherwise the merchants will pass off inferior goods on me. I must have misread your name and thought I had reached the right office." She laughed a little and returned her glasses to her bag.

How could he have been so dim? Dubon berated himself. Lebrun had even indicated the first time he met her that he thought there was some misunderstanding and she was looking for the lawyer upstairs. She had wanted the great social crusader Déon to take on the Dreyfus case, not some lowly solicitor who hadn't tackled anything more serious than a contested will in decades. She had intended to hire the man who would not merely have discovered Esterhazy's name but who would have dragged it through the mud while rallying every left-wing intellectual in the land to the cause. While Dubon was playing dress-up in the Statistical Section, Déon would have got an appeal moving through the courts. He'd probably have had the captain home by now. The lady had climbed the stairs to Déon's office and not realized that she had yet to reach the right floor, because there, on the tiny plaque outside Dubon's door, was a name that—if looked at with bad eyes— might be mistaken for Déon's.

"When did you realize your mistake, Madame?"

"Oh, as soon as you sent me a note from your office arranging a meeting. Your signature is illegible, but your letterhead is not. Then I went and looked you up and found you in a directory of lawyers."

"But you did not think to let me go so that you might pursue the right lawyer?"

"Oh no, Maître. By that time you had sneaked into the Statistical Section. I don't think Maître Déon would ever have dared such a thing. You were the one who found Esterhazy. It will surely not be long before the appeal is granted and the captain comes home. So, in the end, what does it matter if I had the wrong lawyer? I had the right man."

What did it matter? Dubon bit down on his lip as the irony of it threatened to overwhelm him. He thought of the fear he had felt in the Statistical Section and the anger Geneviève had hurled at him for taking on the case and the time he had been away from Madeleine leaving Masson ample opportunity to make arrangements with her. Had it really been worth it? He stared at the widow, hoping for an answer, but she had other things on her mind.

"It's funny, your not being Déon, because that was what I was so worried someone might notice. That was why I came to the office in my widow's weeds. I did not want to be seen visiting such a prominent lawyer, a Socialist and all that."

"Who would notice?"

"Government agents, I suppose. You may think this sounds ridiculous, Maître, but both the captain's brother and Madame Dreyfus are followed continually by government agents, looking to see whom they make contact with or hoping to catch them in some incriminating behavior. There are those who might remember I was an acquaintance of the captain's and I certainly did not want to draw attention to myself. The press would be only too happy to publish a story saying the captain kept a mistress. His brother has been very careful to have almost no contact with me since the captain was deported."

"So you know the family?"

"I have never met Madame Dreyfus, and I only met Mathieu Dreyfus after the captain left France. It was my husband who knew the captain. I was married to an officer, a lieutenant. He was killed during a training exercise. We probably should have waited to marry. His salary was really too small to keep a wife, and the pension . . . well, it was impossible. The captain was so kind, always so kind to me. They have family money, you know, and he started to pay me a stipend, and . . ."

"Certain things were expected in exchange?" Dubon said, trying to phrase it delicately. He was, after all, familiar with the arrangement.

"It was our choice," she replied. "I don't want you to think the captain seduced me or profited from my distress. We had fallen in love."

It was what he had feared. She had hired him to save the man she loved.

"And now?" he asked, almost harshly.

"Now?"

"Are you in love with him now?"

She looked up, surprised at the strength of his tone. "It's been two and a half years since I laid eyes on him, Maître, and I have never received any word from him. I don't suppose he can risk writing to me. I am loyal to his cause, I am heartsick about his current situation, but no, I don't think I would say I am in love with him now."

"Good," said Dubon, and there was a pause while they both thought about what he meant.

"Why did you come to me, then?" he asked, realizing they could not dismiss her last lover quite so easily. "I mean, why did you want to hire Maître Déon to look into the captain's case?"

"I wasn't satisfied that Monsieur Dreyfus was getting results for his brother, and I was frustrated by that, and really, I owe the captain so much. I couldn't stand by and just let him be forgotten." She paused and swallowed visibly, as though coming to the hard part of the story.

"After the captain was deported, the stipend continued. The captain's brother arranged that I would still be paid. Right away when I read the newspapers, I doubted they had the right man. If you knew the captain . . ."

It had been her refrain throughout; if you knew the captain, you knew he was loyal. Loyalty of a certain kind—the same kind he practiced himself, Dubon supposed.

"I wrote to Monsieur Dreyfus, his brother," she said, "and we met. He told me what he knew of the charges and the evidence, and I told him I believed in the captain's innocence as much as he did, but I also told him to stop the money. Well, under the circumstances, I wasn't performing the services for which it was paid, was I." She let out an ironic little laugh. "Also, I worried that now that he was gone, his wife might have access to financial records she would not have seen before, that she might see the stipend going out and guess. I would never have wanted to hurt her. It has been very hard being the captain's mistress. It's like what they say about bereavement: a man dies and his grieving widow gets all the attention, but his mistress has to keep her sorrow a secret. I have often felt invisible, unable to tell anyone of my troubles, but when I imagine what it must be like to be her . . .

"But Monsieur Dreyfus wouldn't hear of cutting me off," she continued. "He insisted that his brother would not want me to be abandoned, although he could never ask for instructions on such a matter in his letters. They do get letters from the captain but, of course, the government reads them all. Monsieur Dreyfus promised me his sister-in-law would not find out about my stipend. And he apologized, but he said he could not risk having regular contact with me. So the monthly check still arrives, but I have felt increasingly burdened by the money: I cannot move on. That's why I was so upset after those stories of the escape, that day at the racetrack. I realized right away they couldn't be true, and that made it all the worse. To have an ending of some kind dangled in front of me and then snatched away . . . As long as the captain was a prisoner, I was too.

"I took the money, but I tried to live very carefully. I found work doing some accounting in an office and managed to put a bit aside each month. As my despair for the captain grew, so did my savings. When I had enough to pay a lawyer, I came to you . . . or to Maître Déon, or someone." She laughed.

Few women, Dubon thought, would have been so scrupulous—but what was the point of her chaining herself to a cause if she no longer loved the man?

"You have been supremely loyal to the captain."

"His wife might not call it loyalty . . ."

"Faithful to his cause, then. That kind of faith can be stronger than personal fidelity," he observed.

"It's probably easier to hold on to abstract principles than to human beings," she agreed. "People can be so unpredictable." She smiled at him.

"Certainly, unpredictable," he said, thinking ruefully of Madeleine. "Easier to worship an idea than a person. They say love is blind, but perhaps ideals blind us even more completely."

"You think the generals have been blinded by their loyalty to the nation," she said, seeing at once into the heart of the question.

"No, Madame, what they have been is mistaken in their notion of what the nation represents. In their paranoia about Germany, they have forgotten that the rights of a man are as important as the future of Alsace and Lorraine."

"The end does not justify the means?"

"Use the wrong means and you'll have no end left worth fighting for."

"You set a high standard."

"You do, too," he replied, and then asked gently, "So are you still being paid?"

"I have urged Monsieur Dreyfus again to stop the payments," she replied. "I have seen him twice recently to pass on information. That's how I heard the captain is shackled now. They had another letter from him, after the stories about the escape. And then last week, I was able to give Monsieur Dreyfus Esterhazy's name. It felt wonderful. I could hand him the real spy, and this time, we agreed the money will stop. I do not owe the captain anything any longer."

Her assertion of her independence hung in the air between them for a moment.

"Good," he said. "That's good." Then something occurred to him and he asked, "Madame, what *is* your name?"

It turned out she had not lied. Her name was Duhamel. Emilie Duhamel.

They lingered over dinner, talking about everything and nothing, and avoiding the topic of the captain's case. They seemed like old friends now, at ease with each other, Dubon noted, as though the knowledge of their real identities had liberated them from their business relationship. Or perhaps it was merely that she did not need to pretend any longer that she was Madame Dreyfus or some supposed family friend. She chatted and joked and told stories at her own expense. That vital energy that he had so often sensed pulsing beneath a surface marked by sorrow and grief came bubbling up now, and her air of mystery dissolved into something sweeter and more familiar. Dubon had to admit that perhaps his fantasies had clouded his view of her and made his behavior stupidly flirtatious. Now, their newfound companionship floated all kinds of hopes inside him. She was free and so was he. Or at least, he thought, as he recalled his conversation with Geneviève the night they had received the news of Jean-Jean's death, as free as he had always been.

It was almost ten when they left the restaurant and he insisted on accompanying her in a cab to her door.

"It was very nice to make your acquaintance, Maître Dubon. I hope I will see you again soon." She shook his hand warmly. "Don't forget to send me your bill."

He turned over her hand and raised it to his lips.

"I am sure, Madame Duhamel, that we can come to some kind of understanding about my bill."

He dismissed the cab and walked home through the streets, thinking over the captain's case and reassuring himself it would not be long now. Justice would be done. The truth was out, marching forward. It couldn't be stopped.

Truth is on the march. He savored the phrase, it had a ring to it. He would offer it to Clemenceau when he went to pay a call on the newspaper editor. Without betraying his bargain with Masson, he still had much to tell him. Clemenceau was the crusader; he would do the work that Déon might have.

He turned the key in his door and stepped quietly into the hall. Luc had left one gas light burning for him, but the household had gone to bed. He took off his clothes in his study, which always doubled as his dressing room, and washed himself in the adjoining bathroom before he pushed through its second door into the bedroom.

At his approach, Geneviève stirred and, as he climbed into bed beside her, awoke enough to asked foggily, "François? Is everything all right?"

"Yes, my dear. Everything will be perfectly all right." He curled his body along the length of hers and together they settled into sleep.

Light seeped slowly into the room, awakening him from a half sleep. He shifted his weight on the bed, aware he must move carefully while not conscious enough to think why. Something pressed against his wrist and, as he winced with pain, knowledge flooded back in: the bracelet knocked against the bandage there. Underneath the gauze was an open wound. He had spent another night shackled to his cot.

In the end, the palisade had proved more blessing than curse. It cut off his view to the sea, but the lieutenant now ordered the guards to take him down to the little beach at one edge of the island for exercise each morning. He was left to pace the small strip of sand or simply sit there staring out at the relentless waves while his guards perched on the rocks behind him, their rifles resting across their knees.

Those days some months before, as the stakes had risen around his hut, he had soon realized the palisade's potential: at any hour other than high noon, it provided shade away from the hot metal of the shed and its little porch. By late afternoon it offered an entire corner of coolness where he soon took to sitting for hours. Eventually, the lieutenant allowed him to move his desk there, and even ordered the erection of a canvas sunshade over the top of it to protect him in the mornings.

The lieutenant was unrelenting, however, on the subject of the shackles. It was as though, the prisoner thought, the man had to make a report all the way back to Paris: as ordered, the prisoner is kept shackled at night and under armed guard during the day. He need not mention the ways in which he eased the prisoner's situation as long as he followed his orders.

The first night they had pinned him to his cot spread-eagled, each arm raised above his head and locked to either side of the metal frame. The position quickly became excruciating. He had managed, by dint of digging in his heels and bending his knees, to inch his trapped body into a more upright position and so lessen the strain on his arms, but by morning his muscles were in spasm.

The next night, he pleaded with them in his cracked voice to allow him to lie on his side with his hands in a prayer position locked together on the frame. It was a position he could hold all night without agony but, repeatedly jolted back to consciousness by the rubbing of the shackles, he never slept deeply again. When it was not his bracelets that pained him, it was the insects that he was powerless to swat from his face. One fly could keep him awake all night. A stinging mosquito could render him half mad.

His guards did not complain when, in the afternoons, he fell asleep without his shackles, his body stretched along the length of the palisade.

Sores soon began to appear on his wrists, where the metal rubbed the skin raw, and his guards kept up a continual campaign of bandages. He wondered at their solicitousness until it occurred to him that, if the wounds became infected and blood poisoning set in, he might die. Not on the lieutenant's watch, the prisoner concluded: the man had been ordered to guard a living prisoner, and that he did.

There was a sound now at the door. The guard was coming to unlock him and give him his bread. The man stepped into the room with more energy than usual, his bearing more upright. The reason followed on his heels: the lieutenant entered with a second guard who carried a duffel bag.

These latter two stood and watched as the first guard unlocked the shackles. The prisoner drew his hands to his body slowly and then stiffly pushed himself to sitting.

"Take off your pants," said the lieutenant, pulling some undergarments from the bag and tossing them on the bed. "Put these on."

The prisoner began to tug at his loose trousers but then stopped and cocked his head toward the corner of the room.

"What is it, man?"

"He wants to pee, Lieutenant."

"Oh. Go ahead."

He crossed to the bucket and simply let his trousers drop. One of the guards snickered.

"Silence! Pass him the underwear."

When he was finished, he stepped out of the trousers at his ankles, took the undergarments from the guard, and put them on.

As he stood there, wearing the new underwear and his old, stained canvas shirt, the lieutenant pulled a tunic and pants from the bag and unfolded them on the cot. The tunic bore no insignia, but the prisoner recognized the clothes instantly for what they were: not the tropical khakis the men here wore, but the blue serge uniform of the army back in France. Slowly, with a kind of wonder, he pulled on the pants and the tunic, his cramped fingers fumbling with the familiar brass buttons. It was an action that once, in some other life, he had repeated unthinkingly thousands of times.

"Boots?" asked the lieutenant, glancing about. "He still has boots?"

"No laces," said the first guard, picking up a well-worn pair of boots from one corner of the tiny room. The laces had been taken away the day he arrived, which did not matter much since he always went barefoot.

"Give him your laces. You can get more later."

The guard did not look happy at the order but bent down and began pulling his laces out of his own boots. The second guard threaded them through the prisoner's boots and passed them to him. The prisoner sat down on the cot and began to pull one on, but quickly drew back his foot. He turned the boot upside down and shook it. A large beetle fell out and scuttled away. The guards laughed.

"Hurry!" barked the lieutenant. "Help him tie the laces."

Once the prisoner was shod and standing before him, the lieutenant drew a cap out of the bag and handed it to him.

"The boat from the mainland docked last night and the captain wants to sail as soon as possible. You are to return to France."

The prisoner croaked out one word. "How?"

"You had better start using your voice, man. You'll need it to plead your case. Your wife has won you an appeal."

"Merci, mon Lieutenant." Dreyfus drew himself up as best he could and saluted, bringing his bandaged hand up to the brim of his new cap. *"Vive la France!"*

KATE TAYLOR is an award-winning novelist and journalist. The child of a Canadian diplomat, she was born in France and raised in Ottawa. Her debut novel, *Madame Proust and the Kosher Kitchen*, won the Commonwealth Writers' Prize for Best First Book (Canada/Caribbean Region) and the Toronto Book Award, among others. She also writes about culture for Canada's national newspaper, *The Globe and Mail*, where she served as theater critic from 1995 to 2003. Kate Taylor lives in Toronto.

A NOTE ON THE TYPE

The text of this book was set in Centaur, an old-style, or Venetian, typeface designed by Bruce Rogers for the Metropolitan Museum of Art between 1912 and 1929.